G000300562

CURSED

Also by John Douglas

The Late Show

CURSED

John Douglas

Hodder & Stoughton

Copyright © 1995 by John Douglas

First published in 1995 by Hodder and Stoughton
A division of Hodder Headline PLC

The right of John Douglas to be identified as the Author of
the Work has been asserted by him in accordance with the
Copyright, Designs and Patents Act 1988.

10 9 8 7 6 5 4 3 2 1

All rights reserved. No part of this publication may be
reproduced, stored in a retrieval system, or transmitted,
in any form or by any means without the prior written
permission of the publisher, nor be otherwise circulated
in any form of binding or cover other than that in which
it is published and without a similar condition being
imposed on the subsequent purchaser.

All characters in this publication are fictitious
and any resemblance to real persons, living or dead,
is purely coincidental.

A CIP catalogue record for this title is available from
the British Library
Douglas, John
Cursed
I. Title
823.914 [F]

ISBN 0 340 63536 3

Typeset by Hewer Text Composition Services, Edinburgh
Printed and bound in Great Britain by
Mackays of Chatham PLC

Hodder and Stoughton
A division of Hodder Headline PLC
338 Euston Road
London NW1 3BH

For my mother and father, Betty and John, for being
everything good parents should be.

Strange is it not? that of the myriads who
Before us passed the door of Darkness through,
Not one returns to tell us of the Road,
Which to discover we must travel too.
Omar Khayyám, Rubáiyát

PART ONE

Introductions

One loyal friend is worth ten thousand relatives
Euripides

1

LEONARD HALSEY WAS a slob. He smoked too much, ate too much and drank too much, but then he could afford to. He sold insurance for a living and was pretty good at it. Most of the people he had to deal with were either stupid or easily dazzled with figures, and with commission at stake, he was prepared to coax and cajole them well into the wee hours. This would often entail his staying away from home but this suited both him and his wife perfectly. Her, because she had grown tired of his untidy and selfish ways; him, because it gave him ample opportunity to pursue his one and only hobby. Sex. Whether on his own, or with a woman – rented or otherwise – he relished sex with all the brio of a revivalist preacher. Getting his end away dominated his thoughts day and night. It was an obsession. So far he had managed to keep his single-minded pursuit of the ultimate orgasm from his wife but soon she would know all about the secret life of her husband's less-than-private parts. And Leonard might even have bluffed his way through this unexpected revelation – *It's a sickness, Dorothy. I can't help it. Dr Haggerty says I need to see a psychiatrist. And I am, honest* – but there was one major drawback, if he did but know it. Leonard was going to be dead in less than six minutes.

However, as yet unaware of his impending demise, Leonard was idly listening to the radio, the announcer continuing to read the news in his disinterested monotone.

'*. . . has been named as Father Alphonse Racimo, thirty-eight, from Cheadle. His car crashed down a steep embankment on the Ollington to Whaley Bridge road near Boothe, some time during Sunday night. Father Racimo left no relatives but a spokesman for his parish council said he would be greatly missed. Now sport. City today announced—*'

Leonard switched the radio off and threw another half-dozen

3

peanuts into his mouth. An overweight man, the hot weather was making him sweat even more than usual. He leaned back against the wardrobe door and surveyed his companion.

She was young, probably seventeen or eighteen, skinny and tall. Not at all to his taste but his plans had fallen through and the man in the pub had got him the girl at short notice. She lay on the bed swilling a can of Diet Vimto, dressed only in bra and suspender belt, the soft mound of her pubic hair in dark contrast to her obviously dyed blonde hair. Leonard had already screwed her and was waiting for nature to take its course. She looked okay but she had spots and though she went through the motions, she'd never win an Oscar. He hadn't had a real woman in a while now, except his wife, but then wives don't really count.

He belched and reached for his half-bottle of Vladivar vodka. He wasn't tanked yet and knew he would be able to drink a lot more before he had to pack it in. After a swig he cradled the bottle in his arm and walked to the bed and sat down. He had pulled his Y-fronts back on and his hairy pot belly flopped out onto his thighs like a dead seal. He idly ran his hand up the girl's leg while she eyed him over the top of her can. He reached her pubic hair and, grabbing a handful, gave it a gentle tug. She smiled a dumb smile.

'Next time, love, try putting a bit more life into it,' he said, toying with her damp curls. 'If I did my job as badly as you I wouldn't be able to afford you. So earn your money.' He let go and took another pull on his vodka.

The girl pouted then switched on the radio and started humming along to a George Michael record. To get him back in a good mood, she attempted what she thought was a seductive smile. It was about as convincing as the news that you had been selected for a special trial double-glazing installation but, strangely, Leonard – himself a professional purveyor of false smiles – appreciated the gesture and beamed a half-hearted grin back.

She was grateful. She knew she hadn't been very good but she'd had the screaming shits in the morning and though she was over it now, she was wondering about the crappy Chinese takeaway the fat git had made her share with him. She tried to make conversation.

'Makes you think, dunnit? Life. One minute you're 'ere, next minute you're not.'

But Leonard had suddenly become preoccupied, looking at the

radio and scratching his belly. He lifted the bottle to his mouth but didn't take a drink. 'What? Yeah, sure . . .'

The girl unhooked her bra and dropped it on the floor. 'You ready then, love?' she said without a trace of interest, giving her nipples a quick pinch to make them stand out from her small, bitten breasts.

Leonard didn't notice. He was still far away, thinking, rubbing the bottle back and forth against his cheek, looking at the radio again for all the world as if the DJ were telling him more bad news instead of announcing a rock and roll revival night at the Ritz.

He sat limply on the bed and she stroked the back of his head even though she didn't want to touch him. 'You all right, Benny? It is Benny, isn't it?'

He turned and looked straight through her, shaking his head.

'I thought it was Benny . . .'

But he wasn't interested. Something was worrying him, something important. It was sat in his head, gnawing away. He looked at the radio. *What was it? That priest in the car crash. What was his name, Racimo? Where had he heard that name before?*

Taking a deep breath he slowly stood up, then walked over to his jacket which was thrown over the back of a cheap armchair.

The girl swung her legs over the edge of the bed. Something was going on here, she could feel it. He wasn't hot or tired or boozed up. He was cold and damp and scared. Really frightened. But by what? He kept looking at the radio, but it was only Piccadilly Gold. It wasn't *that* bad. She scooped up her bra from the floor and slipped it back on, then started to look for her briefs.

Leonard had extracted his wallet, but was still holding it limply at his side. He squeezed his eyes shut as if the sound from the radio actually hurt. *Must remember, must remember.* But he couldn't. He slowly raised the wallet and riffled through its contents.

The girl had put her briefs on and had started hunting for her blouse when she caught sight of him staring into his wallet. His face had gone white. Incredible. She had never seen it happen so quickly before.

'Hey, you all right, Benny? You don't look so good. Something you forgot?' she asked nervously, keeping one eye on him as she fumbled in the sheets for the rest of her hastily removed clothes.

He looked up at her. God, but he was scared. He farted loudly, then offered her a smile so forced that the girl, scared as she was, couldn't help feeling sorry for him. He held out his wallet to her, his hands trembling.

'Yes, yes, I'm fine. Really. Must have been something I ate. Yes. Look, you're a good girl, one of the best I ever had. I – I want you to have this. All of it. All my money. I can afford it. You're such a good-looking girl what with those tits and everything. Here, take it . . .' He was offering her the entire wallet, not just his cash.

She had seen his roll earlier in the evening. He must have had two, three hundred pounds all told, but the man was losing control, she could see it in his eyes. Worse, he wasn't seeing a cheap hotel room any more, or even her. He was seeing something else entirely; something grey and bleak and bad, and he wanted her to be a part of it, to share it somehow, in some way – and that wasn't going to happen, not to this girl.

'Come on Benny, what's up? I d – don't want your money. You keep it. I mean it. You were good. It was fun, really.' She circled the bed, judging the distance to the door; two people lying to each other, and knowing it.

'Come on, come on,' pleaded Leonard. 'I just want you to have this. What's the harm? A good lay deserves good money. Come on, love, you earned it.'

He was almost at breaking point. Any second now and he'd tip right over and she'd have God knows what to deal with.

'No, I don't, Benny. And I don't want it. I—' She bolted for the door.

But Leonard was there first. He pushed his hand into her chest and ran her back to the bed where she fell spread-eagled, his hefty body crashing down on top of her. Pain seared across her chest. He had trapped his hand with the wallet under her and he immediately began struggling to get it out. The terrified girl tried to cough but her chest hurt even more. Leonard continued to mouth hoarse obscenities, pulling himself to one side in order to extricate his arm, his manic flushed face hovering above hers, dripping rancid warm sweat, his eyes wide and desperate.

'*Take it! Take the bloody money, you stupid bitch! Take my wallet, take it!*'

She looked frantically at the door barely ten feet away. Her arms were pinned on both sides and she could hardly move. *Got to get out, got to get out!* Then Leonard shifted his weight a fraction and she saw her chance.

With what little strength she could muster she worked her right hand free and slapped him on the side of the face. It didn't stop him, but he felt it. He pulled desperately at his trapped arm, looking into her face and cursing again. His hot foul breath hit her, making it even harder to breathe. She balled up her hand and punched him in the ear once, twice. The third time he felt it enough to push himself up off her and that was when she raised her left knee and slowly and purposely ground it into his balls.

At first he simply tried to push back down but she kept up the struggle and he had to give way to the steadily increasing momentum of pain. With a cry of irritation and outrage he swung off her and the girl drew back her knee and gave a solid lunge that had him falling to the floor squawking.

In a second she was up and running, clutching at her aching chest. She reached the door and braved a look back. Leonard had managed to pick himself up off the floor but immediately doubled over in agony, clutching at the underside of his belly. The girl guessed rightly that an old hernia had slipped loose and was screaming at his insides in protest. She managed a contemptuous laugh, which hurt, then grabbed her coat and pulled open the door.

Leonard proffered the wallet one more time, looking up at her, tears in his eyes. 'Please take it, please . . .'

For a second she felt something akin to pity, but then the jagged pain in her chest returned and she was through the door and running downstairs as fast as she could.

Leonard watched her leave and started to cry. With the door open the room had suddenly become cold, but he suspected it was more than just a breeze from the stairwell. He heaved himself up straight, the stabbing in his guts trying to drag him down all the time, and stumbled towards the door. The cold was intense, and a noiseless wind had started to blow through the doorway. His steps got shorter and shorter as it got colder and colder. He had just reached the door and was leaning over to grab the handle when it slammed shut and he fell heavily against it, the wallet finally slipping from his shaking hand and tumbling onto the floor, where notes spilled out and swirled clumsily in the cold breeze.

But even though the door was closed, the cold wind still blew. Leonard grabbed at his side, almost passing out in agony, but managing to roll his flabby body into a sitting position against the door, desperately trying to catch his breath, each time finding it

7

harder and harder, and feeling the temperature plummet. He lifted his heavy head up and rested it against the iced surface of the door. Not right, not right. Shouldn't be this cold, not in June.

He opened his eyes and sweat ran into them. He blinked a couple of times, then wiped them with his hand. So cold. He peered at a twenty-pound note as it rolled and coiled its way upwards in the draught from nowhere. Twenty quid. Up up and away. Then a noise stopped his train of thought. It stopped him cold. *So cold.* He looked over to the bed.

No-one heard his scream, not even himself.

2

DUNCAN CANTRILL WAS a deadbeat. His teachers had said so, his friends continued to say so, and his parents knew so. The irony was that Duncan Cantrill agreed with them all. He *was* a deadbeat. But he was good at it.

He had mucked up his 'O' levels but managed to stay on at school, only to bugger up his 'A' levels and so fail to get to university, and had gone to art college instead. Three years later he had dropped out of that. Now all he had was his job at the Sports View Hotel. As deadbeats went he could count himself a roaring success.

After all, how many fathers and owners of their own aerospace-engine companies have sons who are desk clerks in two-rose, no-star bed and breakfast hotels in Ollington? And how many mothers and Conservative Councillors and Chairs of the Education Committees can boast a son who has eight grade C 'O' levels and one grade C 'A' level? So yes, Duncan was a deadbeat. In fact it was just about the only thing he had ever succeeded at. He had no useful education – or rather, no education he intended using – no particular skills, no success with women, no prospects and no ambition and, until 8.30am this morning, no hope of achieving anything approaching fame, but now he was a celebrity. A Media Star.

As proof, he only had to look at the one o'clock News on the BBC and the 12.30pm ITN News. He was more than likely to see himself on the News at 5.40 and the BBC six o'clock News. In addition, BBC Radio Ollington were carrying a brief interview and Peak, the nearest commercial station, had mentioned him though, as yet, had no words from him. Plus he had already spoken to reporters from five national and two local newspapers and was waiting for the man from the weekly *Courier* to pay his respects. Duncan may have been a deadbeat but right now he was famous. After all, it isn't every day you discover a dead body in the hotel you work in.

Room 12 it had been. The occupant, a Mr L. Halsey, had asked for a wake-up call at 8.00am. Duncan had forgotten it. To make amends he had gone up to the room in person with a copy of the *Daily Mail* – he had finished reading it – as a peace offering. There was no response to his repeated knocking. Fearing the worst – that the bastard had skipped without paying his bill – he had fetched the master key and, after jiggling the lock, had entered the room.

The first thing he had seen was the reason for the awkwardness of the lock; the key had been in it and he had pushed it out onto the carpet. The second thing he saw was Mr L. Halsey on the bed, very obviously dead. The third thing he had seen was the inside of the toilet bowl as he reacquainted himself with his breakfast.

It had taken him quite some time to finish retching and steel himself to re-enter the dead man's bedroom. He had finally edged his way back out of the room as if his trousers were stitched to the wall, then dashed downstairs and called the police. And that was when the fun had started.

Mr L. Halsey had very obviously been murdered. What had turned Duncan's stomach wasn't so much being in the presence of death, but the manner of the man's demise. The colour and shape of the man's face for one thing; it was bright purple and blue, as if it were bruised all over, swollen up like a balloon about to burst. His tongue had been hanging out, dark and bloated, as if he was devouring a huge slug, and his eyes had been wide open, offering an expression halfway between horror and surprise. He looked like he had sneezed to death. It was only on the way out that Duncan had also noticed the man's neck. Even now he couldn't credit what he had seen, but it refused to stop replaying in his mind so it must have been true. The man's throat had been squeezed to something about the thickness of one of Duncan's skinny wrists, and yet Mr Halsey had been fat, and the night before his neck had been as wide as his head. Whatever had strangled him had had an unbelievable grip. Other than those two details – the absurdly thin throat and the obscenely swollen head – the man had been propped up in bed in his underpants, as if resting, his hands limp by his side.

The police had come and taken a statement and then Duncan, seeing the reporters, had made his move for fame. He had been warned by the police not to detail the condition of the body and he hadn't, but he had managed to convey his repulsion very convincingly, and his over-rehearsed denials of rumours soon gave the story a macabre edge it might otherwise not have achieved. Almost single-handedly Duncan turned it from 'just another murder' into 'Not Just Another Murder!' His efforts were not appreciated by the Detective Chief Inspector in charge but by then it was too late.

Nor were they appreciated by Mr Brannigan, the owner of the hotel, who was most put out that someone should be so inconsiderate as to die on his premises. Duncan's eye-rolling mime of his discovery of the body on television did nothing to improve his mood and, at two o'clock, when Duncan was due to go off shift, Mr Brannigan informed him that his services would no longer be required.

'I'm sacked?' asked a disbelieving Duncan.

'Yes,' said Mr Brannigan, a big Irishman with enormous teeth that looked like they could dig up peat. They were certainly the right colour.

'But I didn't murder him!' protested Duncan.

'But you found him.'

'I couldn't help that! What if *you*'d found him?'

'Ah, but I wouldn't have found him, Duncan.' And with that inscrutable Celtic reasoning, Brannigan handed Duncan his cards.

Duncan's immediate reaction was to call together the press and announce that he was the second victim of the day, but by then everyone had adjourned to the police station for a press statement so Duncan simply went home.

If he was expecting sympathy he didn't get it. His mother had seen his interview on the BBC one o'clock News – they never watched ITV: too common – and was not amused.

'Did you see me?' he said cheerily.

'Why did you do it?' His mother was aghast. A large woman dressed impeccably in a tweedy two-piece suit – it was Tuesday so it was the green today – and a frilly Victorian-style blouse which, owing to the ample dimensions of her bosom, had all the style of a bedsheet. Over the years, her pinched expression had atrophied to such an extent that she now looked as if her chubby face would pop inside out the next time a shop assistant had the temerity to address her as 'love'.

'*I* didn't murder him,' said Duncan opening a carton of milk in their vast oak-panelled kitchen.

'Not that! Talk to those people. The television.'

'They were asking questions. I gave them answers.'

'But we don't talk to the media.'

'Oh, yes, "we" do. Any time you want to slag off the opposition on the council, you—'

'That is different, Duncan. That is politics. That – ' she pointed at the silent Sony 27″ television in the corner of their even vaster lounge as if it was a member of the Socialist Workers' Party '– is pure sensationalism.'

'No, it's not. It's news.'

'Pardon me, Duncan, but dead people aren't news. They are merely . . .'

'What?'

'. . . disgusting.'

'Oh. Now I know.' He crossed into the lounge and plonked himself down on one of their enormous white leather sofas and continued supping milk from the carton. 'Anyway, what did you think?'

'Of what?'

'Of me. On the TV.'

'I daren't say, Duncan. I was too shocked.'

Duncan was annoyed. Regardless of his motives for talking to the press, he felt righteous indignation at his mother's attitude. 'I'm sorry for doing my duty, mum. Sorry I found someone who had been murdered. Sorry I was asked about it by the police and the television and the newspapers. Cost me my job, too.'

'What?'

'Mr Brannigan fired me. Said I shouldn't have found the body.'

'Quite right, too.'

'Mum!'

'That's what comes from mixing with the wrong sort of people.'

'He was a dead guest!'

'Not the victim . . . Mr Brannigan! Never liked him. Never trust a man who doesn't bother to shave.'

'Like Mr Williams?'

'That's *not* funny, Duncan.' (Mr Williams was their local vicar and Mrs Cantrill was one of his biggest fans.) 'And you know exactly what I mean. So what are you going to do now? Go on the dole *again*?'

'Have to. Job Centre should have plenty of jobs in other hotels. Height of the season.'

'Must you work in a hotel, Duncan? It's so . . .'

'Common? It's all I can do, mum. Besides, I like it.'

This did it for Mrs Cantrill. The concept of anyone actually *enjoying* manual labour was beyond her ken. She announced she was off to a meeting of the Education Committee and left her son to his own devices.

The first thing he did, after making himself a sandwich and finishing off the milk, was to set the video to record the early evening news bulletins on both channels. Then he adjourned upstairs to take a bath.

But it was while he was lounging in the myriad suds of their double-size sunken bath that the full impact of what he had seen in Room 12 hit him. Delayed shock. He started shaking and crying. He pissed in the water and couldn't stop even as he rose unsteadily to his feet and, grabbing the gold-plated taps, hauled himself onto the carpet. There he managed to wrap a bath sheet around himself and stumble to his bedroom where he collapsed on his bed. He had a raging headache and his stomach was gurgling threateningly. He felt awful. He curled up on the bed in a foetal position and willed himself to sleep and, thankfully, it worked.

Had he known it was to be his last decent sleep, he would have enjoyed it all the more. But then, who could possibly have guessed what was soon to happen to him – least of all the rather unimaginative Duncan himself? After all, how many people's worst nightmares become a bloodcurdling reality?

3

WHEN DUNCAN WOKE up it was dark. He checked his bedside stereo-cassette-radio-TV-alarm-clock-calculator. It wasn't plugged in, so he got up and dragged his weary body to the bathroom and found his Rotary watch on top of the toilet cistern. That meant mum wasn't home. Fastidiously tidy, she would rather consign his watch to the dustbin than have it placed somewhere other than on his wrist or in a drawer. It read 11.08pm.

11.08! He had been asleep for eight hours or more. Why hadn't anyone woken him? Well, all right, chances of dad being home before midnight were next to nil. True, he was in the middle of a big take-over deal, but Duncan being Duncan he suspected there might be another reason. Had he been married to his mother he would probably have dallied himself. He didn't feel disgust that his father might have a mistress: he didn't know him well enough to hold any strong opinions about him. He had rarely been home throughout Duncan's life, but Duncan couldn't really complain. Whenever his dad was home he did little but talk on the telephone or read the financial pages. He was a self-made man and it had given Duncan and his mother a lifestyle the envy of anyone on less than a hundred thousand a year, but no matter how adept at manufacturing jet engines his father was, he had proven to be completely inept at forming any kind of parental bond with his only son.

Three. That was the number of times Peter Cantrill had been home for his son's birthday parties. Three out of the fifteen he'd had by his eighteenth birthday. Not a bad average actually. Duncan's father had so far missed nine Christmases, eleven wedding anniversaries, sixteen summer vacations and the entirety of Duncan's appendectomy when he was fourteen. But Duncan wasn't bitter. His father was a stranger after all, and who misses a stranger? These days the gardener was home more than his father and Duncan couldn't even pronounce the man's name.

Polish or Czech, his single idiosyncracy – apart from seeming to be continuously transplanting everything bar the trees from one side of their two acres of garden to the other – was to cast a leery eye at Duncan's mother. Duncan presumed the man had brain damage. Not only was his mother completely asexual – he had always suspected he was adopted: his mother wouldn't have gone through all the degrading activities involved in giving birth – but if she had thought for a moment that the man had dark designs on her body (and they would have to be very *large* dark designs), she would have used his garden shears for something other than topiary. Speaking of which, Duncan still wondered why his mother hadn't noticed that the bush at the bottom far right of their garden resembled an eleven-feet-tall erect penis. His father had never been known to look at his garden, but his mother was very proud of their immaculate lawn and nine-months-of-the-year flower display. Clearly, her many friends had yet to pass comment on the phallic nature of her shrubbery but, then again, they might well be too polite.

Duncan pulled on a pair of black 501s and ventured downstairs. There was a note. His father wouldn't be home tonight – 'Business in Liverpool' – and his mother was attending a special meeting of the local Operatic Society that was likely to 'drag on': code for 1.00am. So he was alone in the house. He raided the fridge but wasn't really hungry so all he took was a flat ginger ale and a handful of ham.

Telly? Snooker, Computers, T J Hooker, Uruguayan prisons. Spot the channel. So, music. He went to the B & O music centre and flipped on the radio. Some dipstick discussing star signs on Radio One. Someone called Cyril complaining about dog shit on Piccadilly. Someone called Eric complaining about dog shit on Peak Radio. Virgin and Atlantic fading in and out. He switched it off. If he wanted to play his own stuff he would have to go upstairs for his cassettes. Sod that. How about a read? He'd just finished Tom Clancy's latest and didn't have anything lined up. What else? Oh yes, the evening paper. It was still on the mat by the front door. He went and fetched it.

There was a full report on the murder. No leads. Nothing mentioned other than Mr Halsey appeared to have been strangled.

(Appeared? That was like saying Terry Wogan *appears* to have a hairpiece.) But all was not lost. Duncan was mentioned:

'The body was discovered by Duncan Catrill, 22, porter at the hotel.' Great. Twelve words and three inaccuracies. It was *Cant*rill; he was 23; he had been the receptionist. Not a lot of difference true, but Receptionist looks a lot better than Porter on a CV. Ah, CV. *Shit.* He'd have to dig that out and amend it. How many jobs was it now? Fourteen? Yes. Unless he also counted that afternoon he worked the ice cream van and everything melted. Projected earnings for the afternoon: £20+. Actual earnings: minus £45 and a black eye.

Now what? The video. Oh yes. The news. He spun the tape back. *What? Oh God, I don't believe it!* he Victor Meldrewed. He had taped *BBC1* from 5.45 to 6pm, then *ITV* from 6 to 6.30pm. *Damn!* All he had were Australian soaps! Oh, and a trailer for Northwest Tonight on the BBC where the murder was mentioned but Duncan wasn't. And that was it. Such is fame. Duncan had had his fifteen minutes. Now for the rest of his life. What a prospect . . .

So what to do? Back to bed? Not after eight hours' sleep. What then? What do you do when there's nothing on TV, and you don't fancy reading or listening to music and there's no-one in the house? Of course. Have a wank!

Duncan ran upstairs and delved under his bed for his box of car magazines then, hefting them out onto the bed, he picked out his two prized videos. Which to watch? *Hotter than Hot* or *Lust for Louise*? *Lust for Louise, I think*. He liked Louise. She looked a bit like Jenny Thompson in the local newsagent. Fantasies are all the better for a little grounding in reality.

He parked *Hotter than Hot* under *Popular Mechanics* for 1986 and made his way downstairs, but as he reached the top of the stairs, he heard a noise. A sort of shuffle. Curtains being moved? A carpet sliding?

He stopped dead, his heart already pounding. Had mum set the burglar alarms before she went out? His being home was, after all, an irrelevance: it was her china and jewellery she worried about. Yes. She must have. Unless it was faulty.

He strained to listen. Not a thing. He took a step, the floorboard creaked – he had always hated the preponderance of bare varnished floorboards in their house – so he stilled again. After thirty seconds there had been no further movement or sound, so he edged his way onto the carpeting on the wide sweeping staircase and slowly walked down.

There were three proper ways into the house: the front door, which he would be able to see in a couple of steps; the kitchen door round to the right; and, of course, the huge patio doors in the lounge that looked out onto the vast garden and its giant penis. Had any of them been breached?

He considered returning upstairs and arming himself, but with what? A loofer? His barbell? Waving that above his head to tonk some raider, he'd more than likely snap his spine. The only really useful weapons were his father's golf clubs but they were by the front door. Terrific. Maybe he could hide? Too late. He had left the TV on. Burglars would know someone was home. Damn. He took another three steps, leaned down and peered at the front door. Shut. Maybe it was mum. Maybe even dad. But if it was they would have made their presence felt, especially mum; she always slammed the front door as if it were a drawbridge. He skipped down the remaining steps, glad for once to be barefoot, and edged his way to the kitchen doorway.

Taking a deep breath he stole a look round the doorjamb. The outside kitchen door was locked and bolted, and the burglar alarm's light was winking away reassuringly. So it had been nothing. Still, better make sure.

He edged over to the lounge and looked in. Nothing out of place. The video had stopped rewinding, and Channel 12 was snowing silently on the TV screen.

He placed his porno tape on the sofa and walked over to the curtained windows. He hated having to do this but he had to be certain. He counted up to three and pulled them wide.

Nothing. The black night leaned against the window and revealed nothing. He moved over to the floodlight switch and flipping it down, bathed the lawn in a harsh brilliance guaranteed to blind anyone foolish enough to be trespassing. Again nothing. Not even Hilda the Hedgehog, their nightly visitant he left a saucer of bread and milk out for. He drew the curtains, switched off the floodlight and returned to the sofa. He was getting too jumpy but, after this morning, was it any wonder? He slotted in the cassette, cued up the counter and fast-forwarded to the good part.

While it spun, he went into the kitchen and checked the back door – this time not in search of burglars, but to make sure he got plenty of warning if either of his parents came home. He was just coming back into the lounge when he smelled something. He sniffed. Fish? Yes. Fish. He hated fish. Was it in a bin? He checked the swing bin. Empty, bar tea leaves and an empty biscuit packet. What then? He checked the cooker. Bare. The fridge? Nothing remotely fishy, not even fish paste, and it was running fine. So was the freezer. But the smell was still strong. He went back into the lounge.

If anything the smell was even stronger there but he couldn't for the life of him think what it could be. It was definitely fishy. Not overpowering but strong enough . . . but not *quite* strong enough to put him off his indulgences. He dropped his pants and, grabbing the two remote controls, lay back naked on the couch and got comfortable. He looked down at his white, near-hairless body.

He was skinny, a fact which had always annoyed him. He had tried bodybuilding and eating lots of carbohydrates but it made no difference. He had a metabolism that burned fuel faster than a V12 engine. It meant that at six feet tall he was only nine-and-a-half stone. That, and a chronic inability to tan, had also put an end to sunbathing, both around their own outdoor pool and on holiday. He was even embarrassed in front of his mother who, whenever she donned her one-piece costume, resembled several joints of pork wrapped in a curtain. He knew that men with slight builds, small bottoms and slim features were all the rage with some women, but looking like an anaemic *No Parking* sign did nothing to boost his self-esteem. Yet, despite his wimpish build, he wasn't ugly.

He had a good bone structure and an intelligent if sharp face with a fine head of curly brown hair and good teeth, thanks to the vast amounts of money spent on them by his mother. He thought his ice-blue eyes were his best feature, but as he often wore dark glasses because of a reaction to strong light, he ended up looking like a junkie. John Cooper Clarke at least had possessed some style; no matter what Duncan wore, he always ended up looking like a Duncan. He also had long thin fingers. 'Piano player's hands,' as his mother had insisted to his piano tutor, even though it was clear to both him and Mr Kern that, whilst Duncan might have had the digits of a young Chopin, he was also tone-deaf. He had always been very self-conscious about his hands: it was like carting around a pair of giant albino spiders strapped to his wrists. He *did* like his willy, though.

It was long and thin like his fingers and it was the one instrument he had learned to play well. He thought it would now be able to give many a girl hours of endless pleasure, particularly if treated as a wind instrument. Fine in theory, but in practice it was practically uncharted territory: an Unstarted – never mind Unfinished – Symphony, in fact. Actually, he had had sex with two different girls. That neither had chosen to repeat the experience had not been lost on his already dented ego. Okay, one had stolen his wallet afterwards, and the other had only done it because her friends told her Duncan was in Wet Wet Wet. (When she found out he wasn't, she'd threatened to claim rape but had taken his motor scooter instead. What kind of girl puts her virtue on a par with a Vespa?) And that was it.

So, for the time being, he had to go on perfecting his technique in a solo capacity. He switched on the picture just at the point where Louise starts getting it from behind and, taking hold of his already engorged penis with his 'pianist's fingers', he started playing his favourite tune.

After a few minutes he noticed the smell of fish was even stronger but now, instead of being unpleasant, for some reason, it was actually quite exciting. Almost stimulating, in fact. Maybe he was getting kinky for cod. He laughed at the thought and missed the vital shot where Big Mick pulls out of Louise and offers her a suck. Being Louise, of course she accepts. Soon would come the part where she discovers the unimaginable bliss of having Big Mick squirt her in the eye. Duncan was getting near himself, his wrist now a blur.

Nearer, nearer. 'Yes yes, come on, come on!' he urged – knowing full well the precise moment Mick's hose would start spraying but no-one was listening, so what the hell.

Only seconds now. 'Come on, Mick, come on! Give it her! Get that monster pumping! Come on come on . . .'

The smell of fish was now overpowering but to Duncan it was merely grist to the mill. *This is going to be a good one, Dunc!* 'Come on come on, that's it, pull it out—'

'What a great pair of tits,' said a voice from behind.

Duncan let out a yell and leapt up off the sofa, too late to stop himself coming. He backed over to the opposite end of the couch, his penis firing on all cylinders and ruining the upholstery. Louise was screaming in ecstasy as she encountered a problem Optrex had no solution for. Duncan was just screaming: not from being interrupted nor from embarrassment but out of sheer bloody terror.

The intruder looked at him equally alarmed. 'Hey, kid, I'm sorry. I didn't mean to—'

'*No!*' shrieked Duncan. '*You're dead! I saw you!*' He stumbled back over the coffee table and fell on his backside. The intruder advanced towards him, the bloated purple balloon that passed for the face of Leonard Halsey staring down at him quizzically.

Duncan's brain took the easy way out and shut down, but even as darkness engulfed him, he recognised the horrifying truth of his situation.

He had just been caught wanking by a dead man.

4

DUNCAN WAS STILL on the floor, on his back. His first sight on opening his eyes was the nightmare that was the man in his underpants with the fractured tomato for a head. He was sat on the white sofa staring intently at the television. Duncan glanced over at the screen. Louise was entertaining three black men at once. It was the climax of the tape, literally. The man was lapping it up, fondling his Y-fronts.

Duncan sat up a touch, then shuffled himself back until he bumped into the cocktail bar. Decanters chinged and the man turned to look at him.

Duncan couldn't help screaming again.

'Oh, shut up with that noise, kiddo,' said the man. 'Good tape, this. Not doing much for me, though,' he said, looking down at his crotch. 'Must be true what they say, despite appearances to the contrary: "There's no life after death."' He let go his crotch with a resigned sigh and lounged back on the couch.

'This isn't happening,' said Duncan, irritating both of them with the hopeless inadequacy of his words.

'Oh yes, it is,' said the man, looking again at the TV. 'And there's worse, I'm afraid.'

Duncan whined and stood up shakily, his own penis wet and now limp.

'I'd have one of those, if I was you,' suggested the man, pointing at the optics ranged on the other side of the bar.

Duncan had never been one for alcohol but he judged the arrival in his lounge of a dead person one occasion when – so to speak – spirits might be appropriate. He grabbed a tumbler and, keeping his eyes on his visitor, edged his way round to the upturned Glenlivet bottle and forced out three measures which he swigged back in one long gulp.

When he had finished coughing and gasping he reached into the mini-fridge beneath the bar and poured a glass of iced water, sipping it in an attempt to quench the burning sensation in his throat.

The man tutted as the tape finished, then turned to Duncan and patted the buttoned-leather cushion beside him.

'Come and sit down, kid. You look unwell.'

'*I* look unwell? You're supposed to be dead!'

'I *am* dead.'

'*What?*'

'You found my body, didn't you? Didn't I look dead to you then?'

'Of course! But the . . . *I'm talking to a corpse! A corpse in its underpants!* I must be mad.'

'Kid, I'll try and make this simple. First things first. Either I'm here or you're off your chump. Agreed?'

'Y – yes.'

'Right. So chuck that water in your face and see if you wake up.'

For want of anything better to do, Duncan did just that. His action elicited more shrieks. It was ice-cold water and he was still naked. He ducked behind the bar and grabbed a bar towel.

'Okay, okay,' he finally managed to say as he dried himself off. 'I'm awake, you're real. Maybe. Could you pass me my jeans?'

'Sorry, no can do.'

'Why?'

'I'm dead. I can't move anything.'

'Oh, cut the crap whoever you are! Who set you up to this? Was it Billy Holland? Andy? Yeah, Andy Baxter. He always had a weird sense of humour. Weird friends, too, the poof. Never liked me much either. Saw me on TV and—'

'—and found out what I looked like and got someone who looked just like me? Persuaded me to strip off and come and give you a fright? Crap. Besides, no actor I ever seen could do this . . .'

The man leaned over to Duncan's jeans and made to pick them up, but instead his hand went straight *through* the crumpled denims. He waggled his hand around to emphasise the point.

'See, kid? Can't touch anything.'

But Duncan couldn't see. He had fainted again, slumping over the bar top.

He came to again almost immediately, however, to find the man lying down on the couch looking up at the ceiling.

'Have we finished now with the melodramatics? Here I am trying to have a sensible conversation and you keep passing out. Now buck up! It's so childish. You're a grown man, well into your twenties I'd judge, so act it.'

Duncan let his left foot crawl across the floor and snag his 501s. Then, dragging them back, he quickly slipped into them and retreated behind the bar again.

'Stay there, then. You going to rewind this tape or what?'

'*You* rewind it,' said Duncan petulantly, looking around for a suitable weapon.

'Can't. Told you. Don't you ever listen?'

'Who are you?' said Duncan, wincing as the man poked his finger through the video remote control. 'What are you? What do you want?'

'More to the point, kid, who are *you?*'

'What?'

'Watt?'

'What?'

'Your name's Watt?'

'No. No, my name's . . . how come you don't know it?'

'*What's your fucking name?*' said the man, angrily.

A startled and frightened Duncan said: 'Duncan Cantrill.'

'And would I be right in assuming you found me in the hotel?'

'Yeah. This morning. About half-eight. You were . . .'

'Yeah. I was, wasn't I? Still, what's done is done. Now to get my own back.'

'On who?'

'On whoever killed me.'

'Well, it wasn't me!'

'I know that! Look, let me explain. My name's Leonard, Leonard Halsey.' He sat up and offered Duncan his hand; he might as well have been holding a gun for all the welcome this action received. He shrugged his shoulders at Duncan's panicked reaction and lay back down again. 'I was murdered by someone last night. I don't know who but I got a few ideas, and until I get the bastard, you're stuck with me.'

'Pardon?'

'I was murdered. Now don't ask me how I know, but it seems when some people are murdered they're offered the chance to come back and haunt someone or somewhere until their murderer is also dead. Of course, I wasn't going to sit around dead while some bastard gets away with killing me, so I came back. Problem is, the only person you get to haunt is the one who finds your body. And that's you, kid.'

'Well, that's all right, then,' said Duncan, without a clue what he was saying. His mind had already run out of the house and was halfway to Macclesfield. 'You're here to haunt me? Until your murderer is caught?'

'Until my murderer *dies*.'

'And you don't know who he is?'

'Not exactly. Got my suspicions. At the moment I don't even know *how* I died.'

Duncan snorted. 'But that's obvious!'

'What do you mean?'

'Well, just look at yourself . . .'

Leonard looked at his hands and body. He was about five feet ten, well overweight, maybe fifteen stone, very hairy all over, and also very pale, but whether that was his natural colour or the result of his predicament . . . The man ran his hands over his arms, chest, belly and balls.

'What?' he finally said.

'Your face.'

Leonard felt his head, then ran his hands round his neck.

'No. What is it?' he said, plainly puzzled.

'Don't you feel anything?'

'I'm bloody dead! Of course I don't feel anything.'

Duncan looked around the bar. The drinks tray. They had a highly-polished silver tray. He cleared the glasses off and held it up for Leonard to look into.

'There,' said Duncan. 'Can you see now? Your head's all purple and puffed up. Bruised. And your neck. It's been . . . *squeezed*.'

'Can't see a thing, kid.'

Duncan walked over to a side table and took a small antique mirror down from the wall and, keeping his distance, held it up for Leonard's appreciation.

'Still nowt. Come nearer, I'm not going to eat you.'

'How do I know that!'

'You've been watching too many movies kid. I can't touch anything, including you. Okay?' To emphasise his point he prodded vainly at the remote control again.

26

Duncan's despairing mind could see some kind of logic in his statement, so taking a deep breath, he advanced slowly towards him.

He held the mirror up again but again the man shook his head. For one horrifying moment Duncan thought it might fall off, or the ludicrously thin neck would snap, but it didn't.

Duncan checked the mirror himself. He couldn't see the man. Puzzled, he shifted it about until he had run the reflection the full length of the couch. He could see the TV and the video and the rug and all five cushions on the couch, but no man. Leonard offered no reflection.

Duncan's mind, for reasons best known to itself, screamed 'Vampire!' He dropped the mirror to the carpet where, thankfully, it didn't break and, holding up his two forefingers, made the sign of the cross in front of him.

Leonard was, at first, clearly puzzled. Despite the loathsome appearance of his face, his eyes and eyebrows were still capable of expressing emotion and Duncan could see the man wasn't reacting in the way he should. Then the man started laughing. He was *definitely* not acting in the manner expected.

'You tosspot!' said the man. 'I'm not bloody Christopher Lee, and with that body you don't even qualify as Peter Cushing! Now sit down somewhere. We've got to talk.'

Duncan was by now too emotionally drained to do anything but obey. Besides, the man's horrible countenance wasn't as bad as it had first appeared. The neck was still incongruous but the face was beginning more and more to resemble that of Alfred Hitchcock with a massive port wine stain.

'I can't touch anything and apparently I don't have a reflection. I didn't know that. You live and learn. Or, rather, die and learn. Ha! Look, kid, my name's Leonard Halsey. I sell . . . I *used* to sell insurance for Arlington Assurance, based in Leeds. I'm forty-six, married, no kids. Me and the wife don't get on so good and I spend a lot of time away from home. Last night I had a girl up in my room. We had a screw, I was waiting for seconds, when all of a sudden – blam! I'm croaked. Next thing I know, everything's white and I'm being given a choice. The room or you. I chose you. Who wants to haunt a bloody no-star hotel room for all eternity? Chances of the bloke I want staying in that room strike me as being pretty remote. So here I am. And anywhere you go, I go.'

'Hang on . . . You died and someone offered you . . . you mean God?'

'Not *someone*. It just, well, happened. I just knew I had a choice and took it. There wasn't any person . . . I don't remember one, anyway. Even if there was someone, I doubt it was Him. I'm no Christian. Exact opposite, in fact.'

'An atheist?'

'Nope. A satanist, supposedly.'

'A *what?*'

'Black Magic. Devil-worshipper,' he laughed. 'I never took it as serious as some of the rest and I think that's what may have pissed them off at me. Who made me the offer I haven't a clue, but I took it. Better this than mouldering in some grave with only worms for company.'

'This isn't happening,' said Duncan. 'You think you were murdered by one of your fellow . . . satanists?'

'Yep. See, just before I got it in the neck' (*the comment was lost on Leonard but it made Duncan feel even queasier*) I found something in my wallet . . . can't remember what exactly but it scared the shit out of me. And before that there was something about a priest . . . Racimo. Yes, that was the name. I knew someone called Racimo from our meetings but I never knew he was a priest. Anyway, he'd died in a car crash and it set me to thinking and I looked in my wallet and lo and behold there was . . . something. Whatever it was, I know it had to be there for a reason and I was right. Looks like the reason was to get me killed. Just how did I die?'

'Papers say you were strangled, but your neck's . . . well, it looks like it was put through a mangle. And your face is all swelled up like a . . . a tomato. Like it's going to pop. It's . . . horrible . . .'

'Thanks. So I *was* strangled.'

'And you don't remember who?'

'All I remember is choking, gasping for breath, and darkness, but that's all.'

'And you think you know who might have done it?'

'Not exactly, I like sex. Who doesn't?' he said, jerking a thumb at the TV screen and making Duncan blush. 'Some time, a few months back, I was offered the chance to get in on an orgy. Witchcraft and all that shit, but the basic thing was lots of fucking. Anyone and anything. I was game, so I went along. And it was great. To begin with. Once a month, regular as clockwork, we got to fuck our brains

28

out. Took me days to get over it. Dick rubbed raw, you wouldn't believe . . . What I didn't realise was some of those arseholes took the whole thing seriously. They really wanted to talk to the dead and summon up the devil and all that stuff.'

'Did they?'

'Course not! It's a load of crap. They didn't even sacrifice animals! But I still made the mistake of letting some of the others know what I thought of it all. And some of them got a bit peeved. I was warned not to treat it so lightly, but as they didn't actually stop me going or threaten me with anything, I thought nothing of it. Until the last time I went, a couple of months back, and I found out one of the girls who used to go had died. Quite a few were scared. No-one said anything but I got the impression that the big boys in the coven had done it. Maybe sacrificed her or something. I decided then and there to give it up. It was getting too heavy. Besides, the sex was getting weird. No fun in it any more, so I quit. Told a couple of people I thought I could trust I wouldn't be back. That might have been my mistake. Now I'm dead.'

'And you think they're involved?'

'Bound to be.'

'So why not tell the . . .'

'I hope you weren't going to say "Tell the police", kiddo. Get it into your head: I'm dead. D-E-A-D. You are talking to a ghost. *Comprenez?*'

For a while Duncan hadn't really *comprenezed*. Despite the man's face and neck and near-nudity, he talked normally and acted normally. But he was dead. He didn't – *couldn't* – exist. Duncan had finally flipped.

Suddenly he stood up, ran out of the lounge and stumbled his way upstairs to his bedroom, where he slammed the door shut, locked it and barricaded it with a chair. He turned, intending to flop onto his bed and do some serious sobbing.

'Until whoever did this to me dies, I'm here to stay,' said Leonard Halsey with a sigh. He was sitting on the bed.

Duncan screamed, turned back to the door and fought with the chair until finally he threw it across the room in frustration, then frantically unlocked the door and ran down the passageway to the bathroom, where he locked himself in and retreated to the glassed shower stall.

Leonard was already there. 'Take it from me, Dunc––'

Duncan screamed again and, gibbering, ran back to the door, unlocked it and ran downstairs. He charged across the kitchen, his bare feet slapping on the red tiles, until he reached the back door. There he turned the three locks and ran into the garden, ignoring the clangour from the burglar alarm.

He didn't look back, even when the floodlights automatically switched on and turned night into day. He charged down the long sweep of the rear lawn, burbled oaths and shorthand prayers tumbling from his lips, until he reached the bottom of the garden. There he stopped to get his breath back, only to find Leonard Halsey standing beside him looking up in astonishment at the floodlit phallic bush.

'Do you know this looks just like a giant cock?'

That was it. Duncan lay down on the grass and tried to bury his face in the earth. Then, clamping his hands over his ears, he began screeching in short sharp bursts at the grass.

And that was the scene which confronted Mrs Cantrill when she came home a couple of minutes later: a kitchen wide open to the night, burglar alarms ringing incessantly, her lawn lit up like a football pitch – and her son lying on his belly, dressed only in jeans, screaming into the lawn. Her first instinct was to find out what he had been up to *this* time, but instead she went inside and checked on her jewellery.

5

DUNCAN COULD HEAR and, just about, see the doctor and his mother on the other side of the room.

'As best we can tell, Mrs Cantrill, he hasn't been taking any drugs. There was a small amount of alcohol in his blood, but it wasn't enough to have broken the law had he been driving. I would like to think it's simply shock from his discovery of Tuesday morning. Encountering death at close quarters takes people in different ways. I've seen some policemen crack after years of duty. Doctors, too. I think the best we can do is continue with sedation if he shows any more violent tendencies, but otherwise, just bed rest and perhaps a holiday?'

Duncan couldn't catch his mother's reply but she nodded. At least that was something. They both looked in his direction and he closed his eyes hastily. They left. He opened his eyes again. He was alone. He was in a hospital all right, and judging by the plush décor and the facilities – TV, cassette radio, telephone, fridge, original prints on the walls, an abundance of flowers – it was a private room. Probably a private hospital come to that. The Pines, more than likely. He sat up. The room smelled clean and fresh, but not antiseptic. Like a good hotel. He thought back to the Tuesday night.

He had been carted in here in the early hours of Wednesday, heavily sedated. So much so that he couldn't be sure now that what had pushed him over the edge hadn't been an illusion after all. *Of course it was!* The dead don't rise and come and slobber over pornographic videos. No. He *had* freaked, just like the doctor said, and now he could look forward to a good rest and, with luck, a decent holiday. Maybe the villa in Portugal or possibly he would be able to weedle a trip to America out of mum. Whatever mess he had made out of his life, his mother still blamed herself to a certain extent and, whenever possible, would exorcise her guilt by spending his father's money on the two of them.

Duncan settled back under the covers. Yeah, best do what the doc says. Rest and recuperation. Good old R & R as they say on *M*A*S*H**. He wondered if dad would pay a call but decided it was highly unlikely. He hadn't been there for his birth – his bloody conception must have been by appointment! – so what appeal would a touch of lunacy in his sole offspring hold?

He pulled the covers up around his neck and turned over. An odour suddenly caught his attention. *Uh-oh*. Fish. Hadn't he heard somewhere that some people, when they go mad, apart from seeing things, also smell things? Like rubber or roses or . . . fish? He opened his eyes to find himself looking at Leonard Halsey sat in an easy chair across the room, still naked bar a pair of baggy Y-fronts. Duncan closed his eyes immediately.

'No fooling me, Dunc. I saw you. Come on,' said Leonard.

Duncan opened his eyes again. So it was true. He *was* insane. He fumbled out a hand and clasped the buzzer for the nurse. She'd take Mr Halsey away. One jab from a syringe and he'd be back in the land of nod, all on his ownsome. Everything would be fine. That said, he kept his gaze on Halsey while he waited.

'Dunc, I can understand your reluctance to believe what's happening. Took me a while to really accept I was dead. Big step, that. Understanding you're dead and gone . . . still, I'm here and now. I'll make it easy for you. Go straight for the big sell. Nursey's going to come in here, right? You carry on as if you're ga-ga and seeing pink elephants and I'll prove to you that I'm really here. Okay?'

Duncan didn't respond because he knew if he did it would be with a high-pitched squawk and a dash for the window.

The nurse bustled in. She was young and quite attractive, Chinese or Japanese, he couldn't decide. Most important though, she was *real*. Leonard seemed to find her attractive as well. He leered. An ugly enough leer it would have been at the best of times, but as he currently resembled a beetroot after a bout of unsuccessful anaplasty, it was a particularly unedifying sight.

'I think I'm going to flip again,' said Duncan to the nurse. 'Do you think you could give me something?'

'I'll have to check with the doctor but I don't see why not. Will you be all right for a moment?'

Duncan nodded. The nurse left. He looked around. Leonard had gone. Maybe he wouldn't need to be zonked after all. Then a hand appeared on the bed covers near his knee. Duncan let out a little whimper as a puffing Halsey hove into view from under the bed.

'God, I might be dead but I ain't lost any weight. Blue. Dark blue.'

'Wha . . .?'

'The nurse has dark blue knickers. Just looked up her skirt.'

Duncan whimpered again. Not only was he imagining a member of the walking dead, but his particular zombie was also a pervert.

'Wha . . .?'

'No way you can know she's got blue panties,' explained Leonard. 'Great legs, by the way. Not unless someone – me – has seen them. Agreed?'

'So what do—'

'Ask her.'

Duncan slumped back on the pillows. *He's dead, he's a pervert, or he's stupid. You should have eaten more vegetables when you were a kid, Duncan.* Then to the ceiling he said, 'How can I ask a nurse the colour of her underwear?'

'Good point, kid. Hadn't thought of that. Got a bit carried away with some of the stuff I can do.' He looked to the door, scratching his backside. 'This might be fun after all. Nice arse . . . Okay, something concrete. Let me think.'

The doctor arrived a couple of minutes later. He was in his late twenties, an athletic blond man with a harried look and a vaguely effeminate manner.

'What seems to be the trouble, Duncan?' he said in an incongruous Geordie accent. It was like hearing Prince Charles speak Brummie.

'I'd like to know what you have diagnosed me as having.'

The doctor smiled a doctorly smile. He might as well have held up a card saying: TIME TO ACT THE PATRONISING PRICK.

'Now, Duncan, we're still not sure,' he said, putting down his clipboard on the side table and sitting on the bed. Duncan fully expected him to start patting his wrist. Out of the corner of his eye he watched Leonard lean over and read the top paper on the clipboard.

'What about him?' interrupted Duncan, nodding at Leonard.

'Who?' said the doctor, patently unaware that there was a dead insurance salesman in his underpants three feet to his right.

'That man next to you.'

'What man, Duncan?'

Trying another tack, Duncan asked: 'What does that sign say on the wall?'

'Which sign, that one by the window?' said the doctor, humouring him.

Duncan nodded. Leonard Halsey would be in direct line of sight. No way would the doctor be able to read it if Leonard was real. Which, of course, he couldn't be, could he?

'Fire regulations,' said the doctor. 'Why?'

'Oh, just . . . curious. So you were saying what's wrong with me . . .'

'No, I was just about to—'

'"*Acute paranoid schizophrenia brought on by trauma*,"' said Leonard with a crooked smile – and with his face the shape it was, it was about the only kind of smile he would ever manage.

'—say that we're not sure, Shock, from—'

'Not "acute paranoid schizophrenia brought on by trauma"?' asked Duncan.

The doctor was plainly fazed by this pronouncement. 'How? No, it's too soon . . . who have you been talking to?'

Wouldn't you like to know thought a simultaneously elated and appalled Duncan. Elated that he wasn't mad; appalled at the truth of his predicament.

'Just a guess. I . . . I was watching Quincy the other night. Same kind of thing . . .'

It took a further three minutes of blether to persuade the doctor that he just needed some sleep – *natural* sleep – before the slightly miffed doctor disappeared to have a serious word with the nurse.

Leonard sat down on the bed and held his hands up. 'Told you so.'

They sat staring at one another for a full thirty seconds, until Duncan reached over to his bedside cabinet and, grabbing a vase of flowers, methodically poured the contents onto the floor, then threw up into it.

6

THE HOSPITAL CHAPEL looked like an old boiler room. The resemblance was easily explained; it *was* an old boiler room. The hospital was fifty per cent new, the rest being the remains of an old preparatory school. As a private hospital constructed during the Thatcher years, faith in the pound had replaced faith in God and the chapel had been provided only as an afterthought.

Still, it was as quiet as a church, and the dusky pink interior, religious adornments, and the dozen or so light oak pews ranked either side of the red patterned carpet helped offset the maze of pipes that festooned the side walls. That, and a startling stained-glass mosaic that hung behind the altar depicting what looked like a dove caught in a nuclear explosion but surely had some deeper symbolic meaning, all lent the room an air of calm reason that Duncan needed.

He wasn't sure of his sanity yet. True, Leonard had read documents which Duncan couldn't have seen, but it wasn't enough. After all, he was being asked to accept the existence of ghosts. He'd read somewhere, *Reader's Digest* maybe, that there had been five trillion photographs taken since the invention of the camera – that's a five followed by *eighteen* zeros – and yet not one shot had produced incontrovertible evidence of the existence of ghosts, spirits or any other manifestations of the supernatural. From UFOs and the Loch Ness Monster to the Yeti and ancient astronauts, not one image was acceptable as proof. So why should Duncan Cantrill, unemployed hotel receptionist and comprehensive failure, suddenly be privileged to witness a visitation by a fully-fledged member of the undead? Why should he be haunted by Leonard Halsey? Perhaps, he reasoned, God had the answer or, failing Him, one of His uniformed intermediaries.

Duncan entered the empty chapel and walked slowly to the front. Leonard was with him, as he always was now.

'What are we here for?' said the nearly-nude man with the aubergine-coloured head.

'To check out if you're real.'

'And then what? Exorcise me? Cast out my evil spirit?'

'Something like that.'

'But I'm not an evil spirit. I'm Leonard. Okay, I'm no saint, but I ain't Hitler either.'

'You sound worried, Leonard.'

'No, I'm not, kid, but *you* should be. If this doesn't work you're running out of options. Just think: wouldn't you rather retain that element of doubt? Maybe you *are* loopy. At least that way you always have a way out, an excuse. Confirm I'm real and you've got to believe in ghosts, reincarnation, resurrection, the afterlife, heaven, hell, zombies—'

'I get the picture, Leonard! But if I leave that doubt, what makes you think I'll do what *you* want me to? If I'm mad, I'm mad – and nothing you do will make me find your murderer.'

'Good point, kid. Go talk to a priest,' said Leonard, sitting down three pews from the front.

Duncan approached the altar. He hadn't been in a church in – what? – ten years at least. He didn't know what to do. Was it a Catholic chapel? Did he bow, cross himself, what?

There was a discreet cough at his side and he turned to find an elderly priest dressed in his vestments looking at him with that kindly expression of understanding all men of the cloth must be handed when they're ordained.

'Oh, sorry,' said Duncan. 'I hope I wasn't . . .'

'It's God's house. You may enter at any time. You don't need permisson.'

Why do priests always talk like priests? 'I need . . . some advice. It's a bit difficult to talk about.'

'Take your time. I'll help in any way I can. Seat?'

He waved at the front pew and they sat down. The priest was white-haired but not as old as Duncan had at first presumed. Maybe fifty-five, he was tall and distinguished and possessed a voice that sounded as if it had been rubbed smooth over the years. He was a comforting presence, there was no denying it. Duncan glanced over his shoulder at Leonard, who simply smiled back.

'Is it sexual? A girl in trouble? A boy?'

Duncan almost laughed. *If only.* 'No. Nothing like that. I don't know where to start—'

'Stick it to him!' shouted Leonard. 'Say your piece, kid!'

'Okay,' he agreed. 'Sir, do you believe in ghosts?'

'I believe in the resurrection through the Holy Spirit—'

Leonard starting laughing.

'No, no, forget religion for now,' said Duncan. 'Sorry, but . . . can you see a man sat behind us, three rows back?'

The priest arched his eyebrows but said nothing and turned to survey the dimly-lit chapel, then shook his head.

'There's no-one there?' said Duncan.

'Just we two, my son. And—'

'Don't say God. Please,' said Duncan.

'I'm sorry?'

Duncan stood up and walked over to the beaming Leonard and stood beside his pew. 'To my right, there is a naked middle-aged man in his underpants who has been murdered. His name was . . . *is* Leonard Halsey. He is haunting me.'

'Well, I did warn you,' said Leonard after they were back in Duncan's room with the door locked.

'I didn't think priests were allowed to swear.'

'Every man has his limit. Especially when you're on top of him trying to make him swallow his surplice.'

'You have a point. Oh shit, what now?'

'The sooner you accept me for what I am, the sooner we can get on with getting rid of me. So what alternatives have you got? No-one else can see me, right? Priests don't know I'm here either and I'm not afraid of religious places or crosses, so I think that means I'm not evil.'

'You don't know?'

'Hey, I've been cheating on my wife for eleven years and I sold insurance. There's two commandments gone for a start! But I don't think I'm evil with a big E, just . . . naughty?'

'"Naughty"? *Your* word. Okay so no-one sees you and you're not evil so that means what? I'm possessed?'

'Good. Like it. "The Exorcist". Ace movie. Just watch where you put the crucifix!'

'Very funny.'

'Father Kelly would've detected the presence of evil in you or me. Mind you, you did try strangling him . . .'

'Okay, let's drop that approach, shall we! The only alternative left, if you're *not* a ghost, is that I must be totally mad. What was it the doctor said?'

'"Acute paranoid schizophrenia brought on by trauma."'

'Yeah. Now what other symptoms do paranoid schizos show?'

'They talk to themselves. Well, if I'm not here, you would be. And sometimes they top themselves.'

'Pardon?'

'They try to commit suicide. Someone I once worked with had it. After a month of talking to his fountain pen he gassed himself in his car.'

Duncan went quiet. Leonard sat on the bed and looked him in the face.

'That's it, kid: your two final options. Either I'm here and I'm dead, or you're going to be dead and gone. Now I may look a mess as you say, but I'm not that bad a bloke, am I? Not so bad you'd go and kill yourself over me?'

Duncan didn't respond.

Leonard stood up and walked to the window. It was dark outside and raining heavily, doing nothing to lift the mood of the conversation. 'Besides, lots of mad people are happy. So why not just relax and enjoy it?'

'Enjoy it? I'm talking to a man with a bloody Belisha beacon for a head; who smells like a week-old tin of sardines; who wants me to check out some of his old mates to see which one of them knocked him off; and who won't go away until the guilty party is as dead as him.'

'That's about the measure of it, Dunc.'

Mad or not, Duncan deemed tears an appropriate response.

7

DUNCAN WAS HOME at last. It was Sunday. They had kept him in hospital for five days before coming to the conclusion that he'd merely had a rather gross reaction to shock, and that with a couple of weeks of taking it easy he would soon be back to his customary deadbeat ways.

Duncan wasn't arguing. Whilst he had come to terms with having a corpse for a roommate, he was in no hurry to do what Leonard was asking him to do. But the last couple of days had amply illustrated the alternatives. He was being haunted by the man – *haunted* – and unless he went along with his ideas, he'd be there forever. It wasn't as if he was even good company! And *in* company, he was just a pest.

As long as he shut up it was all right, but if he started talking or passing comment, then it was very difficult to concentrate. Dinner this homecoming night was the first true indication of how awkward things could get.

'I had Mrs Orr cook your favourite,' said Mrs Cantrill as they entered the dining room. 'Steak, baked potatoes and mushrooms.'

'Yummy,' said Duncan, not meaning it. Mrs Orr was their woman what did. She often cooked meals for them and put them in the freezer for later consumption. Duncan's mother was a lousy cook, but it wasn't entirely her fault.

She had been brought up in a household with a paid cook and had never felt the need or urge to learn. Indeed, with a housekeeper and a maid and a nanny she hadn't had to learn any home-making skills. Her marriage at twenty-one to a rich man had done nothing to change her mind. Her only concession to 'Nineties sensibilities was that she didn't have any live-in staff; Mrs Orr came in every day and Grant, the chauffeur, was always away with Duncan's father.

So they had sat down to dinner in their large dining room.

Immaculately furnished in the Georgian style, it was like stepping into another century, despite their home being less than ten years old. Elsewhere the house boasted the open vistas and unnecessarily large expanses of expensive and too-highly-polished floorboards that its ranch-style design demanded – as if their architect had merely doctored a plan for a library – but this room was actually to the right proportions. The sky-blue walls and gold trim, subdued lighting and beautiful silverware gave it an elegance his mother aspired to and he didn't deserve. For some reason she had lit candles to give the room an atmosphere which, under other circumstances, could have been described as romantic, restful or dignified, but with a dead person staring down his mother's expansive cleavage, became simply spooky. So spooky, in fact, that Duncan couldn't help remembering back to the precise moment in hospital when Leonard had proven he was genuine.

Even had Duncan been guessing, he would never have known some of the facts the man managed to toss his way. He could go anywhere Duncan went, which meant he was able to read papers and files in the same room, even though Duncan couldn't see them himself. The clincher, however, had been the time he had come across the attractive oriental nurse in one of the day rooms.

She had been crying and he hadn't wanted to intrude, but Leonard had insisted as he stooped down and glanced at the letter the girl held in her hand.

'A girl called Penny's been killed in a car crash in Sweden,' he said. 'Ask her.'

Now there was no way Duncan could have known this. The other stuff – doctors' diagnoses, the colour of underwear, second-guessing the menus and so on – all that could have been conjecture or details seen or overheard while he was sedated, but this was something else.

'I'm – I'm sorry about Penny,' Duncan said quietly.

The girl looked up. She *was* pretty. Her mascara was running: proof he was in a private hospital. She muttered an equally muted 'thank you,' and then doubt filtered into her features. Duncan turned and ran before she asked him how he knew. For his part, Leonard had whooped for joy. *At last, the kid knew the truth of it all.*

The sound of his mother pouring wine brought Duncan back to the present. Leonard had finished slobbering over her blouse – she, of course, had been unable to see him – and had sat down at the opposite end of the twenty-feet long dining table in Duncan's father's chair, Cantrill Snr now being in Hong Kong, and watched them eat.

'Duncan,' said his mother after a long pause. 'Do you think you're over this, er, problem now?'

'Yes. It was as the doctor said. I obviously wasn't ready for what I'd seen. Shock, you know. Sorry if I worried you.'

'Oh, she was worried all right,' said Leonard. 'Spent ten minutes checking the safe while you ate the lawn.'

'Shut up,' hissed Duncan.

'Pardon?' said his mother, not quite sure she had heard what she had heard.

'Nothing, mummy. I'm just tired. This steak is excellent.'

It wasn't. It had been cooked in the afternoon, then bunged in the microwave. Warmed-over shoe leather would have been more appetising.

'The doctor suggested a holiday,' she said finally. 'I was thinking the villa in Portugal.'

'So was I,' lied Duncan again. He wanted to go to New England but knew he was on to a loser. His mother was willing to do things for him as long as they didn't involve her *doing* things. The villa was company-owned and everything would be laid on, from a car to take them to the airport, to the airline tickets, to the car at the other end and the servants in the villa itself. A trip to the States, on the other hand, would involve her organising things for herself. Not on.

'Dunc,' said Leonard. 'Not a good idea, this holiday.'

'Yes, it is.'

'What?' said Mrs Cantrill.

'A good idea,' said Duncan.

'The holiday?' said his mother.

'No!' said Leonard.

'Yes!' shouted Duncan.

'Yes, it is,' agreed his mother, somewhat unsettled by her son's firmness.

'*No!*' insisted Leonard.

'*Yes!*' reaffirmed Duncan to his steak.

'All right Duncan . . . I'll arrange it in the morning,' said his mother, eyeing the door.

'Kiddo,' said Leonard, standing up and walking round the table. 'We got work to do.'

'*You*'ve got work to do!' said Duncan.

'Yes,' said his startled mother, peering over her shoulder and wondering why her son was addressing their silver-plated Victorian wine cooler. 'But I can leave it for a while . . .'

'Sorry,' said Duncan, noticing his mother's worried expression. 'Yes, you can. I mean, can you?'

'Course she fucking can, Dunc! But what about my murder?'

'*What about it?*' demanded Duncan through gritted teeth.

'What, Duncan?' His mother's eyes were out of control. She didn't know where to look. She was sharing steak *au poivre* with a deranged person. Worse: he was a relative.

Duncan calmed himself and, smiling, said: 'I meant what work will you be leaving?'

Luckily his mother didn't catch the smile, otherwise she would have armed herself with a fork and started backing out of the room. Instead she seized on the opportunity for normal conversation with all the determination of a terrier down a badger sett.

'Oh, nothing the troops can't handle. There's the ring road; the conservation area extension schemes; the new Tesco's; the problem with the gypsies on Parkway . . .'

She rambled on. Despite her assurances to the contrary, it was clear she was convinced that within three days of her leaving Ollington, the entire machinery of local government west of the Pennines would grind to a halt, such was the integral part she played. But she was brave; she had her son to consider. Who could be re-elected next May with a lunatic for a son?

'Duncy boy!' Leonard had renewed his argument. 'I'm not going until the guy who did this to me has croaked. Wherever you go, I go with you.'

'You won't be going *everywhere?*' Duncan was aghast.

'Not if you need time to yourself, Duncan,' said his mother.

He could see she was starting to panic. On a scale of one to ten she had reached seven, which ranked above the time Winston the collie humped the vicar's leg during afternoon tea – the dog was a guest of the PDSA the next day – and just below catching her naked thirteen-year-old son playing with one of her girdles when she brought her coffee circle up to admire the new canopy on her bed. Duncan tried to make amends:

'I didn't mean that, mum. I could always go off on my own. To Portugal. If you're too busy to spare the time right now . . .'

She obviously thought this an attractive proposition, but immediately envisioned the headlines: 'Prominent Local Councillor's Son Runs Amok With Axe In The Algarve'.

Leonard, meanwhile, had decided to lean against the table next to Duncan, and so obscure his view of his mother.

'It's as simple as this, kid,' he explained. 'Wherever and whenever you go, *I* go. You go for a walk, I'm there. You go to sleep, I'm there. You want a wank? Fine, but I'll be right beside you giving you pointers.'

Duncan dropped his fork and fought for breath.

'Are you all right, Duncan?' said his mother from somewhere behind Leonard.

Duncan didn't answer.

Leonard continued: 'Until the bastard who did this to me is dead, I'm stuck to you like glue. Think on it.'

'*You bastard!*'

'Duncan!' gasped his mother.

'Not you, mum!'

'Who . . . then?'

Oh God! Duncan got up and ran from the room. But Leonard was already waiting for him at the top of the stairs.

'Everywhere, kid,' he said simply.

Duncan ran past him and into the bathroom and slammed the door. He looked around frantically. The shower stall? He'd been there before. No, not this time. The linen basket? No. The medicine cupboard, then? No, thank God. Leonard wasn't here.

He felt his bowels loosening so he went to the toilet, lifted the lid, turned and started skimmying down his trousers.

'Everywhere, kid,' said Leonard's voice.

Duncan turned round and looked up. Oh God! The man was stood on the cistern grinning down at him, his bloated face like the world's biggest haemorrhoid. Duncan tried to stand but nature called and he couldn't help himself. He shat.

Leonard appeared in front of him, smiling. 'Kid, face facts, you've no choice.'

Duncan then had to endure the ignominy of defecating while Leonard stood over him, singing an improvised medley of hits that included '*Shitting on the Dock of Bay,*' '*I'm Going to Shit Right Down and Write Myself a Letter,*' and '*I'm Shitting on Top of the World*'.

8

AFTER HIS ORDEAL in the toilet, Duncan came downstairs and managed to calm his mother by explaining he'd had an attack of diarrhoea brought on by all the medication he had been taking.

'You know I'm allergic to penicillin. I must be allergic to something else they gave me too.'

His mother had accepted his story because she wanted a rational explanation; the thought that her only son could be insane was one she didn't want to consider. Mrs Cantrill felt what any mother would feel when faced with the possibility that her son was unstable; she wondered if it might have something to do with her. It was a thought that lasted approximately four seconds. No, it *couldn't* be her fault. There had to be another cause. True, Duncan had been a disappointment virtually all his life. Duncan's father's visions of an engineering empire passed on to his heir had long been abandoned, but even as he continued to let them down and disappoint them, hadn't she urged Duncan to do better? Hadn't they bought him a good education? Private tutors? And when, after all that expense, he had ended up a common hotel porter, had she thrown him out of the house? No. Even though he was twenty-two now – or was it twenty-three? – whatever, she had spent money on everything a mother possibly could and now, if he was going off his rocker, then she would ensure he got the best medical help money could buy. Though preferably in another county.

After he had gone to bed, she had come up to tuck him in, bringing with her the cassette she had found in the video the night he had gone crazy. She had watched a few minutes of it out of curiosity thinking *Lust for Louise* was that film with Kirk Douglas as Van Gogh, but the screen had painted an altogether darker picture. She had been appalled. So much so that she had suggested to his doctor that perhaps these exercises in fornication had been the deciding factor in his breakdown. She couldn't understand why the doctor thought it amusing as he explained that people who are driven to compulsive behaviour by exposure to pornography tend to perform actions other than eating their back gardens. The best thing, given his hazy state of mind, he had suggested, was to let him have it back and not say anything negative about it. The less criticism he received the sooner he would be back to normal. This had immediately presented Beryl Cantrill with a further problem: what, for Duncan, was normal? But she had complied with the doctor's wishes.

So she had given the tape to Duncan, saying: 'I thought you had better have this filth back, Duncan,' and then she had left, satisfied at her restraint and unaware that her son had turned a colour almost a perfect match for his scarlet duvet cover.

For Duncan, this delivery, and the big broken grin on Leonard's face at the Cantrills' mutual discomfort, had been the final ignominy. Not only did his mother think he was mad, but she also knew he watched blue movies – an activity on a level with roasting puppies alive in her worldview. How could he face her in the future? The woman he had once overheard tell one of her blue-rinsed cronies that she thought page three of the *Daily Telegraph* to be nothing but a guided tour of the lower depths. The *Daily Telegraph!*

Leonard broke Duncan's trance. 'Hey, Dunky boy, why don't you bring the old video up here? We'll have a party.'

'What? My mother has just found out I watch films with girls taking three men at once. The same woman who forbids the use of the word "underwear" in her presence.'

'You're kidding.'

'Nope. So, for her to discover that I watch men being peed on by black girls with big tits is going to come as a bit of a letdown. You know, when I was younger and asked awkward questions about where babies came from, her idea of being open and frank was to open the door and tell me to ask Frank about it. Frank was my personal English tutor. I'll never be able to look her in the eye again. You saw the way she handled the tape. Jesus, she had pink rubber gloves on!'

'Hey, you're right. She did.'

'I bet you she's in the bathroom right now, scrubbing her hands. God, what a mess – and it's your fault.'

'My fault? It's *your* video.'

'Yeah, and I was watching it in peace until you turned up.'

'Sorry, kid, but I didn't have much choice.'

'But you did, you sod. You said so yourself!' Duncan was blazing. 'You could have haunted that room! Other ghosts haunt houses and abbeys and old places but no, you have to come and haunt *me* – and you don't even have the decency to come dressed!'

'I can't help it! You come back the way you are when you die.'

'Why couldn't you have had a heart attack fully-dressed?'

'Because I didn't! I was fucking *murdered*, and until we get whoever did it, I'm here. I don't like it any more than you. You think I like being in my shorts, even if only you can see me?'

'And that's another thing: I've had enough of this "we" crap. I'm not doing anything for you. Your problem is your problem. All I did was call the police.'

'You've no choice, kid, just like me.'

'Oh, I've a choice all right.'

Before Leonard could ask what, Duncan had upped and run through the bedroom doorway. He ran along the landing to another bedroom, spurred on by the sound of vigorous hand-washing from the bathroom. He bounded into a vacant guest bedroom and over to the window.

Leonard was there, of course. 'What you doing?'

'Just watch and see!' shouted Duncan.

He threw open the doors onto the balcony and ran to the balustrade and looked down onto the pebbled drive. He shook his head and looked around. *Aha.*

He scrambled up an ivy-clad trellis and swung himself up onto the gently sloping roof of the house, then walked half bent up the tiles until he reached the apex of the roof. Leonard, as usual, was there.

'This is silly, Duncan.'

'Silly, is it? What point is there in me staying around? My mother will treat me like a disease; the doctors think I'm crazy; you're going to be there every single fucking minute; and dad'll just say "Duncan Cantrill, I know that name from somewhere." But I can save us all the trouble and inconvenience.'

He trotted along the roof ridge to the gable end and peered down. It was a drop of at least twenty feet onto the paved patio next to the swimming pool.

'If I kill myself, no more problems. I've been heading for this ever since you popped up.'

'This isn't the answer, Duncan.'

'Oh yes, it is. For all I know you may still be a figment of my imagination.'

'But how can I be? The stuff I told you. That nurse—'

'If I'm dreaming *you*, I could be dreaming *everything!* For all I know I'm still zonked out back in that hospital, out on some personality-altering drug or other. So if I do jump, nothing's going to hurt me.'

'Hey, Duncan, that's crazy talk!'

Duncan beamed. 'How right you are.'

He took a step nearer the edge.

'Please, kid, I'll do anything you want. No sense two of us dying.'

'Then just go away . . .'

'I *can't*. I told you. I'm sorry but . . . oh God.'

Duncan was one step away from oblivion.

'So it's no use, Leonard. Whether you're real or not I've only got the one choice.'

'But what about your mother?'

'She'll understand. You watch porno videos, you got to be deranged. I'll get a good funeral, too.'

'And your dad?'

'He'll probably get his secretary to send a wreath.'

'But what if your mother finds you?'

'She probably will. Can't be helped.'

'But what if you get the same offer I did?'

'What?' said Duncan, pausing, one foot raised to step forward.

'What if your mother finds you and you have to haunt her?'

'But I—'

'Might happen. Just imagine. Twenty-four hours a day with her forever. *And* she'll be able to see you.'

God, what a concept. Spending every minute of every day with his mother. The Committees. The Associations. The Societies. The coffee mornings, jumble sales, meetings. To say nothing of the trips to the bathroom . . . He'd rather *die*. But then again he'd already be dead! Oh shit.

'Okay. You've talked me out of it, Leonard. There *are* fates worse than death.'

He turned to make his way back along the roof, but his footing slipped, and with a desperate yell he made a grab for support at

Leonard's hand, but both could only look on in horror as Duncan's hand slid through Leonard's bare, plump arm and carried on out into the void above the patio. Then, with a piercing scream, Duncan twisted, overbalanced and plunged headfirst off the end of the roof.

9

GENUINE INTIMATIONS OF mortality are rare for most people. Unless someone close to them dies, or they themselves are in a life-threatening situation, the concept of death and eternal non-existence make little impact. Despite growing up and becoming supposedly mature, responsible individuals, most adults' concept of death remains on a par with that of a child. Hence, when real tragedy strikes, the fragile membrane that holds the average person's life together is apt to be shredded. And so it was as Duncan fell off the roof.

He couldn't say his entire life flashed before his eyes but for the first time he had an insight into the utter nothingness that is the abyss. He didn't want to die. He saw, in the instant that he tumbled over the edge of the roof – when unyielding concrete became the sky, and air his only support – that life was indeed for the living and death was fit only for the dead. He also understood with frightening clarity exactly how angry and outraged Leonard must feel about his own untimely demise. So many people die before their time, like Leonard; Duncan didn't want to join them. Nor, apparently, did Carlsberg Breweries want him to.

One of their sun umbrellas, still open over a poolside table, was strong enough to deflect Duncan's fall before it snapped and he was bounced neatly into the pool.

A scream, a splash, a moment's watery disorientation and then Duncan was thrashing to the surface and hurling himself up onto the more-than-welcoming firmness of the poolside concrete, spluttering and gasping his new-found faith in the Lord above.

Leonard bent down and looked into Duncan's dripping, quivering face. 'I'd give you 5.6 for degree of difficulty, kid, but only 4.8 for style.'

Duncan wanted to tell the man to fuck off but instead he started laughing. He was just grateful he hadn't died. He was also resolved to help Leonard revenge himself. No-one deserved to die; not even an insurance salesman with a bad sense of humour.

Duncan finally hauled himself up and dragged his tired body into the house and up to the bathroom. His mother had adjourned to her bedroom, unaware of her son's recent miraculous escape. There Duncan stood under a scalding shower for fully ten minutes, then towelled off, brushed his teeth and stumbled back to his bedroom, where he dressed in a crisp pair of clean cotton pyjamas, slid in between the sheets, and turned out the light.

'Goodnight, Leonard. We'll start tomorrow.'

'Thanks, kid. I'm sorry about the accident, but I just couldn't stop you from falling. You understand.'

'I know. Thanks anyway. One thing, though . . .'

'What, kid?'

'Don't call me kid. Kids don't deserve to come that near to dying. Only adults, and even then not them. Call me Duncan.'

'Sure, Duncan.'

As sleep enveloped him, he could hear someone crying. He couldn't tell if it was himself or Leonard. It could well have been both.

PART TWO

Investigations

Your friend is the man who knows all about you, and still likes you.

Elbert Hubbard

10

THE NEXT MORNING, while waiting for his mother to finish bustling about in the kitchen with Mrs Orr, and head off to whatever her crowded schedule allowed her to do on a Monday, Duncan got Leonard to explain in more detail about the people he wanted him to see.

'I went to these meetings once a month, regular as clockwork. Whenever there was no moon—'

'Full moon, surely?' corrected Duncan, pulling on his shirt. 'Witches and stuff is always at the full moon.'

'Not our lot. Exact opposite. When the moon was at its darkest, that's when we had our orgies. We held them in the basement of an abandoned cement factory out on the Buxton Road. Do you know it?'

Duncan did. It had closed down about five years ago. It was big and ugly and had been a centre of local controversy ever since. He thought his mother might even have campaigned about it. But then again, she'd campaign about anything, including the colour of a Labour councillor's socks if she thought there was political mileage in it.

'Well, we went down there after dark once a month and . . . did our thing.'

'And what was your thing?'

'Sex. Leastways, that's what I was after. Had some great shags, those nights . . .'

'A religious experience. I can tell.'

'Don't knock it, kid. I'm not the one who has to wank in front of the telly.' (That hit home). 'I must have got to jump the bones of a dozen or so women. All ages, all sizes, didn't matter. Every one of them was crying out for a fuck and we all obliged. And I picked up a few tricks, too. Soon found it easy to pick up birds anywhere

I went. Class, too. Money and cars and such. They couldn't get enough of me.'

This Duncan seriously doubted. Alive or dead, Leonard would hardly match the definition of stud, even in a Braille dictionary.

'Did you know any of the others?'

'Some. We weren't supposed to but I recognised some of them. Couple were almost friends.'

'Almost?'

'To be honest they were all a bit weird.'

And you weren't? thought Duncan.

'I spent some time with two of them. A sculptor called Kimmel and a teacher called David Beaumont. He had a boat. I also knew one of them was called Racimo. I didn't know he was a priest, though.'

'A priest?'

'Catholic priest. He was killed in a car crash last Monday. That's when I thought something was up. Too much of a coincidence – and I was right; just look what happened to me. Racimo had some tackle on him.'

Duncan felt vaguely nauseated. It had become clear over the last few days that Leonard was obsessed with sex. So much so that it had blinded him to the consequences of his involvement in the orgies. Plainly he was invited there for a reason above and beyond his own satisfaction, but he didn't know what. One of the few pieces of advice Duncan's father had ever given him was: *You never get anything for nothing. Everything costs.* So what had Halsey paid for his fun? The man didn't know, except he was dead. Some price.

'And that's it?'

'Yeah. I stopped going two months back. Haven't seen any of them since. I know Racimo wanted to leave, and they said he could, no problem. I took that as my cue to leave, too. Sex is one thing, but the other shit they started . . .'

'Like what?'

'Rituals. Lots of Latin and stuff. Sometimes an hour or more before we got down to business. Fair puts you off your stroke all that . . . and the sex wasn't as good any more . . .'

'How?'

'You're not married, Duncan, so you mightn't understand. Lots of people get married because it means access to unlimited supplies of nooky. Day or night, they can get a shag. But you soon come to realise there's more to marriage than getting your end away.

Boredom sets in, even if you love your wife. There's a limit to what you can do with one woman. I know it sounds sexist, but there's nothing more guaranteed to perk you up than a fresh bit of skirt. Same goes for women, too. A new prick can make up for a lot. That's why the meetings were so much fun. But the last few times the fun had gone right out of it.'

'No, er, "fresh skirt"?'

'There wasn't, but that isn't the point. It was like we were . . . having to do it for someone else. Like we were, well, in a sex show, *performing* . . . I've always wondered what people in porno do to get their rocks off. If you're on the job all day, the last thing you want to do is have it off at night. Well, it was like that for me, and a few others too. No fun, just hard work. Well, sod that. I left.'

'And now you're dead . . .'

'Yeah.'

'Sounds like a good argument for monogamy.'

'Very funny. Now, are you going to help me or just make sarcastic remarks?'

'Okay, but before we go anywhere. I think we'd better just check out what you can and can't do.'

'Fine.'

It didn't take long to determine the precise limits of Leonard's tactile abilities. He couldn't touch or move anything without going straight through it, unless it was a solid object, firmly fixed. That meant he could stand on floors, sit down in chairs or, as they soon found out, ride in a car, but he couldn't lift so much as a paperclip. Nor could he touch Duncan and vice versa. But for all his intangibility, Leonard couldn't *walk* through walls or doors. He also didn't exist anywhere other than in view of Duncan.

'It's like a cut in a movie,' Leonard tried to explain. If he didn't actually walk after Duncan, he simply found himself wherever Duncan had gone. They tried a test. Duncan walked out of his bedroom into the hall while Leonard stood by the window. Duncan shut the door. Leonard was in the hall. He hadn't run past; he'd just 'jumped' instantly. Duncan then walked back into his room, keeping his eyes fixed on Leonard, and shut the door on him. But Leonard was already beside him.

Duncan tried closing his eyes but Leonard was still there. Even when Duncan had been sleeping, Leonard confirmed that he had been sat somewhere within sight. He had no choice. He couldn't leave. He was stuck there twenty-four hours a day. He could avert his gaze, as when Duncan went to the toilet, but he still had to be in the bathroom itself. It did not make life easy.

But Duncan found he was getting used to it. After all, what alternative did he have? Leonard was like a nagging pain that won't go away: as long as you kept busy you didn't notice it so much. Duncan realised that if he treated Leonard like a real person instead of some phantom, then his horror could be sublimated to little more than nervous indigestion. As a result, he started sucking Setlers regularly, but it was better than going ga-ga. He was even getting used to Leonard's grotesque appearance.

From behind, Leonard's head was perfectly normal. Greasy brown hair, thinning on top, and small ears that stuck out. Only his horribly thin neck gave the game away. Even in profile his face maintained a relatively normal outline, albeit in purple and blue. His eyes had become hooded but nothing excess weight mightn't have caused. His cheeks were also rather bulbous but, again, fat could have been responsible. However, face on, Leonard was a real disaster.

His forehead had escaped unscathed, but his eyes were both bugged out and hooded by the bruised flesh above and below the pupils. It made him look as if his eyes were fighting to escape. His nose was bloated, and could well have been broken. His cheeks had swelled, the skin shiny and distended, a raving mix of bruises, broken veins and underlying dark discoloration. The worst part was his mouth and jaw. It looked as if he'd had something implanted into the bottom half of his face that was half-a-dozen sizes too large. His tongue was swollen as well, though thankfully it wasn't hanging out. It gave him a slight lisp, as if he were talking with his mouth full (which he probably was). The contusions were worst here, almost all natural skin tone vanquished, and like his eyes his skin, stretched as taut as possible, looked as if it would burst. His face looked like a very large angry boil just set for lancing.

Duncan tried taking a photograph, but the Polaroid film ignored Leonard. It wasn't faulty either. Using all ten shots in the pack, alternating views of his bedroom with portraits of Leonard, he simply produced ten reasonable pictures of his room. Studying Leonard's face closely it occured to him that a black and white photograph might show him as a very fat negro rather than a white man.

Next he tried sketching him. It didn't work. He'd never had much talent as an artist – one thing art courses at technical colleges never demand is ability – but he simply couldn't get a handle on the shape of the man's face. Besides, whilst he could cope with Leonard's face, the one thing that still turned his stomach was his neck.

The more he looked at it the more he came to think that all the flesh and muscle and sinew and whatever else there is in a person's neck had somehow been squeezed up into his head. The equation seemed to balance out: his neck was a third its proper size and his face was twice as fat.

As for the rest of his body, he looked like any other middle-aged man in his underpants. The comically classic 'short, fat, hairy legs', a generous tyre around his waist, the beginnings of tits and general flab all over. He was also fairly hairy, but his body hair was grey, which betrayed the hair colouring he had used.

Duncan was glad that the man's underpants were both capacious and clean: they at least afforded a semblance of decency. That said, with his white body and purpled head, he still resembled the world's largest safety match.

A door slammed downstairs.

'That's sounds like mum's gone. Let's get my car.'

They walked downstairs, through the kitchen – Mrs Orr was off somewhere dusting – and out to the four-car garage where they got into Duncan's own car and drove off.

'I thought you said you had a car,' said Leonard, as they made their way along the sweeping curves of the main road to Tilworth Reservoir.

'What's this? Scotch mist?' said Duncan.

'A wreck, that's what this is.'

'It may look a wreck, but it shifts when it has to.'

'Yeah. Behind a tow truck. It looks like a turd and drives like one, too.'

'You want to walk?'

'Okay, kid, sorry. Sorry . . . never knock a man's car, or the size of his dick. They're the best he can offer and you're not the one who has to use them.' And with those words of wisdom, they drove on in silence.

Duncan was fully aware that his brown Riley Elf was a breakdown waiting to happen, but since wrapping his Toyota MR2 round a tree at Christmas, both his parents had refused to finance his motoring. He had little alternative. Still, it went, after a fashion. As they waited at a level crossing for the 10.40am to Manchester to trundle past, Duncan checked over the piece of paper he had scribbled on earlier.

'And you think one of these two will have the answer?'

'Got no-one else to ask. They'll have to do.'

'What if they don't know anything?'

'Be optimistic, will you? One of them must know something. Which one are we going to first?'

'Like I said, this David Beaumont's the nearest,' said Duncan. 'The Rezzy's only a couple of miles. If he's there.'

'He lectures in child psychology at the local teacher training college, but as it's the summer hols he shouldn't be at work. And in all the time I knew him all he talked about was his damn boat. "The Young and in Love" it's called. Weather like this he should be on it.'

Duncan hoped he wasn't, but then he wished the other name on the list was unreachable as well. Ludo Kimmel – what kind of name was that? – had a farm out on Cavalry Edge, which would be a bitch to find; he'd been lost out there before. How the hell was he supposed to broach the subject of Leonard's murder with them? And what had it to do with him anyway? It was all so . . . absurd.

The train had passed. They drove on.

'What if I say the wrong thing and one of them attacks me?' said Duncan, still looking for an out.

'I'm not saying *they* did it, just that they might have some idea who could have done it.'

'But just suppose one of them *did* do it?'

'I'll watch out for you.'

'Yeah. That's about all you can do, isn't it? Watch.'

Leonard didn't say anything.

It was as they drove on that the one other characteristic of Leonard made its presence felt. The smell. It was definitely fish, but neither of them could explain it. Mind you, neither of them had ever smelled a dead body before, so for all they knew it was normal, though they doubted it. Leonard's crack that *'There are only two things in the world that smell like fish, and one of them's fish!'* did nothing to improve the tone of the discussion, so Duncan let the subject drop and opened his window wider. Luckily it was a bright, sunshiny day; a day when windows demanded to be opened wide.

They reached Tilworth Reservoir at 11am and Duncan set to work in his new rôle: Private Investigator.

11

TILWORTH RESERVOIR WAS a wide expanse of water that served the dual purposes of providing Ollington and its surrounding district with drinking water, and acting as a popular venue for water-based recreation. About five miles long and almost a mile wide, it formed a lazy 'C' nestling in the high hills of the Pennines. On a day like today – hot, bright, calm – it would be easy to believe you were in the Lake District. Its northern end was the focus for most leisure activities. Here there was a campsite, shops, a restaurant and a small marina, as well as concessions for boat hire and watersports, and it was in this crowded area that they found themselves.

Threading his way along the rutted dirt track between multi-coloured tents and equally colourful campers, Duncan found himself leaning on his horn almost continuously.

They eventually reached a small car park beside the sparkling water only to find it already packed with canoeists, swimmers, anglers, windsurfers, dinghy owners and lots of other people in swimwear obviously only interested in the sun and other people in swimwear. Duncan abandoned his car on the verge and stepped out.

Leaning back into the car he said, 'You coming?'

'I've a choice?' said Leonard glumly, making no attempt to move.

'Well, come on, then.'

'I don't need to get out. As long as I can see you I can stay here. When you disappear I'll meet you.'

'So why not just walk anyway?'

'I can't. Not dressed like this. In front of all these people.'

Duncan laughed loudly, but stopped when he noticed people looking at him. *Look at that man, mummy, laughing at his car.* He got back in.

'We know no-one can see you—'

'It's the principle. I thought it might be fun but now, with all these people . . . it doesn't feel right.'

'Of course it isn't right! You're *dead*. I'm sorry . . .'

'I know my head's a mess, but even if it wasn't, I'm only dressed in my underpants.'

'So what? Look around. Lots of guys are wearing less than you. And some are even fatter. Not many, I'll grant you . . .'

'But they're in swimming cozzies. I'm in Y-fronts.'

Duncan understood Leonard's discomfort. His underpants were bigger, more substantial and more modest than many of the trunks and bikini briefs being worn by some men around them, but they had swimming togs and Leonard was in his underpants. It was like the difference between a bra and a bikini top: one had obvious sexual overtones, the other was a costume. But it didn't alter the fact that no-one could see the man!

'Leonard, I'm not going to argue with you. You and I both know no-one can see you, but if you're shy, I understand. I'll see you in a couple of minutes, wherever I am.' And with that he stepped out of the car, locked it, and made his way down to the busy landing stage that was home to a boat-hire company.

It *was* a nice day. Duncan realised that this was the first time he had been out in the daytime since Leonard's appearance. It cast their relationship in a new light, literally. How on earth could it be true, when here he was surrounded by happy holidaymakers and gorgeous semi-clad girls, with the temperature in the seventies and every prospect of sunburn by noon? Surely it was all some sick joke, or a bad dream?

But it wasn't. The counter of the hut faced the water and was out of sight of the Riley but, sure enough, as he walked round the small creosoted shed, Leonard was stood waiting. Duncan smiled and stepped up to the counter, then paused.

'Where's Beaumont's boat?' he whispered behind his hand to Leonard.

'What?' said Leonard.

'Where's his boat?'

But Leonard was looking round, ogling the bikini'd women.

'What, Dunc?' he muttered vaguely, his predicament over his attire already a distant memory.

'Where the fuck is the boat?' Duncan shouted.

The attendant in the small hut pointed over Duncan's shoulder. 'Behind you, stupid. In the water like boats should be.'

'What?' said a startled Duncan. 'Oh . . . oh, sorry.'

'Beaumont's boat?' said Leonard, still staring at a teenage girl trying not to fall out of two strategically-placed bootlaces. 'It's out there. The blue one. See it? Two masts?'

Duncan shaded his eyes and looked over the crowded water to the middle of the reservoir. There was a two-masted motor launch there.

'You want a boat or what?' said the surly attendant. Duncan didn't want to argue. It generally pays to avoid arguing with a man who has 'Muther' tattooed on his forearm.

'Er, any motor boats?'

'Nope. All out.'

'Rowing boats?'

'Nope.'

Duncan looked at the splashing, shrieking chaos that passed for inshore relaxation. 'Canoes?'

'Nope.'

'What have you got, then?'

'A pedalo. Red one over there. Number eight.'

Duncan had said he'd take it before he looked at it.

And that was how he found himself half-an-hour later near to exhaustion, covered in sweat, his legs aching, barely a hundred yards from shore on a giant red duck.

'I'll get you for this, Leonard,' he huffed, holding his side.

'Oh, yeah? What you going to do? Beat me up? Keep pedalling and stop moaning.'

Duncan felt like abandoning duck. He was knackered. He had peddalled himself in circles for fifteen minutes, trying to manouevre his oversized mallard through the shoals of windsurfers and swimmers that swarmed around the dock like stupid fish. Why on earth, when they have a lake twelve miles and more in circumference, does everyone congregate within a hundred yard area? But, finally, he had perfected his technique and had started to head for Beaumont's boat. Throughout his exertions, Leonard had sat back, for all the world as if he were perfecting a tan.

Another ten minutes of earnest struggle and he had reached the side of the boat. The boat was actually called the *Jungandinlove*, no doubt a psychologist's joke. It was a large motor launch painted powder blue. Leonard informed him that it was a thirty-two footer, built in the Forties, and that it had been on the lake since it was built and still had the original Thorneycroft diesels. As he explained, you learn to remember what your potential customers talk about, and all Beaumont had ever talked about was his damn boat.

It was a bit of a haul getting up onto the deck, since it was a good five feet higher than the pedalo, but eventually Duncan made it.

It was an old boat with two masts, neither of which had a sail, and where the wood hadn't been painted light blue it bore fading and cracked varnish. There was a wheelhouse to the rear on what appeared to be a large cabin, and an ancient sunlounger sat forlornly on the deck, the remains of a half-eaten meal on a tray beside it.

'Someone's home,' said Leonard, nodding at the stew.

'What now?'

'Call him.'

Duncan shouted for Mr Beaumont but got no response. Leonard pointed at the wheelhouse.

'See if he's inside.'

Duncan tried to protest but it was pointless. He made his way through the wheelhouse to the hatch leading to the cabins.

It was fairly dark below, but Duncan could see well enough. It was obviously well-lived in, full of clutter and junk, but the kind of stuff you would usually find in a house: letters, crockery, bottles of drink, a radio cassette player, magazines, books, a portable TV, and framed photographs including one of a man in a fur-trimmed scholar's gown. The boat was obviously Beaumont's home.

The first area was a galley. Duncan felt the coffee maker and it proved to be warm. The name *Marie Celeste* sprang unbidden into his mind, and he fought the urge to turn tail. The floor had broken glass on it but nothing that his clumsy boarding couldn't have produced. He stooped through a doorway into another small cabin with two woodframed couches and a table and bench. The place was neatly decorated, the walls hung with various sailing prints and marine bric-à-brac. The table was covered in papers and books, some of which had fallen on the floor. Suddenly the boat shifted slightly. The swell, Duncan supposed. On a reservoir?

The floor creaked as he leant over to pick up a sheaf of papers. Students' essays. Something about bed-wetting. How edifying. He looked around and spotted a torch hanging on a hook. Taking it down he tested it. It worked. Suddenly the boat gave a frightening lurch tó one side and he was thrown against one of the couches.

'What the fuck's going on?' he asked Leonard, but Leonard wasn't there.

'Leonard? Leonard? Where are you?' He started panicking. Darting back to the hatchway, he looked up into the bright sunlight. Leonard was there, standing stock still.

'What is it?' asked Duncan.

'I wish I knew, Dunc. Something's holding me back.'

'What do you mean?'

'I mean I can't go down there. I just can't.'

'What's to be scared of? I'm the—'

'It's not that. It's like there's a glass wall stopping me. I just can't follow you down.'

'Oh, great. Well, I'm not going down, then.'

'Oh yes, you are. The fact that I can't means something must be up.'

'All the more reason!'

'Dunc, all we've got is what's down there and Ludo Kimmel. Unless we get some kind of lead, we're a team forever.'

'Shit!'

Leonard didn't comment.

Cursing again Duncan turned and went back into the cabin. The boat gave another jolt and, struggling to regain his balance, he felt the boat slowly angling to one side, groaning and complaining as it listed. He heaved himself up towards the table in the second cabin and grabbing hold of it, swung the torch round to illuminate the final cabin at the fore of the boat. Something glinted back at him. Water. He took a couple of cautious steps. Splashes. He looked down. Oh God, the boat was sinking. He shouted back to Leonard:

'The bloody boat's sinking!'

'Beaumont might need help.'

'What about me? Oh, shit.' Duncan turned and advanced into the forecabin to finish his tour of inspection.

It was bigger than he thought it would be, containing a double bed that jutted out at an odd angle from the left bulkhead; clearly the cabin was supposed to have a bunk along each wall and Beaumont had had it converted, but the result was an off-centre look, as if too much had been put into the room. The walls were again garnished with naval memorabilia, but it was something in the centre of the room that held his attention.

There were several inches of water now, and it appeared to be gulping up from the base of something jammed into the floor. It looked for all the world like one of those carved figureheads from the prow of an old sailing vessel and, for a moment, Duncan accepted that that was exactly what it was – just the kind of artifact the man would keep on his boat, given his rather predictable and unimaginative ornamentations – but shining a light over it revealed something far less substantial than wood, and a lot more out of place. It was a man.

Duncan tried to keep the beam steady but it shook violently as the boat shivered again and a fount of water spurted into the cabin from the splintered decking around the figure. Duncan crouched down. The man was facing away from him, jammed into the deck up to his waist except for one leg that came straight up his back, the foot level with the face, pointing at Duncan. The left shoulder was slumped and the right stiff, its arm crooked into the body, giving him the appearance of a grotesque man-size teapot.

The boat shook again and more water gushed up around the body. Duncan wanted to leave but something urged him to move round and shine the torch on the man's face. As the boat trembled and shifted again and a loud crack echoed through the boat's bowels, Duncan stumbled and fell onto the bed, his hand landing in something soft and cold. He looked down, fearing the worst. It was a damp towel. He let out a cry of relief.

Pulling in a deep breath, Duncan shone the torch onto the man's face. It was worse than anything he could have imagined.

At first it seemed that the man was looking up at him, his face screwed up in concentration, much as he might have looked burning the midnight oil marking his students' essays. Even his eyes were open, though clouded with blood. Duncan didn't know what Beaumont looked like but this man matched the photograph he had seen on the wall over the bar dressed in gown and mortar board. But it wasn't until he had been studying the poor bastard for a few seconds, almost thankful that something more horrendous wasn't confronting him, that he noticed the dull white gleam under the man's chin. Duncan stooped down and shone the torch full on the man's neck.

Except it wasn't his neck. It was his skull. The man's face had been pulled off his skull and left on the top of his head like a discarded mask. Beaumont's whole, complete, *entire* face had been pulled off.

Out! Out! Out! Duncan's brain screamed as he scrabbled for the doorway, but his sudden movements made the boat rock all the more and, very quickly, just as he crawled up the hatchway to the wheelhouse, the front of the boat, the forecabin, the body, that face gave a dreadful sigh and water swirled up around his ankles and his calves and then his knees.

Duncan lunged up the steps for the relative safety of the deck and didn't waste a moment in throwing himself over the side of the boat and into the reservoir.

Less than a minute of frantic threshing later and he was able to grab hold of the pedalo. Leonard, naturally, was already sitting aboard, dry as a bone. Duncan managed to haul himself up into his seat, then turned to see the launch tilt forward until water reached the wheelhouse window. Then, with a loud groan, the stricken vessel rolled over sideways as if trying to spew its sordid contents at them, and quickly sank.

12

THE INTERVIEW ROOM was a dull, grey cube. Take away the furniture and it could have been turned any way, including upside down, and have looked the same. And right now, Duncan would have been very happy if it had done just that: turned upside down and shaken him out.

After the *Jungandinlove* had sunk, he had managed to pedal back to the shore to a reception committee that seemed to number every tourist within a ten-mile radius. He couldn't have had more witnesses if he'd sold tickets. The police were also waiting. What could he do? He couldn't deny he had been on the boat when it sank; at least a hundred people had seen him jump off. So he had gone along quietly to 'help them with their enquiries'.

For once Leonard shut up so as not to confuse the situation further. Only as they walked the short distance from the patrol car into the police station did he speak:

'Duncan, listen. You went out for a paddle and got into difficulties. You reached the boat and got on. It started sinking immediately and you jumped off. Nothing else. You had no reason to be there and you didn't see the body.'

'Why?' he whispered

'Well, I presume your brain isn't so waterlogged that you're thinking of telling them about me?'

'Obviously!'

'"So why were you on Mr Beaumont's boat, Mr Cantrill?"'

'Er . . . for a paddle and I got into—'

'What?' snapped a sergeant as he opened the door to the interview room.

'I said I don't know why you've brought me here. I was just—'

'Save it for the Chief Inspector. He'll be along shortly.'

End of conversation.

They asked him to strip – he was still soaking wet – and provided a towel, blankets and a cup of tea. Quite civilised, really.

Leonard stood in a corner, watching. Occasionally he would suggest Duncan cheer up, but Duncan ignored him. Once he was out of there, Leonard could go fuck himself. Bad enough he was bosom pal to a corpse; now he was finding more. Shit, there was a thought. Was Beaumont going to pop up next? He'd been the first to find his body, too. Duncan let out a little cry of fear. The constable sitting across from him looked up. Duncan offered a smile. The man refused to accept it and stared back.

Ten minutes later the Detective Chief Inspector came in. The *same* DCI who had interviewed Duncan after Leonard's body had been found. Oh dear.

DCI Chater was a blond-haired man in his forties. He was slim and athletic, with a boyish face that reminded Duncan of someone he couldn't place. He had about him a polite, non-officious, friendly manner, helped by a strong north Manchester accent, possibly Rochdale (which he would have pronounced *Rotshdeel*). Rather incongruously, however, he started with a quote from Oscar Wilde about 'losing one parent being unfortunate but losing both being careless' and then proceeded to spend two hours demanding to know why Duncan had this unfortunate knack of being in the wrong place at the wrong time. They still hadn't traced the boat's owner and were having to wait for the police divers to arrive before checking out the submerged boat itself.

Again wisely, Leonard let Duncan handle it, and he handled it rather well, despite the tears and the pleading and the begging and the apologies.

Finally they let him leave – 'for the time being' – and a panda car ran him back to his car out by the reservoir, with Leonard riding shotgun.

The area was still crowded so Duncan said nothing, just got into his car and drove away. Once out of sight of passers-by, he turned to Leonard, who was sitting in the passenger seat.

'That's it, Leonard. Over. No more. Finished. I'm sorry you were killed, and no doubt so's that Beaumont guy, but at least you now have one less suspect. But if every time I call on one of your mates he's going to be in bits about his home, then I'm not interested.'

'But Dunc, unless we sort this out I'll be here forever with you.'

'How do I know that? You might be lying. I might still be off my trolley.'

'So how come you went to his boat and you—'

'A dream! All of this is some fantastic nightmare. Some time I'll wake up and everything'll be okay.'

'Dunc, pull over.'

'What?'

'Pull over. Now!'

Duncan did as ordered.

'Right, get out the car. Follow me.'

'I can't follow you. You have to stay within sight of me. Or had you forgotten?'

'I mean come with me, and don't start getting clever all of a sudden. I've been around a week now, Duncan. No dream lasts that long. Just do as I ask; it's time we had a good talk.'

'What, haunter to hauntee?'

'No. Father to son, you little prick.'

Duncan stopped in his tracks. They were halfway up the path to a small church.

'Father to son?'

'It's time you grew up, Duncan. Heard a few home truths.'

'Oh yeah?'

'Oh yeah, unless, of course, you're not up to hearing the truth?'

'I'm up to hearing anything, especially from a fat git like you. A fat dead git at that!'

'Fine, fine, keep it up, kid. Sticks and stones can't break my bones, and words can't hurt me either. Now come on.'

'Where?'

'Just over there. There's a bench round under that willow tree. It's nice and quiet. We can talk without being disturbed.'

'If we must. How do you know there's a bench?'

'Because I used to come here sometimes. To think.'

'Rare event, was it?'

'Shut up, Duncan.'

There was a bench and they sat down on it. Duncan found himself looking out through the drooping branches at a small churchyard which was dominated by a small brick-built chapel of undistinguished style. However, the graves were well-tended and the rustling leaves of the many trees bordering the cemetery cut the place off from the rest of the world. Like the quadrangles in an Oxford college, it didn't matter what traffic there was outside; once inside the colleges you entered another world: a quiet capsule out and away from the hustle and bustle of reality. This churchyard had about it the same air of tranquillity. There was a busy motorway within half-a-mile and Ollington barely a mile beyond that, but they might as well have been in another country.

'I don't want any more antagonism between us, Duncan.'

'Fine. Leave.'

'I can't! Please, just shut up for a moment and listen . . . I left school at fifteen with no qualifications, nothing to help me on in life. My dad was a miner but he died when I was four. I was brought up by my mother and gran. They were very strict. Too strict, probably. When I left school I was given a choice: get a job and pay rent or get out. I found work *and* I got out. But I had no education worth mentioning, no special talents other than the gift of the gab. I could talk to people. I soon learnt I could talk people into buying things from me. First it was door-to-door, then in shops, finally I got into insurance. Been doing it twelve years now. I've been offered promotion lots of times, but any move up in this game means sitting behind a desk. I'm no good at that. All I can do is talk to people. Sell them things. So I keep working in the field. I pull in a good whack. Thirty, thirty-five grand on average. One person who won't be suffering is my wife. We never had kids; one reason why we've drifted apart. That and my dick. She'll have picked up better than a hundred-and-fifty grand on my death, together with the house being paid off. Big house at that . . . She's better off now with me dead than she ever was with me alive. Ironic, really . . . I loved her, you know. Really loved her, specially for the first couple of years, but when she found I couldn't give her any kids, she became cold, uninterested. Now I might have fired blanks but I still had the gun and so I started looking around.

'When you look it's easy to find, as long as you're not too choosy. I wasn't choosy but with my build and looks how could I afford to be? But it meant I was soon shafting a different bird every week. Just sex, nothing else. No romance or any of that shit. Just get into the sack and fuck. Now that may be bad and a sin, but I can't believe it's evil. I've never hurt anyone, never stolen anything.

'Okay, so I sold insurance and I'd say anything to sell a policy. My commission was usually most or all of the first year's payments on a policy. That's anything up to seven hundred quid for a night's work. I'd say *anything* to get that. And I did. It wasn't a con or a scam. Stuff I sold was legit and as good as most other policies, but I would always have to pretend it was the bee's knees. And because I have a way with people, they fell for it. I was Salesman of the Month sixteen times, and of the Year four times. By my own terms I was successful. I was using my own talent to make a decent living, and I was getting laid any way I could. That's all I ever did wrong. I'm not a bad person.'

'What about the orgies?'

'Okay, so I was stupid. Naïve even. I honestly thought they were using the witchcraft as an excuse for fun. So they burned a few candles and we dressed up in robes. Half-an-hour into the meeting the robes came off and you boffed who you wanted. No different from chucking your car keys onto the kitchen table, or spinning the bottle. Even when I realised they meant what they said, I simply tried to leave. I hadn't any intention of informing on them or anything like that. I'd made a mistake, I was sorry, I left. Seems they took it even *more* seriously than I thought. Even to arranging my death.'

'Are you sure it was them? Couldn't it have been anyone? A random murder?'

'It could, but it wasn't. Don't ask me how I know, I just do. Whatever happened to me was evil. I wasn't just topped by some nutter. My murder was planned and I was executed. And I don't think it's fair.'

'Obviously . . .'

'I don't remember it too clearly. All I know is that my wallet meant bad news. I tried to give it to the girl who was with me, then blank – and I wake up dead.'

'That's tough, but what can I do? You think it might be one of these two guys, but only because they're the two you know. How many others were there?'

'Twenty or more.'

'See? It's hopeless. I'm sorry, Leonard, but finding you put me over the edge. If every time we make a house call I find another corpse I'm not going to be able to cope. And the police are going to get mighty suspicious. I'm already in the shit when they find Beaumont's body in that boat.'

'I know it's tough, kid, but I'm stuck here until it's sorted. I don't like being dead, and I sure as hell don't like being a ghost. You any idea how boring it is being awake twenty-four hours a day with you? No offence, but you ain't the best of company.'

'And neither are you . . . beetroot face!'

'God, that was cutting,' said Leonard clutching his chest. 'Another thing you're going to have to change is your line in jokes. Puerile isn't in it.'

'Oh, come off it. I'm quite happy with the way I am and I'm not changing anything I do, least of all for you.'

'Well, that's a pity, because you need to change.'

'Oh? How?'

'You told me you messed up your education. Not once but three times. 'O' levels, 'A' levels, art college, right? You've done a succession of deadend jobs which haven't required thought or talent, right? You've no savings, no home of your own. You're twenty-three and you still live at home, right? You've got brains: haven't you ever stopped to figure out why you're living the way you do?'

'Because I want to.'

'Bullshit! Even those poor sods who can't do anything but shitty jobs don't want them. You're just running away from life, and punishing your parents into the bargain.'

'Oh, cut the amateur psychology, Leonard. Leave it with Beaumont at the bottom of the Rezzy. This from a man who couldn't control his dick and lied for a living.'

Leonard stood up and made to punch him. Duncan flinched but then realised the punch would never, *could* never, land.

'Ha!'

'Ha yourself, Duncan,' said Leonard sitting down again. 'Your mother and father may be shitty parents, but in their own eyes, and those of their peers, they're successful. Your mother in politics and charity work; your father in business. Even *I*'ve heard of Peter Cantrill. So he's never home; so he's a rotten dad. Still gave you a home the envy of anyone; paid for a private education you pissed away. Buys you cars, holidays, clothes . . . *everything*, in fact, that you have comes from your father. Maybe he never made it as a dad but at least he makes your misery comfortable. Same with your mother. Despite her faults, she's a whole lot better than my mother ever was. She doesn't hit you or humiliate you . . . And remember I was chucked out at fifteen: you've every possibility of living at home forever! You know what I think? I think you resent your parents. Not hate; that requires too much commitment: the one thing you're obviously lacking. You resent them so you make them suffer as much as possible by doing all you can to be a failure and an embarrassment.'

'Oh, do me a favour . . . I like the jobs I do. I just don't want to be a part of the rat race—'

'Utter crap, kid! You can't enjoy the work you do when you're obviously as bright as you are. You should be in the professions – a lawyer, an accountant, *anything* – instead of portering in cheap hotels. And I think I know the reason for that. You believe you'll never be able to match your parents' success, or live up to their hopes for you. Whatever you do, in *their* terms, you'll always be a failure, so you're making sure that you fail on *your* terms. *You* fucked up school; *you* blew getting into university; *you* choose the lousy jobs. I guarantee both your parents have offered you jobs through their contacts. Don't deny it.'

'Yes, they have, but I—'

'But you being a man of principle have refused, of course. Nepotism isn't right. It's immoral.'

'Right.'

'Wrong! You live in a house that must be worth more than a quarter of a million. You've got a garden bigger than some housing estates. A bloody swimming pool. A four-car garage. Those leather couches in your lounge must have cost more than some families earn in a fucking year! Some principles! You're just a lazy bastard who wants everything on his own terms but isn't prepared to take any risks. If you'd gone to university you'd have to learn to stand on your own two feet. Instead you're still sucking your mother's tit, with daddy paying for the nappies. To you, success is being a failure at what you choose to fail at. Twisted logic, kiddo.'

'Your twisted logic,' said a red-faced Duncan.

'Prove me wrong.'

'How?' Duncan was almost in tears.

It was clear that what Leonard had been saying was hurting the boy. Thirty-odd years in the selling game had provided Leonard with a valuable insight into human nature. Duncan was basically a good kid who'd had the misfortune to inherit his parents' selfishness, but had chosen to exercise it in a negative manner.

'Help me.'

'How the hell does that prove I'm not what you say I am?'

'Because if you fail, it won't be your fault for once. If you succeed, then you'll have done something even your super-successful parents haven't done: avenge a murder victim. Dad may own a big company, and mum may run Ollington, but neither of them has ever helped anyone out of friendship or honour. This is your chance to be a good guy for once.'

Duncan shook his head. 'You don't really believe that crap, do you?'

'Not really,' sighed Leonard, burying his head in his hands. 'But I can't think of anything else that'll convince you. But what I've been saying about you is true, Duncan – and you know it, don't you?'

'I suppose so . . .'

'Well *do* something then! For someone else, even if only this once. I may be dead, but I used to be someone. Help me, Duncan, I'm begging you . . .'

'Father to son?'

'No, Duncan. Man to man.'

Duncan nodded slowly, then burst into tears.

Leonard's hands fluttered as helpless as moths as he tried futilely to hug the boy, but Duncan stood and turned away.

'All right, I'll help, all I can, whatever happens.'

'Thanks,' said Leonard, letting out a big sigh and shaking his head. *Just think of the commission you could have earned on* that *selling job, Lenny boy.*

13

'WHY'S IT CALLED Cavalry Edge?' asked Leonard.

'Something to do with cavalry . . .'

It was the next morning and they were driving out to the farm owned by Ludo Kimmel, Duncan again at the wheel of his Riley Elf. Kimmel's house was some six miles from Ollington, way up in hills, nestled in the shadow of Cavalry Edge, which could be seen for miles, but was awkward to get to, roads always managing to turn off just as they seemed to be getting near. Eventually Duncan confessed ignorance and consulted a road map, his pride at knowing the local area dented.

They arrived at about 10.30am. It was as hot as any day so far, and the farmyard was dry and dusty. The farmhouse itself was an old, plain, two-storey building in traditional stone, its design so simple it could have been a child's idealised view of a house. There was a central door with two windows on either side, two matching windows upstairs, and a slate roof stained green by moss and time.

Duncan stepped out of the car. It was very quiet, and the whole place looked abandoned. Apart from the two low outhouses and a delapidated corrugated iron open-sided barn, the farmhouse stood alone, its windows obstinately facing away from the magnificent view down into the valley. Tilworth Reservoir glinted in the distance, its constant winking a promise of cool breezes and even cooler bathing. Duncan promised himself a visit as soon as he had gotten over his encounter with Beaumont in his boat, if he ever could.

'Hive of activity,' said Leonard, wandering over to the outhouses and looking in. They were pig sties but, like the yard, were devoid of livestock and, thinking about it, neither could remember having seen any sheep or cattle as they had driven up the long, rutted track.

'Nothing here. Maybe he left,' suggested Duncan.

'Maybe.'

Duncan spotted something on the ground by the far corner of the house. He walked over and picked it up. It was telephone wire which ran across the yard to a telegraph pole. He looked back up at the roof of the house and, sure enough, a foot length of the wire dangled limply from the eave of the house. Odd.

He poked his head round the corner of the house. There he saw the remains of half-a-dozen rusted and wrecked cars and vans, and one slightly more complete tractor which, despite its decrepit appearance, at least looked vaguely functional. But the scene did nothing to dispel the impression that the place had been deserted.

He returned to the front door with Leonard and rang the bell. No-one answered. Leonard stepped back and looked up at the windows. They were still curtained, but the windows were grimy; they told no story. Leonard looked at Duncan and shrugged.

'Try the back, then give it up,' said Duncan.

So they ventured around the side of the house, trampling through a riot of weeds and wild flowers until they came to the back door. Leaning against the step was an oxyacetylene kit with its two tanks and burner on a wheeled trolley. Two more cylinders lazed in the grass nearby, safe in the cool shadow of the house. Further on, under a big chestnut tree, sat a large jumble of car parts welded into a shape. What it was supposed to represent was unclear but it was decidely unappealing.

'A sculptor, you said. That would explain the lack of animals,' said Duncan.

They found that the back door was wide open.

'Hello, Mr Kimmel. Anyone home? Mr Kimmel, I'm a friend of Mr Halsey; I'd like a few words . . . Anyone there?' shouted Duncan.

Still no response. Duncan peered inside. It was an old kitchen, with a large stone sink, an Aga-style cooking range and a huge wooden table that looked sturdy enough to dance on. The table was bare. Duncan pushed the door open all the way and walked in.

A couple more shouts, still without response, and Leonard urged Duncan to continue exploring. On the stove sat a battered saucepan containing milk. Duncan felt it to see if it was warm. It was hot. He yelped in pain, pulled his hand back and dashed to the sink to run it under the tap.

No water. Instead he blew on his hand and rubbed it against his thigh.

'Hot, was it?' said Leonard, and walked through into the hall, Duncan following.

The house was oppressively warm, as if a fire had been stoked up in the cellars. It was dusty as well, motes sparkling in the shafts of light that stabbed white against black through the windows, the contrast between the gloomy interior and the invading sunlight so strong it seemed to drain all colour out of the house.

Another shout, another silence.

They entered the first room on the right.

It was empty. Completely and utterly empty. Only naked floorboards and bare stone walls remained. It was strange. Someone, presumably Kimmel, had removed the plaster, leaving just a thin veil of dust clinging to the century-old stone. Duncan examined the wall nearest to him. There was no light switch or light fitting, though there was a hole visible in the ceiling from where it had been removed. Leonard stepped into the middle of the room. A piece of sacking fluttered lightly on the furthest wall. He walked up to it and nodded. Duncan joined him and drew it aside.

It was the window. Or rather, it wasn't. The glass and wooden frame had been removed to leave just a gaping hole.

'I've heard of getting back to nature, but this is ludicrous,' said Duncan. 'No telephone, no water, no light. Now no window.'

'There's not much else to get rid of.'

'You any idea what's going on, Leonard?'

'None. Honest. I'm just glad I'm dead because it'd be damn spooky if I were still alive and kicking.'

'I'd like to kick you sometimes.'

'Charming.'

They stepped back into the hall and tried the next room on the right. Duncan went in first but with a startled cry, suddenly disappeared from sight. Leonard looked down.

There *was* something else to get rid of. The floor. Duncan had slipped between the exposed cross beams and was having to hold himself up with his arms. Leonard was unable to help as Duncan fought to get himself back into the hall.

Once sat safely on his backside, Duncan looked back into the room. True enough, all the floorboards had been removed and they were able to look straight into the cellar, which was itself as empty as the previous room. This room faced the front of the house so clearly whoever was at work hadn't yet removed the glass from the window.

Duncan pulled up his trouser leg to reveal a scrape. Nothing serious. Then they both heard a sound.

A small sound.

A furtive sound.

The sound of someone trying *not* to make a sound. It came from behind the closed door of the other front room. What to do?

Duncan's automatic reaction was to run, but Leonard stopped him in his tracks.

'No! This is my last chance, Duncan. Run out now and I'm stuck with you. Behind that door might be the answer we're looking for.'

'Behind that door,' whispered Duncan, 'might be a mass murderer!'

Leonard shrugged. 'So we all have to take risks some time.'

'It's *my* risk.'

'And it's your choice. How old are you? Twenty-three? Say you live to be eighty. That's another fifty-seven years with yours truly by your side—'

'All right!' hissed Duncan. 'All right, you made your point. But if I die, I'm not only going to come and haunt you, I'm going to kill you. Again!'

Duncan leaned against the wall beside the closed door. 'Mr Kimmel? Is that you? My name's Duncan Cantrill. I'm a . . . I was a friend of Leonard Halsey. I understand you knew him. I'd like a few words? Hello? Are you there, Mr Kimmel?'

No more noises. Shit.

Leonard said, 'It could be the wind, or a cat. Anything.'

'Well, can't you go and look?'

'I have to be in sight of you, Duncan, remember? Open the door and I'll go and have a look.'

'Open the door?'

'Yes. It's this big thing in front of you with a knob on.'

'Oh, I thought that was you . . . Okay, let's do it.'

Duncan took hold of the doorknob and turned it carefully, then gave the door a gentle shove. Contrary to both their expectations, it didn't creak, but glided all the way open to offer them a clear view of the room. It was empty. They both edged their way in, Leonard in the lead, fully alert to the smallest sound, but all either of them could hear was the rapid tattoo of Duncan's heart.

The room was as empty as the first, except for the floor. The bare boards here bore a large symbol in either paint or whitewash. A five-pointed star inside a circle. A pentagram, fully ten feet across. Duncan dabbed at it with his toe. The paint smudged. It was fresh.

They surveyed the rest of the room. The grimy window, the bare stone walls and the curtain that covered most of the wall to their left. Nothing. But then Duncan realised something: the curtain must be hanging on an inside wall; there were no windows there for it to cover.

Leonard advanced to the side of the ancient red velvet curtain. Once lush, it was now as threadbare as the farmhouse. He found a faded gold cord on one side and called Duncan over. Duncan took hold of it and pulled down.

The cord simply fell limp to the floor, like a dead snake. The curtain didn't even twitch. But then that sound came again from behind the curtain. A click. A *metallic* click. Before either of them could shout, the shotgun had fired, exploding the curtain into a whirlwind of red shreds and dust. The window behind them shattered and the boom of the gun echoed across the farmyard.

Both men instinctively dived to the floor. Duncan's brain was buzzing with possibilities. First he had to check that he hadn't been hit. He appeared to be whole.

They looked up but could see nothing but the shivering curtain, a large black hole decorating its centre, and a swirling cloud of dust and fragments of velvet. Duncan scrabbled forward on his hands and knees, but before he could get out of the room, he had to know where their assailant was standing. He snagged the hem of the curtain and pulled.

It came away surprisingly easily and thudded to the ground, sending up yet another choking cloud of dust, but it also revealed the gunman.

He had been as surprised by the removal of his cover as they had by his shot, but now they had temporary advantage because the sun was shining directly into his eyes and had blinded him. But Duncan too was equally immobilised by his bizarre appearance.

'Come on, Duncan, run for it,' said Leonard.

But Duncan didn't hear him. He was staring at the apparition before him. A thin, middle-aged man, with long straggly hair and beard, like an ageing hippie, he was also completely naked apart from what encased his entire head. His hair, face, ears, neck, and even down onto his shoulders, all were painted bright scarlet.

Duncan was stunned. The contrast with his sun-starved milky white skin made the man look like a lollipop. And a complete idiot. Except this idiot had a gun and, even though he couldn't see properly, he had just remembered the fact.

'Show me your fire, show me your fire!' he screamed, his voice hysterically high.

Duncan shrieked, 'What fire? What fire?'

The man rounded the gun on his voice. Duncan immediately realised his mistake and moved into the relative safety afforded by the middle of the room.

Thankfully the man kept waving his shotgun where Duncan had been standing, and continued his strange tirade. 'What fire? What fire? Your master's fire! *His* fire! Show me, show me!' And before Duncan or Leonard could react he let off another barrel.

He missed, hitting the wall almost at ceiling height. Now he was disarmed and would need to reload. But as Duncan stood panic-stricken, oblivious to Leonard's shouted warnings, the man danced back as if on hot coals and grabbed another shotgun he had leaning against the wall. It was clear from this action that the man had also regained his sight and was not about to miss a third time.

Duncan turned towards the door but knew the man's buckshot would reach it well before he did.

'Distract him! Distract him!' screamed an hysterical Leonard from the doorway.

Duncan pointed over the man's shoulder. 'There's his fire! Behind you! Behind you!'

As if by a miracle, the man believed him and turned.

Duncan ran for the shelter of the doorway and on towards the front door.

'Oh, fucking hell! It's locked!' he yelled as he wrestled with the handles.

He had no choice but to charge back past the open doorway, and had just crossed the gap when another shot boomed out and he was showered with plaster. There was nothing left to do now but run for it along the hallway and into the kitchen, ignoring the bumbling form of Leonard. Scrambling over the large table Duncan charged out through the back door.

Even in his terror, he knew he needed cover so the man wouldn't be able to take a pot shot at him, Both he and Leonard looked around frantically.

'There, there, the bushes!' yelled Leonard, pointing to the left. Duncan instantly sprinted a diagonal course across the backyard towards the large bushes beyond the sculpture. But just as they were about to reach Kimmel's artwork, the madman with the red head came hurtling through the open space of the window in the back room and, executing a perfect roll, came up clutching his gun, ready to fire. Duncan swerved to his right and doubled back around the sculpture, putting it between him and the gunman.

A shot rang out and Duncan heard it ricocheting around the metalwork, a stray pellet whistling straight through Leonard's head, another hitting Duncan on the back of the hand, the livid pain giving him even more impetus.

He broke from the cover of the sculpture, hoping to gain breathing space before the man could reload. Unfortunately the man had decided to throw away his shotgun and had got a pistol from somewhere and was assuming an expert, two-handed stance to take careful aim at Duncan. He'd just reached the side of the house when the madman let off two shots.

The first whistled over Duncan's right shoulder and smashed into the corrugated iron sheeting of the barn. The second shot was drowned out by the massive crack of an explosion which bowled him over. Almost immediately there was a second equally loud explosion and a horrible scream, and then pieces of hot metal were raining down on his head.

The madman had shot straight through his oxyacetylene cart and, being less than ten feet away, had gone up with it.

Duncan didn't care. He and Leonard were in the middle of a metal hailstorm and he could only think of getting to the relative safety of his car, so he kept running and didn't look back. Only when he had run straight into the bonnet of the Elf did he stop to think.

As they both looked back at the house there was a third, duller explosion and then everything went quiet. Duncan was too breathless to speak and spent the next couple of minutes simply trying to calm down. Leonard said nothing. Finally, Duncan walked to the house and stole a look round the back.

The tractor was on fire, and so was a lot of the grass. The stupid bastard must have blown himself up. Oh shit, *fire*. It's June, and it hasn't rained in two weeks! He waved Leonard over as he ran round to see if he could do anything.

The whole back of the farm seemed to be ablaze, but then he realised the flames were leaping out from inside the house. The floorboards must have been like tinder waiting for a spark. Most of the grass was on fire by now too, as was the upper half of a tree a good twenty yards away.

'Christ, we better get the fire brigade out!'

They turned to go, and it was then that Leonard saw the man. He shouted at Duncan and pointed through the blazing grass. On the sculpture hung the blackened, smouldering remains of the gunman, pierced through in at least three places by metal rods, his red head now a seething mass of orange flames. He had also lost both his arms.

Suddenly something collapsed inside the house and sent a cascade of sparks shooting into the sky.

They ran back to the car and Duncan got in, started it up and wheeled it round the yard and down the drive in search of a telephone.

14

'LOOK AT IT from my point of view, Duncan.'

Detective Chief Inspector Chater turned his chair round and sat astride it as if it was a horse, his arms folded on the back, and looked at Duncan sympathetically.

'Last Tuesday Leonard Halsey was found, by you, dead in his hotel room. Murdered. You called us and we started our investigation. Despite my specifically asking you not to, you talked to the newspapers and TV and generally made an exhibition of yourself. Now I never thought you were responsible for his death—'

'How could I be? His door was locked on the inside.'

'Precisely, Duncan, but you know that hotel, don't you? Someone murders Mr Halsey, they have to leave. Dr Nelzen, our pathologist, says Mr Halsey died on the bed and would have been incapable of getting up, locking the door, then staggering back to his bed to die. Therefore his murderer must have left by another route.'

'So? There were windows.'

'Indeed there are, Duncan. Two to be precise. Unfortunately the main window, overlooking the front of the house, was painted last year, inside and out. As a result it is now impossible to open. No-one could have come in through it or left through it last Tuesday night. So that just leaves the bathroom window. Not very big, true, but a small person could get through it, at a pinch. However, there is then a twenty-two foot drop to the car park at the rear of the hotel. There are no drainpipes and no footholds, not even another window on a lower floor. A sheer drop of twenty-two feet onto concrete. Would *you* jump that?'

'No, but I might lower myself by rope.'

'But you would have had to leave it tied to something in the bathroom, wouldn't you? I presume you didn't find any such rope? We didn't.'

'No! No . . . so what are you saying? I did it? Me?'

'Not necessarily.'

'Well, thanks for the straight denial, chief inspector. Look, if what you say is true, why the hell would I claim the door was locked on the inside in the first place?'

'A good point. Either because you're telling the truth; you're lying; or your memory fails you. However, we *did* find Mr Halsey's key, with his fingerprints, exactly where you said it had fallen. Unless, of course, it was placed there by you.'

'Fascinating,' said Leonard. He was sat on the table to Duncan's right and had been enthralled by the story of his own demise. 'Real mystery, eh, Duncan? Ask him how I died.'

Duncan was too tired and too nervous to think for himself. 'How did Mr Halsey die?'

'He was strangled. Died of asphyxiation but as you yourself observed, it wasn't an ordinary strangulation.'

'How so?'

'Confidential, Duncan.'

'Ask him about the fish smell,' said Leonard.

'What?' said Duncan.

'I mean, plainly a man's hands didn't do the damage,' expanded the chief inspector, puzzled why Duncan had addressed his question to empty mid-air.

'I'm sorry, inspector . . . what was the fish smell?'

'Pardon?'

'Mr Halsey smells . . . smelled of fish. I wondered what it was.'

'We don't know. It was probably the Chinese takeway. It had been there all night.'

'Since when does sweet and sour chicken and beef chow mein smell of fish?' muttered Leonard.

'At least they smelled it too,' said Duncan.

'What?' said Inspector Chater.

'At least you smelled it too. I thought you might have believed it was another of my little lies.' Duncan sat back tight-lipped. It was proving very difficult to concentrate with Leonard butting in. But Leonard wasn't finished:

'He knows something he's not telling. Ask him is he sure.'

'Are you sure?'

'What are you getting at, Duncan?'

'Oh, nothing.' *What am I supposed to be getting at?*

DCI Chater stood up and started walking round the room. 'Enough of Mr Halsey. Yesterday you were seen jumping from a sinking boat in Tilworth Reservoir. Divers have since recovered a body – or at least the remains of a body – from the boat. He has been unofficially identified as one David Beaumont, the owner of the boat. He was a teacher at Ollington College of Education. Did you know him?'

'Course not! I told you what happened. I got knackered peddalling that bloody duck and went on board to ask for a drink. I couldn't find anyone on deck or when I shouted and then the boat started sinking so I jumped off.'

'And you never saw Mr Beaumont?'

'No.'

'How long were you on the boat?'

'Two minutes at most.'

'We have a witness who says you were on board for at least five minutes, most of them below deck.'

'Well, they're wrong. If Mr Beaumont drowned I'm only sorry I wasn't able to save him.'

'Good one, Duncan,' said Leonard. 'Never let on you saw him.'

'Mr Beaumont didn't drown. He was dead before the boat sank.'

'*Before?* You mean he was dead when I was on board?'

'Yes.'

'Well, I didn't see anything . . . I . . .'

'To be honest, he'd been dead for at least ten hours by then.'

'*Ten* hours? So what the hell are you questioning me for? I told you what happened.'

'But we didn't have a body then.'

'But you say he was already dead.'

'You might have returned to the scene of the crime.'

'Crap!' shouted Leonard, making Duncan twitch.

'Crap!' echoed Duncan, perhaps a touch too vehemently. 'Why return? And in daylight?'

Inspector Chater smiled. 'Good point.'

He sat down again and opened a file. 'And so we come to Mr Ludo Kimmel. You see what I'm driving at, Duncan? Three deaths and you're the first one on the scene in each case. A terrible coincidence or more?'

'Ask him how Beaumont died,' said Leonard.

'You ask him!' said Duncan.

'Pardon?' said the inspector.

'Er . . .'

'Terrific, Dunc, terrific,' said Leonard, peering over the detective's shoulder at the file. 'Section 28 coming up.'

'I meant . . . I . . . er, how did Mr Beaumont die?'

'Extremely violently.'

'Tell us something new,' said Leonard.

It was hard trying to ignore Leonard's presence. Apart from anything else, he was Duncan's only ally in the room. 'Like Mr Halsey?' he finally said.

'Why do you ask? Is there a connection?'

'No! Obviously not, otherwise—'

'*You'd* be the connection,' said Leonard. 'Never try and con a cop. Try and keep your mouth under control, kiddo.'

'You bloody shut up, then!' *Oh God . . .*

DCI Chater was surprised. 'Pardon, Duncan?'

'Big mouth strikes again,' sighed Leonard.

'I'm sorry. I'm nervous . . . what I meant was . . . could you shut up asking me questions when I ask questions.'

'Nice one, kid,' allowed Leonard.

'Oh, I see. Mr Beaumont was the victim of an extremely savage attack, but not the same kind as Mr Halsey. Okay?'

'Yes. Thanks. Sorry.'

'Now, why were you out at Mr Kimmel's?'

This was the question Duncan had been dreading.

Leonard looked up from the file he was sneaking a read of and said; 'Mum and dad. Wedding anniversary. Commissioning a sculpture. Dad'd pay.'

Brilliant. 'I'd heard of Mr Kimmel somewhere and I thought it would be a nice idea to commission a piece of sculpture as a present for my parents' wedding anniversary.'

'Spot on, kid,' said Leonard. 'As good as a news reader.'

'What?' said Duncan to Leonard, puzzled.

'What?' said Chater to Duncan, equally puzzled.

'What?' said Duncan to the detective.

'Pardon?' said the inspector to Duncan.

'You read your lines perfectly,' said Leonard. 'Just like someone reading the news. You see that film with William Hurt? *Broadcast News?*'

'What?' said Duncan, completely lost. Here he was trying to avoid being charged with murder and Leonard was impersonating bloody Barry Norman.

Chief Inspector Chater was worried. The boy kept addressing his right shoulder. He turned to look just in case. No-one there.

'Are you all right, Duncan?' he said, writing something down on the pad in front of him.

'I, er . . .'

'"Mad?"' said Leonard.

'Uh?'

'He thinks you're mad, Duncan. Not surprised, the way you've been—'

Duncan leapt up. 'Will you shut the fuck up!'

DCI Chater raised his eyebrows. The uniformed sergeant raised his fists.

'Anything wrong, Duncan?' said Chater warily.

Duncan slumped down. 'I'm sorry. I, it's just . . .'

'Three bodies,' said Leonard quietly.

'Three bodies,' repeated Duncan. 'Finding so . . .'

'Would you like a drink? Tea?' said Chater, already nodding the sergeant out of the room.

'Yes, please,' said Duncan. 'Anything.'

It was five minutes before conversation resumed. Duncan drank the sweet tea even though he disliked it.

'Are you all right now?' asked the chief inspector.

'Yes,' said Duncan. 'Sorry. Pressure . . .'

DCI Chater nodded, looked down at his pad, and then said, as if the tea-break hadn't happened: 'When is your parents' anniversary?'

'Pardon?'

'You wanted a sculpture for their wedding anniversary. When is it?'

Oh, shit. 'December. The eighth.'

'Six months away?'

'Well, I didn't know how long it would take.'

'Good one, Duncan,' said Leonard. 'Hadn't thought of that.'

'What was it going to be?'

God knows. Help me, Leonard, help me. But Leonard was leaning on his elbows beside Chief Inspector Chater, absorbed in reading the file. 'It . . . I was . . . going to leave that to him. I wanted it symbolic of dad's involvement in aircraft and industry . . . and mum's social work and . . .'

'And just how were you going to pay for it? I understand Mr Kimmel's sculptures fetch anything up to ten thousand pounds.'

'Do they? They do! Oh . . . dad! Yes, dad, he'd pay.'

'So he knows about this?'

'Not exactly. No.' *Be honest.* 'He doesn't. I was going to ask him.'

'You were going to spend his money on an expensive piece of art as a present for him and your mother and then ask *him* to pay for it?'

'Yes. My father's a very busy man. He often forgets anniversaries and such. I thought he'd appreciate the gesture.'

'Despite the cost.'

'Two grand to dad is twenty quid to anyone else.'

'Including hotel porters?'

Duncan didn't answer. He was tired. And angry. Angry at the presumption that his misfortunes could be construed as something more sinister. Angry that Leonard had got him into this mess. And angry that he couldn't call Leonard as a witness on his own behalf.

'Okay, so you went to ask him to do some work for you,' continued the detective. 'Then what?'

Duncan repeated his experience exactly as it had happened, only leaving out Leonard's involvement.

The chief inspector listened intently, occasionally taking notes, and only asking questions that clarified details. All the while, Leonard stood behind him, urging him to turn the pages of his file but it remained open resolutely on the first page.

Duncan finished and sat back and took a sip at his cup of tea. It was cold. The chief inspector asked the uniformed sergeant to go and get them some more.

'And that's what happened? He was just there waiting with a shotgun and went mad?'

'*Two* shotguns *and* a pistol, yes. I think he would have shot anyone who had come in. You, a neighbour, anyone.'

'Quite possibly. And you didn't know Mr Kimmel at all prior to going out to his farm?'

'No.'

'Did you know he had a record?'

'No.'

'For drugs,' said Leonard, reading as much of the file as he could when Chief Inspector Chater finally opened it. 'Half-a-dozen convictions. Marijuana, mainly.'

'He was into drugs,' said Chater. 'Caught a few times with marijuana, nothing stronger. He may have been high.'

'He certainly acted like he was.'

'We may be able to establish if he was, but there wasn't much left of him. Why did you return to the farm?'

'Why shouldn't I? He'd tried to kill me!'

'True.'

'Remember I told a constable at the scene he had tried to murder me. That's why I'm in here.'

'True again, Duncan, but then that police officer didn't know you had been involved in two other deaths.'

'Involved? Involved? I found one body and was unlucky enough to be on the boat of another. Then this bloody Kimmel decides to go nuts and shoot me. That's not involvement, that's bad luck.'

'But mightn't it also be too much bad luck?'

What?

Chief Inspector Chater stood up and stretched and closed the file.

'Damn,' said Leonard.

Despite his tiredness, Duncan smiled at Leonard's annoyance but Chater caught the smirk.

'Yes?' he asked.

'Nothing,' said Duncan sheepishly. 'I was just wondering what mum would say . . . that's if she knows I'm here yet.' He had phoned her earlier about his "problem" but had had to leave a message with one of her cronies on the council.

Just then there was knock at the door and another sergeant popped his head round the door and had a few words with the chief inspector, who nodded and turned to Duncan.

'Seems she does, Duncan. She's here now with Mr Klein.'

Good. Solomon Klein was the most expensive solicitor in Ollington. A very big gun.

'No doubt the Latin is already tumbling from the great man's lips. I hate to spoil his fun but you're free to go. You'll be needed as a witness at the inquest into Mr Kimmel's death but otherwise . . . Come on, I'll see you out.'

They left the interview room and walked down a dingy corridor until they reached some stairs. One flight down and they walked along another corridor filled with the chattering of typewriters, then turned left into the foyer of Ollington Central Police Station.

Duncan nodded his thanks and went to greet his mother, who fussed over him as only a mother can, and Solomon Klein (a man to whom food and drink were a religion and who, consequently, resembled an average-sized synagogue) who peered at Duncan over his half-rimmed spectacles as if he was Jack the Ripper's apprentice. (Solly Klein worked on the assumption that anyone who could afford his prices had to be guilty otherwise they wouldn't be able to afford him.)

Apologies were offered from every quarter and accepted by all, then Duncan found himself and his mother being swept out to Solomon Klein's Rolls Royce, Leonard whinging away behind the three of them about not being able to read any more of Chief Inspector Chater's notes.

'Duncan, couldn't you just ask some more questions? Just a couple. Find out something—'

'Shut up, Leonard!' shrieked Duncan, near to breaking.

It was fortunate that Solomon Klein's chauffeur was himself called Leonard, a man whose lifetime of obsequious compliance to his employer's every whim had rendered him impervious to insults of any kind, however undeserved. He simply doffed his cap and opened the doors to the limousine.

As the car set off Mrs Cantrill nodded discreetly in the direction of the chauffeur and sternly admonished her son in hushed tones: 'It's "Shut up, Leonard, *please*."'

15

'I'M SORRY, DUNCAN, but the holiday's off,' said Mrs Cantrill, a
slight tremor in her voice, as if fearing any comment she made would
send her only son off into a fit of rage that could only end in yet
another murder. Not that she believed Duncan was responsible for
any of those nasty deaths but . . .

'It's all right, mother, honest. I didn't think we would somehow.'

'Well, it's the inquest; you heard the chief inspector. And I've
work to do. And your father may be coming home at the weekend.
And Dr Menzies says he thinks travel would put too much strain
on you. And Mr Klein—'

'It's all right, mum, I get the message. No holiday. I don't mind.'

'You don't?'

'No, I just need a rest, that's all.'

'Yes. A rest. Dr Menzies said rest was vital if . . .' she trailed off.

'You don't think I've got anything to do with these mur— these
deaths, do you, mummy?'

'Of course not. No. You're my son . . . you wouldn't, no . . .'

'Honest?'

'Honestly, Duncan. It's not your fault you discovered that first
body in the hotel. Or that you just happened to step onto that boat
where that man had been killed. Or that a man you went to visit
tried to murder you and blew himself up. I mean it's all so . . .'
(*There was a pause like the distance between the planets as his mother
fought to find the appropriate word. She failed.*). . . .'

'Of course it is,' prompted Duncan. 'You know me.'

That was the trouble. His mother didn't know him, and only now
was she beginning to realise the truth of it.

'You're my son, Duncan. I love you and believe you. Tomorrow
this will all seem like a bad dream and we'll be able to put it
behind us.'

'That's right,' said Duncan, eyeing Leonard. 'Tomorrow everything will look all right.'

'Yes,' repeated his mother, as if reading from a cue card. 'Everything will be all right.'

'And you believe me? Everything?'

'Of course I do, Duncan. You're as innocent as a lamb.'

Like a lamb to the slaughter, thought Duncan. But he said: 'Exactly, mother. So why have you locked yourself in your bedroom?'

'Because . . . because I'm very tired . . . in fact I'm going to go to sleep now. Goodnight, Duncan.'

Duncan said goodnight to her bedroom door and made his way along the passage to his own room.

Inside he stripped and got into bed, as exhausted as his mother was pretending to be.

'I'm sorry about all this,' said Leonard.

'I bet.'

'No, I am. Sorry for the danger, sorry for the mess. Sorry even for your mother. When the papers get hold of this, she—'

'Don't even think it. She'll be the one who'll need Dr Menzies.'

Leonard sat down on the bed, his head as bloated as ever, his body white and flabby. 'I'm also sorry for myself.'

'What?'

'All I had was Beaumont and Kimmel and I was on the right track, but—'

'Right track?'

'Oh, come on, Duncan. Someone murders me and the only two people I know are dead. One murdered, the other obviously expecting to be killed – so much so he's prepared to shoot anyone who comes near him!'

'That's a point; he didn't know who was coming for him. He kept asking us to show him our fire, but he didn't know who we were so —'

'So he didn't know who wanted to kill him, either.'

'Right,' said Duncan. 'Which means . . .'

'"Hello, Leonard" for the next fifty years.'

Duncan slumped back on his pillow and wrapped the sheets around his head, a muffled refrain of '*Shit, shit, shit*' punctuating the ensuing silence.

He suddenly threw off the sheets and walked over to the window, pushed it open and breathed in deeply. Turning back to Leonard, already so accustomed to his presence that he was unabashed at being naked in front of another man, he said: 'It's not that I don't like you, Leonard, but the sooner you're gone, the better.'

'I quite agree.'

'So we've got to sort this out. No Beaumont, no Kimmel and no – who was the other guy?'

'Father Racimo.'

'Right, Racimo. And we've got no other leads, other than assuming that whoever killed – or was going to kill – you four is the same person and the only link between you all is these orgies you went to. Where did you say they happened?'

'Abandoned cement works on the Buxton Road.'

'Where exactly?'

'In the basement. It's just a big, empty room. They used to light it with candles. It was always cold, I remember.'

'Well, it might give us a clue. Is it worth a visit?'

'What else is there?'

Nothing else, except the sound of his mother sidling along the passageway to sneak a listen at his door. Duncan noisily climbed back into bed intent on sleep. What else was there?

16

THE SITE WAS a mess. It had obviously been a large complex with two main buildings, and a jumble of covered conveyor belts, huts and loading areas. Mounds of waste provided a backcloth, the whole covered in a coat of white dust that dazzled Duncan in the mid-morning sunlight. It looked like the surface of the moon, dotted with the shattered remains of fantastical spacecraft, lounging dead and decayed.

It was also as quiet as the moon, with only the odd bird call giving proof of life. Duncan pulled up outside the main building and stepped out of his Elf into a slowly settling cloud of dust. The large building stood blindingly white and he donned a pair of sunglasses as he strolled around.

There was nothing out of the ordinary. He heaved himself up onto what must have been a loading bay and made his way into the body of the biggest building, Leonard following behind him. Whatever had been there had been removed, leaving a large empty shell that echoed every footstep. Duncan also kicked up a choking cloud of dust that slowly but surely crept up the legs of his 501s. Cursing, he retreated and continued his travels around the inside wall of the building.

It was still very quiet, and the lack of sound and the white surroundings reminded him of a hospital, where everything is so clean and white and every action is so muted that simple ordinary sounds become exaggerated. The scuffing of his shoes on the bare ground and the relentless chatter of a lone bird way up in the rafters were his only companions. Apart from Leonard, of course, but even he still seemed in awe of the quiet.

Duncan came out of the building and made his way over to a smaller cube-shaped structure. Inside was a large open space surrounded on three sides by offices and workshops. Judging by the tumble of chairs and tables, it must have been some rudimentary canteen.

He stood in the centre and turned through three hundred and sixty degrees. Nothing but broken windows and damaged doors. One particular doorway caught his attention. He walked over to it and looked in.

It led to a basement. He took a couple of steps down but it was so dark, despite the blaze of sunshine streaming through the broken roof, that he decided to give it a miss.

Leonard finally piped up. 'That's it, Duncan. Down there's where we went.'

'Great,' said Duncan, eyeing the darkness.

He stepped back into daylight and returned to his car and got a torch. Then, once back at the entrance to the basement, he removed his sunglasses, switched on the torch, and set off down the steps.

Straight away he noticed Leonard wasn't with him.

'Leonard?'

'I've got that problem again.'

'You can't come down?'

'No. Don't know why. It's just like when we were on—'

'That bloody boat! Right. And look what happened then!'

'I'm sorry, but I can't move.'

'Fuck! I'm not going down there on my own.'

'You've got no choice. Down there's all we've got.'

'But it's so bloody dark.'

'And I'm bloody *dead*, Duncan. Get your priorities right.'

'My priorities are simple, Leonard. Get rid of you – and keep rid of you.'

'Couldn't agree more, but this is the only place left. Now get the fuck down there and see if there's anything we can use!'

'Like what?'

'Like a signed bloody confession! I don't know. Just do it. *Please*.'

Duncan knew he was in trouble when he heard Leonard say 'please'. He hesitated, but he didn't have much choice. He set off down the steps.

He counted eighteen of them. As he reached the last one he noticed with dismay how the light from the torch seemed to spill out and fall to the floor in a small pool, the darkness sucking all the brightness out of the beam and leaving it concentrated in an impossibly small circle at his feet. It was next to useless and Duncan considered giving up and going back upstairs but chided himself for his reluctance. He pressed on, but after ten steps found himself confronted by a wall and he had to turn to his left. He took another dozen steps then shone the torch round the room but it wouldn't reach the opposite wall. *What the hell kind of a torch is this anyway?* He ran his finger along the wall. It was relatively smooth and looking at his fingertips in the beam, he could see that it had also escaped most of the ubiquitous chalky dust upstairs.

He took a few more steps then pointed the beam at the ground. Concrete. Then up at the ceiling. More concrete and some rusty pipework. He shone it on the wall again. Blank. He tried it again across the wide space of the basement but it still failed to reveal how wide the room was. He decided to give it up; the torch was next to useless and appeared to be growing dimmer by the minute, but that might just be his mind playing tricks. Sure, that was it. *Okay, I'll take three more steps, then pack it in.*

How adult.

One: he pointed the torch down. Nothing on the floor.

Two: he pointed the beam up. Nothing but pipes up there.

Three: he swung the torch around the room. Again nothing. Sod it.

'Nothing here, Leonard, just like you said,' he shouted, his voice impossibly small in the dark chamber.

He turned back, letting the beam play across the wall. It was then that he saw the face screaming at him, eyes mad with hatred, pointed teeth dripping blood!

Duncan yelled and dropped the torch, immediately diving after it. *Ohgodohgod. Who is it? Where is he?* Crouched down on the floor, scrabbling for the torch, he tensed, fully expecting a man's weight to come crashing down onto his back. But it didn't come.

He rolled to one side, fumbled for the torch, grabbed it, switched it back on and then, bracing himself, shone it back on the wall.

The face was still there. Still screaming, still full of hate, still dripping blood from its fangs, but this time Duncan took long enough to see that it was only a painting. He let out a none-too-sure sigh of relief and stood up straight, studying the face more closely.

He could see that it was actually quite crudely done, almost comic art, and that the look was one of terror rather than hate. He played the beam down and saw why the man was screaming; his throat was being slit by the razor-sharp fingernails of an ugly naked old woman, her face showing what could only be described as glee. It made Duncan's stomach turn over. He was in the presence of real sickness. He shone the torch further along the wall. *Oh God in heaven* . . .

More appalling scenes met his gaze. Babies being dismembered. Women eating shit as it came out of a man's anus. A man slicing off his own penis. A woman feeding her breast to a dog. Duncan felt sick, but couldn't tear his eyes away from the kaleidoscope of perversion. And, unconsciously, he started walking further into the basement, like an art lover absorbed by a Hieronymus Bosch exhibition.

There were men being crucified upside down; women speared on poles through their vaginas; children with their eyes gouged out, weeping tears of blood onto copulating adults. Scenes of bestiality, sodomy, torture, pain and fear . . . all painted in garish colours in a primitive and repellent style that was too crude to be the work of a talented artist, but which nonetheless was the work of a dedicated amateur. These were not the juvenile inanities of a public convenience, but the product of a truly sick mind who realised every little detail with obvious relish. It was a comprehensive catalogue of every conceivable pain and perversion it was possible for human beings to inflict on one another.

Duncan felt himself shivering, and even heard his stomach rumbling its disgust. He felt sick. He wiped the sweat from his eyes and tried to walk away, but his eyes seemed to be drawn to the horrors, drinking in every gory, gratuitous detail. The decapitations, castrations, eviscerations, mutilations . . . and everywhere, the sure, dead hand of graphic sexual excitement. Erections, ejaculations, engorged nipples, slavering tongues. This was where Leonard came? And Beaumont and Kimmel? What in God's name did they *do?*

He wanted to shout his horror, to give vent to his overpowering disgust, but he didn't trust himself to open his mouth, afraid that if he started screaming he wouldn't be able to stop. Or worse, someone, in the dark, might laugh. So instead he forced himself to look away and concentrate on getting back to the stairs. Even so the torch beam would occasionally offer him brief glimpses of the bottom twelve inches of the wall.

It was after he had taken just a few steps that his torch caught something shiny and red. Just for an instant, down low, and gone as quickly as it had appeared. He stopped and played the torch back over the spot. No. Nothing there. His mind was playing tricks.

He took another step but the light caught something again. Two bright red points of light, low and against the wall. Oh no . . . eyes. *Eyes!* Against the wall. Not on it or part of it but away from it, in the basement. *There was something in here with him!* Whatever it was, it was between him and escape.

Duncan jabbed the torch straight at the twin pinpoints of pink and suddenly a white blob appeared behind them, hissing. The sound made his spine freeze. Then there was another hiss behind him.

He spun round and his torch caught two more pairs of glaring red eyes barely six feet away. He also detected a movement above him and looked up. More hate-filled red eyes glinted evilly above him. Even as he watched they started to advance along the line of a pipe towards his exposed head. He could also hear more animals hissing and spitting in the background, and behind the eyes he could see large white bodies, bloated and spiky. Cats!

Normally he liked cats; they were good fun, a bit stand-offish, but nothing to fret about. But here, with these cats, he felt nothing but fear. These cats were not at all friendly; they weren't even being territorial. They were stalking him, as if he were a sparrow. Except he didn't have the benefit of wings to lift him out of trouble.

He stepped back against the wall, the loathsome pictures seeming to claw at his back. Out of the darkness came yet more eyes, and more hissing and a chilling screech. Wherever he played the torch there were more shapes and more eyes; white indistinct forms just keeping out of range, but their red baleful eyes boring into him, daring him to move. Duncan had put his arm out along the wall and was slowly starting to edge back towards the stairs when the crying began.

Duncan held his breath. It was the most horribly unnatural sound he had ever heard, like an old woman pleading for mercy, or a baby being slowly crushed. It started low then rose and rose until it became a gut-wrenching squall that seemed to revolve like a screw, boring its way into his brain. And then another cat joined in. And another. And another, all wailing and whining, in front of him, behind him, above him, all mocking him and beginning, slowly but surely, to advance on him, their eyes like eager little pits of fire on a field of black velvet.

Duncan started to swing his torch around as if it were a flaming brand, trying to keep the screeching beasts at bay, but they continued to creep towards him regardless, their ululating cries growing louder and louder. Now he could see their teeth – small and sharp and yellow, snapping and grinding, evil rictus grins sizing him up. And then his torch went out!

Duncan *laughed* out loud in terror. It had to be a nightmare, it had to be; this kind of bad luck only ever happens in bad dreams or bad movies. Yet still the wailing and mewling grew and the eyes came closer, twenty or thirty pairs of them now. Then Duncan realised that even without the torch he could see them. Big albino cats, with horrible reptilian pink eyes, claws scratching and fretting on the concrete. He had no alternative. He estimated the distance to the stairs and ran.

The noise was insane. Cats hurled themselves at him in fury, clawing at his legs and back and arms, one even landing on his face, but he tore it off and sent it squealing to the floor. And still he ran blindly, covering his eyes for protection until he crashed into the end wall, spun ninety degrees and charged towards the steps, oblivious of the bodies he trampled and crushed underfoot and their hideous protests of pain and agony. Then he tripped on the first step and went down.

Cats ran over him, nipping at his hands and ears and elbows, spitting and snatching at him, their feet drumming over his back and legs, trying to smother him.

He struggled up, crushing one cat with his hand, breaking its neck, seeing its eyes pop out as he forced his full weight down on it to gain enough purchase to lift himself and a dozen clinging cats off the ground. Once up he spun round, frantically beating at his back with his hands, kicking out wildly at anything that dared to approach, but the cats were oblivious to everything except their need to attack.

He regained his sense of direction and was about to mount the steps when he heard a sound above him and, in the new light from outside, he saw four absolutely enormous cats sitting smugly on the stairs, teeth bared, waiting for him. For what seemed an age he and the four cats stared deep into each others' eyes, all parties lost in a world of black fury and blind hatred. Then they leapt; the cats at Duncan, and he at them.

Duncan ducked, and that saved him. Three of the cats passed right over him, their demented shrilling pulling at his ears, but the fourth snagged a paw in his hair. He screamed out in pain as the cat whipped his head back, tearing out a large chunk of his hair before falling to the floor. Immediately two more cats ran up his body intent on getting his eyes. His hands got there first and he grabbed them by their necks, one in each hand, and dashed their heads into the wall, feeling the skulls crack and hot blood squirt over his hands and into his face.

He turned again to the stairs and started the slow inexorable climb up, the cats wriggling and shrieking and slithering underfoot. Flailing about him, he caught a glimpse back into the basement. There seemed to be hundreds of them, the floor heaving with their bodies, their eyes like lit matches at a rock concert.

He fell, got up, fell, got up again and gradually clawed his own way to the top of the stairs. One cat dug its claws into his groin and an electric pain shot through his legs and up his back as the cat attempted to destroy his testicles. Without thinking he started pounding at it with his bare hands, oblivious to anything but the need to get the cat out of his flesh.

Eventually it gave in and fell back onto the threshing carpet that now made up the floor of the basement and the bottom three or four steps. And that was when he noticed that they had stopped following him. He felt two on his back and he grabbed behind him with both hands and flung them away, then turned and fled into the sunlight, only to trip over a broken chair and sprawl in the dust.

He rolled onto his back and looked down past his feet at the black maw of the basement entrance. Nothing moved; no eyes, no white forms, nothing, except a receding mewling and squawking, as if the cats were in retreat like some malignant tide. Then there was silence.

He sat up straight and peered further down over the lip of the stairs. Nothing. He leaned back on one arm and wiped his forehead with his sleeve, the sweat running into his eyes and stinging him, but he didn't care. He felt at his mouth and his fingers showed blood. It acted as a spur and he stood up, but just as he turned away there was a loud hysterical shriek. He half-turned back in time to catch sight of a white blur and then the cat thudded into his chest and he toppled over again onto his back.

The cat was trying to claw his eyes. He covered his face with one arm and batted futilely at it then, realising his actions were no use, grabbed instead for the loose fur around its neck. After a couple of misses he got a handful of skin and jerked the cat away from his head. The cat's fearsome face was now about a foot from his own, the eyes blood-red and bulging like open wounds, its mouth so wide as to almost conceal the rest of its face. Its paws were splayed, vicious yellow claws like miniature meat hooks fighting to impale themselves on his face and in his eyes. He grabbed it round the neck with his other hand and then, two-handed, started to strangle it.

The cat's eyes opened even wider and it started kicking frantically but he refused to give it an inch. He howled back into its face as he squeezed harder and harder on its throat, listening to the bones cracking and the cat's gurgling with his own demented laughter, determined to bring his hands together.

The cat gave a couple of spasms and spat in his face, its lips curling back to reveal luminous pink gums as livid as its eyes. Its paws flexed weakly and then it stopped struggling, its hot bitter urine pouring down over Duncan's jeans.

He merely laughed all the louder, then whipped the cat round and down onto the ground next to him. Letting go momentarily, he grabbed its back legs and swung it up and down again onto the ground, dashing its brains out, the head exploding like a ripe tomato. Then he got up and kicked it back towards the basement entrance. As it landed, it shook furiously, seeming almost to crawl, then lay still. Duncan stared at it blankly for a full ten seconds, then ran.

He didn't look back, just jumped into his car, slammed it into gear and roared off, his spinning wheels spraying the building with a fury of gravel and covering the site in a cloud of choking white dust which served to obscure whatever other horrors might still be leering at him from the debris.

He zoomed onto the main road without checking for other traffic and roared on towards Ollington. It was only after a minute had passed that he noticed Leonard sat next to him.

'Duncan? What happened down there? I heard—'

Duncan turned slowly to look at Leonard, his face set in a sick grin, his eyes wide with fear.

'You know full well what happened down there, you FUCKING BASTARD!'

Duncan let go of the wheel and lunged for Leonard's throat, missed, and slammed his head hard on the side window. He was too stunned to sit back up straight away and consequently could do nothing to stop the car lurching to the right, ploughing through a hedge and plunging two hundred feet to the bottom of a disused quarry.

17

Déjà vu.

Duncan opened his eyes to find himself in a hospital room. He was alone, the bed across from his empty. It was a private room again, but not The Pines this time. It must be the Cottage Hospital, Ollington's big and inaptly-named general hospital. What now?

He sat up, the throbbing in his head bearable, and surveyed himself for damage. He seemed intact; no broken limbs, movement where it counted, no tubes or splints or bandages. Then he remembered: the cats, and driving away and lunging for Leonard and then . . . nothing.

'Leonard, are you here?' he said through gritted teeth.

'Yes,' said a voice. 'Do you really want to see me?'

'Not particularly. Just answer me two questions.'

'Sure.'

'What happened to my car?'

'It drove through a hedge then over a cliff. Long drop. You fell out just in time – good thing you hadn't shut your door properly or put your seat belt on. I'd have pushed you out myself if I could've but, well, you know . . .'

'How long is a long drop?'

'Couple of hundred feet. Your car didn't make it. You're okay, though. Minor cuts and bruises and a concussion. You lay there for a couple of hours until someone noticed the hole in the hedge and they found you. You've been in here about five hours now. Your mother had hysterics, naturally. And that Inspector Chater paid his respects as well. Does the term "deep shit" mean anything?'

Duncan groaned. 'Second question: why did you say there was nothing down in that basement?'

'The cats, you mean? I saw the little fuckers come up after you. I swear on my life there weren't any cats when we went there.'

'How can you swear on your life? You haven't got one.'

'Okay, smart arse, I swear on my *death* then: when we used that place it was just big and dark and empty. Honest.'

'No cats?'

'No cats.'

'No paintings on the wall?'

'Paintings? No. What sort?'

'Sick, that's what sort. You telling the truth?'

'Why would I lie? You're all I got.'

'Ditto,' sighed Duncan under his breath.

'Can I come out now?'

'Suppose so. Where are you?'

In answer Leonard scrambled out from under the bed and stood at its end, as naked and as absurd as ever.

'Hello, Leonard.'

'Hello, Duncan. I'm sorry about what happened. And the car. You've got to keep control; I don't recommend being dead.'

'Thanks. I'll bear it in mind . . . Hey, how come you could hide under the bed? I thought you had to be in sight—'

'I could see your hand. There, the left one, hanging over the edge. It's enough.'

'Great. One other thing: how come you couldn't come down into the basement with me?'

Leonard sat down on the bed. 'Don't know, Duncan. That's twice now. The basement and the boat. Beats me.'

'Happy days.'

They sat in gloomy silence for a long while as, outside, dusk claimed the day. Finally Leonard spoke up.

'Duncan, I've got a favour to ask you. I heard the doc and your mother and the cops talking and they all agreed tomorrow you could be moved to a private rest home, for the foreseeable future. For your own safety, apparently. They think you're ga-ga and that cop Chater wants you under strict supervision. That fat solicitor – Klein, is it? – persuaded him that this hospital they knew would be best.'

'Perhaps it would. I need a rest. Besides, that basement was the last chance we had. If you're telling the truth then they've had the Dulux out since the last time you were there. And as for those fucking cats . . .'

'Right. But I found out one interesting thing, Duncan. Ollington's morgue is downstairs.'

'What?'

'Downstairs is where they stash all the bodies, including yours truly. Where there's bodies there's case notes and—'

'Oh no – ' said Duncan, pulling the covers over his head.

'– where there's case notes, there might just—'

'– no way—'

'– be clues.'

'No, Leonard,' he insisted, sinking deeper and deeper under the blankets.

'So I was thinking, as this is your—'

'No no no,' came the by now muffled rejoinder.

'– only night here, me and you could—'

'No!' the bed pleaded.

'– take a gander—'

'NO!' the bed insisted.

'– downstairs.'

The bed whined pathetically. And lost.

Just after midnight Duncan was awakened by someone screaming in his ear. Of course, as it was Leonard, no-one else could hear this alarm call from beyond the grave. Letting Leonard act as lookout, they sneaked their way past the nurses' station and down the stairs to the ground floor. There they avoided the porter on duty and followed the discreet signs to the morgue. It was indeed downstairs.

The well-lit stairwell provided a relatively cheerful introduction to the bowels of the hospital, but on leaving its reassuring brightness, Duncan's trepidation returned. He was about to break into a morgue! A roomful of corpses. Hadn't he got enough problems with dead people already? But as his 'problem' urged him to move it, he speeded up, walking briskly along the long corridor to the morgue.

Overhead a myriad of thickly painted pipes gurgled and creaked, and distant voices echoed through the labyrinth of passages, the two-tone brick walls, grey concrete floor, dingy lighting and heavily antiseptic air only serving to add to the rather sinister atmosphere. The abandoned trolleys and drip stands gave the journey a slightly surreal aspect, as if everyone had suddenly run away from some nameless horror. Duncan, despite having a dead person as a companion, was scared shitless.

As Leonard had guessed, the morgue was both empty and unguarded, but also locked.

'It's locked. That's that, then,' hissed Duncan with no effort to hide his relief.

'No problem,' said Leonard. 'You learn a lot about people, selling insurance. Keys is one.'

'Keys?'

'When there's no guarantee that the keyholder will always turn up on time, there's usually a spare key hidden so staff can get in.'

'Don't talk daft.'

'Assume there are assistants ready to work but the pathologist's car breaks down. Are they just supposed to stand around? Rather than let everyone have a key, the easiest thing is to have a spare hidden. Now, no point hiding it high. And,' said Leonard scanning the floor. 'There's no mat. So where would they put it?'

Duncan looked around. The walls were empty, the floor bare, all pipework too high even for him to reach.

'Aha,' said Leonard pointing at a fire alarm.

Duncan saw a red metal box with a key and a notice saying *In Case of Emergency, Break Glass*. 'So?'

'Where's the exit door?'

True. Duncan touched the casing. 'More to the point,' he had to admit, 'where's the glass?'

He scooped out the key and fitted it into the morgue door and let them in.

It was pitch black.

'Put the bloody light on,' said Leonard.

'What if someone sees?'

'No-one in here's going to have their sleep disturbed.'

'I meant outside, you prick.'

'Just do it, Duncan.'

Fumbling in the dark he finally found a switch and pulled it down. Duncan didn't know what he was expecting but it wasn't art deco.

Obviously the morgue reflected the age of the building; hence the vaguely oppressive off-white and green glazed décor and antiquated lighting that served to reinforce the illusion that the outside world was a fantasy. Never mind the colourful posters of the pyramids of Egypt and Mexico – they were tombs, after all – or the absurdly incongruous burgundy British Railways sign for Ollington station: this was a charnel house. On the right was a darkened office behind a large window with vertical blinds, and ahead of him on the opposite wall were three large metal doors behind which was obviously where the bodies were stored. The left-hand side of the room, about thirty feet to his left, was dominated by cabinets containing instruments and jars. The centre of the room was given over to a brace of metal tables, the only modern-looking feature of the room. Thankfully they were empty. Duncan edged into the room until he was by the first table. So this is where they did it . . .

He had read up on post-mortems (as well as Japanese war crimes, Nazi atrocities, the Marquis de Sade and the history of torture – what teenage boy doesn't?), and he had a good idea of what happened to a body during the impoliteness of an autopsy. It sent a shiver through him; eyeing the chill cabinets he started to edge back to the door. What was he doing here? It was spooky.

Then he spotted Leonard standing by the cabinets. Spooky? What the hell could half-a-dozen disembowelled corpses do to him that the ghost with him couldn't? He started to relax.

'Let's get this over with. And, as it's your bright idea, you tell us what we're supposed to be doing,' said Duncan.

'First thing: see who they got stashed in the drawers. See if Beaumont and Racimo are there.'

Duncan looked askance at Leonard. 'You've got to be joking!' He pointed a shaking finger over at the cold store doors. 'You want me to root around in there until we find your dead friends?'

'No, dickhead. Check the reports. There must be some filing system which can tell you who's in which box . . . like that board by the doors.'

Duncan walked over to where Leonard was standing. There was a small blackboard divided into twelve lines, each with a number corresponding to a corpse in the store. There were eight bodies in residence at present, including Kimmel, L; Beaumont, D; and Racimo, A. There was also a Halsey, L. Leonard saw this and became very quiet.

'Creepy,' said Duncan, relishing the man's discomfort. Serve him right, making him come down here . . . then the situation hit home; here was a man stood next to his own *corpse*. Damn it; Duncan had no way of understanding just how it would feel for Leonard to see himself laid out, post mortem stitching and all – but he could imagine what would happen if he had been badly burned in a fire and saw his melted face for the first time in a mirror . . .

Duncan turned to the office. 'Files, you say?'

Leonard followed, his eyes watching the cabinets.

'Damn! Looks like everything's locked.'

'What?' said Leonard. 'Oh, filing cabinets? No problem. They operate with a bar that runs top to bottom. Get a ruler or a paper knife, then slide it in at the top and move it across the top of the lock.'

Duncan did as suggested, and it worked.

'Years of practice getting a look-see at other salesmen's returns,' explained Leonard. 'The secret of my success. That, and a magnetic personality.'

'And a good line in bullshit.'

'That too, yes.'

Duncan riffled through each drawer until he found the files. Extracting those marked 'Racimo' and 'Beaumont' they read through their contents.

They were autopsy reports, both odd, but nothing to connect the two men. However, there were also photocopies of police files included. Incomplete, but they were obviously there for a reason.

'What've we got, then?' asked Leonard, scanning Racimo's file fanned out on the desk. 'Alphonse Caesar Racimo, 43, unmarried – surprise, surprise – a Catholic priest working and living at the St Gabriel's Shelter for the Homeless in Ollington. Goody two-shoes; if only they knew. He died of trauma and blood . . . well, obviously. God, his head was cut off. Decapitated in that car crash.'

There were photographs of a car crash taken from several angles and a police traffic report with measurements. It appeared that his car had gone off the road and run down a hill for three hundred yards before coming to a halt against an embankment. The car was not seriously damaged except the front end where it had gone through a dry stone wall. All the glass was intact, the doors locked and Father Racimo inside, his corpse headless, the head itself on the back seat. There was blood inside the car but, oddly, none outside. The car had left the road between 11.30pm and 1.45am when it was discovered. Analysis of débris in the priest's neck wound found traces of iron, which suggested the use of a weapon of which there was no trace. There were also photographs of the body, sat clasping the steering wheel as if still motoring; and of the head, its face set in a terrified grimace. Duncan put the shot down as soon as he had picked it up.

'Christ,' he said, fighting the bile.

'Don't think He was there helping His boy. Not this time.'

'What do you mean?'

'Look at this police report. The man was interviewed . . . what? six . . . *eight* times about molesting children over the last fourteen years. Once in Ollington, twice in Ludlow, once in Dudley . . . And every time he's not been charged.'

Duncan took the sheets. 'Yes, but he moved on – or was moved on. And look at his jobs. He started out in Coventry; three years later Leicester. Every time he's spoken to by the police he's shifted. Bastard must have been getting away with it for years. Never any evidence, just accusations.'

'Well, it doesn't tell me anything I didn't suspect,' said Leonard. 'He always seemed to go for the young guys; some got hurt, obviously not gay, but they couldn't protest.'

'And what about you?' asked Duncan a bit too harshly.

'Girls, women, any woman who wanted to. Hey, whatever they were up to I was only after getting my end away with skirt that wanted it. I never forced anyone.'

Duncan shook his head. He hated to admit it but he still felt vaguely jealous. What he wouldn't give to have a woman who wanted him, never mind the plural . . . but then again, Leonard had been mixing with sick scum.

'Okay. All that's left is a list of the contents of his pocket and wallet, and this photostat.'

They studied what looked like two rows of Chinese characters, neither making any sense of it.

'Shopping list for a takeaway?' said Duncan. 'Sod it. Let's try Beaumont.'

David Mark Beaumont, 36, had been a lecturer in child psychology. Unmarried, his official address had been in Ollington College. His autopsy report ran three times as long as Racimo's. After reading through the incomprehensible medical jargon, Duncan was surprised to realise that he had just read the man's cause of death was *poisoning*.

'Look at this,' he said to Leonard. 'Beaumont was poisoned as well as beaten to death. He'd have died of respiratory failure brought on by the poison anyway but he had fifty-seven *pre*-mortem injuries. He was poisoned *then* beaten to death. The poison resembles "scorpionida venom". They're waiting for Home Office tests to confirm the precise type. *Scorpionida*. Where have I heard that before?'

Leonard let out a big sigh. It sounded like air escaping from a tyre. 'What does it sound like?'

'Scorpion . . . He was poisoned by a scorpion?'

'Report says fatal levels. In fact it says "abnormally high concentration".'

'Some creep injected him with poison, then . . .' Duncan stopped, the picture too graphic – and too dangerous. He looked at Leonard, his head, his neck. There was one serious maniac on the loose.

'I don't think we should—'

'You know we have to, Duncan. I promise you if it gets too dangerous we'll stop, but right now all we've got is some corpses. Corpses can't hurt people.'

'Hey, I'm talking to one now. How do I know *Night of the Living Dead* isn't just as real?'

'Read some more, okay?' said Leonard, pointing at the police documents attached to Beaumont's post mortem report.

'He's a bad driver. Got lots of speeding fines and endorsements. Been banned three times. Only speeding, though. Couple of dangerous drivings. Nothing else. Pulled a couple of times on complaints from students. Nothing proved.'

'What kind of complaints?'

'Sexual harrassment. One by a girl who believed he was having sex with her friend against her friend's wishes.'

'That's rape.'

'Word's not mentioned here. They interviewed the girl: nothing.'

'Nothing else?'

'Just a hand-written note. Paper's not headed. Signed Dr B. Harrison. "Mr Beaumont exhibits classic signs of psychopathic behaviour. Manipulative, open yet evasive, charming yet self-possessed. Good-looking man, he could easily use his position in the college to take advantage of vulnerable students. Suggest college authorities take any complaints against him extremely seriously." That's all. Dated eighteen months ago. Wonder who Dr Harrison is?'

'Doesn't matter. I knew Beaumont better than Racimo. I'd say that summed him up. He always came with a young girl, eighteen, nineteen usually. He'd fuck her, then watch others use her. I put it down to him being a voyeur but, thinking back, he used to have a look on his face: he liked the way the girl was used . . . come to think of it . . .'

'What?'

'Remember I told you some of us started to get worried because one of the girls had died?'

'Yes.'

'She was a girl Beaumont had brought a couple of times.'

'Coincidence? How did she die?'

'Don't know.'

'Doesn't help.'

'No,' said Leonard. 'Okay, let's try Kimmel.'

'Why? We saw how he died. He wasn't murdered.'

'Yes, but he was expecting to be killed, wasn't he? "Show me your fire" and all that shit. Let's see if there's any link between him and Beaumont or Racimo. If the only link is the orgies, then we know where the murderer's at, don't we?'

'Ludo Kimmel, 51, Czech immigrant, single. He was high on drugs when he was killed, no surprise there. The police record was small time stuff, sex and drugs mainly. Possession and pushing. Served two jail terms of a year each. Also a suspended sentence for child pornography; he'd made a couple of videos with teenagers. Lived on his farm for three years, before which he'd lived on another farm in Henshaw in Shropshire. While there he'd been arrested as a suspected child molester but no charges were made. A couple of weeks later he moved to Ollington.'

Shropshire. Why did that mean something to Duncan? He pushed aside the files and found a *Financial Times* diary on the desk. Flicking to the back he found a map of the UK. A minute's searching and he had found another link.

'Kimmel and Racimo knew each other before they came to Ollington,' said Duncan.

'When?'

'Racimo worked at a children's home near Ludlow. Kimmel lived on a farm only four miles away. They were both questioned at the same time about abuse in a children's home. They were both paedophiles. And that gives someone a motive. Maybe they had abused some kid, the parents or relative found out, decided to take the law into their own hands?'

'What about me? I never touched kids. And Beaumont? His girls may have been young but they were over the age of consent. Kimmel or Racimo introduced the other to the orgies – that's it.'

Duncan was stumped. 'It's grinding to a halt. The only thing that links you four is those bloody orgies and we don't know anyone else who went.'

Duncan slowly closed up the files and put them back in the cabinet. He sat down in the chair, his head in his hands. He had a headache and he knew it wasn't going to go away. Not as long as Leonard was there.

'Come on, Leonard,' he said finally. 'Let's lock up and go back upstairs. It's after one. I'll try and talk my way out of the nursing home idea but that's it. We'll just have to get used to each other.'

Leonard didn't answer. He stood by the freezer cabinets staring at the list of names of occupants. Duncan presumed he was staring at his own name.

'That girl who died. Someone said it was the week before the last meeting I went to. That puts it . . . middle of April. Check the files again. See what girls they brought in between, say, 1st of April and the 21st.'

Duncan couldn't be bothered to argue, so he slipped the lock on the cabinet and went through the relevant drawer.

Only two young girls had died in that period who had required an autopsy. A fourteen-year-old in a joy riding accident and a Jane Dalton, a nineteen-year-old student at Ollington College of Education. She had taken a drug overdose and then hanged herself on the moors. Her body hadn't been found for thirty-six hours. Poor bitch. The file contained post mortem photographs. He showed a head and shoulders shot to Leonard.

The man drew in a heavy gasp of breath, then nodded his head. 'That was her. She came . . . three times. First time I can't remember her. Second time I was . . . I was going to, you know, but she . . . she was scared. Like I said, I only wanted fun; she didn't, so I left her alone. Third time I remember Beaumont watching as others took her. He encouraged them to do . . . well, everything. She seemed zonked, out of it. Might have been drugs but, well, it could have been shock, I suppose.'

Duncan could tell that Leonard was genuinely sorry for what had happened and decided not to pursue it. 'So how does it help us?'

Leonard didn't know. He was still thinking back to the last night he had seen her. What torments she must have gone through to actually kill herself . . .

'Anything in the report that might help?' he said.

'She lived on campus; her roommate said she had been depressed but didn't know why. She denied she did drugs, but then she would, as her roommate . . . Her father identified the body, she was buried in her home town of Chester. Coroner's verdict, suicide. Hmmm, that's interesting. There's a note from the pathologist. He wanted the police to investigate why she was depressed. Apparently she, ugh, had cut up her vagina prior to killing herself. In his opinion this indicated sexual disgust which could result from sexual abuse. Either in the family . . .'

'Or from someone she trusted.'

'Like Beaumont.'

'Still doesn't get us anywhere. The man deserved to die – unlike others I could mention,' said Leonard.

'They *all* deserved to die. As for you . . .'

Leonard hung his bloated head in shame.

'Oh come on, I believe you.' And Duncan did. How many times had he fantasised about attending an orgy, of having wild abandoned sex with a group of like-minded individuals, often with older, bigger women? While their husbands encouraged him? Would he have done it for real and if he had would he have noticed if one or two of those in attendance were perhaps less than keen? Yes, you could have couples who agreed wholeheartedly with the *idea* of swapping partners, but put four couples in a room and at least one of them is bound to be less enthusiastic about the reality. Take that to the extreme: a girl trusts a man enough to let him let others use her to satisfy *his* desires, then he probably uses psychobabble bullshit and his own psychotic charisma to convince her he was right to do so. The poor cow . . .

'Get her name – and her roommate's,' said Leonard.

'Why?'

'Only lead left. She may have said something to the girl that could help us.'

'Oh come on, that's a bit of a long shot, isn't it?'

'You said yourself she would probably have lied to the police about drugs if they both took them. What if she knew about Beaumont? Was scared of him or of losing her place at the college if she talked? She wouldn't have said anything to the cops, would she? Well, now Beaumont's dead, she might be more forthcoming.'

'Forthcoming? Now there's a word. I just—'

Suddenly there was a loud crash in the corridor. Something metallic.

Duncan grabbed the file and stuffed it back in the drawer then flipped off the office light.

Leonard was standing by the morgue doors. There wasn't another sound but that didn't mean no-one was outside.

Duncan came up behind him and flipped off the main light and there they stood in the dark, only Duncan's ragged breath for company.

They waited a full two minutes before Duncan dared to edge the door open and peek into the corridor. He let out a long sigh as he realised what had caused the noise: a stretcher handle had rolled off a trolley. Nonetheless, he was resolved to get back to his room.

He locked the morgue doors, replaced the key in its box and made his way cautiously back up the corridor and then up the stairs. Once on his own floor, and sure there was no nurse about, he slipped back into his bed.

'Tomorrow we go and see the girl,' said Leonard.

'Tomorrow I'm supposed to be going to a loony bin.'

'Don't. Persuade your mother, run away, get better, *anything*, just don't let the men in white coats get you.'

Duncan didn't answer. Maybe that was just what he needed, even if Leonard was real and all this insanity was happening; it was getting just too damn dangerous to continue. Christ, Kimmel had shot at him, he'd almost drowned on that bloody boat, cats had nearly ripped him to pieces and he'd driven over a cliff, his mother was convinced he was insane and the police held much the same view. Someone, somewhere, was trying to tell him something.

He looked at his watch. 1.26am. Last time he'd been up this late he'd been in his bedroom, his earphones on, the volume turned to max, trying to come down from the only 'E' he'd ever taken. That experience had put him off drugs for good; he wondered what it would take to stop him doing Leonard's dirty work? Chances were it would be far worse than an overpowering thirst and legs that wanted to climb the walls. Then, just as he managed to drift off to sleep, a thought jolted him awake:

If paedophiles like Kimmel and Racimo and mysogynistic bastards like Beaumont wanted out of the orgies, what was so bad that even their twisted minds couldn't cope with it?

18

'HONEST, MUM, I'M okay now. I've had a long think and I've decided to do something constructive.'

'What?'

'Become a teacher.'

It had been Leonard's idea: to get out of being sent to the clinic by concocting a positive reason not to go. Blethering on about feeling okay wouldn't be enough; he'd had his chances to sort things out and his mother was prepared for the worst, but this . . .

Mrs Cantrill was plainly flummoxed. She sat down on the chair by Duncan's hospital bed. 'I – I don't know what to say, Duncan. I . . . do you . . .?'

Duncan, fully dressed and packed, crouched beside her.

'Look, mum, I know I've been a pain. Wasted my education, messed about with dead-end jobs. I had my reasons but I know they're not important now. Finding that dead man, well, it made me see . . . see the value of living. I know I can never match up to what you or dad have achieved but I do want to do something useful with my life.'

The argument had been prepared by Leonard. Inserting key phrases like 'Wasted My Education', 'Dead End Jobs', 'What You Or Dad Have Achieved' and 'Do Something Useful' not only massaged her ego but would also concur with what the psychiatrist had been telling her: that until Duncan took responsibility for his own life, he would not improve.

Mrs Cantrill looked at Duncan, then turned round to the doctor. 'What do you think?' she said.

'Duncan, what is it you want to teach?' he asked, unconvinced. 'And how—'

'I'm not sure. My two best subjects were art and design. I'm going

117

to go to Ollington College and talk to the Tutor for Admissions, see if anything can be arranged.'

'Mr Phelps?' said Mrs Cantrill, her face brightening.

'Yes. That's the name I was given.' God, you're a genius, Leonard, he thought. He looked over at the window where Leonard gave him the thumbs up and what his damaged face could concoct as a smile.

Mrs Cantrill worked on the Education Committee and therefore was bound to be well in with the college authorities. More than that, she would probably be able to pull strings; she would be able to play a part not only in getting her son back on the rails, but also getting him a decent job.

'I know Anthony well,' she said to no-one in particular.

Duncan could see her mind working, could imagine her fingers twitching to get at a telephone.

'I'm going to see him this morning, chat it through,' he said, icing the cake.

Whatever faults Duncan thought his mother had, indecisiveness was not one of them.

'I think we can forget the clinic, don't you, doctor?' she said, standing up, clearly ready to leave.

The doctor was surprised. He could see his fee about to walk out of the room. 'I think it's a bit premature to—'

'Good, that's settled. Would you like a lift to the college?' she said to Duncan, the doctor already dismissed.

Before Duncan could say no, Leonard shouted over that he should accept her offer.

'Okay, thanks.'

He picked up his belongings and followed his mother out to her car, he too ignoring the glowering doctor.

'And if all goes well with Mr Phelps, I'll see if I can persuade your father to sort another car out for you.'

'Thanks.' Duncan was genuinely thankful. His mother was far from perfect but she did have his interests at heart.

He settled into the passenger seat of the white BMW 730i and belted up. He couldn't see Leonard in the mirror so he turned to see him sitting smiling in the back, as impressed with the car as Duncan was with the success of his plan.

'What is it?' asked Mrs Cantrill, also looking into the back of the empty car.

'Nothing. Just I haven't been in this one before, have I?'

'No.'

Mrs Cantrill changed her cars the way some women change their hairstyle.

As they drove the couple of miles out to the Ollington College of Education on the south side of town, Duncan asked his mother to put off calling Mr Phelps.

'Let me do this for myself, mum. Talk to him, see what's required. I may have to re-sit some exams before I get in but I can do that at the local college. I appreciate the offer but . . . well, part of the problem has always been that I've never had to do things for myself. You and dad have always looked after me, even when I've fuc – sorry, messed up. I'm sorry I've put you through it the last couple of weeks. Honest.'

Mrs Cantrill tapped his knee. 'It's all right, Duncan. What are mothers for?'

His mother's reaction had Duncan biting his lip. She normally shunned physical contact so for her to touch his knee was a moment of deep maternal intimacy. That it was the result of yet another subterfuge by him made him feel bad. What he was doing may have been in a good cause, but his mother would never know that and what would she feel when she realised his idea of being a teacher was just a ruse to avoid incarceration? That although he had rung the college to find out the name of the Admissions Tutor, he had no appointment with him that or any other day?

He stared out of the window, his gloom clouding the sunny morning.

Ollington College was a refugee from the Sixties, all glass blocks and coloured panels; functionalism bestriding a gentle wooded hillside like Lego bricks strewn across a child's bedspread. Duncan's mother dropped him outside the blandly titled Administration Block and he waved goodbye as he entered, the invisible Leonard by his side.

The first problem was how to find the roommate of Jane Dalton. There were over a thousand students. Leonard came up with the answer. They were in the Gents toilet, Duncan careful to keep an eye on the door in case anyone came in as they talked.

'The roommate was called Gwynedd Proudfoot. I remember it from the report; mind you, difficult to forget a name like Gwynedd Proudfoot,' said Leonard, puzzling over his inability to see himself in the mirror that ran the length of one wall. 'But college staff will be reluctant to give out information in case you're a weirdo.'

'And I look like a weirdo?' he said, eyeing himself in the mirror. He was wearing blue jeans, a James sweatshirt and had a CONS striped cap. His hair was greasy, his skin was sallow and he looked like he needed a good meal, but he also looked like a typical student.

'You look like a weirdo *student*, which is a help,' confirmed Leonard. 'So, go to the Students' Union, find a secretary in an office – any office, it doesn't matter – and say you're looking for this Gwynedd Proudfoot. When she asks you why, just act real embarrassed and tell her your doctor told you to tell her something "personal". No way is this secretary going to ask you what; she'll just assume one of you has given the other a dose. I bet she'll give you a room number before you can say "Venereal Disease".'

It worked. The girl blushed more than Duncan was supposed to and even pointed him in the right direction for the correct hall of residence. Soon Duncan was knocking on the door of room 48 on the fourth floor, unsure what he was going to say to whoever answered the door.

A girl answered, pretty in a big-boned way, dressed in black from head to toe. Black cardigan over black blouse, long black skirt, black DMs, to say nothing of black shoulder-length hair and jet earrings and cameo choker.

'Yes?' she said with a slight lisp, her accent Welsh.

'Umm,' mumbled Duncan.

Leonard leaned to his ear. 'Nice pods, eh? Okay, here's the story. Repeat after me . . .' (What Duncan wouldn't have given to be able to dig the annoying slob in the ribs.) 'I'm sorry to bother you . . .'

'I'm sorry to call like this . . .' parroted Duncan.

'I've been away at university . . .'

'I'm studying up at Lancaster Uni . . .'

'And I used to slip Jane Dalton a length way back . . .'

Duncan almost hurled abuse at Leonard but could see the girl's initial openness fast disappearing. She was beginning to wonder if he was a whining socialist or a religious nut trying to convert her.

'Jane and I knew each other at school and . . .'

'. . . I've only just—'

'And I've only just heard what happened to her. I couldn't believe it. She seemed so level-headed when I . . .' He let himself trail off, as if overcome by emotion.

Leonard was peering into the room past the girl.

'Keep it up, Duncan. She's got a Simply Red poster; she'll fall for the slushy guff.'

She did. Five minutes later Duncan was in, supping tea and explaining how he hadn't really known Jane all that well but how she was the first person he actually knew who had 'actually died' and it had 'really really' affected him. She was very sympathetic and both Duncan and Leonard soon realised that no-one else had bothered to talk it out with the poor girl.

Her accommodation consisted of a small lounge with two small sofas, a desk and chair, coffee table and a wall unit, with a small kitchenette to the right and two bedrooms to the left, one door ajar, the other shut. The room obviously belonged to a student but seemed too neat, not so much because the occupant was tidy but because they were unsure of when decoration became defacement. There were posters on the wall of Mick Hucknall, Michael Hutchence and Kevin Costner. There were also a couple of plastic fans and a corn dolly, and the room was tinged by just a bit too much fragrance from the dried flower pot pourri on the coffee table. Next to it sat issues of *Sky*, *More* and *Marie-Claire* and there were framed photographs dotted around the room, all of them family shots.

'I didn't really know her too well, despite us living together,' the girl was explaining, all the time avoiding Duncan's eyes. 'She was out a lot, we did different courses, had different interests, friends. Some nights she didn't even come back. Even working, I like to work in the library, she'd work in her bedroom . . .'

Leonard was sitting on the two-seater sofa next to Duncan watching the girl as she fiddled with her tea cup. Nothing they had seen since they had come in, or the girl had said or done, would dissuade him from his initial impression that this was a girl a long way from home and trying hard not to admit it. He expanded on his theory to Duncan.

'I've met her type many times, especially when dealing with life policy payouts. She wants to talk about it and she feels guilty that maybe she could have done something more.'

Duncan took the prompt. 'Do you want to talk about it?'

The girl put down her tea cup, rattling it in her saucer as she did so, and let out a big sigh. She started to fiddle with one of her five rings, each of them with a different shaped black stone. 'I didn't really like her. I know I shouldn't say that but we never, well, connected, know what I mean? She was very cynical, didn't seem to be here to learn, just to have a good time. I know what everyone says about students but I always thought that if you studied to be a teacher you had to take it fairly seriously because at the end of the four years you're trained for a job with real responsibility. University students still have to learn how to do a job when they leave so they can afford to . . . oh, sorry, I didn't mean . . .'

'S'alright,' said Duncan. 'I know just what you mean. That's why I never tried to do teaching; I want some fun. Sounds callous . . . sounds like Jane, I suppose.'

'Well, yes . . .'

'Good call,' said Leonard. 'Now, be blunt, Duncan. Ask her why she thinks the girl killed herself.'

'I can't do that,' he said.

'Pardon?' said the girl, her downcast eyes making her think the remark was aimed at her.

'Oh, I meant I couldn't do what you're doing,' said Duncan hurriedly. 'You know, take it seriously. I should but . . .'

'Ask her, Duncan. She's not going to volunteer it. Ask her. Trust me.'

'Gwynedd . . . do you know why Jane killed herself?'

Gwynedd burst into tears and ran into the adjoining kitchenette, hiding herself behind the eye-level cupboards that split the room.

'I'm sorry,' said Duncan, glaring at Leonard. 'I didn't mean . . .'

'No, you're right,' she sniffled. 'I've asked myself that so often; why did she do it and could I have helped, but you can't, can you? Not unless someone confides in you; not unless they're actually bloody there to talk about it to.'

'So you really didn't see her often?'

'The last month or so I hardly saw her at all. She was living with that bastard on his boat.'

'Beaumont?' said Duncan.

'Yes. He was the psychology tutor, supposed to teach us how to handle awkward children, root out reasons for learning difficulties, but he and she started . . . well . . .'

Leonard had walked over to the bedroom doors. One was open. 'Lots of fluffy bunnies in here, Duncan. This girl's a girl, all that punk shit's just so much make-up. She's just a young virgin up from the valleys. God knows what she made of Dalton shacking up with the course tutor.'

'Did she tell you anything about the tutor?'

'Only that he was a wonderful . . . a wonderful lover. And that he had taken her to places she didn't believe existed.' Gwynedd said this last sentence in a harsh, sneery voice.

'She's a virgin, all right,' said Leonard.

'How do you know?' asked Duncan, amazed at the man's mind.

'Know what?' said the girl.

'That . . . that she was telling the truth?' said Duncan.

Leonard sat down again. 'If she was getting it she wouldn't have said "wonderful lover": too coy.'

Duncan wiped his hands over his face. Man oh man.

'Why should she lie?' said Gwynedd.

'To shock you,' offered Duncan. 'I remember she used to say some ludicrous things to me just to see me go crazy.'

The girl emerged from behind the cabinets, her make up running. She was young, he could see what Leonard meant now. Despite her intelligence she was no sophisticate. Her fashion sense was based on the need to shock and say 'I'm here' rather than to appear attractive. She had a weight problem, though nothing major, but enough to affect her self-esteem. How many kids had he met who dressed up for a part they couldn't live up to, including himself? He caught sight of the wording on his sleeve. He'd never even been to a bloody James concert and only had Goldmother on CD. Kids, the pair of them. Leonard knew what he was talking about.

He stood up and pulled a couple of tissues out of a pastel Kleenex box and handed them to Gwynedd. 'Your make-up. Look, I'm sorry for upsetting you. I think I'd better go.'

'No!' shouted Leonard and Gwynedd together.

Duncan was surprised at the stereo effect.

Leonard pleaded. 'Go for broke, Duncan. She knows Beaumont was a shit; go for the bastard.'

Duncan turned and shrugged a 'how', but then inspiration struck.

'To tell the truth, Gwynedd, what I really had on Jane was a crush. I did know her at school but when we went to different colleges I tried to keep in touch by letter but she never answered. Then I found out from someone else that she'd been seeing this Beaumont guy. I had intended coming here and dropping the pair of them in the shit about it; you know, blabbing to the principal or whatever you have here, but I . . . I got glandular fever and couldn't go anywhere for the best part of a term. Then I found out she'd killed herself; and then I read that the Beaumont guy died on his bloody boat. I had to find out if there was any connection, see if that bastard had anything to do with her killing herself and . . . and if I found out he did then I was going to find his grave and . . . well, to be honest, um, piss on it.'

The look on Gwynedd's face was a picture. As he had burbled on her eyes had got bigger and bigger until, as he confessed to his desire to pee on Beaumont's final resting place, she had burst out laughing.

'I wish I could! I wouldn't have the nerve. Piss on his grave, now there's an idea.'

'Nice one, Duncan,' said Leonard. 'She's on your side now.'

Duncan appreciated Leonard's comment, but what most pleased him was the simple fact that the girl was laughing. It was probably the first time she had done so in weeks. She begged him to excuse her for a minute as she rinsed her face in the sink and towelled her face dry.

When she came back and sat down again and supped her lukewarm tea, her face was plainer but brighter. Sparkling eyes mean so much more than perfect cheekbones or a rosebud pout, Duncan thought. Besides, she had a pretty face. Round, with wide hazel eyes framed by thick, natural eyebrows, a small nose and a slight overbite which kept her wide mouth open most of the time. Sexy. He decided that even if he found nothing that could help them, then at least he could leave the room knowing he'd helped a nice girl to peek through the grey shroud of self-doubt she had wrapped herself up in.

'I was wondering,' said Duncan after a long pause, 'If I could see her things. I don't want to take anything, just look . . .'

'No problem. Everything that was hers is in her room. I keep it locked.'

She retrieved a key from a drawer then opened the late girl's bedroom. As Duncan followed her, he caught a glimpse of Gwynedd's own bedroom. Leonard had been right: fluffy bunnies, costume dolls, flower bedspread, lots of lace. This was a girl reluctant to leave her old self behind, despite the new model who stood next to him.

Jane Dalton was clearly another matter. Her room was identical in size to Gwynedd's – perhaps ten feet square and consisting of a bed against one side of the room with a couple of shelves running its length above it, a bedside cabinet, an in-built wardrobe and chest of drawers and a desk and chair. It was spartan but cosy and whereas Gwynedd had used hers to remind her of her bedroom back in Wales, Jane had turned hers into a cell.

Two walls were covered in dark rugs, the window on the right sealed with a blanket, and the bed covered in black sheets and a black duvet. There was no bulb in the main ceiling light, instead candles were dotted around the room. The air still seemed hazy and smelled of incense. The only decoration consisted of three wooden carvings hung on the wall by the door. They looked African and the exaggerated breasts and penises blatantly stated their symbolism. It was a very depressing room; God knows what the girl thought about locked in here, with only candles for light.

'Jesus,' was all Duncan could manage.

Leonard said, 'This was one fucked-up girlie.'

Gwynedd shook her head. 'I hardly ever came in here, even when she was out. She locked it. Her dad came up a few days after she died. Took one look in there and laughed.'

'Laughed?'

'Yes. I got the feeling he knew what to expect.'

Duncan thought back to Gwynedd's own room and the comforting reaction it would no doubt provoke in her parents when they saw it: *That's our girl; never mind the silly make-up and clothes, that's our Gwynedd.* But this . . .

'Ask if he took anything,' said Leonard.

'Did he take anything?'

'No. I offered to help him carry stuff to his car but he said he didn't want any of this "crap". He checked the wardrobe and drawers and offered me her clothes. He pocketed a bit of jewellery, looked at the books then knocked them onto the bed. Oh, and he took a silver picture frame with her picture, ripped out the picture but kept the frame, then he went.'

Duncan looked at Gwynedd. The memory obviously hurt her. People from happy families sometimes find it hard to understand just how cold some homes can be, or how uncaring parents can act. Whatever his own hassles at home, he felt more grateful for his circumstances.

'What happened then?'

'The college said they'd clear the room but they haven't got round to it yet.'

'Police?' said Leonard staring at the books, his bulky form dominating the room but offering no indication to Gwynedd of his presence.

'What did the police do?'

'They went through everything, looking for a diary or letters they said. Clues to why she would kill herself. I told them about Mr Beaumont and how she boasted about doing it with him and they said they'd look into it.'

'And?'

'And nothing. They never came back. Then Mr Beaumont was killed and, well, I was pleased, though I shouldn't say that.'

'Don't worry; he was everything you thought.'

'How do you know?' she asked.

'Big mouth,' said Leonard.

'People I've spoken to, while I was trying to find you . . .'

'Do you want any of her things?'

'No,' he said too quickly.

'Yes,' said Leonard.

'What?' said Duncan.

'Pardon?' said the girl.

'Check out these books, Duncan,' said Leonard.

'Er, can I look at the books?' said Duncan.

'Sure. They're creepy; horrible pictures. I just left them there.'

There were twenty or so books, all of them to do with sexual disorders or witchcraft. A very queer combination. He pulled down a couple of volumes – *The Black Arts* and *Occult Practices in the Eighteenth Century* – and flicked through them. Dense text, graphic illustrations, most of them historical in nature, details of rituals and occult history. Few of the books were new, and most of them had yellowed pages and smelled musty. Odd.

'What was she studying?'

'English. Though you wouldn't know it . . .'

'No.' He put the books back and selected another two. Same stuff; either the girl had a morbid fascination with the darker side of the occult or, worse, she believed in it. Must have been some surprise when Beaumont gave her to his friends . . .

He threw the books down in disgust. No-one deserved that, even a stupid girl. What had she been? Nineteen? Christ, at that age he had been refusing to wash his hair because it annoyed his mother, and wearing ripped jeans in mid-winter 'to make a statement'. Who the hell to? And he also kept coming back to Leonard's attitude on the orgies: what would he have done if someone he knew offered him the chance of a good time with no comebacks? People who live in glasshouses shouldn't preach about nudity . . .

Gwynedd had backed out of the room. 'Would you like another tea?'

'Yes,' said Leonard as if she could hear him.

'Yes, if it's no trouble,' said Duncan.

She busied herself in the kitchen.

'What do you want to stay in here for?' asked Duncan, appalled at a picture of a broken corpse on a wheel being carved like a Sunday joint by two old women. Judging by the style, the picture was an etching from the Middle Ages.

'If we leave this room without anything we go nowhere. We've got to find something.'

Duncan sat on the bed, tried the drawers. Clothes, trinkets, nothing untoward. He got up and looked in the wardrobe: more of the same. The desk drawers were almost empty; some pencils and pens, Sellotape, a punch, spare paper and, in the bottom drawer, her college papers, exam certificates, grant details, union membership and a wad of bank statements and receipts. Junk.

He shut the drawer and sat back on the bed next to Leonard.

'She knew what she was doing,' said Duncan, eyeing the books above him. 'At least that there was satanic shit going down.'

'I told you there was that stuff but it wasn't heavy; just robes and some chanting.'

'Robes and chanting! You never mentioned robes. If someone said "Do you want a good fuck, oh, and by the way, just put this robe on and chant a black mass" I might get a pretty good idea these people weren't exactly Methodists!'

Gwynedd called through: 'Sorry, did you want something?'

'No. Sorry. Talking to myself, bad habit.'

'Isn't there something in your life you're absolutely obsessed about?' asked Leonard, now standing by the window, only his outline visible, silhouetted by the dim light that filtered through the blanket pinned across it. 'Something that you're willing to risk everything for – or are you too fucking lazy even for that?'

'Not to the extent of signing up with a coven, no!'

'Nothing? Football, pop music, drink, drugs, sex?'

Duncan thought for a while. 'No. Well, I remember as a kid missing the bus home from school so I could spend the fare on bubblegum cards. Mum got upset about it, but I kept on doing it. Alien Invasion, I think they were. But that's kids' stuff.'

'Duncan, surely you've learned now that an adult is just a kid that got taller? Look at you and how your life is: look at me and mine. Look at little Miss Fluffy Bunny out there; in a couple of years she'll be teaching kids not much younger than she is now about life. What you want to do with your dick is decided by the time you're sixteen; you've no control over it. All I knew was I wanted a lot of it – and how I got it didn't really matter. Just like a drunk ignoring all the warning signs because he has to have a drink. Same with me and sex. Same with your bubblegum cards. Same with Jane and the kicks she thought she was getting.'

Duncan was about to argue when Gwynedd brought in tea.

As Duncan got up and followed her into the sitting room, Leonard called after him. 'Sit so I can see you from in here. That way I can still look.'

Duncan did as he was asked although he didn't know what Leonard could do, given that he couldn't touch anything. So polite conversation ensued as Duncan and Gwynedd found out about each other.

He was grateful to be talking about mundane things like pop music and jobs and fashion and to be away from Leonard. It was so *normal*, and it was obvious Gwynedd was equally pleased to be talking to someone. Initially her conversation seemed to come out in a rush, as if she was afraid he would leave, but eventually she assumed a natural speed and they were talking like friends.

He learned that her father had been a teacher but had retired with back trouble. She had two sisters and two brothers, all younger than her. Teaching was something of a family tradition going back two generations – and although it seemed pre-ordained, she actually wanted to teach primary school children. All her family could speak Welsh, which she proved, but, of course, Duncan couldn't understand a word.

Duncan was going to lie through his teeth but instead settled for something nearer the truth: he still lived at home and was aiming to manage a hotel, and was working his way through the business prior to gaining the necessary qualifications. He explained his late interest in a career – after all, he was four years older than her – by saying he had mucked up his time at school.

It soon became clear that they had a lot in common. They both liked Indian food, disliked smoking and alcohol, and weren't interested in politics. They also both hinted that they weren't going out with anyone. Under other circumstances, Duncan would probably have got up the nerve to suggest they go for lunch somewhere but, as Leonard's increasingly noisy interruptions underlined, there was more pressing business. So, finally, he had to make his excuses.

Truth to tell he was beginning to feel a little guilty about his false pretences. He liked her and felt sorry for her but knew if she suspected anything underhand it could set her back even further – and the longer he stayed the more chance there was of him putting his foot in it.

'Look, I must go, Gwynedd. I've kept you too long.'

'No, you haven't. I've enjoyed the company. I don't see as many people as I should. Not since . . .'

'But why? The only reason you knew her was because some clerk put her in the same room. You don't owe her anything; there's no need to feel guilty. Whatever she got into, she seems to have wanted to get into it. The books, her room.'

'But still. We were friends . . .'

'Did she ever try to get you involved in all that?'

'No. She didn't.'

'Good. That's something.'

'For someone who had a crush on her you seem to have taken a bit of a dislike to her.'

More a liking to you, he thought. 'Well, I obviously didn't know her as well as I thought.'

He looked over his shoulder at the room. Leonard waved at him.

'Come here,' said the man.

Duncan stood up. 'Can I just take another look?'

'Sure, anything.' She started to gather up their cups.

Duncan stepped into the bedroom, his eyebrows raised in question.

'Check the books,' said Leonard. 'See if they're library or her own.'

Duncan did as he was asked. No library marks.

'Okay, now these are pretty old books, don't you think?'

'So? Beaumont might have given them her,' said Duncan quietly.

'Or she might have bought them. And if she did, where? Not W H Smith.'

'So they're secondhand.'

'So where's the shop? Someone sells this stuff, they might just have something to do with all this.'

'Oh come on, that's pushing it.'

'What did you say?' called Gwynedd.

'I said "I'm a bit pushed for time". Got to be going.'

'Oh.' She sounded disappointed.

'Look in the bottom drawer, there were receipts there,' said Leonard. 'See if there are any for books.'

There were. Fazey's Bookshop on Tyler Cop in Ollington.

'Ever heard of it?' asked Leonard as he watched Duncan fan the four receipts out, each dated about a week apart. Perversion on a budget?

'Nope.' He had lived in Ollington all his life and was having difficulty placing the street, never mind the shop. He thought it might be somewhere near the market, one of the steep backstreets tourists found quaint and residents found tiring. 'But I suppose we can always look it up.'

'Attaboy,' said Leonard.

They exited the bedroom and Duncan pulled on his coat.

'Look, Gwynedd, Jane's gone, her father doesn't want her stuff and the college don't seem in any hurry—'

'Take whatever you want. I don't—'

'No, no, what I was going to say is why don't you throw it out? Bag it and bin it; get the room back to normal.'

'Seems such a waste. Some of it could be worth money.'

'Well, sell it. You've been through enough—'

'No, I don't want the money.'

'Well, sell it and . . .' he spotted a PDSA sticker in the window. 'Give the money to charity. Or give it to a charity shop. Get some use out of it.'

'Okay, that makes sense.'

'Good. Well, we'll . . . I'll be off then. Thanks for seeing me and the tea and everything.'

'No problem. Come . . . come again if you want.'

'I will, if I'm round this way again.'

'Right.' She moved past him and for the first time Duncan could smell her soap. It was nicer than the stuff she had soaked the pot pourri in.

She opened the door and there was embarrassed shuffling as he edged into the corridor and walked off. At the corner he paused to look back but she had shut her door. What was he expecting? More to the point, *why* was he expecting it?

Leonard saw his disappointment. 'I'd give her one.'

Duncan had had enough. 'Do you have to reduce everything to the same level? You'd fuck a stoat if it wore a dress.'

'Who needs a dress . . .'

'Gwynedd is a nice kid, not happy being away from home, who's landed in the middle of sordid shit because of that creep Beaumont. You heard her talking about home. Imagine being away living with strangers and the one person you thought you could trust to help you with any personal problems can't keep his dick – and those of his "friends" – out of your roommate's cunt. Just have a little respect.'

'Sorry,' said Leonard. 'Me and my big mouth.'

'Right.'

'She *was* cute though.'

'If *I* say she's cute, Leonard, it means I like her. It does not mean I wish to remove her undergarments.'

There was a pause. 'Bet you wouldn't say no, though?'

Duncan started to laugh. 'To be honest, given my sex life, I'd probably have a go at that stoat of yours.'

'Sloppy seconds?'

'God, you're gross!' Duncan stormed off but, of course, there was nowhere to go: Leonard would always be there.

19

THEY LEFT OLLINGTON College at about 11am and caught a bus back into town, Leonard extremely reluctant to be out in public. It had only struck Duncan as they waited in the bus shelter, avoiding the rain, that Leonard had only once had to venture out in crowds. Every time, except when they had visited Beaumont's boat, he had been indoors or in a car. As long as he was in sight of Duncan, he could go where he wanted. So he had been able to 'jump' from Mrs Cantrill's car into the college building without setting phantom foot on pavement, but here there was no escape. Although the two punks sitting next to them were unaware of the middle-aged murder victim's presence, the incongruity of the situation, and Leonard's sudden re-appearance behind the hedge on the opposite side of the road, set Duncan laughing. He stopped when he saw the two beleathered lads looking at him.

The double-decker bus appeared and Duncan went upstairs. The deck was empty except for Leonard, who was sitting on the back seat. Duncan sat next to him. They travelled for a while in silence until, prompted by Leonard's leering down at any female that the bus passed, Duncan's curiosity got the better of him.

'Did you really sleep with as many women as you say?'

Leonard looked amazed at the question. 'Yes. Why, are you jealous?'

'No, to be honest.'

'Says Mr Video.'

'Oh, I don't deny I'd like a bit more practical experience,' admitted Duncan. 'But once I found a girl I liked, then I wouldn't want anyone else.'

'Like that Gwynedd?'

'Leave her out of this.'

'Ooh, touchy. Okay . . . Anyway, it's natural for men to want a change.'

'To want a change you have to have something to change *from*. Did you ever stick with one for more than a night?'

'They were all one-nighters. Even when I was staying somewhere for a few days, I'd find a different woman each night.'

'Why?'

'Why not?'

'No, why?' said Duncan. 'You go to bed with someone and it's good, so why not go to bed with her again?'

'No woman's that good.'

'Oh yes, they are – you *know* they are. You said you and your wife were happy until she dumped you because of your . . . problem.'

Leonard stared at the floor for a long time. 'I have to do it. To move on. Can't let myself be trapped again.'

'Trapped? Like your marriage?'

'Yes. I loved her, trusted her, but as soon as we had the test results she refused to have me in bed. As if I was only there to impregnate her, like some farmyard animal. And all that time I . . . well, I went out and found myself another woman. And another and another, safe in the knowledge that they wouldn't get pregnant. Lot of women out there willing to put out, either because they're desperate or they're as ugly as me or they just want to prove a point. Why should I care?'

'So you don't trust women?'

'Wasn't it Groucho Marx who said: "I wouldn't want to be in a club that would have me as a member?" Well, I wouldn't want to be with any woman who'd have my member.' He laughed, but Duncan could see he was hurting.

'And you never tried—'

'No! Women . . . my mother, grandmother, all they wanted was my wages when I left school. My wife only wanted babies . . . All those women I've had just wanted fucking . . . None of them wanted *me*. Well, fuck them! I'm not violent, I just use them. They have fun, I have fun – that's it.'

'And you've never been tempted to stay with one?'

'Course I have,' said Leonard. 'But next day another piece of skirt would pop up and so would my cock and bingo! Live for the moment. Anyway, what right have you to—'

'Hey, I may be no good with girls, and I don't believe in marriage but I do believe in love.'

'I wouldn't bank on it.'

'Do you hate women?'

'No, course not.'

'You sure?'

'Hey, I'm the one getting his end away; you're the one sharing your knob with the Panasonic.'

'Thanks,' said Duncan.

'You started it.'

'Fuck off.'

'Charming.'

They didn't speak for the rest of the journey.

Once in the town centre, Leonard popped in and out of shop doorways, behind parked cars, once even into an upstairs office, in his vain attempts to keep out of the crowd.

After a while it got tiresome, like trying to keep track of an unleashed terrier. Duncan called in at a newsagents and bought an A-to-Z and found Tyler Cop.

A dog-leg lane, steep, cobbled and barely wide enough for a car, Tyler Cop ran for less than a hundred yards and contained solicitors' and accountants' offices, a vegetarian cafe, a stationer's, an art gallery, a number of private residences, a cheap B-&-B and, hidden away near the top, the doorway to Fazey's Bookshop. Its presence was only announced by a hand-written notice of some age: 'Fazey's Bookshop. Second Hand Books. First Editions and Rarities Welcomed. Open 10–4 Mon, Tues, Thurs, Sat. No food or drink on the premises please. Absolutely NO Smoking.'

Entering, a bell tinkled above them and they walked up a half flight of narrow stairs until they found themselves in a small bookshop with ceiling-high shelves of old dark oak crammed with hardback volumes, the room gloomy and musty, the floorboards polished and creaky. Another world, another age.

Turning left, they found the shop opened out into a more spacious area, with sturdy tables of books in the centre, and shelves on three walls, the fourth giving way to narrow gangways lined with yet more shelves. The silence, the gloom, the lack of paperback books and their bright colours and gaudy designs leant the shop the air of a library. Indeed, although it boasted three other customers – a middle-aged man, a middle-aged woman and a young hippy male –

they each looked at Duncan as would readers in a library expecting some disturbance. Duncan, anxious not to attract attention, picked up a book from the nearest table – *Egyptian Gods* – and pretended interest.

The light in the shop came from weak fluorescent tubes, apparently hung at random from the high ceiling, and a dirty skylight. It was cosy and quiet, relaxing even, but it also made it damn difficult to read. A quick skim of the titles on offer on the table before him revealed an overwhelming belief in the power of reincarnation and the validity of ancient religions. Oh dear . . .

He turned and glanced at the shelf immediately behind him. Crop circles. Loch Ness Monster. Strange beasts. He edged further into the room, and ventured down one of the narrow gangways, wide enough only for one person. More strange beasts. Bigfoot. Yeti. Japanese sea monsters. Legendary creatures. He turned to the opposite shelf. Telepathy. Poltergeist activity. Telekinesis. Something called SHC. He stepped back into the room, slowly scanning the shelves. There must have been hundreds, thousands of books. The words 'special interest' took on a whole new meaning. This was serious stuff, even if it was all crap, but then he caught sight of Leonard peering at books to the left of a small doorway at the furthest end of the shop, and realised he shouldn't dismiss anything in the shop out of hand. After all, for the last couple of weeks he had lived with a ghost, proof of life after death, teleportation, a murderous belief in the occult . . . which meant some of the stuff in these books was true.

Just then Leonard hissed at him. 'Over here.'

Duncan walked over and stood beside him.

'What?'

'These are all on witchcraft. I recognise one of the books that Jane had.'

Duncan followed the man's finger. True enough, there was *Demonology : The Black Pathway* and a whole case full of books on witchcraft. Duncan pulled a fat volume down at random and flicked through it. *Invocations and Evocations of Evil*. It was musty. He checked the print date: MCMXI. 1911. It seemed to be an earnest study of the Black Arts by someone who plainly believed in their efficacy. If the writer believed, presumably he practised – his text didn't contain any negatives – and if he practised in 1911, where was he now?

Two more volumes showed the same story. These were books by people who would have no truck with doubt or balance; they were written by believers who wanted others to believe.

Duncan looked around and, sure he couldn't be seen, he spoke to Leonard: 'This is serious shit. If Jane had had just the smallest interest in this stuff, this would have convinced her.'

'And she'd go along with Beaumont's wishes.'

'Like a lamb to the slaughter.'

Leonard didn't answer; the simile was as apt for his fate as for that of the girl.

Just then the door to their right opened and a small rotund man with a gleaming bald head, thick glasses and thick lips walked through, a pile of books cradled in his arms.

Instinctively Leonard made to grab Duncan's arm but his fingers clutched at nothing. Before Duncan could question his action, the little man had turned.

'Excuse me, young man, could you help me?'

'What?'

'These books. Heavy. Could you put them on the table?'

Leonard shouted into Duncan's ear, startling him. 'Duncan! Don't mention anything you know. Trust me, this fat bastard went to the orgies! He's in on it!'

Duncan took a step back as if the man had a knife. The man noticed the action.

'Are you all right, young man?' he said, lowering the books to the table with some effort.

'Y – yes. Sorry. It's . . . pins and needles. In my leg. I've been standing in one place for so long . . .'

'Know the problem, know the problem. Were you looking for anything in particular?' The man's voice was high pitched, his age probably in the fifties. For some reason he reminded Duncan of a eunuch from an old Arabian adventure film, though his shabby Help the Aged grey trousers, stretched bronze cardigan and open-necked red shirt made him look more like a seedy newsagent.

'Anything but witchcraft, Duncan!'

'You . . . UFOs! Flying saucers. I . . . I was wondering if there have ever been any around here. I know Todmorden's got a reputation. I just wondered if—'

'You've seen one, haven't you? Haven't you?'

'Go with it Duncan, for fuck's sake.'

'Yes . . . Couple of nights ago. I called the police but they, well, they weren't interested.'

'Where was it?'

'Reservoir. Tilworth Reservoir.'

'Ah . . . I can see why they weren't interested. Not a good place, not a good place.'

The man held out his arm and Duncan had to force himself not to flinch as he let the man guide him to a shelf near to the entrance.

How Duncan got through the next five minutes, or why the man didn't see anything odd in his sweat or mumbled descriptions, he didn't know. Mr Fazey, as he revealed himself to be, ended up selling Duncan a small, privately published book called *The Peaks Speak* which explained, apparently, that while the Peak District was alive with unidentified flying objects, most sightings near water were to be rejected as they involved too much chance of reflections. However, there were places where sightings had occurred and the book catalogued them.

As he was paying what he considered an outrageous £10.50 for what was little more than a pamphlet, he caught sight of Leonard nosing round the man's office. The door was only open a short way so Leonard's field of enquiry was very restricted – he had to keep Duncan in sight at all times – but something had caught his attention and he could see him counting out something on his fingers.

Mr Fazey, ever keen to convince a possible convert, handed Duncan a half dozen handbills about various local organizations involved in Ufology – '*Well worth attending, well worth attending*'. Duncan thanked him and hurried out of the shop, trying not to look as if he was escaping rather than simply leaving. At the door he paused to look back at Mr Fazey, but he was already engrossed in conversation with the hippy who was holding a book on crystals.

Outside, Duncan huddled into the doorway of an accountants' office and tried to get his breath back. From the moment Leonard had shrieked at him not to give anything away Duncan had been a bundle of nerves, convinced that everyone in the shop was in on the conspiracy and at a signal from Mr Fazey would have sprung on him and dragged him away to some dark place, there to indulge in a little ritual sacrifice.

'You did good,' said Leonard.

Duncan threw his books at him. Although they passed right through, Leonard flinched and that helped.

'Don't ever do that again,' said Duncan through gritted teeth. 'I nearly kekked myself when you shouted like that.'

'Sorry, but if you'd mentioned anything about witchcraft or that Jane girl, then he might have got suspicious. As it is, I think we've got a lead.'

Duncan was afraid to ask. 'What?'

'Remember I said we had our meetings on the new moon night, the opposite to the full moon.'

'Yes.'

'I didn't go to the last one and I was killed about ten days later. That means there's another due. It's the fifteenth today, isn't it?'

Duncan checked his watch. Damn.

'Mr Fazey's got a calendar on his wall and once a month there's a little black dot. The dates tally with the meetings. And the next black dot is—'

'Tonight. So, er, what are you saying?'

'Fazey lives in his shop. There was a bedroom off his office. We wait and follow him. He needs to be wherever they're going before midnight, so he'll leave before then.'

Duncan needed an excuse. 'What if he's got a car?'

'He doesn't. He's got a bicycle. And a bus pass. They're both in his office.'

'So we follow him and then?'

'We see who else is there.'

'And?' said Duncan.

'And . . .'

'Exactly. And nothing.'

'Okay,' said Leonard brightly.

Duncan looked at him. 'Okay?'

'Yes. If you don't want to go, we won't.'

'Oh, all right.'

'No, we'll just go back to your house, watch some TV – and I'll watch you watching. Then when you're tired, you can go to bed, and I'll watch you sleeping. If you want a wank, I'll watch that, too; I'm no prude, as you know. Toilet? No problem. Sit in on your chats with your mum, stare at those big tits of hers, maybe catch a look up her skirt. Then when you get married, I'll be there. I hear even the best of men are nervous on their wedding night—'

'All right!!' shouted Duncan, startling a woman and child as they hobbled past. The woman saw the books by his feet and hurried on: drugs, obviously.

'All right,' he said quietly. 'We'll go to your damn meeting. It just better be worth it.'

'Depends what you want to see,' said Leonard.

'I suspect it won't be nice.'

'So do I. Believe me, Duncan, when I started it was just a bit of fun.'

'Obviously someone else has had other ideas since.'

20

DUNCAN WENT HOME, grateful to find his mother out, made himself something to eat then got his mountain bike out of the garage and made his way back to town. And waited.

It was a very long, extremely boring wait. Mr Fazey didn't leave his shop until 10.15pm. Duncan had never realised just how enervating it could be to do nothing. When it came to action he found it a struggle just mounting his bike to follow their quarry.

Mr Fazey was a very leisurely cyclist, always using the lowest possible gear on his ancient racing cycle. His build was his main impediment, his round shape leaving him to balance on his thin bike like an orange on a knife edge.

He headed through town then north towards the moors. He cycled for over forty-five minutes, Duncan wondering how he would have the strength left to do anything when he got to his destination.

Eventually he came to a halt, a good two miles into the country, the last house fifteen minutes back, the lights of Ollington an orange smudge over the hills. Ducking down behind a bush, Duncan watched the man conceal his cycle behind a hedge, then waddle across the narrow lane and strike out across a patch of empty moorland that led gently uphill to a dark screen of woods.

Duncan hid his own bike and followed at a discreet distance. It was after eleven o'clock and the lack of a moon and an abundance of cloud rendered his route almost invisible. Several times he felt himself tripping and had to stop himself crying out while Mr Fazey – apparently equipped with night vision – bobbled along, his route as plain as day.

However, as soon as they had entered the wood and couldn't be seen from the road, Mr Fazey switched on a small torch and used it to guide himself. It didn't help Duncan but at least he was able to keep sight of the waddling beachball.

Thirty minutes passed as they plunged further into the woods. The path seemed to be rather convoluted and soon Duncan had lost all sense of direction. Leonard was of some help: a couple of times Duncan had lost sight of Mr Fazey but a shout from Leonard set him back on the right track.

Duncan finally began to get angry. He had come to realise that if he ever did lose sight of Mr Fazey completely he would be truly lost. He knew the woods and moorland went on for miles around here. Indeed people had *died* while out walking here in deepest winter because no-one knew which path they had taken. Suddenly, it all got rather scary.

'Leonard, don't lose Fazey, for God's sake,' he whispered. 'I don't know where we are.'

'Don't worry. What's the time?'

It was a struggle but Duncan eventually managed to read 11.38 on his watch.

'Must be nearly there,' said Leonard. 'The shit always starts at midnight.'

'Bloody hope so.'

A minute later and Leonard abruptly stepped into Duncan's path, nearly giving him a heart attack.

'Stop! It's just over the next rise, a hundred yards. Come this way off the path.'

Duncan was too worried about his heart rate to argue and followed Leonard to the left through some bushes, then down into a shallow dip that he found overlooked a wide clearing – and there he found light. Torchlight.

Duncan huddled down further behind the bushes and gave silent thanks that his trip hadn't been a waste of time. He watched torches waggle their slow but certain way from several directions to the clearing in front of him, the surrounding hills and trees ensuring that no-one would see them. Mind you, he thought, who in their right mind would be up here at this time of night anyway, particularly without moonlight? He avoided answering his own question.

He counted the torches. Eight, maybe nine; they kept slipping behind trees or intervening rocks. Some were heading up the same path that Duncan had taken and passed within ten feet of him before veering right and taking a steep path down into the clearing. He eased himself back out of sight even further and debated what to do next.

The clearing, about twenty feet below him, was completely surrounded by hills, most of them densely wooded. Forty yards or so across with, at one end, three large rocks that formed a platform at the front with a standing stone behind, it was well away from prying eyes. If something as large as a bonfire was lit, the light wouldn't travel, even on a jet black night such as this – and, as Duncan could see, bonfire there would most definitely be.

Some ten feet high and well constructed, it was sure to burn for quite a time while they did whatever they intended to do. Duncan hadn't a clue as to what precisely they would get up to and Leonard had been reticent about it.

Soon the fire ignited with a mighty *whumph* and Duncan could see the arena as well as if it were daylight. He almost burst out laughing when he saw the robes.

There were twenty people all dressed in white robes with cowls pulled over their heads, and they shuffled around the fire until they had ringed it. Then they started singing, or rather humming, their discordant chant rising above the rough crackling of the fire. They kept up their monotonous song for a good ten minutes until another figure appeared, this time dressed entirely in black. He made his way over to the platform of rock and stood in front of it, then raised his hands and all the others present lowered their hoods.

Good grief! To a man – and possibly woman, it was difficult to tell – their faces, and hair, were bright red. They looked just as if they had dipped their heads in a bucket of signal red paint, just like that lunatic Kimmel. At one and the same time they were totally silly and disturbingly creepy. Then they started dancing and whooping around the fire, like a bunch of Red Indians in a Grade Z western. Duncan sat back and made himself comfortable. It looked like being a long night.

'And you didn't find this odd?' Duncan asked Leonard.

'We didn't have the red paint.'

'But you had the robes, the dancing?'

'Only the last time. All the other times there was just a quick sing-song, then on with the humping.'

'The "humping"?'

Leonard refused to rise to the bait and instead they sat in silence.

After five minutes the man in black raised his hands and they all stopped, not a few of them a little out of breath. The man then picked up a long silver staff and turned it around above his head three times and then pointed it at one of the assembly. The man in question was Fazey and he looked pleased as he bounded up to the rocks and stood by the man in black. Together the two shouted in a foreign language, then Fazey stepped behind the rock and brought out a large wooden chest. The two of them heaved it onto one of the flat boulders. Duncan decided this was their altar and, sure enough, they took out of the chest four large silver chalices, a large crucifix and a large book, which the man in black opened and proceeded to read from. Again it was in a language he couldn't place, but it seemed to hold the audience's attention.

Another couple of minutes passed and Duncan yawned. He had been missing his sleep, and if they kept up this boring display he would probably be snoozing before they got around to anything interesting.

The man in black suddenly stopped speaking and closed the book, Fazey returning it to the chest. He then handed the crucifix to the man in black, who held it above his head, turned it upside down and spat on it – and not a little spit either, but a large wad of phlegm he must have been saving up all day. Then he stepped down from the altar and moved towards the fire. Midway he knelt down and rammed the silver cross into the ground upside down so that all that was visible was an inverted 'T'. His supplicant then brought over the four goblets and the man in black held each one up in turn to the ebony sky, then to the altar and to the fire, then he placed them around the crucifix to form a square.

He beckoned the dancers to him and they formed four neat queues five deep behind each of the goblets. Then the first four in each queue took off their robes and stood naked. They were all men, one young, one old and two middle-aged. It looked like this was where the sex part might begin.

It wasn't. Instead the four men grabbed their penises and together urinated all over the cross and goblets. When they had finished, the next four had their turn. Women this time and, once naked, equally unappealing. They held their arms around each other as if they were at a knees-up and, bending their legs, also peed on the cross and goblets.

The third group repeated the exercise as did the fourth and fifth until there was a large steaming puddle of urine around the crucifix, its bitter ammonia smell wafting across the clearing, making Duncan hold his nose.

The naked piss artists then adjourned to the altar, and in the wavering orange light from the fire they struck Duncan as being just about the most unappealing bunch of people he could have imagined. Men appeared to outnumber women two to one, and all were obviously starting to feel the relative cold of the night. He could see blotchy skin, erect nipples, taut breasts, and testicles clambering up for safety. Some were rubbing their hands or upper arms to keep warm, or edging surreptitiously towards the welcoming heat of the flames.

While they waited expectantly their leader, the man in black, stepped into the quagmire of urine and pulled out the steaming cross and without any ceremony tossed it into the fire, where it hissed momentarily. He then picked up one of the goblets and . . . *oh no* . . . drank from it.

Duncan found this hard to grasp, the mere thought sending his stomach into spasm. However, the man in black seemed almost to relish his tipple and was generous enough to pass it around the assembled onlookers.

As they each took a hearty sup, Duncan found he was having difficulty handling what they were up to. He was no wide-eyed innocent, and could appreciate that people had their little fetishes and fantasies; he knew all about water sports and men who liked to dress up as babies and pee their pants. He even accepted that some weirdos got turned on by lying under glass tables and being shat on, but at least that had some kind of sexual content, however perverted. But this lot weren't getting turned on or getting off on what they were doing; they might just as well have been down the *Dog and Partridge* swigging on G-and-Ts.

He glanced at Leonard and could see that he too was disgusted – but then that might have been with himself if he had actually indulged in this stuff.

'Leonard,' he asked. 'Did you ever—'

'You've got to be joking!' said Leonard, his voice trembling with disgust.

Duncan turned back and watched them all take their turn.

When they had all had a drink of their combined pee, their leader clambered back onto the altar and addressed them once more. They started singing again but pretty soon started to grope each other as well. Aha. *This* must be where the orgy starts, thought Duncan.

As if reading his thoughts, about half the crowd fell to the floor and started feeling each other, one pair mounting straight away. And then they were all at it.

There were men on top of women, women on top of men, men jerking off men, women frigging women. They were grunting and moaning too, their actions seeming to intensify by the minute, as did their frantic and somewhat theatrical cries of pleasure. In fact, so persuasive was their communal ecstasy that Duncan couldn't help becoming aroused.

He sat back against a tree, and adjusted his trousers to accommodate his erection. He was embarrassed to admit he was excited, particularly with Leonard leering just feet away, but there was such a sexual charge in the air that, had he been alone, he might well have succumbed to his urge to masturbate. But then he started looking more closely.

One unfortunate woman was on all fours being attacked from behind by an amazingly withered old hag with breasts like stretched chewing gum. She was pulling for all she was worth on the younger woman's nipples, seemingly intent on prising them off. Up front two men were trying desperately to insert their rigid members into any available orifice and the way they were going she would soon lose an eye, but she was enjoying it! Jerking all over the place, banging her face onto their penises, and pulling her breasts away so they would hurt all the more.

Another woman nearby was on her back stuffing a broken branch as hard as she could into herself. It made Duncan's eyes water just to think of the damage she was doing; already blood was splashing her thighs. It was horrible, her tongue snaking in and out with each thrust as if the branch was pounding up her throat.

Duncan looked away to the other end of the crowd, but the story was the same. One middle-aged man was screwing the ground. He winced at the thought of what the man's dick would be like the next morning. And there were others.

A woman sat on a man's face, humping up and down, the man writhing about, kicking his feet as if he were choking, but pulling on his prick like he was trying to put out a fire. Then she leant over it and took the whole length into her mouth in one gulp, right down to the balls, and started bearing down even more.

Nearby a large matronly woman was on her back and a young man and another older woman were biting her breasts again and again, every time drawing blood. Pretty soon her tits resembled two large cuts of meat. And she couldn't get enough, her fingers raking her thighs and lower stomach in a frenzy, fingernails dragging raw skin with every sweep.

Duncan looked at Leonard but could see the man was equally appalled. Either things had got worse since he had been involved or he had never realised how bad it had been – or how horrible. If you're not in the mood, sexual activity looks at best comical and, at worst, as here, downright degrading. Maybe he had been too involved to appreciate how sick it had all been but, as if reading his thoughts, Leonard said:

'Never like this. Never so . . . sick. This isn't sex, not fun, not fucking . . . It's sick, crazy . . .'

Duncan was too shocked by what he was watching to even nod; he had just spotted one cameo that was almost surreal.

A skinny man had himself pinned to the ground, his knees over his shoulders, sucking his own penis whilst being rooted in the arse by the most stupendous cock which could just be seen under its owner's elephantine beer gut. And more, much more, and worse, much worse.

Duncan's erection faded as quickly as it had appeared. There was something desperate about the sexual activity he was watching; it was *too* keen. It wasn't humping for fun or in the heat of passion. It was if they were trying to prove something; they might be fucking but they were behaving just like little kids trying to show off how big their prepubescent winkles were, or how far they were filling out their training bras. What's more, they were too preoccupied to be showing off to each other, so who were they showing off to? Their leader? Possibly, but he himself had disrobed and was urgently sodomising Fazey. The fat little shopkeeper seemed to be in some pain but wasn't complaining.

And still it continued. A few had disengaged and were masturbating furiously, trying to reach an elusive orgasm, as the air filled with the odours of sexual activity; smells that were even stronger than the reek of urine; smells that slowly tumbled and uncoiled on the warm air from the fire. It made Duncan retch, and he turned away, trying not to throw up. He wasn't entirely successful.

Then they stopped, just like that, and everyone got up off the floor and edged back towards the altar, not a few of them in considerable discomfort. Then Duncan heard a dog. Nearby, but muted, and clearly afraid. Oh God, what now . . .?

The crowd looked cold again, their exertions obviously having taken a heavy toll. The smell of sex was less intense as well and a rising breeze started to swirl about the clearing. A wraith of smoke from the fire swept over Duncan making his eyes water anew, and he had to blink away tears for some moments.

When he was finally able to re-focus, he could see most of the crowd were craning their necks to the right. He also noticed a few of them had lost a little of their previous interest in the proceedings, not least two men who clutched their ripped and bloodied penises forlornly in their hands, and another who prodded warily at his torn foreskin, which flapped and fluttered like a warning flag. The woman who had used the branch on herself had a thin stream of blood coursing down her left leg. Madness, utter madness.

Then it went quiet. Very quiet.

Too quiet.

They brought in the dog. A black German shepherd. A big lithe animal, one of nature's perfect creations, like a thoroughbred stallion, or a tiger or dolphin. So purposeful, so handsome, which made it all the more worrying that such a fine beast should have its ears down along its cowering head. It sensed something was wrong and for an animal that proud and that powerful to be afraid of a bunch of middle-aged, piss-drinking nudists was perhaps the saddest aspect of the evening so far.

Fazey got to his feet and revealed a raging erection that was nothing to shout about but which seemed to please him. He kept shifting from one foot to the other which may have been the cold or nerves or possibly the searing pain up his backside, it was hard to tell. He then took the dog's lead and pulled it up to the man in black, who stared it straight in the eye.

The man tugged on the lead and tried to get it up onto the rock, but the dog dug its claws in and whined softly; it knew it was losing but some instinct told it still had an element of pride. The dog put up a brave if futile struggle and eventually a couple from the audience had to come to their leader's aid and heave the dog up onto the altar. It hugged the rock for all the world as if it were a precious bone but was quickly forced to roll over onto its back, its four legs lightly pawing the air. Then the assistant walked around to the tail end of the dog and took up position.

Oh God, he's going to fuck the dog! The fucking little creep is going to fuck the dog! Duncan almost broke cover and ran over to the assembled perverts but restrained himself. He was totally outnumbered and miles from any possible help, so it would be pointless – and dangerous. He knew the dog had more morality than the whole bunch of them put together. He didn't want to watch but a sick horror overtook him.

The frightened dog looked at the crowd upside down, a pitiful expression on its face, made all the more sorry by the flickering light from the fire. It was too petrified even to whimper and instead could only shiver and tremble. Then the naked Fazey looked over his shoulder to his leader, as if waiting for a signal to go ahead, and then the man in black was there with a fucking *huge* knife and then it was down and *into* the dog's belly and it was *ripped* back and a fountain of *blood* and an awful *squeal* came from the dog and its legs were *threshing* and kicking and its head was *jerking* from side to side as its tongue slithered *in* and *out* of clenching teeth as its *guts* welled up and *steamed* into the night and *spilled* over its side onto the bare rock and then the little creep *bastard* leaned forward and . . .

Duncan turned away and vomited. A deep, violent upchuck that seemed to tear half his stomach with it, and before he could gasp for breath, he retched again and again, the fumes of his bile booming around his ears. He leaned forward, resting his forehead on the floor, whimpering, sobbing, shaking, drool from his quivering mouth looping down to slip and slide over his hands, his senses drowning in the bitter stewed stink. All he could hear was the pounding of the blood in his ears and deep searing *haaws* as his diaphragm ejected vomit, and all he could see was the image burned indelibly in his brain of the poor dog's paws flexing and clawing at the air as it twitched and died. Nothing, *nothing* had prepared him for this.

It was a long while before he could push himself up onto all fours. His eyes stung and his attempts to wipe them were defeated by the puke on his sleeve. He sat back on his haunches, slowly regaining something resembling normal respiration. He tried to clear his mind but the utter horror of what he had seen defied rational thought. Instead he tried to see if any of the cunts had seen him but his vision was still blurred.

Then, over the rushing in his ears, another noise caught his attention. In the dark, to his left, very close. Then an unfamiliar voice whispered hoarsely in his ear:

'Hello, sonny. Feeling better now?'

Duncan's heart missed a beat. Two beats.

He spun round to find himself staring at an old man, his twisted face a livid red that danced in the light from the fire. He had no teeth and his gums glinted orange, echoing the yellow flares in his wild eyes. His sparse hair was plastered down by sweat, his face twisted in an evil sneer. He must have been three feet from Duncan's face and his naked body stank and his breath was worse. Duncan couldn't help thinking what the man had swallowed. Then he saw the man's knife, small and stubby, like its owner. Duncan froze, then pissed himself, peeing his pants like a little baby.

Then he hit the man. He hit the rat-faced old bastard right on the nose and he felt it crumple up like newspaper, and he felt hot blood shoot across the back of his hand, and just as the old man started to squeak Duncan hit him again across the right eye. And again he felt something give and there was more blood and the man was falling sideways but Duncan swung his right arm round in a fast long arc and smashed it full force into the old man's head. It flipped him back upright and the man's whole face sort of *shifted* and even under the red paint Duncan could see the skin blackening across his forehead like ink on a blotter. Then, with blood *squirting* out of his pulped nose and dribbling darkly red on red from his left ear and eye, and a really surprised look on his face, the old man fell backwards, his spindly naked arms and legs flumping every which way.

Duncan looked down at him. He didn't feel anything; no fear, no triumph, no satisfaction: he'd had to do it and it was done.

'Jesus Christ, Duncan,' said Leonard, his voice hoarse from surprise. 'You've fucked him good.'

'Thanks for the warning.'

'Sorry. I was watching them. You were puking. I wasn't going to watch that.'

Duncan tried to stop shaking. He wasn't a violent person but he now knew what he was capable of, and he didn't like it, even if it had saved him. Or had it? He turned slowly and looked at the clearing.

Everyone was looking in his direction. But not all *at* him. They had heard something and maybe the old man had simply been the nearest, but as yet no-one else had pin-pointed Duncan. He still had a chance.

'Better leave now,' suggested Leonard.

Duncan tutted in annoyance then, without taking his eyes off the assembled crowd twenty yards away, edged back further into the bushes. All he could hear were querying shouts so he was pretty certain they hadn't seen him yet, but they would soon find the old man, so he had to get away.

He stumbled up against a tree. Feeling behind him he edged his way around its circumference, keeping his eyes on the revellers silhouetted against the fire. They seemed to be getting organized now and their leader was handing out the torches. Duncan stepped back and stood on a branch on the ground. It cracked like a rifle shot and to his dismay he saw almost every head swivel as one and peer in his direction. Shit! Then someone shouted *'There!'* and he had no choice but to run.

It was blacker than he had ever known away from the lambent glow of the flames and he was soon running blindly, branches and bushes snapping and snatching at his face and arms and legs. He seemed to stumble with every other step, convinced that at any moment he would feel someone grabbing his shoulder and dragging him to the ground.

Duncan ran, his only instinct being to avoid the path they had all used to reach the clearing. He had no idea where he was going; he didn't know the area and was certain some of the group would be sent to cut him off by some short cut he couldn't know about. He could hear Leonard's voice urging him on occasionally but, in the dark, he was as blind as Duncan.

So he ran and ran, unable to remember ever being so frightened in his life, not even when he had been drowning off the coast of Crete and he had been saved in the nick of time by a passing fisherman. But now there was no helping hand, no solid comfort afforded by a rolling deck; just his legs and the relentlessly unyielding Pennine landscape.

Duncan ran and ran and ran, desperate to scream out, to give vent to his horror and terror and outrage. He had witnessed the most sickening degrading acts and wanted to bring the culprits to book, to let the world know what a bunch of sick bastards they all were, but instead he was running for his life. He had no alternative; they wouldn't let anyone who had seen what he'd seen get away, and after they found the man he had brained they would have no compunction whatsoever about disposing of Duncan permanently. Out here on the moors his body could be buried and never discovered – or they might devise an even worse fate for him.

He ran on, his lungs screaming for relief, the stitch in his side wrenching him at every step, his hands cut and sore from the punishing bushes, his feet painfully aware of every sudden change in terrain, all the time terrified that he would catch his leg on a rock, or come down too hard or too soon and break his ankle.

After what seemed an eternity Duncan had to stop, his body refusing to take any more. He leant against a tree and tried listening for his pursuers. At first he could only hear his own desperate fight for breath and the blood rushing in his ears, but gradually he was able to catch the odd sound and confirm his suspicions that they *were* still in hot pursuit. Judging by the oaths and shouts they didn't have him in their sights, and the way their voices were spread out over a broad front seemed to underline the fact that they were following the noise of his escape rather than any path he might have left. Suddenly, Leonard was with him again.

'Got to keep going, got to keep going!' was all he said.

'Fuck . . . you!' managed Duncan. Leonard had got him into this shit and the last thing he needed was the fat bastard stating the bloody obvious. But the refrain continued:

'Got to keep going, got to keep going . . .'

Duncan took a deep breath and plunged on regardless into the deep grass and bracken. Logic might have called for him to try and be as quiet as possible, but his adrenalin was in charge and it dictated flight rather than strategy.

Another minute, another pause. It might have been his imagination but were they farther behind? Didn't matter. Run. *Run!*

Another minute and another pause, longer and more painful this time. They *were* falling behind, which wasn't all that surprising. At least half of them appeared to have been old or in bad condition: they simply wouldn't have been in a fit state to chase him for any great length of time, especially over such tough terrain. He might still have a chance.

He ran on again, but had to slow his pace from a dash to a jog, then to a lope until finally settling into a painful walk. The countryside was still deep in darkness, but he found himself on a path through a densely wooded valley. He reckoned he had been running for ten minutes, maybe a touch longer. He must be at least half a mile or more away from the fire. He stopped again and looked back. He couldn't see any glow. Presumably they would have put it out anyway by now, those that had given up the chase either waiting for instructions or making their way home. He listened hard but couldn't hear any sounds of pursuit. No shouts, no undergrowth being trammelled; no sign of torches either. He bent forward, holding his waist, aware for the first time just how drenched in sweat he had become. He thought of removing his jacket but decided not to leave any clues to his route.

He counted to sixty. No sights, no sound. Then to sixty again. Still nothing. Maybe I'm safe, he thought, almost laughing at his lack of conviction.

Leonard said, 'Can't hear anything.'

He appeared by a tree about fifty feet away looking for Duncan's pursuers. He came back. 'Think they've stopped. We might be okay.'

'We? We? What's this "we" shit?' hissed Duncan. '*I'm* the one still alive; *I'm* the one who can still get fucking killed. We? Ha! If it wasn't for "we" I'd be in bed asleep and none of this shit . . .' He gave up, his throat sore.

Leonard also chose to keep quiet.

Duncan turned and jogged down the track he had found, pausing every so often to check if anyone was behind him. No-one showed. Things were looking up. His first priority had to be finding a phone to get—

Sudden panic took him and he fumbled through his pockets. Wallet, money, still there. Thank Christ, he might have dropped something with his name on it; if they had found it they could decide it was easier just to make a housecall. Right, okay, a phone it was.

Easier said than done. He had no idea which direction he was heading and out here in the hills it would be quite possible to trek for several miles and several hours without seeing a single farmhouse or village. Jesus, what a mess.

He looked up at the sky. It seemed slightly brighter, but that could just be his eyes getting used to the dark, so it was too early to hope for dawn. He checked his watch and cursed the advent of digital watches: no luminous faces. Mind you, the fact that he couldn't even see his watch six inches from his face told him that dawn was a good way off yet. He estimated it might be one-thirty, two o'clock if he was lucky. Dawn? It might just as well come next year.

He considered sneaking into the bushes and bedding down for the night but dismissed it almost immediately. They could still be after him and if they passed him he would be trapped within their circle and even if he remained undetected until sunrise, he had no guarantee they wouldn't just wait to attack him in broad daylight.

It was a good fifteen minutes of slow progress later, with Leonard looming out of the dark every so often like some spectral traffic cop directing him along the path, when he came over the crest of a hill and spotted a familiar-looking shape – an angular outline – against the skyline. Some of the cloud had cleared now, but as he had been walking under the cover of trees he hadn't noticed until now. It was a farm. It was also a miracle. He deliberately edged off the track and ventured back into the trees for his approach. If he could find this farm without knowing the lie of the land, then those bastards would almost certainly know of its whereabouts. They could even be waiting for him.

He came within fifty yards and, crouching down low, peeped through a bush, letting his eyes become accustomed to the gloom so he could make a careful study of the building.

It *was* a farm; there were outbuildings and what could be a tractor parked around the side. There was a TV aerial as well, perched on the chimney, and a wire leading to a pole – a telephone! But there were no other signs of life. It was late; they'd be in bed. What to do, what to do?

Sod it. He could lie there all night and still be exposed crossing over to the farm. Besides, he didn't know where he was; he could travel miles before he reached another farm. No, he'd have to risk it. Then Leonard was beside him again.

'Bit risky, Duncan.'

'They've got a phone.'

'Still . . .'

'Still, I could be walking for bloody hours. Better call the cops now and lie low.'

Before Leonard could respond, Duncan had sat up, stooped down, and crabbed over to the nearest wall of the house where he slumped down and studied the surrounding landscape. He could hear nothing and see nothing. Good. He edged his way around to the front of the house.

He reached the front door. It had a porch and offered some protection from people who might look along the side of the house.

The door had a big brass knocker, and a bell, lit by a little light. Which to use?

He unlodged the knocker and considered his next move. No, too much noise; better risk the bell. It might be noisy, but it might also be quiet, whereas the bloody knocker was going to be loud whatever he did.

He pressed the bell lightly. Nothing. Damn. He pressed harder. It rang. Like the fucking bells of Westminster fucking Cathedral it rang! Jesus Christ! He looked around in a panic, convinced he was centre stage at a witches' homecoming party. But there was no sound or movement out there, and none in the house either. What now? If they're in they have to hear the bell to answer the door. If they're out, he'd be like an ice cream man on a hot day ringing his bloody chimes! He almost laughed. Almost. Oh hell! He rang again – and again the outrageously loud doorbell clanged out and again there was no response from the house nor from the great beyond. He tried the door. Locked.

He worked his way around the front of the house trying every window. No go. He had finally reached the back door when it occurred to him that a farm had to have a dog. He'd never been on a farm that didn't. Why wasn't Rex barking at him now? He tried the door. Locked. He looked down. A metal grille instead of a door mat, and next to it a large plant-pot. He remembered Leonard's comment about people and keys at the morgue. He looked at the man and saw him nod down at the pot. *No, no, don't be absurd, they wouldn't* . . .

He lifted the pot and picked up the key and put it in the lock and turned it and opened the door and entered the house and shut the door behind him and locked it again and put the key in his pocket and then lay down on the cool tile floor and tried to remember how to breathe.

He didn't know how long he lay there sweating and shaking and quietly trying to regain his sanity. He didn't hear anything. He didn't see any torches outside the window. No-one got up out of bed upstairs. No dog whined. Nothing happened. For the first time in what seemed years something had gone right. Eventually he forced himself to sit up and lean against what he took to be the sink. Right, first priority the phone. Where would it be? Hall? Lounge? Bedroom? Pray it's downstairs.

He stood up and walked slowly into the body of the room. It was in total darkness. He bumped into something solid and unyielding. He felt down. Wood, flat, with a lip. Table. Yes, the kitchen table. He was sorely tempted to strike a match but that one small flame in here would be seen like a beacon outside for miles. Better safe than sorry. Besides, he didn't have any bloody matches, did he!

'Leonard,' he said into the dark. 'Can you see a phone?'

'I can't see anything, Duncan. I can only just make you out. You'll have to find it yourself.'

Duncan edged his way around to the left, then turned right, then right again until he judged himself about centre of the table. He hoped the door out of the kitchen was on the opposite wall to the back door. God but it was dark. He took one step, two steps, three *shit!* Something rattled as he bumped into it. A dresser. Plates and stuff. He waited for the gentle but ominous jingling to stop and then felt along its edge sideways with both hands until he was bending over, almost touching the thing with his nose. His right hand reached an end before his left so he stepped that way, fingering the side of the dresser until he touched a wall. He then moved along, feeling with both hands. Suddenly his right hand was feeling nothing. He stopped, leaned forward further, waving his right hand about. It still felt nothing. A doorway, had to be. He edged further to his right then walked straight ahead, holding onto the door jamb with his left hand.

Once through he turned left and followed his hand. Only a couple of feet and he felt another wall. Good. Progress. He turned to walk parallel to the wall and slowly moved forwards. He tried shutting his eyes then opening them and found he was unable to tell the difference. He couldn't remember ever having been anywhere so dark; having spent almost all his life in towns and cities there had always been street lighting and the reflected glow on the sky from other parts of the city, but here he was in no town, and there was no light *at all*.

'Leonard, are you still there?'

'Yes, but I'm still blind.'

Damn. Duncan might as well have been alone.

He reached another gap. So, another door. Would the phone be in the hall or in a room? He thought back to his walk round the house. Whatever this room was it would run to the front of the house, he was pretty certain of that. Oh God, decisions, decisions. Okay, try it. He turned to face the door and walked forward.

Six steps brought him bumping into another hard piece of furniture, and more rattling. What is it with farmers that they have Welsh dressers everywhere? He felt along the edge, then turned to face the room. He thought he could just make out the barest outline of a window but a blink and it was gone. Bugger. He edged along with the dresser to his back, feeling behind him for the comforting outline of a telephone but only found an ashtray with ash in it. He paused. Sod it, let's take the chance.

He walked into the body of the room, almost immediately coming up against another, lower obstacle. Moving his fingers down he found the arm of a chair. It was thick pile, cut into a pattern like flock wallpaper. He felt one way and then the other until he found the back of the chair. He moved around the front of it, his right hand on the chair back, his left still on the arm. He was in a slightly awkward position, bent at the waist about thirty degrees, but the fact that he was holding onto such a familiar object was oddly cheering. He started to edge his way along.

The chair had a tight velvety ruche running along its edge and its soft touch was almost comforting. He tried to imagine what colour it was. He decided against red – the wrong connotations tonight – and instead chose blue, a deep royal blue; it helped to give his surroundings some kind of reality. He moved further along.

It was bigger than a chair; so, a couch. The back dipped slightly then rose again and, moving his left hand down, he ran it along the front of the couch until he found the crease between the two cushions. He then trailed his fingers further along to the edge of the second cushion where he expected a groove which would signal a third cushion, but no, it was another arm. A two-seater, then. He shifted his feet along and lifted his right hand over the arm of the chair so he could steady himself before lifting his other hand off the back, but instead of finding thin air, it touched another chair arm. Two arms? Odd. Maybe they had pushed a couch and a chair together, or maybe two couches.

He moved his left hand along the back and touched something else. An obstruction. Even odder. He felt around the object. It had the same close-cut pile as the rest of the couch, but the pattern had disappeared or been worn away and it seemed somehow harder, as if the springs had gone. And round; it was round. Duncan moved his hand down. It was bumpy too, and bare. Funny, the other end of the couch hadn't had a wing back . . .

Then something dreadful dawned on Duncan, but before he could stop his fingers from their journey, they had moved further down and onto a sharply erratic surface and then two thin strips. Then the strips parted and Duncan's hand delved inside and felt a row of small hard flat objects, and a wetness. And then the thin strips parted even further and so did the teeth and the man smiled in the dark and Duncan screamed and tried to pull away and the man switched on the torch in his lap and the harsh white beam shot upward to illuminate his smiling red face with the crewcut hair and then his other hand grabbed Duncan's arm as he tried to let loose the man's thigh and Duncan's terrified scream was suddenly cut short as he fell backwards and cracked his head and the lights went out again.

21

THERE WAS A rattling. It thrummed at the edge of Duncan's mind, insistent, comforting. Still there was darkness; he liked that. But there was also pain. A pain in his head, deep and hard. Pain? Pain meant feelings meant alive . . .

Wake!

Duncan sat up with a start, his cry of pain echoed by a shout of surprise as the crouching Leonard was sent tumbling back into the fireplace.

Duncan's heart raced again as he frantically scanned his surroundings for any threat, but there appeared to be none.

'Leonard, Leonard! Where is he? The man?'

'Gone,' said Leonard. 'Long gone. God, I thought you'd gone, too. Couldn't see you breathing, couldn't feel you for a pulse. That was some knock you took.'

Duncan leaned back against the couch. He remembered. The ceremony, the chase, *the man* . . . The memory made him shiver and he hugged himself. Slowly it dawned on him that he was cold as well. He looked up at the window.

Light. The curtains were partly open and he could see rain blatting against the window. He used to find the sound of rain on a window pleasant; now it would forever be a coda to the worst night of his life. He had been mugged once wearing his Walkman: he still couldn't listen to the Clash without feeling queasy; it had been blaring out 'Police and Thieves'. Not funny.

He felt his head. It was matted with blood at the back. He was glad it had dried; had it still been wet he might have panicked. As it was he heard a noise in the hall and he scuttled back round the side of the couch.

'He's come back!' he hissed at Leonard.

Leonard was stood by the door. 'No, and there was only ever that one guy in the house,' he said.

'Who was it? Did you know him?' said Duncan, relaxing.

Leonard shook his head. 'All the time he was here he only used the torch. I never saw his face.'

'I did. For a second.'

'Yeah, but I wasn't watching him during that second.'

'So, what did he do?'

'He shone the torch over your face, then pulled out your wallet to check who you were.'

'So he knows who I am?' Duncan felt inside his jacket pocket and was surprised to find it was still there. He pulled it out.

'Must do,' said Leonard quietly.

'Shit. But why put the wallet back?'

'Don't know. He took your wallet and left the room. I couldn't follow him because you were still on the floor. When he shone the torch on your face I saw the blood where you'd hit your head. I didn't know . . . you could have been dead. Anyway, he came back after a few minutes and put your wallet back. Still couldn't see his face. He checked your neck for a pulse then left. I remember he had long fingers and very well manicured nails, but that's all.'

'That's it?'

'Yeah. Oh, and he ripped the phone out. So it looks like you're walking.'

'Have you seen the rest of the house?' said Duncan forcing himself up, despite the hammering in his head. He sat down on the couch.

'No, I have to stay in sight of you, remember. But judging by the dust, it's not been occupied for a while.'

Duncan caught sight of the fireplace and the dark stain on the green carpet. There was also blood on his jacket, though it didn't show up much on the black. He touched the scab on his head. Pressing it hurt, but things could have been a lot worse than stained clothes and a raging headache.

He looked round the room. It smelled musty, and there was dust everywhere. It looked like an elderly person's home, everything aged and out-of-date. Maybe they had died here and the house had been left untenanted.

'So what do we do now?' asked Leonard peering out of the window at the rain.

'Walk it. Find a road, cadge a lift or get a bus. Fuck knows where we are.'

'Then?'

'Could get the police. Tell them about the dog and what those fuckers got up to.'

'Prove it. Whatever those bastards did, I guarantee it's not there now. You won't even find the ashes. We always had to clean up after.'

'Shit.'

'Besides, how come you found them? Because you followed Fazey all the way out here from his shop? Why? Because of your interest in that girl who topped herself. Which girl? The one who was mixed up with Beaumont. Oh, the same Beaumont you claim to have found dead on his boat by accident? It would soon get very messy, Duncan. Besides, that Chief Inspector wanted your mother to put you away. You start coming on with orgies and dog sacrifices and witchcraft you can't prove and he'll get a court order and bang you up himself!'

Duncan hauled his weary frame out of the room and back through the kitchen and out into the open air. It was pouring with rain, the sky overcast. Looking around he realised he really was in the middle of nowhere. He remembered his watch and checked the time. It was broken.

'You don't think anyone will still be hanging about, do you?' he asked, scanning the walls and clumps of trees that seemed to be huddling together against the elements.

'In this weather? Why? If they were going to do you in they had all the time they needed last night.'

'So why didn't they?'

Leonard didn't know. 'Let's be nasty for a minute.'

They set off walking. Duncan had already accepted that he was going to get soaked to the skin so didn't bother to cover his head. 'What do you mean?'

'Assume the worst and pretend you're that guy last night. Obviously no-one wants to be revealed as a dog-killing sexual pervert – what would it do for Mr Fazey's business? – so they chase you and find out who you are. They could cover their tracks and let you blab about it; they could bribe you; they could hope you're scared enough to leave well alone; or they could kill you.'

'Quite a choice,' said Duncan, trying to avoid the deeper puddles, his trainers already leaking.

'They didn't kill you last night so they're not going to kill you. There's no way they can link you to me – I don't exist – so you're just some kid in the wrong place at the wrong time. Even if you talk they've hidden the evidence.'

'So you think that's it?'

'If you got caught again I doubt they'd let you go again. No, they know you know they know who you are; I reckon they'll bank on you being too shit scared to interfere again.'

'And they'd be right.'

The rain continued to hammer down as Duncan trudged along the long, unkempt lane that led away from the house. It was fifteen minutes before they reached a wider lane and another thirty minutes before that joined a road. Two cars passed, both ignoring his thumb – not surprisingly – so Duncan walked on until he found a bus stop.

Leonard was unaffected by the weather or walking, though he chose to keep pace with Duncan. He was pleased that he had managed to calm his friend, and get him through this latest crisis, even if he himself remained unconvinced. Given that there had been three deaths – four, if Kimmel's reaction was anything to go by – why should that man let a nobody like Duncan leave after seeing what he had? It didn't add up.

Ten minutes later, Duncan was sitting under a hedge next to a bus stop, water dripping into his underwear, the same conundrum running through his mind. It made him shiver even more. If Leonard had been telling the truth, things had taken a turn for the worse; instead of an excuse for a gangbang, the orgies were now serious ceremonies designed to do – well, what? Leonard went there because he wanted sex. Someone in charge was after more than that now and if they were that sick, why let Duncan off so lightly? There was more to this than just scaring him away.

A bus came after half an hour and, ignoring the looks from the driver, Duncan paid his fare and sat down. He was too cold and tired to ask where he actually was. The bus destination sign had said Ollington and that was enough. He sat at the back of the empty bus and fell asleep.

He was woken by Leonard shouting that they had to get off and jolted awake to see they were in Ollington Bus Station. Duncan checked the clock at the end of the bay: 9.50. He stumbled out to the taxi rank and caught a cab home.

His mother was out, but Mrs Orr was in. He chose to ignore

her questions and ran a shower instead, doused himself warm, then fell into bed and let his fatigue take him too deep even to dream.

Leonard, seeing how exhausted Duncan was, made no protest and let him sleep.

Mrs Orr had gone, his mother was still out and so Duncan had the run of the house. He had given in to his new found paranoia and put on the burglar alarm even though it was mid-afternoon. He was sitting in the kitchen in his dressing gown, scarfing down chicken pieces from the fridge.

'Duncan, I've been thinking,' said Leonard, seated across from him at the kitchen table, vaguely disgusted by Duncan's table manners. Okay, the kid might be hungry but it was usual to finish one piece before starting on the next.

'That's the problem with all this,' managed Duncan between mouthfuls. 'You thinking. It's your thinking got us into this mess.'

'Forget the personal shit for a mo. Something's been nagging at me since last night.'

'Don't fret,' said Duncan touching his scalp. 'It's just called a conscience.'

'Ha ha. No, something that guy did to you and something that happened to me the night I died.'

Duncan stopped eating. His stomach turned over. It was the word 'died' that did it. He put down his chicken, the heels of his palms resting on the table, his greasy fingers hovering like birds frozen in flight. 'What do you mean?'

'You fell over, when you stepped back. He didn't touch you, but he checked your wallet then put it back and left.'

'So?'

'Night I died I remember . . . I remember hearing about Racimo on the radio then I got all uptight, God knows why. Tried to give the girl all my money . . . No, I tried to give her the *wallet*, that was it; I looked in my wallet and . . .'

Duncan was hanging on every word. 'You looked in your wallet and . . . ?'

'. . . and . . . something. I saw something.'

'In your wallet?'

'Yes. I don't know what but it . . . I didn't like it.'

'And that guy took my wallet out then put it back.'

'No. He took it out, left the room with it, then came back a couple of minutes later.'

'A couple of minutes?'

'Might have been longer. Shorter. I thought he was going to kill you, Duncan. I was shouting at you, trying to get you to wake up.'

Duncan slid his chair back from the table, his stomach actually grumbling, and looked over at the tumble dryer. He had put his clothes in to dry and left the contents on top, including his wallet.

'You think he put something in it?'

Leonard shrugged his shoulders. 'Something in mine . . . I don't know.'

'But I've looked in it. Nothing's missing. Maybe he just went to copy out my address.' He shot a glance out of the window at the driveway. It was as empty as ever.

'Or he had a change of mind.' Leonard was as anxious as Duncan to find nothing wrong.

'Best check, though.'

'Yes.'

Duncan walked to the dryer, wiped his hands on a tea towel then gingerly picked up the wallet and brought it back to the table.

It was a pocket wallet, four inches by three, that folded out to reveal credit card slots, a zipped compartment and a back pocket for bank notes. He carefully extracted his Barclaycard, his Connect card, his old NUS card, his driving licence and a video club card. He pulled out three tenners and a fiver from the back pocket then, pulling open the zipper, he extracted three Visa receipts, a Connect receipt and a W H Smith receipt. And that was it.

Duncan hadn't realised how badly his hands were shaking. He dropped the wallet and rested his hands on his lap out of sight.

'Empty,' he said. 'Nothing that shouldn't be there, though what the hell we were looking for . . .'

'Just a thought. Sure it's empty?'

Duncan picked it up and opened each flap for Leonard to see. It was empty.

'Lining?'

'Pardon?'

'The lining, in the back pocket. Is it stuck in?'

'No, it's stitched.'

'Check it.'

Duncan did and the look on his face told Leonard that there was

164

a problem. He slowly pulled out the brown satin lining and turned it inside out. It was frayed along the bottom, slit open. Duncan slid his fingers inside the cut then ran them along both sides of the pocket until he found something. Pulling it out he set his find down on the table, letting go of it as if it was hot.

'What is it?' said Leonard.

'How the fuck do I know?' yelled Duncan edgily.

They both sat and stared at the two-inch-square folded piece of paper until Leonard persuaded Duncan to open it.

He unfolded it carefully – the paper felt brittle – and laid it on the table. It was eight inches long by two inches deep and it carried two rows of indecipherable characters, about twenty to a row.

Duncan looked up at Leonard and found the man was transfixed by the paper.

'Well?'

'It's coming back,' said Leonard. 'When I opened my wallet, there was something like that folded up behind my Access card. I pulled it out . . .' Duncan could see the man's eyes focusing on a past scene. 'Unfolded it, realised something was . . . *wrong* and I had to get rid of it. I don't know how but I knew it was there for a reason so I tried to give it to the girl; to get her to take the wallet.'

'So you're saying you—'

'—had one of those when I died.'

Duncan swallowed hard, tasting bile. 'Tell you something else. So did Racimo.'

'What?'

'Racimo had one of these in his wallet. There was a photocopy of it in his file at the morgue.'

22

THEY WERE STANDING outside Fazey's bookshop. It was a little after 3pm and Duncan was angry, his emotions fuelled both by his fear of what the piece of paper might mean and by Leonard's continued harping on about the need for action. Because by 'action', he meant talking to Fazey, which required Duncan to walk into the lion's den.

If Leonard was sure that only the man with the torch had seen him, then Fazey wouldn't know what the intruder at the ceremony looked like – so reasoned Leonard – so Duncan could still pose as the curious ufologist of the day before. But Leonard was also a pragmatist:

'Duncan, if he starts suspecting who you are, you've got to get him to tell you the truth, whatever it takes.'

'Meaning?'

'Meaning last night you punched out that old bastard who found you. You better be prepared to do the same to Fazey.'

'But that was different—'

'It wasn't! You saw what Fazey did to that dog after the head guy cut it up. The man's a fucking sicko, as deep in that shit as anyone. And he may well know what that paper means – and not want to tell you. You've got to find out because two people who had one just like it are dead.'

The implication was obvious.

Duncan leaned his head against the building. He felt sick; sick and scared. 'What if he just clams up?'

'Unclam him. Remember, this is life and death. You can't come out of there *without* knowing.'

Duncan turned to face the alley, and immediately turned back to throw up. Chicken pieces splattered the pavement.

'Deep breaths, Duncan, deep breaths. Now it's up, it's up. Take your time—'

'Will you shut up!' coughed Duncan. 'Just shut up.'

Satisfied he had retched his last, and that there were no passers-by, Duncan steadied himself, wiped his mouth on his sleeve, took the suggested deep breaths and marched up the alley to the bookshop's door.

The sign said Closed. It was Wednesday. Duncan almost burst into tears.

'It's only a sign, kid. Try the door!'

It was open.

'The bell!' reminded Leonard but too late: it had tinkled. 'Fuck it, get upstairs.'

Duncan mounted the bare wooden steps two at a time and had just reached the top when a familiar high-pitched voice called out.

'Sorry, we're shut. Sorry.'

Duncan turned into the body of the shop and saw Mr Fazey standing by the door to his office.

'Sorry, son, we're shut. Wednesday, you see. Wednesday we shut. Open tomorrow.'

Duncan didn't move. He didn't know what to say.

Mr Fazey took a step forward, a small letter opener in his hand. He was dressed rather incongruously in just an oversize dark red towelling robe and black brogue shoes. 'I'm sorry, but we're . . . oh, it's you.'

Duncan's heart began racing even faster. *He knows me*, his brain screamed, *he knows me!*

'Yesterday,' said Mr Fazey. '*The Peaks Speak*. Well?'

'Well?' said Duncan, his voice barely a croak.

'Interesting, was it? Was it interesting?'

'Answer the man,' said Leonard, now standing by the open office door.

'Yes. I was wondering . . .'

'More books, more books? Certainly. I said I was shut but I'm always ready to help a believer.'

For some reason the word 'believer' angered Duncan. That horror from last night was because of 'believers'.

'Actually, I wanted your help with something else.'

'Something else,' said Mr Fazey, eagerness personified. 'Certainly, certainly.'

He looked at Duncan expectantly. In other circumstances he might have been an interesting person to know, but . . . Duncan stared at him and realised he, Duncan, had the advantage: he was taller, fitter, motivated and fully clothed and this fat dog-fucking necrophiliac was half-naked and on his own away from witnesses. Duncan felt courage – or was it just adrenalin? – surge through him.

'Yes. This,' he said.

He took out his wallet, removed the piece of paper, slipped the wallet back into his pocket, then held out the unfolded scrap, gripping it between the thumb and forefinger of both hands, about three feet from Fazey's face.

The man's shiny red face seemed to shrink, changing colour with a chameleon-like facility to a waxy white, his eyes widening and his bottom lip trembling as if he was going to cry.

'What is it?' asked Duncan.

'N – nothing. Paper. Nothing.'

Fazey stepped back and Duncan thrust the paper towards him and the man shrieked like a girl.

'No! I don't want it, I don't *want* it. Keep it away! Take it away!'

'Why? It's only a piece of paper.'

The man shook his head and backed further away.

Leonard stood beside the two of them, studying Fazey. 'Get tough, Duncan. He's a creep but he's also a coward. Get heavy.'

Duncan made to grab the dressing gown lapel but his attempt was half-hearted and Fazey tugged his shoulder out of the way.

'Remember the dog, Duncan! Remember what this fat creep did to that dog!' hissed Leonard.

Duncan lunged for Fazey and, grabbing both lapels, he swung him to the left and slammed him into the table of books in the middle of the room, where he twisted and slumped face down.

'Do it, Duncan!'

Duncan leaned down, thrusting the paper into the man's face, their closeness making him aware of his vomitous breath. 'What is it?'

Fazey let out a little squeak then went limp. Duncan stood upright and let go, watching astounded as the man slumped to the floor. He had fainted.

'Get him in the office,' said Leonard. 'Time to get rough.'

'You sure?' asked Duncan, slipping his hands under the uncon-scious man's shoulders and starting to drag him to his office.

'You saw how he reacted,' said Leonard.

Argument enough.

Five minutes later Fazey was slouched in an upright chair in his office. The man had refused to be roused and Duncan had had time to make a cursory exploration of the other rooms.

The office was cramped and crowded with heavy furniture and filing cabinets. Almost Dickensian in atmosphere, it led through to a small kitchen, and a studio flat with a fold-up sofa bed, ageing TV and stereo and a pair of well-worn deep leather armchairs. Beyond that was a surprisingly large, echoing bathroom with a deep cast-iron bath on legs, an old-fashioned geyser, a toilet and a sink. Damp underwear and socks hung on a line across the room rendering it dank.

But it was the office that held the attention of Duncan and Leonard as they waited for their captive to regain consciousness. The room again had only a skylight for daytime illumination, and a single fluorescent tube hanging at the end of two metal rods from the high ceiling. One wall was covered by shelves of books; another had a table piled with stacks of folders and file boxes pushed against it, a small fish tank to one side; a wide oak writing desk with the upright chair Fazey was slumped in occupied the third. The fourth wall contained the centrally-placed door and supported four grey filing cabinets, chipped and scratched with use. Either the man made little money or simply couldn't see beyond his books. Yet, somehow, he looked at home here: a fat little eccentric pursuing his life's work oblivious of the outside world. In fact, it was quite possible Fazey could go entire days without having to see the world outside at all, simply relying on his customers for contact with reality.

He started to come round, slurping on the drool from his mouth, his hands clutching at the tattered dressing gown that had gathered around his crotch.

'Wake him up,' said Leonard, pointing at the small aquarium.

There were four or five electric-blue fish in the tank, extraordinarily beautiful and, incidentally, the only bright colour in the entire room. Duncan scooped up a handful of water, the fish scurrying for cover, and flicked it into Fazey's face.

He spluttered, then shook his head and opened his eyes and tried to take in the scene before him. Immediately Duncan held up the slip of paper again.

'You're going to tell me what this means and you're going to tell me now.'

The man twitched and pressed his lips together.

'Scare him some more, Duncan,' urged Leonard.

'Otherwise, I'm going to . . .'

'Get extreme, we haven't got the time to—'

'I'll do to you what you did to that dog last night.'

The man's eyes bugged out and he swallowed with a gasp.

'Slowly,' Duncan added, surprised to find himself relishing the power he had over the little man.

'I can't. Can't.'

'There's no such word as "can't",' said Duncan, not believing he would ever have repeated one of his mother's favourite sayings; and certainly not as he poked a sweating pervert in the chest. 'I'm not going to piss about, Fazey. You tell me what this means, I'll go. Don't tell me and I'll pretend *you're* man's best friend. Like last night.'

Duncan pictured the German shepherd being ripped open and remembered the horror and anger that had welled up with his vomit. Then he remembered Racimo had been carrying one of the slips of paper and he saw the photograph of Racimo's head lying on the back seat of his car. And he looked over at Leonard – a movement Fazey saw but obviously couldn't understand – and saw a dead man, his face destroyed by something evil, a man he had come to like despite his faults, a man desperate to solve his own murder.

Murder: that was the key word here. It wasn't about sick sex or sacrificing dogs or witchcraft – but murder: the removal of someone's life. Racimo and Beaumont and Kimmel might have been shits, but Jane Dalton had just been a stupid girl and Leonard a dick-driven twit, and it had led to their deaths, their lives snuffed out for no reason other than the fact that the fat cunt sat snivelling in front of him wanted to play at black magic. People were *dying* so this bastard could get his jollies.

Suddenly, and unaware that he was doing it, Duncan started punching the man in the stomach. He was on to the fourth blow before he realised what he was doing. It didn't stop him. The man was whimpering on the floor, coughing hard, before Duncan stopped.

'Tell me what it means!' he screamed into the man's twisted face.

'No, I can't. Won't,' he spluttered. 'Hit me all you like, I won't tell, I won't.'

Duncan hauled him back onto the chair and raised his fist to punch him on the nose. The man stared at the fist.

Leonard spoke. 'Could be he enjoys this stuff. Got to try something else.' He looked around the room.

He could see spikes for paper, heavy paperweights, letter openers, a stapler, scissors . . . no, pain wasn't enough. It had to be something that meant more than personal suffering; it had to have a consequence beyond the now. He remembered one time a friend of his had broken his legs in a fall and because he was in some weird religion he had refused painkillers, despite the obvious agony. Leonard had asked him how he put up with it and he had said he thought of tomorrow. Pain was transient; it was the one thing the mind couldn't recall. Sights, sounds, smells, emotions; the brain could dig into its memory and produce a reasonable facsimile of them all, but pain was impossible to remember. His friend had simply thought of that time when he wouldn't be able to remember his legs hurting. But, as he had admitted, had it been his daughter's pain, the fear and worry could not have been banished. To get Fazey to co-operate they had to do something that he would have to live with after they had gone, long after a bruise had cleared up or a scar healed. They could set fire to his shop, but that could have serious consequences for Duncan, so what else? Then he saw it . . .

He told Duncan what to do. At first he refused, basically because he thought it was stupid, but Leonard persuaded him. All the time they argued, Fazey watched, his terror increasing. It was quite clear that Duncan was insane, conducting imaginary conversations. Then he crossed the room to the fish tank.

It had been a struggle but eventually Duncan had done as Leonard insisted and he had come back to Fazey.

'Don't hurt him, please,' Fazey begged. 'Don't hurt him.'

'Oh, I won't hurt him, if you tell me—'

'No! I *can't.*'

'Well, then, you'd better open wide.'

'What?'

'You're going to eat your fish.'

The man started gibbering, as if he couldn't quite contemplate what Duncan was going to do, so Duncan brushed the blue fish he had managed to pull out of the tank across the man's cheek, struggling to keep a grasp of the squirming creature. Fazey slapped at the wetness on his cheek.

'Get his nose!' shouted Leonard.

Duncan grabbed Fazey's nose with his left hand and pinched it. Fazey tried to bat him off but Duncan pinned his arms to his chest with his knee.

'Open wide,' Duncan whispered as the man began struggling for breath.

The fish flapped between his fingers, its lips opening and closing as if instructing its owner what to do. Eventually, his face turning red, sweat coursing down his brow, Fazey's resolve burst and in a shower of saliva he blurted:

'I'll tell you, I'll tell you! Just put him back! Put him back, please!'

Duncan stared at the man. He had never seen fear up close. Yes, he had been scared a few times: his near-drowning, a mugging, a couple of car crashes, his O-level results, *last night*, but that had been himself, inside. Here he was looking into the eyes of a man in terror; it was not a pleasant sight but, he told himself, whatever he was scared of, Duncan had every reason to be as terrified: he might be looking at his own face when he had learned the truth.

'Put him back, put him back!' pleaded Fazey as he watched his fish losing its fight for life.

Duncan darted over to the fish tank and dropped the fish in the water where, after initial reluctance, it started swimming round its world.

Duncan returned to the gasping Fazey, pulled out the piece of paper and waited.

Fazey tried to regain his composure, pulling himself upright, but his hands were slick with sweat and they lost their grip on the seat of the chair and he slid back into a submissive slouch.

'Last time,' said Duncan. 'What is this? Who gave it me? Why?'

He didn't answer.

'I wonder what it feels like to swallow a friend?' said Duncan.

'Make sure he knows you mean the fish,' said Leonard.

'Will you shut up!' Duncan shouted over at Leonard who was sat on the edge of the desk.

Fazey followed Duncan's eyes, saw he was shouting at no-one, and any resistance he had left crumbled.

'It's a curse.'

'A curse? Like a spell?'

'Yes, if you want.'

'We don't want,' said Leonard. 'What is it, exactly?'

'What is it? Like voodoo?'

'It's a runic incantation; a curse. Whoever accepts it is doomed to fulfil its promise.'

'Accepts it? I found it when I woke up.'

'You haven't got rid of it. It is yours.'

'Who gave it to me?'

'I can't . . . don't know.'

Duncan raised his hand, but Leonard interrupted.

'Forget the who for now, get the what. What does it say?'

'What does it say?' asked Duncan.

'Nothing special . . . just a warning.'

'You can read it?'

'Yes.'

'What's the point of a warning you can't read?' said Leonard. 'There's more to it than that.'

'Good point,' said Duncan, Fazey seeing again his eye contact with thin air. He turned back to Fazey who flinched. 'Is it the same warning Racimo, Beaumont and Leonard Halsey received; the same warning that ended up killing them?'

Fazey threw up. He just leaned forward and vomited onto Duncan's shoes, moaning like a wounded animal.

'Bingo!' said Leonard.

Duncan was used to the smell of vomit; his own sleeve was smeared with it, after all. He grabbed Fazey under his slobbery chin and pushed him back upright.

'Translate it.'

He shook his head.

'Tell you what, you fat fucker, how's about we *fry* your little chums before you eat them? Right now, on your cooker. You got a frying pan?'

Fazey's eyes fixed on the fish tank, then on the paper Duncan waved in his face. 'It says "The Black Wind will come at the next midnight hour to avenge its priest." Nonsense, really.'

'Sure . . . Is that all it says?'

'Yes . . . it also says you received it willingly and are pleased to be called upon to be . . .'

'Be what?'

'Sacrificed.'

'Like that dog last night?'

'No, not like the dog. That's all I can tell . . . No-one has ever seen . . .'

'The black wind?'

'Yes.'

'No-one who has survived, you mean? Does your priest put on some kind of Batman costume before he butchers his victims?'

Fazey laughed bitterly. 'You don't understand.'

'Ask him about midnight,' said Leonard.

'Midnight? I got this some time this morning. Does that mean tonight?'

Fazey nodded, casting an eye at the wall clock. 3.21 pm.

'So eight hours from now the black wind comes and . . . and what? Racimo was beheaded, Beaumont poisoned, Halsey strangled. What will happen to me?'

'Whatever you fear most . . . I can't tell you any more.'

'Oh yes, you can. What if I gave you this paper?'

'*I refuse it, I refuse it, I refuse it. I don't want it. I will not accept it!*'

Duncan stuffed it into the man's dressing gown pocket and he became hysterical, thrashing and cursing, insisting again and again that he hadn't accepted it, that he didn't want it. To calm him down Duncan took the paper back.

'Who gave it to me?'

'I don't know . . . I don't . . .' he started to faint again, but Duncan slapped him awake.

'I don't know who our—'

'The guy fucks you up the arse and you don't know who he is?' said Duncan.

Fazey stared at him. 'You *were* there; he was right.'

'He? You do know—'

'Duncan, look out!' But Leonard's warning was too late. Fazey had reached for a pile of books beside his chair, picked up a large leatherbound volume and swung it round into Duncan's head.

Duncan felt the impact and lost his vision and balance. Another blow told him he had hit the ground and a third that Fazey was hitting him again. He tried to crawl away but blows kept landing on his back. He could hear Leonard shouting to him to get up but it was just so many words so far away from the hammers that were jarring his body.

But he kept crawling, his eyes slowly clearing, moving under the table, Fazey only able to hit his back. Aware that his head was protected by the table above him, Duncan forced himself over onto his back only to be hit full square in the balls, a white light exploding in his head and a deep sharp pain in his abdomen making him shriek. Anger and agony made him lash out with his feet, catching Fazey's hand and forcing him to drop his book.

Duncan tried to squirm further away but there was no more room and the pain between his legs made every movement a torment. He could see Fazey's legs cross the room, pause, then come back. Then he stabbed down at Duncan's exposed stomach but missed, the paper spike sticking into the floor. Terror fuelled Duncan's response: he kicked wildly and blindly, making contact with books and table and floor and, he hoped, parts of Fazey. Then a high-pitched shriek told him he had struck home and he forced himself out into the open, aware that he was making himself vulnerable again.

He sat up, the deep untouchable pain in his groin forcing him to breathe through clenched teeth, his head swimming. Fazey was sprawled underneath his fish tank, blood dripping from his nose, seemingly crying.

'You fat bastard!' said Duncan, all self-control lost.

He got to his feet and steadied himself to kick at the man's face. He wanted the little fuck to pay; for his pain, for that dog, for Leonard's death, for everyone who had been corrupted or destroyed by his filth. But even as he raised his foot, Leonard was shouting a warning and Fazey pulled out a large screwdriver from behind his back and jabbed at Duncan's shin. It made stinging contact and he yelped and danced back, but Fazey dragged himself up and lunged at him.

Duncan hadn't any choice: he stumbled across the office and fell headlong into the studio flat. Fazey yelled again and charged at him. Duncan rolled over and was lucky to kick the door to and slam it in Fazey's face. Duncan then scrambled up, locked the door and leaned against it.

Leonard was beside him. 'God, he can move when he has to.'

There was a shout and a thump and, expecting the man to keep battering at the door, Duncan looked around for a weapon, but suddenly silence fell.

'Can you see what he's doing?' Duncan said to Leonard.

'Got to stay in sight of you, kid. No windows.'

Duncan strained to listen. There was a shuffling, maybe a chair leg being scraped along the floor, then nothing more.

'Maybe he's just going to run.'

'Maybe,' said Leonard. 'But his clothes are here.'

Duncan kneeled down, the pain in his groin roaring back, stealing his breath, clawing his fingers. With a shaking hand he pulled the key from the lock and tried to see through the keyhole, but something was blocking his view.

'No good. Let's see if there's another way out of here.'

There wasn't. The only windows were both painted out, the only accessible one, in the kitchen, too narrow to afford escape, even if it opened onto something other than a sheer drop into the alley. He returned to the door to the office and listened. There was no sound.

'What do we do?' said Duncan, his face scrunched up as his testicles continued to throb.

'Got to get more info from that fat creep.'

'Easy for you to say.'

They waited another three minutes until there was a sudden clatter, a strange gasp and then more silence.

Two more minutes and Leonard said to try the door.

Duncan carefully re-inserted the key and slowly turned the lock, every tumbler click like a gunshot, until the door was unlocked. He turned the handle; it squeaked with all the subtlety of a car skidding round a bend. Pulling the door open, he stood back so that Leonard could take a look and see what threat Fazey posed.

'Oh shit,' was all he said, his shoulders slumping.

Duncan was about to slam the door shut again but Leonard shook his head. 'No need.'

Duncan peered round the door.

A naked Fazey was hanging by his neck from his dressing gown cord which had been tied round one of the rods holding the fluorescent tube in place. His eyes were wide open, his purple tongue clenched between his teeth, blood on his chin, his face a horrible red, like a balloon about to pop atop the white blimp of his body which slowly revolved like a bloated pear too long on the tree. His hands were clenched spastically at his side and there was a pool of urine on the floor, next to the chair he must have kicked over. A brown stain coursed down the back of his right leg. An ugly little man, his death had rendered him uglier still.

'Oh God, now what do we do?' said Duncan, near to tears.

'Nothing. He's dead, he did it himself, his problem.'

'But we were here. The fight . . .'

'If we leave, no-one will be the wiser.'

'Oh, okay . . .' Duncan was in a dream; he wanted to believe anything Leonard told him as long as it relieved him of any responsibility for Fazey's suicide. 'Let's go, then.'

'Not yet. We've—'

'But what if anyone comes?'

'He's closed. The shop's shut.'

'Oh.' *Yes, Leonard, whatever you say, Leonard.* Duncan didn't know what to do; he just stared up at the rotund bookshop owner as he slowly turned one way then the other, as if the cord was patiently trying to work its load free.

'He knew what that paper was,' explained Leonard, looking round the room. 'And he knew who gave it you. He also said that whatever happens will happen at midnight. We've got till then to find out what's going to happen and stop it.'

'So what do we do? He's dead!' It was Duncan's turn to get hysterical. 'The fucking bastard's dead!'

He punched Fazey on his flabby knee – it felt like suet – and the body revolved quicker. It also let go a fart foul enough for Duncan to step back.

'He kept a record of when the ceremonies took place; maybe he has other stuff.'

Duncan didn't react, just kept staring up at Fazey, his mouth open. *Another* death, *more* mystery, *more* fear . . .

Leonard stood between the two of them, trying to get Duncan's attention. 'If I was alive I'd slap you,' he said.

Duncan looked at him. 'If you were alive I'd punch you.'

'If I were alive we wouldn't be here. But I'm dead and so will you be if we don't find more.'

'I will?'

Leonard nodded. 'I'm sorry, kiddo, but from now on it's about saving you, not finding out who killed me. I'm . . . I'm sorry; if I'd guessed it would have ended up like this . . .'

Duncan looked up at Fazey, a ball on a string, then at Leonard, a man who'd had his life choked out of him. Two dead men. He really, honestly, truthfully, didn't want to join them: he wanted to live, to survive, to *be*. And he didn't have time for recriminations. It didn't matter for now who had started the war: winning it was what counted.

'So what are we looking for?' he said.

'Good lad. I don't know. Stuff.'

Duncan scanned the room. It was five feet deep in 'stuff'! It would take forever.

'Check drawers, diaries, address books . . . stuff.'

Duncan did as he was asked, all the time plagued by the suspicion that Fazey was only faking and, like some avenging monster, would slip free from his noose and hurl himself onto Duncan's back, his teeth digging into the younger man's skull. More than once he had to stop looking and check that Fazey was still there, hanging three feet from the ground.

Ten minutes produced an address book and little else. It was like the hunt through Jane Dalton's drawers, but taken to the *n*th degree.

Duncan found a drawer of polaroids, most involving animals and blood; a collection of porno magazines with titles like *Grunt* and *On All Fours* (none of which, a cursory glance concluded, contained two members of the same species having sex) as well as gay S & M material. Fazey certainly wasn't restricted in his perversions.

As Leonard couldn't physically touch anything, he could only urge Duncan on. It soon grew tiresome, not least because all they were turning up was sex-related material.

'Don't you think it's odd?' asked Leonard as Duncan stared at a polaroid of a teenage girl being double fist-fucked by two middle-aged men.

'Odd? It's impossible.'

'No, it isn't, no. All this sex shit, it's way out there, real sick, but what's strange is that none of it involves black magic. There's no robes or pentagrams or black candles.'

'True. So?'

'So, what's the one thing you don't mock if you believe in it?'

'Religion.'

'Right. That bastard was a true believer; all this stuff was just a hobby: the real stuff was serious.'

'So where does that take us?'

Leonard pointed at a small safe in the corner. 'He must use some gear on those nights. Robes, the paint. Remember he left here with a bag last night. Serious stuff gets hidden.'

'But I can't open a safe!'

'No tumblers, just a key. It must be here somewhere.'

Duncan held his hands out in defeat. *Where?* They might as well have been on a rubbish tip looking for a particular can ring-pull. It was hopeless.

'But if it's in a book . . . Or a file of clippings . . .' he trailed off. There were literally hundreds of places it could be, and that was just in the office. It could also be in the shop itself, hidden under the floorboards, in his mattress, in any of his clothes, *anywhere.*

'We're fucked.'

'No, Duncan, *you're* fucked. That's why you *can't* give up. This isn't some bloody school test or shit job. This is your *life*, so keep looking.'

Duncan looked at the clock. 3.42. Eight hours and a bit. He turned to Fazey, now almost used to his dead presence. 'Where would you hide it?'

'Try his pocket.'

'Oh, come on.'

'Try it. You'd be surprised how careless people are about security. Remember those keys at the morgue?'

Duncan went through the dressing gown pockets. Bingo! He knelt down by the safe. It was small, the door barely eight inches square. He inserted the small brass key, turned it, then pulled the handle down and edged the door open.

Inside, bundled up tight, was the robe Fazey had been wearing, a book, several hundreds of pounds in twenty-pound notes, property deeds, insurance papers, VAT forms and a ledger, presumably for sales.

Having put everything on the floor, the two detectives surveyed their find. Duncan unfurled the robe but it had no pockets. The book was old and in Latin and had no illustrations. The money added up to five hundred and eighty pounds. The ledger showed average daily sales of about £100, but the property was insured for £80,000, the contents for – here they both let out a whistle – £200,000, and the shop and premises of 1B Tyler Cop were rented on a 99-year lease – which had 76 years still to run – from a company called Tanfeld Estates. The annual rent was £100.

'A hundred quid? You could rent this apartment out for that a week, never mind the frigging shop,' said Leonard. 'Whoever these Tanfeld Estates are, they either haven't got any sense or . . .'

'Or they're big chums with fatso. And have been for some time. Check the address book.'

Tanfeld Estates just had a number, 887632, which meant it was local, but no address. The deeds had an address in Market Street, but the area had been redeveloped in the Eighties so that office was probably a part of the Peak Shopping Centre.

'What now?'

'Get a Yellow Pages, see where Tanfeld Estates are now,' said Leonard.

They looked around the room but couldn't find one.

'Put it all back in the safe, except the book,' said Leonard. 'Get a cloth and wipe everything you've touched.'

Five minutes later, they were ready to leave.

'Will they call it a suicide?' asked Duncan as they walked into the shop.

'No reason not to, unless they think there's a link with some of the creeps he must know to get hold of that porno. Either way, what's it got to do with you?'

Reassured and relieved, Duncan led the way, but halfway across the shop they heard the doorbell tinkle. Someone was coming into the shop!

Leonard pointed Duncan behind the tables that filled the centre of the room. 'Get down there. Maybe they'll leave when they see it's empty.'

Duncan crouched down, his heart pounding, convinced his next sight would be of a policeman's boots.

He peered through the stacks of books under the tables to the entrance, listening as the visitor slowly walked up the stairs, a step at a time. Leonard couldn't position himself to see down the stairs without Duncan revealing himself, so they both had to wait.

Slowly the steps came closer until finally they paused at the top, then they walked into the shop, the creaking floorboards like thundercracks, drowning out Duncan's heartbeat and the tick-ticking of the clock on the wall above him.

Then he saw they *were* boots and he almost choked, clutching at his chest and sucking in what he was convinced would be his last free breath. The boots paused, big and black and shiny, then slowly walked into the shop until they were level with Duncan. He wondered if their owner would be able to see him crouched down, but then he heard another noise. A door creaking open, behind him. Then all hell broke loose.

Leonard shouted for him to run even as the office door was opening and Duncan looked back to see Fazey hanging and knew that whoever was in the room could see him as well and then Leonard said *'Oh Christ, it had to be'* but Duncan was scrambling on his knees towards the end of the table nearest the exit and then there was a stifled scream and it was now or never and he stood up and started for the door but the polished floorboards betrayed his feet and instead he careened into the shelves and fell back onto the floor, his feet above his head, and landed on his coccyx but even as he got up again there was another louder scream and as he rubbed the base of his spine and swore and looked up towards the visitor their eyes met and he himself let out a cry:

'Gwynedd!'

23

'GWYNEDD! WHAT ARE you doing here?'

The girl didn't answer. Instead she continued to stare into the office and at Fazey's corpulent corpse as it continued to revolve slowly.

'Oh, don't worry about that,' he said lamely. 'Why are you here?'

She held up a plastic carrier bag. 'Jane's books. I brought some of them back. To sell. Charity. Oh God . . .'

She started to tremble, then she dropped the bag and started to walk backwards to the stairs. Duncan intercepted her – he could see she might tumble down the stairs – and guided her sideways so that she was against the shelves.

'Look, Gwynedd, I don't want you to get involved in all this. It would be best if you just left.'

'What happened?' she asked, her voice toneless. She was dressed in her regulation black, and her clothing, make-up, pallor – and now her demeanour – made her look as lifeless as Fazey.

'Mr Fazey killed himself,' said Duncan.

'Did you find him?'

Duncan looked at Leonard who nodded.

'Yes. I came to ask him about Jane's books, to see if he knew anything about her and Beaumont and when I came in I found him like that.'

'Have you called the police?'

'No. I was going to leave him.'

Her eyebrow twitched. 'Why?'

'Why?' He looked over at Leonard again.

Leonard shrugged. 'Beats me.'

'Thanks.'

'What?' said Gwynedd, puzzled.

'Thanks . . .' Duncan fumbled for an answer, but everything had caught up with him. 'Oh, thanks nothing.' His world collapsed. *What was the point?* He sat back on the table and buried his head in his hands.

What could he do except wait until he was carted away to explain to Chief Inspector Chater why he was, once again, first on the scene of a suspicious death. His *fourth* suspicious death. God above! Maybe it *would* be better if they locked him up: safer for the public and safer for him, particularly in view of what Fazey had been babbling about.

'Go on,' he said. 'Call the police. I've had enough.'

'No!' shouted Leonard.

'And you can shut up, Leonard. I've just had it. It's over. Get a policeman, Gwynedd. Save yourself a lot of grief, just forget Jane's books, okay? Just say you were curious; it was a bookshop you hadn't been in before.'

There was silence in response. Duncan looked up and saw Gwynedd looking around the shop.

'Who's Leonard? Where is he?' she said anxiously.

'Don't worry about Leonard. You'll not find him. Just go get help.'

She shifted uneasily. 'No, not until you explain.'

'Explain what?'

'Leonard. When you visited me I caught you talking to someone—'

'I told you I talk to myself. Habit. Maybe I'm schizo, maybe just soft in the head. I'm nervous. Wouldn't you be?' He jerked his head at the office. 'Finding someone dead: it's getting to be a habit.'

'What do you mean?'

'Please, Gwynedd, you don't want to know.'

'Oh, but I do.'

'Why? You have no idea what I'm like. I could be a raving – I could have done *that*, strung him up myself! I've already stopped you leaving. Do yourself a favour; go get a policeman.'

'No.'

'Why?' He was exasperated.

'I trust you. You were worried about Jane.'

'Trust me? You stupid girl. I don't give a fuck about Jane. I don't even *know* Jane.'

'What?' She froze.

'I wanted to find out more about Beaumont. A friend was murdered and Beaumont had something to do with it.'

'Well . . .' She was lost, Duncan could tell. 'Why can't the police handle it?'

'Exactly! So go get them.'

All this time Leonard had been quiet, studying Gwynedd. As she seemed on the point of leaving, he spoke up. 'Duncan, the last thing you want is the police. If you can get out of here without being spotted, you've got a chance of sorting things out.'

'"Sorting things out"?' he exploded. 'Sort what out? I've got a piece of paper we can't read which that fat git said means certain death, but he won't say how or who. *Can't*, now. There's bodies all over the place, sick sex . . . I've just had it, and whatever happens I don't want someone like Gwynedd involved – she had enough crap rooming with Jane Dalton.'

'Who are you talking to?' Gwynedd demanded.

'A fucking ghost! *Now* will you leave?' Duncan was at the end of his tether.

The girl was visibly shaken. It seemed to be dawning on her that whatever she might have thought she had seen in Duncan, he was, in fact, rather unstable.

'Don't let her go, Duncan, it'll fuck everything!'

'I'm not stopping her!'

Gwynedd began edging to the exit and Duncan held up his hands as a signal that he wouldn't interfere.

'Duncan!' shrieked Leonard standing in the girl's way. 'Stop her! Convince her!'

'How? How do I convince her?'

'Prove I'm here!'

'How?'

Gwynedd was near to tears, trapped in a room with a lunatic who was bellowing at thin air, for all the world as if someone really was there.

Duncan caught her wild eyes. Oh Jesus . . . 'Gwynedd, I'm sorry. I'm not mad, though it feels like it sometimes . . . I'm being haunted by a man who was murdered just like Beaumont. Until I find out who killed him he's with me all the time.'

'Yes,' she said. Never had the word been used more negatively.

'Duncan, you've got to prove I'm here.'

'All right, all right,' said Duncan to both of them, frantically trying

185

to think of an easy way to prove Leonard's existence. 'Gwynedd, do me a favour. Take any book from the shelf behind you. Any book. I'll go over here,' he said backing round the table towards the office – both to make the one-off experiment work and also to give her the chance to escape should she choose to do so. 'Take a book, turn to any page, point at any sentence and I'll tell you what it is.'

'Pardon?'

'Look, Gwynedd, you're a nice girl, I –

'Don't patronise me.'

'I'm sorry. It's the only way I can prove I'm telling the truth. If I can tell you what you're pointing at, you'll have to admit that it's not just a trick. I won't know what book it is, the page, anything, will I? If I can prove there is a ghost in here with us, will you listen to what else I have to say, to convince you not to get the police?'

'But you just told me—'

'I know, I'm sorry. I need time to think – and I haven't much time. Midnight is all . . . please, do you want to help me or not?'

There was a very long pause as Gwynedd judged the distance to the door and the distance to Duncan. He continued to walk back until she was certain she could escape if she had to.

'All right, just this one chance,' she said, shivering as she eyed the hanging Fazey. She felt behind her and fumbled out a book without taking her eyes off Duncan. She pulled it from the shelf, thumbed it open and pointed at a line half way down the page. Leonard leaned in and read it out.

Duncan repeated it. '"Only the fall on the twenty-first of March was bigger. Dr Hodgson expected the . . ."'

Gwynedd glanced down at the page, let out a little gasp and dropped the book, then hunched up against the shelves as if expecting an attack.

'It's all right,' said Duncan. 'It's all right. His name is Leonard. He read the book when you opened it and told me.'

'You mean . . . you mean like in *Ghost?*'

'Yes, sort of. But it's *true*, Gwynedd. Please believe me. I can see him and hear him, but no-one else can – and he doesn't look like Patrick Swayze.'

'Where is he now?'

'Next to me,' he lied. If he told her that Leonard was standing right beside her she would probably freak.

'I don't think I can take this in . . .' she said.

'Will you let me talk to you about it? Explain? If you still think I'm mad, you can walk away.'

'Talk about it now?'

'Yes, now – but not here. Somewhere else. Somewhere safe for you.'

'Safe?'

'Gwynedd, I could be a homicidal maniac. Look at Mr Fazey. Leave now and go to . . . go to the Deep Pan Pizza on Oriel Street; know where it is? Right. I'll join you in a couple of minutes. Find a booth if you can; somewhere we can talk but where I can't do anything. If you ever feel I'm dangerous, just get up and leave or call a waiter or scream, anything. I don't want to hurt you, Gwynedd, but I need to explain to someone. If you'll let me.'

She nodded. 'Deep Pan Pizza?'

'Yes. Five minutes. If there's anyone downstairs in the alley, just leave like nothing's happened. Difficult, I know, but . . .'

She nodded again and made to pick up her bag.

'Leave the books. That way you're shot of them whatever happens, okay?'

Gwynedd walked to the stairs then ran down and out the shop door.

'You'll not see her again,' said Leonard.

'No thanks to you.'

'You wanted her to call the police, for God's sake!'

'No, not for His sake; for my sake. If there's some loon out there killing people and I'm locked up in police custody, he's not going to get me, whatever that piece of paper or Fazey says.'

'So what now?' said Leonard.

'We leave and see if she went to the pizza place.'

'I hope she is in the Deep Pan, or we're in deep shit.'

'We're not already?' groaned Duncan as his groin stabbed a reminder of Fazey's assault.

'Where have you been, Duncan?' said Mrs Cantrill from the kitchen.

'Out. Town,' said Duncan, unable to tell what kind of mood his mother was in. 'Dad?'

'Malaysia. Four days. Come here.'

Uh-oh, a summons. Usually she let Duncan settle before talking to him.

His mother was standing at the cooker, watching a pan of soup. Another diet. He sat down and waited for the interrogation.

'What did Mr Phelps say at the college?'

Leonard peered closely at Duncan's mother. 'Oh dear, she's about to sort you out, Duncan. Better tell the truth.'

'The truth?' spluttered Duncan, thinking back over the last thirty-six hours.

'Yes,' said his mother. 'The truth.'

'I, er, didn't see him.'

'Go on.' It was clearly a dare to him to enter the minefield of her wrath. Duncan would have to tread very carefully.

Leonard was about to speak but decided instead to let Duncan handle it for himself. Besides, he'd never been much good at handling his own mother.

Duncan tried to work out a plausible story about Mr Phelps being out but it was more than likely Phelps had spoken to his mother and confirmed his total ignorance of Duncan's teaching ambitions. Worse than that, of course, would have been the fact that his mother would have been made to look stupid and, the Education Committee being the way it was, soon all would know about the communication breakdown between the Chair and her son.

'I was lying. Sorry. There's this girl . . .' (And sorry, Gwynedd.) 'At the college. I've been seeing her and I didn't want you to send me away, so I made up the . . .'

'You lied to me.'

'If you want to put it that way, yes.'

'What other way is there to put it? I don't think you realise just how pleased I was when you said you were thinking of training to be a teacher. To say I am disappointed . . .'

Oh shit. Her voice had dropped, always a bad sign: Duncan really was in for it.

Leonard could sense the atmosphere and tried to joke about it. 'Get ready to duck, she's armed with hot soup.'

Duncan managed to still his tongue and walked over to his mother. 'I'm sorry. I have been thinking about it, honestly, but I said too much too quick.'

'You just used me as a taxi to see your, your—'

'No! I told a white lie – a premature truth – and couldn't get out of it. If I'd refused the lift you'd have wondered why.'

Duncan could see his mother's grip on the saucepan handle tense then relax.

'So do you *ever* intend talking to Mr Phelps?' she said.

'Yes. I will ring him and make an appointment. Promise.'

'And this girl?'

'What?'

'Who is she? Her parents? Local?'

'No. They're . . . from Wales.'

The hand tightened again. His mother did not like the Welsh. Why hadn't he lied? Indeed, why wasn't he lying? Was it wishful thinking, that by saying so it might come true?

'I think her father's retired.'

'What from? The pit?'

His mother could be spectacularly prejudiced when she wanted to be. Asians, Irish, Jews, Americans, even the French – Mrs Cantrill never had a bad word for them. But the Welsh and Italians, well, the gorge rose at a frightening rate. Duncan had never found out why.

'I think he was a teacher.'

'And what's her name, this girl?'

'Gwynedd.'

'I suppose she can speak Welsh.'

'No,' Duncan lied. He wanted this discussion over as soon as possible – he did, after all, have more to worry about than his mother's prejudices, not least a midnight date with God knew who.

'How long have you been seeing her?'

'A month or so.'

'You never mentioned her.'

'I was too busy being ill. Remember?'

'There's no need for that tone.'

'Sorry.'

'I've done my best. You have been extraordinarily difficult, Duncan.'

'I know and I'm sorry. But I'm over it now and I give you my word that I intend to "pull myself together". (Using one of her own phrases wasn't exactly subtle but it seemed to dissuade her from pursuing the matter.)

'I do hope so.'

She turned the hob off and poured the soup into a bowl. 'I'm going to take a shower and then I'm going to the Operatic Society: final dress rehearsal. Could overrun.'

'Okay.'

Duncan watched his mother go upstairs. It was only as he heard her bedroom door close that it occurred to him that she might never see him again, or he her.

'Leonard, what are we going to do about tonight?'

'Does your dad have any guns.'

'What?'

'Guns. You know, boom sticks. Twelve bores, pistols . . .'

'Yes, he does. Shotguns, double-barrelled. For shooting clay pigeons, I think. Why?'

'You never know, Duncan.'

What Duncan did know was that sometime soon his mother would be out and he could set the alarms, put the garden floodlights on, double-lock everything and cocoon himself somewhere in the lounge with a clear view of any assailant – and the shotguns would certainly afford him some bargaining power. Having a mobile phone to hand would also be a good idea, the re-dial button programmed to 999.

He walked into the lounge and flicked on the TV. Local news, but after ten minutes there had been no mention of a suicide in Ollington so he switched off. However, as Leonard reminded him, suicides usually weren't news unless they were very young or very public. So he sat and waited in silence, his mind running through the possibilities, hoping deep down that Gwynedd had decided to save him from himself; he was secretly waiting for the doorbell to ring and for it to be the police. Mind you, thinking back, he had done a very convincing job of proving Leonard's existence to Gwynedd over the course of the two hours they had been together at the Deep Pan Pizza.

It had started with her scribbling messages on her napkin while Duncan looked the other way, and had then progressed to listing the contents of her handbag, telling her what salad she had chosen at the salad bar before seeing it, and reading from the newspaper on sale outside the pizza parlour.

She had taken it extremely well, considering, and it wasn't until Leonard gave Duncan a wink that he began to see why she wasn't running in terror. She liked him. This was unusual; most girls thought his appearance the result of substance abuse, or he would fumble his chat-up lines and come over as an inept idiot.

'She fancies you, Duncan,' confirmed Leonard during a lull. 'Can hear her juicing up from here.'

Duncan coughed his Pepsi back into his glass. 'You gross bastard! One more crack like that—' but Leonard was smirking and Gwynedd was looking puzzled.

'You don't want to know,' explained Duncan. 'He's an extremely disgusting individual.'

'Charming,' said Leonard.

Duncan stared at the still uneasy Gwynedd. He liked her too. A lot. She was cute, despite her attempts to conceal the fact. Cuddly and cute. What some might see as a weight problem he saw as extra squeezability; what others might find social naivety, he saw as appealing shyness. In any other circumstances, this could have been the start of something special; if she liked him half as much as he liked her, they could have been a couple very soon. But then his predicament reared its ugly head again.

Having proven Leonard's existence – or at least Gwynedd had given the impression she believed the ghost was real – Duncan had then told her the whole sordid story, and once he had started he hadn't stopped, even though he could see from her expression just how deep he had managed to submerge himself in filth. Even as he had raved on, he remembered parties he had attended where, too pissed to care, he had regaled his intended paramours with tales of wanking contests at school and Jimmy Piggot's ignited farts and the time they had caught Vince the coach driver with a sheep on a school geography trip: their glazed expressions had soon matched his – and without the aid of alcohol.

Eventually Leonard had pointed out that Gwynedd's initial curiosity had dissolved into a growing horror. The tale that tumbled uncensored from Duncan's mouth had soon become the aural equivalent of date rape: she didn't want to hear any more and Duncan simply wouldn't shut up. Only the cold-eyed glaring of the waiters and Leonard's insistent demands that he cool it and shut up silenced Duncan's verbal diarrhoea. And so, as he was paying at the till, Gwynedd had slipped out the door and hurried into the rush-hour crowds. Duncan hadn't been able to find her and had made his disconsolate way home.

Not content with being haunted by a dead salesman, or being in the middle of the hunt for a serial killer who had targeted him for midnight, he had now alienated his only potential ally and – so the stirring in his trousers had told him as he had taken sneaky glances at her body – maybe even a potential girlfriend. To say he was having a bad day would be a gross understatement. Then, to top it all, his mother had been in.

Mrs Cantrill had taken a taxi – 'might be drinkies' – a little after 8.30, leaving Duncan to his thoughts. Leonard left him to them as well. Much as he wanted a resolution to his problem, it was obvious he had dragged the kid into a situation he couldn't cope with: guilt began to gnaw at him as terror gnawed at Duncan.

Time passed. Duncan found himself dozing, the tension of the previous night and that afternoon sapping his strength. He was tired, so tired. All he wanted to do was sleep; to slope off up to his bedroom, slip between the sheets and –

No! Stay awake, stay alert! There's serious shit going down, you've got to be ready. But to rest . . . to drift off into that other world where there were no problems, no blood, no –

'Wake up!' yelled Leonard.

Duncan jerked upright, his eyes wide, cold sweat on his face. God, what time? 9.40. Must stay awake. Watch the clock. Tick. Be ready. Tick. Stay awake. Tick. Stay. Tick. Awake. Tick. Stay. Tick. Awake. Tick tick tick . . .

The doorbell rang, its two-tone chime jabbing at the quiet like the clatter of dustbin lids in a dark alley. Duncan jumped anew at the noise, then tried to dissolve into the couch. He looked at the clock. 10.14. *10.14!*

'Well?' said Leonard.

'Well what?' gasped Duncan, his heart threatening to beat its way out of his chest.

'Aren't you going to answer it?'

Duncan laughed.

'It's only quarter past ten,' said Leonard. 'It could be anyone.'

'Precisely,' said Duncan.

The bell chimed twice more.

'Got to answer it,' said Leonard. 'Besides, I don't think murderers use doorbells.'

'Not funny. Remember, you've got nothing to lose. I'm the one whose heart is still beating.'

'Sorry. Have you got a spyhole in the door?'

'Yes.'

'Go look through it.'

Duncan did as asked. Truth to tell, he was on automatic pilot. The last half hour he had been staring at the clock as if hypnotised, counting down the minutes to, well, he didn't know what, but his mind had made too many guesses at any one of a hundred fates.

He edged his way to the front door and cautiously peeked through the spyhole, then quickly unlocked it and let Gwynedd in, slamming the door behind her and bolting it.

'What are you doing here? We said we'd meet tomorrow.'

'And read about what happened in the paper?'

'That's what I like, a positive attitude.'

'She's just positive you're doomed,' said Leonard.

'Leonard, shut up. Look, Gwynedd, we had an—'

'Look,' she said, holding out a book. 'It's Jane's diary. The police dropped it off; asked me to pass it on to her father. Well, we know that's a waste of time, so I've been looking through it.'

'Invite her in,' said Leonard. 'See if she needs a drink.'

'But the time?'

Leonard said: 'Midnight, kiddo. I was on the job till the last minute. Plenty of time to get rid of her before then.'

'Don't worry about the time,' she said, thinking Duncan was talking to her.

'Oh, you'd better come in to the lounge, then,' said Duncan. 'Do you want a drink?'

'Diet Coke'd do,' she said.

He watched her walk into the lounge. She was dressed as ever in black, but wore tight jeans instead of a long skirt and under her coat she wore a tight black jumper. The girl had curves. Leonard spotted Duncan's interest but Duncan silenced him with a finger.

One Diet Coke later – Duncan was too edgy to drink – they were scanning Jane's diary.

'As you can see,' said Gwynedd, 'most of it's empty and what's there is appointments, lectures and stuff. Except for one night each month where there's a big black dot.' (Leonard confirmed the dates as those of the ceremonies.) 'And there's these entries the week she died. Obviously it meant nothing to the police but I thought it might mean something to you. Or Leonard.' She looked around the room.

'He's sitting opposite,' said Duncan. 'You know, I can't believe you believe he's there.' He put the diary down.

'It took some . . . when I left the Deep Pan I had every intention of never seeing you again. What you had done in there had to be some kind of sick trick, and the story you told me was just so weird, so . . . frightening. I . . . well, I went back and sat and thought about it and I realised what you had done *couldn't* have been a trick. I think the thing that confirmed it was when you read out the letter from my mother. I hadn't even read it myself – it had been in a sealed envelope, remember? There was no way you could have . . . anyway, when I had convinced myself you were telling the truth I remembered all the other stuff you had told me and then the police dropped off the diary.'

'You'd think they'd have kept that longer; tied it in with Beaumont at least,' said Duncan.

'No,' said Leonard. 'The girl's death was a suicide; everyday routine stuff: case closed.'

'Leonard says they wouldn't be worrying about Jane now. She committed suicide.'

'Suppose so,' said Gwynedd. 'So, this is what I found. There were two entries, one I can guess at, one I don't understand. On the Wednesday before she died she's written: "*D showed me paper he's giving to bastard PD. Says it will fix him.*" Next day she's written: '*PD! God!*' The day after that she hanged herself. This is probably why they gave it back: if I was a policeman and knowing she was a student I would just assume that meant D was giving someone a test or an exam. It means nothing.'

'Exactly,' said Duncan. 'It probably does mean that.'

Leonard said: 'You can be one thick twat when you want.'

'What?'

Gwynedd continued her explanation. '"*D*" could be David Beaumont. "Paper" could be the thing you've got and "FPD" someone Beaumont didn't like.'

'And the "*PD! God!*" means he's dead and she's realised what Beaumont said would happen actually happened?'

'And the next day she kills herself,' said Leonard. 'Couldn't cope with it.'

'Next day she killed herself, because she couldn't cope with it,' repeated Duncan.

'Yes. Maybe,' said Gwynedd.

Duncan sat back. 'So who's PD and why's he a bastard?'

Gwynedd shrugged. 'Can't think of a PD.'

'He's probably someone who fucked Jane at one of the ceremonies,' said Leonard. 'Maybe she didn't like it or he did something weird.'

'Leonard says he may be someone she met at the orgies and didn't like. Good enough reason; there were some real creeps there,' he said, smiling at Leonard. 'When did he die?'

'The eighth.'

'That's a Tuesday. The *Courier* comes out Thursday afternoon. Mum keeps every copy because it has reports on her Education Committee, and she likes to keep track of what other counsellors say.' He stood up. 'Couple of weeks back she got all excited because one of the Labour guys contradicted something he'd said eighteen months ago!'

He dashed upstairs. Five minutes later he had the *Couriers* for the 10th and 17th from his mother's filing cabinet. They went through the issue of the 10th first, looking for any deaths involving someone with the initials PD.

Gwynedd spotted it first. 'It's in the Stop Press. Peter Donaldson, a bookmaker, was found drowned on the banks of the Wealot River on Thursday morning. No other details. Police refuse to say if the death is suspicious.'

'They'll follow that up won't they?' suggested Leonard.

Duncan found the subsequent story in the next week's issue: STRANGE DEATH OF BOOKMAKER. Uh-oh, *'strange'* . . .

'Peter Donaldson, 46, a bookmaker with two betting shops in Ollington, was found dead on the bank of the Wealot by two anglers just after 6am on Thursday morning. The post-mortem found cause of death to be drowning; the odd thing was he was actually found on the bank and not in the river.'

'Washed up?'

'No, he was at least ten feet from the water. He couldn't have crawled out and drowned, so he must have been fished out. Police believe someone was there, rescued him but, when they found him dead, panicked and ran.'

'Odd. Who would panic?'

'Someone who didn't want to be there,' said Leonard.

'Like?' said Duncan.

'Pardon?' said Gwynedd.

'Sorry, Leonard was about to suggest who could have been with him.'

'Three possibilities: he was having an affair and the woman freaked; he was gay and his boyfriend did it or didn't want the world to know what he and Peter were up to; or he was with a hooker who likewise didn't want any trouble.'

'He says it could have been an affair, a prostitute or he was gay
and none of them wanted to get involved. Or maybe one of them
did it themselves. Or a business rival; you know, gangsters. Or . . .
or it was whoever Fazey wouldn't tell us about. But given that Jane
says Beaumont was going to give him a piece of paper, and we know
Racimo and Leonard also got one and were killed, it seems pretty
conclusive.'

'Pretty conclusive you're in the same trouble as they were?' said
Gwynedd. 'Sorry. Didn't mean it to sound . . .'

'She's right,' said Leonard. 'Me, Racimo, this Donaldson, probably Beaumont . . . and if Kimmel knew what the paper meant,
his reaction makes sense. And Fazey certainly didn't want to get
involved, did he?'

Duncan sat back and shivered. The clock ticked to 10.35. Less
than an hour and a half until . . . until what?

He turned to Gwynedd who he found had sat right next to him.
She was warm, smelled nice, a comfort; in any other circumstances
he'd have had a boner as big as his hopes, but now was not the
time. 'You'd better go. If anything is—'

'No. I didn't just come to bring you the diary. I'm also here
because I still feel guilty about not helping Jane.'

'We've been through all that—'

'I know I'm useless with people. Too stand-offish. If I'd been
friendlier towards her, maybe . . . I mean, look at me now. I'm
sitting here quite happy to accept your word there's a ghost here
with us. If I can accept that from you – someone I've only known
a few hours – why couldn't I get close enough to Jane to help her?
We roomed together for six months, for heaven's sake. If I'd . . .
anyway, that's one, and you can't argue me out of it. The other,
well, I don't know how to . . . I was hoping you wouldn't be in,
actually. Just tell me one thing: why, when you're expecting someone
dangerous to come and see you at midnight, you're sat here?'

'What?'

'You could be hiding anywhere, but you're home. He knows
where you live, so why are you here? Is it part of a plan?'

'When you come to think of it, that's not a bad question,' said
Leonard.

'So why didn't you think of it?'

Five minutes later, Duncan had located the spare car keys and they
were driving away in Mrs Cantrill's BMW, the shotgun in the boot.

'We'll drop you at the college,' said Duncan. 'Then Leonard and I will find somewhere to hide out. Unless we're being followed, there's no way whoever it is could find us.'

'Sounds fine by me, except the dropping me off bit,' said Gwynedd. 'I told you I want to stay.'

Duncan didn't answer. Instead he drove across town to the college, only speaking again as he drew to a halt outside the college gates.

'I'll call you tomorrow,' he said.

'Tomorrow? So why am I getting out?' she asked logically. 'If nothing's going to happen?'

'What I mean—'

'Duncan, someone's following us,' said Leonard.

'What?'

Leonard pointed out the back window from where he sat in the rear seat.

Duncan checked his mirrors. True, there was a car pulled in on the other side of the road at the bus stop, but so what?

'It stopped when we stopped,' said Leonard.

'Might be dropping someone off.'

'And it might not. It might be after us or it might be some perv after a girl. It's a big campus . . .'

Gwynedd agreed, though plainly because she wanted to stay in the car rather than from fear of attack should she leave.

'So what do we do?'

'I could go take a look,' said Leonard. 'Keep your hand out of the window and I'll look into their car.'

Duncan explained what Leonard was doing. It seemed to impress her, as if Leonard had a use. But, unfortunately, her faith was misplaced.

'There's a fucking disco in there. Four kids, maybe teenagers, definitely eyeing up this car.'

'They could be hired by whoever,' said Duncan. 'We'd better drive on.'

'You should,' said Leonard, looking at the clock. 11.03.

But there was no shaking the car behind them. It followed them for over twenty minutes, even though they drove around a housing estate at random. Duncan accelerated out onto the by-pass, wound the car up to sixty but was dismayed to see the other car keeping pace with him.

'What now?'

'First chance you get, take a turn and keep turning. If they stay with us, get back into the centre of town and park near the police station. Even if it's not who we think it is, it could be bad news anyway. Carjackers, for one.'

'Carjackers?' said Duncan.

'Carjackers?' said Gwynedd.

Leonard explained to Duncan, who passed the information on to Gwynedd (without thinking how much it might scare her), that the car could contain a bunch of yobs who, first chance they could, would overtake their BMW and force them to stop, then they'd pile out armed with bats or knives and take the car away from them, either for fun or for profit.

'In Ollington?' said Duncan.

'Hey, you mean that town without strange murders or suicides?' said Leonard sarcastically.

Duncan shut up and concentrated on driving, his nerves just about frazzled.

Unfortunately, wherever Duncan drove, the Escort XR3 followed and it was inevitable that Duncan's fear would force him to make an error. It happened at the last roundabout on the by-pass: he took the third right instead of the fourth right and, instead of driving back into town, found himself heading out into the countryside on a road that ran a good ten miles before the next town. And still the XR3 followed.

Terror coursed through him, and reached new heights when he saw the dashboard clock reach 11.40.

'Oh God, where do we go?'

'You've got to get back. Got to turn round,' said Gwynedd.

'I will, I will, when I find a proper turn off.'

'Well, get ahead of them enough they don't see you turn.'

For once Duncan was glad to have a backseat driver. Luckily the road started to wind as it headed towards Leek. After a couple of minutes an opportunity presented itself and Duncan slewed the car down a dark lane, switched off the lights and slowed so they could see out of the back window, his foot on the accelerator, his hand on the light switch, ready to let rip if the other car followed.

There was an agonising pause during which Duncan was sure the car behind them was slowing to take the turn but then there was a blur of lights – white-red – and it was gone. He drove on slowly, all the time his eyes on the mirror, expecting the car to reappear, but it didn't.

'Okay,' said Leonard, 'let's turn this round and get back to town. There's still time.'

Duncan was all for doing as he was told. They motored for about half a mile before Gwynedd spotted a turning point, the entrance to a field.

Duncan stopped, reversed the car back towards the gate, then slipped into Drive and pressed the accelerator. Nothing happened. He pressed harder. The engine roared and the wheels whined but still nothing happened.

He stepped out and found the back of the car was stuck in mud and the wheels had dug themselves in deep – and there wasn't even room to reverse back out of it: the gate was in the way.

He stooped into the car door. 'It's stuck. Mud. I don't know what to do.'

Gwynedd stepped out of the car and Leonard joined them.

'We'll either have to open the gate and try reversing further to get a run through the mud, or get some stuff under the wheels for grip.'

'Try the gate,' said Leonard. 'It's quicker.'

Gwynedd unhooked the rope holding the gate. 'Oh bugger,' she said. 'It opens outwards.'

Duncan banged his head on the roof of the car. 'Okay, something under the wheels then.'

He and Gwynedd gathered branches and clumps of dry grass and forced them under the wheels. Leonard suggested Gwynedd push the car and when Duncan told her this she readily agreed, despite it meaning standing in mud up to her ankles.

Duncan took it really slow and for a brief moment the car moved forward, but then something slipped and the car's wheels dug in even further and mud was blasted against the gate, just missing Gwynedd.

Duncan gave up. The clock said 11.50. He switched off the engine but kept the lights on, then clambered out, removed the shotgun from the boot, and got back in. Gwynedd climbed into the passenger seat and they shut the doors.

By now Duncan was in a blind panic, his mind seeing only blood and pain. He was incapable of coherent speech, his eyes locked on the clock before him.

'Snap out of it!' shouted Leonard, himself feeling an old fear he couldn't place.

'Duncan, Duncan, talk to me!' ordered Gwynedd, but she could get no response.

Duncan pulled the piece of paper from his inside pocket and stared at it, his hands shaking uncontrollably. He could feel his bladder stretching, ready to release at the slightest provocation. It came. He caught a movement in the rear mirror: a face, a shape, *something*.

He shrieked, pissed himself and raised the shotgun, but its barrel hit the side window and all he could do was clunk it impotently against the glass.

'Behind!' he screamed.

Gwynedd instinctively ducked, but Leonard looked straight behind them. There *was* something there. He too felt like screaming, but he took a moment to study the apparition.

It was a horse.

'It's a horse!' he shouted, but Duncan wouldn't hear him – and Gwynedd couldn't. 'Duncan, it's a fucking horse!'

Duncan slowly turned to look at him, his finger twitching on the shotgun triggers.

'It's a horse, a frigging gee-gee. Be careful, or you'll shoot out the bloody window!'

Duncan looked in the mirror and slowly relaxed his finger. *Shit a brick . . .*

He looked over his shoulder. 'It's a horse . . .?'

Gwynedd looked over the back seat and saw it as well.

All at once Duncan was out of the car. He ran back to the horse which was bathed red by the car's rear lights. The startled creature whinnied and stepped back into the darkness.

'Don't go,' said Duncan, as if it was some protective talisman.

Gwynedd joined him and she kissed air and cajoled the horse back to them. It was big and dark and old; probably retired and living out its days in the field.

Gwynedd patted its nose, its nostrils flaring steam into their faces. It was comforting, like a giant teddy bear. Duncan's tension eased, and he pointed the gun to the ground. Leonard joined them.

'Five minutes, Duncan,' he reminded. 'Here's as good as any-where. It'll have to be, anyway. Keep the gun handy, I'll watch out.' Leonard walked into the road and looked up and down the lane.

Duncan surveyed their defences. A high hedge ran both sides of the lane, the car's headlights shining across onto the opposite verge. Any traffic would be visible for quite a distance, and behind them was the high gate and the horse but, beyond it, the inky blackness of another moonless country night filled the world.

'Good thing he's here,' said Gwynedd nodding at the horse.

'Why?' said Duncan, his voice as shaky as his hand as it stroked the horse's nose.

'Anyone comes, he'll react,' she said. 'Like a guard dog.'

Duncan nodded. It wasn't much comfort.

Gwynedd suddenly hugged him, her body trembling, her eyes darting left and right, but the familiarity was lost on him.

'Nothing coming, Dunc—' Leonard stopped mid-sentence.

Duncan spun round. Leonard wasn't there.

'Leonard! Leonard?'

There was no response.

'Oh God, no,' said Duncan, pushing Gwynedd away so that he could raise the gun again.

'What? What's wrong?'

'Leonard's gone! The only time that's happened before is when there's something bad.' His mind rewound to Beaumont's boat and his run-in with the cats. 'Oh God,' he said. 'I'm going to be sick . . .'

'No!' Gwynedd said. 'You've got to get through this. Face it, whatever it is. Do what you can, just don't give up.'

'Yes, but what? What the fuck can I do? I've got the paper, whatever that means. All we know is Fazey said it was a death sentence.'

'Think. What did Fazey say exactly?'

'I don't fucking—'

'Yes, you do. Now think! *Think!*'

'He said . . . I had willingly accepted it. And he kept saying he didn't want it. Whenever I tried to give it to him he freaked out. Almost as if . . .'

'As if what it said could be passed on? Like a disease?'

'He certainly got het up about it.'

'So if you'd given it to him and he'd taken it, he'd be the one pissing his pants now?'

'Yes, but it's rubbish! He's out there somewhere, whoever the bastard is, with a gun or a knife and he's—' But Gwynedd wasn't listening.

'The horse!' she suddenly shouted.

Duncan spun round, smacking her in the face with the barrel of the shotgun. For a split-second he thought it would go off and he jerked it back away from her, his heart banging in his chest.

'S – sorry!' He peed himself some more as he aimed the gun at the ground.

Gwynedd pulled an object from her pocket, then threw away something shiny. 'Quick, wrap your paper round this!'

Duncan pulled out his piece of paper and did as he was told, his mind now beyond reasoned action, his terror for himself overlaid with the horror of having nearly blasted Gwynedd in the face.

'Now give it to the horse!'

He walked over to the animal, not questioning his bizarre action, and held out the chocolate wrapped in his paper.

Initially the horse shied away but then curiosity took over and it came snuffling up to his hand. After a couple of tentative licks it bared its teeth and pushed its mouth into his hand, scooped up the chocolate and chewed it, paper and all, then swallowed it.

Gwynedd then clapped her hands and shooed the horse away. At first it thought it was part of the feeding game, but then it took fright at the flapping and cantered away into the dark, its horsy breaths disappearing into the crisp night.

'Now what?' said Duncan unable to appreciate what they had just done or why.

'We wait,' she said, checking her watch.

They edged closer in the ominously bloody light from the car's tail lights, Duncan holding the gun at the ready, his finger on both triggers. He knew he would have no time to finesse one shot then a second; it would have to be both barrels, so he would have to be certain he had the fucker in his sights before—

The horse let out a terrified whinny somewhere behind them, a noise that goosepimpled their flesh. They hugged for warmth and comfort like frightened children during a thunderstorm as the horse whinnied again. Then there was a horrible squeal from the animal, high-pitched and desperate, followed by a soft thud and then silence. They both looked edgily towards the field but all they could see was eerie darkness in all directions. They both started at a thrashing noise, somewhere off in the field to their right, then silence reigned again.

They turned back to the lane. No sounds, no other lights and still no Leonard. Then the wind began to blow, rustling the trees and hedges, its sound like the rushing of water; a freezing wind that made them shiver and seemed to worm its way under their clothes and into their very pores, as if they had both been dunked in iced water. So cold was the chilly blast that Duncan's hand could no longer stand the touch of the shotgun's metal and he dropped it, but neither cared about their sudden lack of defence: the cold was all-encompassing, encroaching even into their minds, its blackness treading on their thoughts.

Then just as suddenly as it came, it was gone and they both fell to their knees gasping for breath, the air alive with the spiralled plumes of their breath.

Duncan grabbed for the gun but it was iced and it stung his fingers. The side of the car was the same, but he forced himself to pull the door open. Then he saw the clock. 12.04 – and they were alive.

It took them both five minutes to rub each other warm, hugging and holding and crying with relief and fear at what had happened.

Another couple of minutes of sitting in the car with the heater blasting full power and Leonard reappeared in the back, his face pained and sorrowful.

'What happened?' he asked.

'Gwynedd made me give the paper to the horse. Then there was this really cold wind and everything iced up and then . . . where were you?'

'I don't know. It just went black, like I fainted. There was something evil . . . I can't be near it. Like that cellar and the boat . . . I'm sorry but there was nothing . . .'

'The horse,' said Gwynedd. 'What happened to the horse?'

'I don't know,' said Duncan. 'And I don't want to know.'

'But we have to know,' said Gwynedd.

'She's right,' said Leonard. 'I'll go look, if I can. But I need you to be in sight Duncan.'

Duncan climbed onto the boot of the BMW and pointed the torch at his chest, a human lighthouse for Leonard. He watched as the man walked across the field into darkness, his disappearing act pointless as he didn't know where he was looking. After a minute or so, he came back.

'Can't see anything. Too dark. You're going to have to come yourself.'

Duncan felt his knees trembling and found it difficult to get back down off the car, nearly falling into the mud.

'You wait here,' he told Gwynedd.

'You've got to be joking!' she said, looking up and down the road. 'I'm staying with you.'

'But we might find . . . there could be . . .'

'And you want me to stay *here?* On my own?'

There was no argument. They climbed over the rickety gate and set off into the field, darkness soon enveloping them, their world a thin beam of light.

'Why are we doing this?' Duncan asked Leonard.

'Because we have to know. If something happened to the horse we have to know what.'

'But why would they attack a horse just because I gave it the piece of paper?'

'Exactly,' said Gwynedd.

Her comment stopped Duncan in his tracks.

'But that doesn't make sense,' said Duncan, the shaking torch beam betraying his hands.

'Does any of this?' said Leonard, passing his hand through the torch.

They walked on, Duncan sweeping the torch from side to side, praying the beam wouldn't alight on anything more sinister than horse droppings. But it did.

The first thing they saw were the teeth. Just that, the teeth. The horse's lower jaw had been ripped off, the tongue next to it, like a fat man's arm. To its left the torchlight found the rest of the head, the skin ravaged to the bone by deep slashes, one mad eye staring. The rest of the horse lay ten yards further on, its insides strewn about like wrapping paper on a Christmas morning, steaming into the night, its fetid smell insinuating itself into their noses and throats like the questing fingers of some rancid pervert.

The poor horse had been slashed to death; slashed and cut to ribbons, through tissue and muscle, then decapitated and its head smashed. Duncan found he couldn't take the light off the horse's belly, with its coils of pink and purple offal, thin vapours drifting into the cold night air like smoke from some hideous stew. It reminded him of the dog – how long ago had that been? God, just last night . . .

He fell to his knees, the torch tumbling from his hand and landing so that the beam illuminated the gaping rawness of the horse's neck, dark blood black in the black night, the grass stained and matted as if by spilled paint.

Gwynedd let out a little cry, a noise of distress, then threw up, apologising between every retch. *Sorry, sorry, sorry*, she gasped, as if she had killed the horse.

Duncan thought he would also be sick but for some reason his stomach refused. He was beyond mere physical reaction; his senses had been battered to numbness, his mind taking comfort in gratitude for his survival. *That could have been me*, he told himself, *that could have been me*.

Leonard watched his two companions, unable to say anything of use, then realised he was struggling to be with them. A blackness approached, his vision greyed, his thoughts . . .

He found himself back at the car, his only point of reference a small point of light in the distance, like a single full point on a black computer screen. The night was silent still, except for distant apologies and oaths. He turned away and stared at the car.

What had it come to? He should have stayed in the room, stayed out of people's lives. Whoever had killed him and why was not enough reason to endanger the lives of Duncan and Gwynedd. They were good kids – Duncan a bit messed up but he'd get over it – and now they had missed death by a matter of moments – and no thanks to him. And still they were no closer to solution. All those deaths, all that fear . . . if he could have wept he would have.

Duncan forced himself to his feet and walked unsteadily over to Gwynedd. She had stopped vomiting, but her apologies continued. He crouched down and put his hand round her shoulder and he too began to apologise. She hugged him and wept into his chest. He patted her back and lied that it would be all right, that it was over now.

But he knew it wasn't over. He knew that he had now stepped over some boundary; he had gone too far and the only way out would be to carry on until he found the answer.

Or until the answer found him.

PART THREE

Incantations

What is a weed? A plant whose virtues have not been discovered.
Ralph Waldo Emerson

24

ONCE THEY HAD got over the shock of finding the dead horse, they had gone back to the car and, amid a torrent of oaths and frantic scrambling, had managed to reverse the car back far enough to drop a large branch under the rear wheels. It had given the car something to climb before it fell into the mud again, but its momentum was enough for it to shoot forward across the lane and bury its nose in the hedge on the opposite side of the road. Duncan had then reversed back onto the road and driven them back into town. It was Leonard who had suggested Gwynedd's room on campus.

'There's no way I can break this gently, Duncan, so pull the car over and listen.'

Duncan eased the car over into a side street and pulled up behind a Transit van. It belonged to a company called 'Rippers', but he was still too numbed to react to the irony.

'What happened back there was unnatural, understand? It was not a gang of car thieves or a hired assassin or some pissed-off dog fucker. It was occult.'

Duncan paraphrased what Leonard had said.

'Supernatural?' offered Gwynedd, her first words since the attack.

'Yes, supernatural. Some *thing* did that, not somebody,' said Leonard. 'Get that clear. Some unnatural force was called up by that piece of paper and sent to kill you. Instead it killed the horse. Just passing on the paper doomed the poor animal.'

'Oh shit.'

'Precisely, but it's worse than that: whoever gave you that paper has got to be stopped; look how many people have died. Now, some of them may have deserved it but you didn't, Duncan, so how many others are there?'

'But we don't know who gave it to me.'

'We'll have to find out – and for that we have one advantage.'

'We have an advantage?'

'Whoever it is thinks you're dead,' said Leonard.

'That's an advantage?' said Duncan.

'What?' said Gwynedd.

'He says the man thinking I'm dead is an advantage.'

'Yes. Unless he finds out you're alive, he's not going to be after you, is he?' explained Leonard.

'Meaning?'

'Meaning we can still try and find him.'

'Oh no, I'm not looking for him any more. That's it, that horse, all this . . . I don't care if you're here till doomsday, Leonard, we . . . I'm not doing anything more. There's a loony out there topping people with curses? Tough. He wants to kill animals? Fine. He wants to cut the heads off paedophiles? No problem. Each to his own.'

'Duncan, think it through,' said Leonard. 'Look, I don't want to piss on your chips but *the guy knows who you are.* And as soon as he finds out you didn't snuff it, he's not only going to come after you again, but he's going to want to know *how* you got away with it – and the only way you could get away with it is if you knew how to, and *that* makes you even more dangerous to him than some kid who saw him gutting an alsatian.'

'I don't know what Leonard's saying,' said Gwynedd watching Duncan's reaction to the empty back seat. 'But if the man finds out you're not dead, he'll try again. He has to, now we know how it was done.'

Duncan rubbed his forehead. 'Shut up, the pair of you. I don't care any more.'

'Well, that's tough,' said Gwynedd, getting annoyed. 'I'm in this crap as well now. Leonard, that horse, the man in the bookshop. When whoever's behind this finds out you've cheated him he's going to get you, but as long as he thinks you're dead, you're okay.'

'So how do I pretend to be dead? Get fake scars? Arrange a funeral? Put a notice in the paper?'

Gwynedd slapped him across the face. 'Sorry. Just calm down and stop acting like a prat. If you go home, he'll know you survived, so you keep out of sight instead.'

'Where?'

'Her place,' said Leonard.

'The college?' said Duncan.

'Yes!' said Gwynedd. 'You can stay there while we try and find out what to do.'

'And Duncan,' said Leonard. 'Don't call your mother. You are officially dead, or at least missing. You've got to keep it that way.'

'But the car?'

Leonard laughed. 'You stole the bloody thing, why get guilty now?'

'The car?' said Gwynedd.

Duncan explained Leonard's plan. To his surprise Gwynedd agreed wholeheartedly – and that was why they had parked the BMW in the furthest reaches of Ollington College of Education's main car park and made their way up to Gwynedd's room.

Supping tea they tried to formulate a plan, but too much had happened and, despite their fear, Gwynedd and Duncan soon succumbed to sleep, he on the couch, she on her bed. Leonard had protested that they should stay awake, that there was work to be done, but he realised he hadn't a clue what to do, so he let them rest, envy coursing through him as he faced another night in the dark on his own.

Duncan had woken first and Leonard had talked their situation through with him in detail and, once Gwynedd was awake, Duncan explained it to her.

'There's still time for you to throw me out and not get involved,' he said.

'I want to be involved.'

'With all this madness?'

'No . . . with you. I . . . want to help you.'

'Oh.' That took the wind out of his morally righteous sails.

'Well, we know the how – it's cold and it's violent, capable of ripping apart a horse, strangling Leonard, decapitating Racimo, poisoning and smashing up Beaumont . . . Jesus. What we don't know is the what or the who: what it is and who sets it loose.'

'Or the why. Why is he – or she – doing it? And why those people and why you?'

'Okay. We need to know the what, the who and the why.'

Leonard piped up. 'We also know the when.'

'The when?' said Duncan.

'Midnight, last night. And midnight for me too. Beaumont had been dead how many hours before they dragged him from the lake?'

Duncan cast his mind back to the interview with Inspector Chater. 'Fifteen hours.'

'And they hauled him up five hours after you were there and that was 3pm. That makes it midnight.'

'And Racimo went off the road sometime between 11.30 and 1.30 – midnight.'

Duncan informed Gwynedd of the 'when'.

So it went on, their limited knowledge tumbling out like the babblings in Bedlam, one fact leaping on to another, the picture becoming all the more confusing. It was like trying to piece together a jigsaw without any reference and with no edge pieces to show them the limits of the puzzle. Add to that shaking hands and a nagging terror that made them jump at the slightest noise and their discussion soon proved to be more an exercise in fear-reinforcement than mystery-solving. Gwynedd finally made the intelligent suggestion of writing everything down.

'When I'm writing an essay I find the best thing is to make notes, then put them into some order. Get the facts down on paper then you can get the overall picture.'

'No arguments there.'

Gwynedd fetched a pad and pen from her desk, then sat down expectantly. 'So, what do we know?'

After half an hour, they had taken their first rough scribbles and transformed them into a list. Duncan wished they hadn't.

VICTIMS	– Racimo * Beaumont * Donaldson * Leonard * (Duncan) (PLUS Dalton * Kimmel * Fazey???)
CAUSE?	– Paper with runes
GIVEN BY?	– DON'T KNOW
WHY GIVEN?	– DON'T KNOW
WHEN GIVEN?	– Day of death
WHEN WORK?	– Midnight
WHERE?	– Wherever victim is at midnight
WHAT HAPPENS?	– Something not human + cold wind * D & G felt it/L remembers it * Fazey called it 'the black wind'

```
                          * BUT Kimmel said 'show me
                            your fire'
ANY LINKS IN TYPES OF DEATH?
  – Beheaded/strangled/poisoned/slashed/drowned
     NO PATTERN
WHAT LINKS VICTIMS? – Occult ceremonies
CLUES?                    * D poss. seen man who gave
                            him paper
                          * Fazey knew the man and had
                            cheap rent
                            NEED ADDRESS BOOK
PROBLEMS:                 1. D supposed to be dead: can't
                            go home
                          2. Horse will be found: tyre tracks,
                            broken headlight, paint on gate
                          3. BMW will be reported stolen
                          4. Fazey will be found: poss
                            fingerprints
                            PLUS he was kicked = suspicious
                            PLUS till receipts, could find
                            D's name!
ACTION:                   1. Find out more about 'black wind'
                          2. Get Fazey address book FROM
                            HOME!!!!
                          3. Avoid getting caught with stolen
                            car
                          4. AVOID POLICE – NO
                            EXPLANATION THEY'LL
                            BELIEVE!
```

'So where does that leave us?' asked Duncan as he rinsed his face in the sink.

Gwynedd shrugged her shoulders. Scanning the list she couldn't help wondering if she had wandered into a rehearsal for some gothic melodrama. Unbeknownst to her, Leonard was peering over her shoulder, his eyes flicking from the list to her cleavage. Duncan saw what he was doing.

'Well, Leonard?'

'Ah . . . we need to know the what and the who, right? So, I know it's a long shot, but we might find the "what" in reference books.'

Duncan laughed. Gwynedd looked up at him.

'Leonard says we might find out what it is by looking it up. What under, Leonard? "Oddities in Ollington"? "Weirdness West of Whaley Bridge"? "Murderous Things Wot I Have Seen by A Local Expert"?'

Leonard ignored him. 'Ask Gwynedd if she has any of the Dalton girl's books left.'

'Did you take all Jane's books back to the shop?'

'No. They were too heavy. There's nine or ten left, the biggest ones. If that man . . . had bought the first lot, I'd have taken the rest.'

'It's a start,' said Leonard. 'Look at the list. Fazey called it a "black wind". Check the indexes.'

Duncan was going to protest, but Leonard had been right about the obvious so many times now, he didn't want to lose face again.

Gwynedd brought the books in and she and Duncan looked through them. Only one had a reference to a 'Black Wind'. Rather worryingly it was in a fat volume called *Daemonology: Perfidy's Listing*.

Written at the beginning of the century, it was an alphabetical list with descriptions of demonic entities in world religions. 'The Black Wind' was a cross reference to a story from the Welsh borders about how local priests in 1908 still blessed the doors and windows of new households to stop the 'black wind' insinuating itself through the gaps. That was all. Mr Perfidy had been unable to trace the source of the legend but speculated it might have had something to do with the Black Death and an old belief that the plague was carried on the wind. He mentioned Eyam in Derbyshire, a village virtually wiped out by the plague in 1665 when a consignment of cloth from London arrived containing fleas. Mr Perfidy, an American, seemed to think Derbyshire was in the same general vicinity as the borders.

'Bloody Americans. Eyam's only a dozen miles from here, but the borders are fifty. He probably thought Dick van Dyke was the local vicar: "Cor blimey guvnor, up the apples and pears, strike a bleeding light!"'

Gwynedd laughed at Duncan's atrocious Cockney accent and that pleased him. Getting a girl to laugh – as long as it wasn't at your body – was always a good sign. And she had a good laugh; it also made her bosom wobble. Oh dear . . .

'If it's in his book, it may be in others,' said Gwynedd.

'True, but where? Can't go ask Mr Fazey, can we? And I don't suppose the town library has a big occult section.'

'Mr Beaumont?' said Gwynedd.

'No, his boat sank.'

'His study. Here, in the college. I went in a few times. He had books.'

'On the occult?'

'I didn't notice.'

'Worth a try,' said Leonard.

'Can we get in without hassle?' said Duncan.

Gwynedd didn't know, but was willing to try. Anxious not to be shown up as a wimp, Duncan agreed, but cautioned that if there was any chance of trouble they were to forget it.

Ten minutes later they were outside Beaumont's office. It was in a small modern block, built for economy rather than style. Beaumont's office was on the third floor midway down a corridor containing a dozen or so similar rooms. Unfortunately, the door was locked.

'Pick the lock,' suggested Leonard.

'What with? My teeth?'

'Pardon?' said Gwynedd.

Duncan explained.

'Force it, then,' said Leonard.

'Just kick it in?' said Duncan.

Gwynedd did so, the door flying open.

'Good girl,' said Leonard. 'Come on, Duncan, before someone notices.'

An aghast Duncan scooted in after Gwynedd and shut the door, listening for any sound in the corridor. Nothing. He turned back to the room.

It was small, about fifteen feet square, one wall given over to a waist-high window with a desk in front of it. There were only two bookshelves, running the length of the right and left walls, a hundred books or so in all, mostly paperbacks. On the wall behind them were certificates, qualifications and photographs of school and university. Beaumont had also been a rower; he had gone to Cambridge. There was an oar at the top of the wall, victories from 1975 and a college crest painted onto the blade.

'Check the books,' said Leonard, already running his eye along the titles on the left hand shelf. 'Anything occult.'

Gwynedd checked the same shelf, Duncan the one on the right. Not surprisingly there wasn't a single book on the occult – after all, Beaumont wasn't going to boast about his habits; it would be a bit like a transvestite having a Nightingales catalogue on display.

'The desk?' said Gwynedd.

'Locked,' said Duncan testing the three drawers on each side. 'In for a penny . . .' he said, aware of what Leonard was about to say.

He picked up a letter opener and slipped the simple catch at the top. All the drawers were empty.

'Police?' said Gwynedd.

'Yes,' said Duncan. 'He's a murder victim; they'll have cleared out everything looking for a possible motive: debts, threats, whatever.'

'So nothing to help us.'

'Seems not, and there's no other way to find out more.'

Duncan sat down in one of the two chairs that faced the desk, Gwynedd in the other.

'Any ideas, Leonard?'

He was sitting on the desk, looking around the room. He shook his head. 'Nope. We should have thought; even if he had hidden something the police would have found it.'

They sat in silence for a couple of minutes, but no-one came up with any suggestions.

'Okay, let's go!' said Duncan suddenly, startling Gwynedd. 'Sorry. All we've got left is Fazey's address book and that's back at my house. I'll have to go get it.'

'Remember you're dead,' said Leonard. 'You'll *sneak* in and get it; your mother mustn't see you in case she tells someone checking out what happened to you last night.'

'Thanks for reminding me.'

Duncan got up and walked to the door and was about to open it to check the corridor when something caught his eye on the wall. What was it? He stepped back and studied the frames and the oar.

'Something up?' asked Gwynedd.

'I don't know. There's something . . .' What was it?

The oar filled the top fifth of the wall, then underneath that were six certificates, and five framed photographs. The certificates were degrees and diplomas from various places, including his MA certificate from Cambridge, but the most recent was the MA from 1983.

And the photographs: one of a rowing eight; a freshman year photograph from 1973; a school shot with several hundred boys in it from 1972; a group of students in hiking gear posed like a football team; and a rectangular frame with an oval, leather-framed picture of Beaumont shaking hands with a tall, thin man in an ill-fitting suit.

The man's face was looking away from the camera, as if he was reluctant to pose. His long grey hair was matched by an equally straggly beard, his apparent disguise topped off by a pair of heavy framed glasses. For his part Beaumont had an eager, self-satisfied look on his face, as if he had achieved something and wanted proof, regardless of the other man's wishes. Beaumont also looked older than in his other shots, so the picture had been taken more recently, but that fact was no help.

He carefully looked over the photographs again until he came back to the congratulatory shot. There was something wrong with it, but what?

'This photo here, the one with the older guy – do you see anything odd about it?'

Leonard and Gwynedd both studied it, but could see nothing. Duncan took it off the wall and sat down again, holding it in his lap. He turned it over and opened the frame and pulled the shot out. Odd. The background around the figures had been painted out. *That* was why it looked strange: at first sight it was simply a posed shot against a bland studio grey backdrop but now he could look at it in detail, they seemed to be floating in mid-air, their feet not touching the ground, because it wasn't there. Silly, but was that it? Not all the photograph had been coloured in, only enough to leave the oval on view. The four corners of the shot revealed that it had been taken indoors, wooden shelves and books on the right, a table on the bottom left.

He flipped it over. No photographer's sticker or stamp.

'Well, what is it?' said Gwynedd.

'Just the way it's masked; must have caught my eye.'

He started to put it back in its frame then stopped and stared at it again. It wasn't the background or Beaumont, it was the other guy. Take away the beard and glasses, give him a crewcut and it was him.

'What is it?' asked Gwynedd. Duncan had gone white and was holding his stomach.

'It's him. The guy. The one who killed the dog and fucked Fazey. The guy who gave me the piece of paper!'

25

A THOROUGH SEARCH of the room produced no further clues as to the man's identity. Finally Leonard called a halt: Duncan was working himself up into a state.

'We're leaving now,' he insisted. 'Duncan, keep the photo, but put the frame in a drawer so it doesn't attract attention, and let's go.'

Gwynedd edged over to the door and, finding the coast clear, they left, Duncan pulling the door shut behind them. They then made their way back to Gwynedd's room where Duncan sat and stared obsessively at the photograph.

The man seemed reasonable, ordinary, yet he had sentenced Duncan to death. Leonard too. And all the others. That chiselled, handsome face was the face of a mass murderer, a black magician . . . the face of evil.

Leonard also looked at the photograph. He thought he recognised the man from the ceremonies but couldn't be sure; the man was usually cowled and whenever he had disrobed, Leonard had usually been too busy doing other things. There was something else, however, around the border: the room in which the two bastards were standing.

'Ask Gwynedd if she's got a knife, something sharp. See if you can scrape off the paint, see more of the room.'

It took two more prompts before Duncan responded, so deep was his concentration on the bastard who had tried to murder him. Gwynedd found a pair of scissors and although they weren't very good, they scraped enough away to reveal to them that the room Beaumont and the man were in was Fazey's shop.

'We need Fazey's address book,' Leonard said.

Even Gwynedd could guess what he had said.

The plan was simple. They would park up in the lane at the bottom of the Cantrills' long garden and Duncan would scale the wooden fence and make his way up the garden under cover of the border shrubs.

It would then be just a short dash to the side of the house where he would clamber up the drainpipe to the low roof, make his way to an open window, then along the upstairs landing to his bedroom, all the time keeping an ear out for where his mother might be. Although he could disable the burglar alarm – he knew the code – there was no guarantee that either his mother or Mrs Orr would be out. After all, he had his mother's car!

Having retrieved Fazey's address book, he would retrace his steps across the roof, down the drainpipe again then back down the garden to the lane and away they would zoom, back to Ollington College and the relative safety of Gwynedd's room. That was the plan. However, the need to steal a car could have killed the plan stone dead, but with Leonard's help, it was simple.

While Duncan and Gwynedd dawdled by the college car park, acting like two students having a chat, Leonard kept his eye on each arriving car, checking if the owner was careless enough to leave the car unlocked or unalarmed. Barely ten minutes had passed before a girl parked a battered 'C' reg Nova and surreptitiously pushed the door to until it stuck without using the key. Leonard could see the lock had been tampered with and the girl hadn't been able to replace it. Once she had disappeared from sight, Duncan retrieved the shotgun from the BMW, hid it under his arm, strolled over to the Nova and got in with Gwynedd. Leonard then showed him how to hot-wire the car – a trick he had learned to show customers how easy it was for someone to steal their car.

Careful to take the long circuit out of the college, Duncan then drove steadily through town towards his home. The sight of a police car had him involuntarily stamping on the brake but Leonard calmed him and they drove on unimpeded.

Parked up in the lane behind his home, Duncan got out and clambered over the fence. It wasn't much of a deterrent to tres-passers, but the house was alarmed and the floodlights at night were bright enough to confuse aircraft heading for Manchester International.

The gardener wasn't working, which helped, and he scrabbled his way up the left hand side of the lawn, ducking and weaving among the shrubs and bushes. Reaching the outdoor swimming pool, he scanned the windows. He couldn't see any movement, but that didn't mean anything.

He dashed across the concrete patio to the side of the house and hugged the wall, getting his breath back. Well, so far, so good . . . then he looked up the drainpipe.

To the roof was about twelve feet, but it meant clambering over the guttering onto a sloping roof. Why had he thought he could do it? He was almost tempted to walk round to the front, but Leonard appeared on the roof above and tutted down at him.

'Get your arse up here now, Duncan. No time to waste.'

It was hard work, but the only real difficulty was swinging his legs up onto the tiles. He ended up facing down onto the unrelenting concrete patio, but some earnest crabbing sideways got him to the chimney stack and he was able to haul himself upright.

'Right, shift it!' hissed Leonard.

Bastard! But Duncan got onto his knees and crawled to the apex of the roof, immediately aware of how nakedly obvious he would be to passers-by. He quickly crawled along the top of the roof to the landing window, swung himself down onto the balcony and checked the window. It was open. That was good, because it meant no alarm – but it was also bad because it meant someone was home, and they could be upstairs.

He pulled open the window, reminding himself that when he came back here to live he would make sure the house wasn't so easy to enter. If he, a mere amateur, could sneak in in broad daylight, what could a couple of pros manage?

He edged along the passage to the landing and listened. There was a radio on downstairs. Classical music, either Radio 3 or Classic FM. Mum's choice – Mrs Orr always had Radio 4 on. He keened an ear and thought he could detect clattering – someone cleaning up the kitchen. What day was it? Mrs Orr always had Thursdays off. He found it rather disconcerting that he couldn't actually remember what day it was. Rack his brains as he might, he couldn't place the day. God Almighty! He broke out in a cold sweat: he didn't know the day of the week!

'Get on with it,' urged Leonard.

'See who it is,' said Duncan.

Leonard went to the bottom of the stairs and peered into the kitchen.

'Your mother. Dressed to the nines. Green suit. Wiping the counter with Dettol.'

Wiping kitchen surfaces? She only did that when—

'Get a bloody move on, Duncan. Your bedroom!'

Duncan moved down the passage to his room, pushed the door open carefully to avoid any squeaks, and closed it behind him. It hadn't changed, other than the bed being made. He reached under the mattress, located the thin volume, pocketed it and made his way back to the door.

Just as he was about to pull it open, the doorbell rang downstairs. He let out an involuntary gasp and let go the handle as if it was wired to explosives.

'Who the fuck is that?' said Duncan.

'I have your mother's appointment diary?' said Leonard. 'Open the door, let me look down the stairs.'

Duncan grabbed the handle and slowly pulled the door open. *Now* it squeaked. He stopped but the small gap was enough for Leonard to see him through as he appeared at the top of the stairs. However, it didn't take Leonard to confirm what Duncan heard.

His mother opened the front door and said, 'Yes?'

'Mrs Cantrill,' came back a Northern accent. 'Detective Chief Inspector Chater, my colleague Detective Sergeant Hampsey, I wonder if we might have a few words with your son, Duncan.'

Duncan didn't hear the rest of the conversation: his heart was beating in 8/4 time, his ears pounding. He stepped back into the room and the door closed.

'Damn!' said Leonard next to him. 'I didn't catch it all.'

Duncan mouthed the word 'what?' but the sound refused to disgorge itself from his constricted throat.

'They didn't say what it was about, but it wasn't the car your mother reported stolen.'

'She *did* report it. The cow. How does she know I won't bring it back?'

'Because you haven't! Twit. Come on, let's go.'

'No! Let's wait. When they—'

'When they come up here, Duncan, led by your mother who is obviously at the end of her rope with you. "Could we have a look at your son's room?" they'll ask. "Why certainly, Detective Chief Inspector," she'll say.'

'Fuck.'

'Yes. So go – now.'

Duncan pulled open the door, his teeth grinding as it squeaked, and listened. Leonard was at the top of the stairs waving him forward. It sounded as if they were in the kitchen.

It was as Duncan reached the top of the stairs to turn towards the open landing window that they came out into the hall. They didn't see him but his mother heard his footsteps as he dashed for the window.

'Help!' she screamed, even though the detectives were standing by her. 'There's someone in the house!'

Duncan was off the balcony and onto the roof before he heard running footsteps up the stairs.

He dashed across the roof, his feet uncaring of the slope, then up over the apex to the other side, heading for the drainpipe. Behind him he heard shouting, but he paid it no heed.

He reached the edge of the roof and slipped, kicking out wildly to stop his slide. His left foot caught the gutter which broke free with a loud crack, taking the top eighteen inches of the drainpipe with it.

He rolled over and kicked himself away from the edge.

'Come on!' shouted Leonard.

Duncan was too scared to respond. He froze, grateful not to have fallen from the roof.

'They're coming!' shouted Leonard. 'Get up, come on!'

'Fuck off!' said Duncan. He could hear the policemen calling to him to stop from somewhere across the other side of the roof.

'Come on, Duncan!'

'How?' hissed Duncan. 'The bloody drainpipe's gone.'

Leonard looked around. 'The pool,' he said, suddenly standing at the end of the roof looking over the edge.

'What?'

'The swimming pool! You've done it before, remember?'

'No! No way!'

'Duncan, it's that or give up now. If they're not here about the car, they must be here about Fazey. Think on!'

The policemen were on the apex of the roof, edging gingerly along. Duncan caught a glimpse of someone's head around the side of the chimney. *Shit*. Crouching down he ran to the edge of the roof, another shout from behind lost as he leapt feet first into space.

A second of flight then cold water smashed his body and swallowed him whole. His feet touched bottom and he let out a scream, water fighting to enter his mouth.

He kicked himself to the surface, got his bearings, then reached the side of the pool. Even in his shocked condition he realised he had leapt so far he had almost landed on the opposite side of the pool, a landing that would certainly have killed him.

He pulled himself out of the water, the weight of his sodden clothes threatening to drag him back down, then loped across the lawn towards the rear of the garden.

From the roof he heard orders to stop and curses, and from the house he heard his mother shouting:

'Stop him! Stop him!'

Half way down the garden Duncan stumbled and fell on his face, the breath knocked out of him. He couldn't move, the urge to vomit cramping him double.

Leonard could see the two policemen heading back to the window. Both were fit; once in the house they would run downstairs and out the patio doors in no time.

'Get up, Duncan! Get moving!'

Duncan couldn't answer. Didn't want to answer. Let them come, let them come.

Suddenly there was a crash and a roar and Duncan and Leonard looked up to see the stolen Nova hurtling across the lawn towards them, broken fencing showering its wake.

'Jesus,' said Leonard.

The Nova angled to the right, sliced through a flowerbed, then spun to a halt side on, barely inches from Duncan's head. The passenger door then flew open and Gwynedd shouted to him to get in.

The policemen crashed through the patio door, demanding that they stop, followed by Mrs Cantrill, shrieking:

'My lawn! My lawn!'

'Get up, Duncan, now!' said Leonard.

Duncan crawled forward, then summoned the strength to get to his knees and pull himself into the car, Gwynedd setting off before he was settled.

The Nova slewed across the lawn, its wheels fighting for grip, and plunged through more shrubbery before straightening on a course for the hole in the fence.

'Stop! Police! Stop!' yelled the policemen.

'My flowers! My flowers!' screamed Mrs Cantrill.

The car clipped a lawn sprinkler, careered to the right and, missing the gap in the fence, crashed through the hedge, its passenger door finally slammed shut. Onto the road, Gwynedd touched the brakes and spun the wheel, turning the car a perfect 90° then, dropping into first and stamping on the accelerator, she set the wheels spinning on the loose gravel of the verge. Then, slowly but surely, they got grip and the car roared out of sight.

The policemen skidded to halt in the middle of the lawn, fighting for breath, the sergeant struggling to get out his radio. Duncan's mother came to a halt half way between them and the house and surveyed the damage to her beloved garden.

'My garden! My garden!' she shouted, the tyre marks as appalling as ground-in dog dirt on a Persian rug.

The Nova exited the lane onto the main road leaving Ollington for the north, Gwynedd skilfully juggling brake and accelerator.

Duncan squidged his way into the seat, fighting to find the seatbelt. 'You didn't tell me you could drive!'

'You never asked,' said Gwynedd, gunning the engine as she overtook a Scania.

26

IT WAS DARK, the sun having set an hour before. They had a torch but they didn't want to waste the batteries, and they didn't dare risk a fire in case it spread. The house still reeked of smoke, spelling a warning they heeded, but the weather was reasonably warm and dry and what wind there was whistled through the eaves and round the walls outside so, whilst it wasn't very comfortable, it was at least tolerable. Besides, what choice did they have? They were on the run, car thieves, vandals, burglars, suspected horse killers . . . the list went on.

That was why Duncan and Gwynedd were huddled together in the corner of the front room of Ludo Kimmel's house. After escaping from his own garden, Duncan realised it would be unsafe to go anywhere in town in the Nova, or back to Gwynedd's room. (All it would take would be for Mrs Cantrill to mention a 'Gwynedd' at the college to the police – how many of them could there be, after all? – and for them to realise Beaumont had known her dead roommate: even the slowest DC Plod would reckon something suspicious was afoot.)

It was Leonard who suggested Kimmel's house: it was out of the way, empty and unlikely to attract visitors. It would also give them time to go through Fazey's address book and find any leads. Easier said than done, however.

Although Fazey's book had survived its dunking in the Cantrills' swimming pool – Fazey used pencil and ball point pen, so once it had been dried by the car heater, little had been lost – it didn't make much difference. An address book is an address book: unless you know who the people are, they're just so many names and numbers. Duncan did recognise some names: councillors his mother knew, a few prominent local business people, including two people on their 'B' Christmas card list (they got a card but no signatures).

Leonard recognised some other names, but none that helped. It was a pretty bizarre mix but, as Gwynedd pointed out, it didn't make them satanists, just people who had met Fazey either in his shop or socially. Chances were Duncan's name would have gone in the book soon enough if he had bought any more books. Jane Dalton's name was not in it, but those of Beaumont, Racimo, Donaldson and Kimmel were.

They sat in the gloom, mulling over their situation. Duncan felt Gwynedd shiver next to him – although he had managed to dry out, he still only wore the same as her: jeans, trainers, sweatshirt – and he asked if he could hold her. Leonard laughed but Duncan ignored him as Gwynedd huddled closer and he put his arm around her shoulder. There had been a rug in the back of the car and although it smelled of dog, it was warm and it covered their legs.

Soon it was wrapped up to their necks, helping to keep their heat in.

'I'm sorry about all this,' said Duncan, his arm going numb but not caring. 'I shouldn't have involved you.'

'Doesn't matter. Once you start something you have to finish.'

'Yes, but you needn't have started at all – if you hadn't come round last night to the house . . .'

'But I did. I wanted to help you.'

'Why? You don't know me from Adam and I'm not exactly a prize catch.'

'Depends what you're after. You're rich for starters, judging by your house.'

'Is that—'

'Grow up. I didn't know where you lived till I got there, did I? But you're also, well, cute.'

Duncan looked at her in the twilight. She wasn't looking at him, but she wasn't laughing either. Maybe, God bless her, she meant it. The feeling was certainly mutual but he wasn't going to make a fool of himself by admitting it. He'd always blown it in the past by coming on strong too soon; he would bide his time.

'Cute? Me? I'm just a beanpole.'

'A *skiving* beanpole,' said Leonard.

Duncan ignored him. Sat as they were he couldn't see Leonard on the other side of the room and, credit where it was due, he was giving them some privacy, even if he was all ears.

'Wiry,' she corrected. 'Slim. Slender.' She was laying on the adjectives too thickly for it to be a piss-take. 'Unlike me.'

'Ah, but you're cuddly.' *Cuddly? You twat, Duncan.* Cuddly to a girl meant fat loathsome elephantine cellulite nightmare. The fact that he had meant it as in sensual womanly curvaceous sexy would be lost on her. It was.

'Fat. A 16. Plump. Bloated,' she translated.

'No. Cute. Like me.'

They both laughed. He felt her warmth, her breath on his cheek, the yield of her breast. Oh God . . . He also felt movement in his underpants: understandable but unwanted. He tried to shift himself but it would have meant breaking his hug and he would rather break his arm than let go of her.

'Okay, so we're both cute,' he managed. 'Doesn't help us with all this stuff. "Cute" never helped anyone against Dracula.'

'Or beat off Frankenstein, no.'

An owl hooted on cue, giving them both the creeps. Gwynedd shivered some more. *Oh God*, thought Duncan, *I'm not going to be able to get through tonight.*

'What are we going to do?' she asked quietly, as if afraid of the answer.

Duncan shrugged as best he could. 'I don't know.'

'Find the man,' said Leonard.

'How?'

'Pardon?' said Gwynedd.

'Leonard said we have to find the man.'

'How?' said Gwynedd.

'His name must be in Fazey's book. That photo was taken in his shop; he's had the bastard up his arse.'

Duncan laughed. 'Nicely put, Leonard. He says the name's in the book somewhere, but there's two hundred names.'

'Tanfeld,' said Leonard.

'What? Oh you mean the company owns the shop. So?'

'Tomorrow you find out where they're located.'

'And?'

'And . . . wing it.'

'Good thinking.'

Gwynedd stared at Duncan, her eyes wide in the dim light. Big brown eyes. *What was that phrase about drowning?* He wondered if she really believed Leonard existed or if she just accepted he was mad. Duncan had never seen the problem with madness; as long as the person was happy with their delusion and didn't hurt anyone, what's the problem? Look at the time he decided he was married to Kim Wilde; the times they'd been in bed . . . But this was more than madness; it was blood, murder, *death*.

'Do you trust me?' he said suddenly.

'Yes,' she said. 'I don't know why, but I do.'

They kissed – it just seemed the obvious thing to do – and it was wonderful. And their tongues told them it would have gone a lot further if Leonard hadn't been around. *The Chaperone From Beyond The Grave*, thought Duncan bitterly, as they finally parted after five minutes, both accepting the commitment, content in the knowledge that when the time was right, Mr Thin-and-Cute and Ms. Cuddly-and-Cute would go all the way. But before that could happen, they would need privacy and for *that* they would need to solve the mystery at hand because the alternative was unthinkable.

Duncan woke up stiff – in all senses of the word – and, reluctant as he was to let go of Gwynedd (he had never held a woman overnight) his bladder ached as much as his bones and he had to make a move.

He managed to extricate himself without waking her and cranked himself upright, his bones creaking. Rubbing his thighs he walked out of the house into the morning.

It was cold and crisp, making him shiver, but the memory of the warm sleep he had enjoyed cheered him. He walked round the side of the house and had a pee, Leonard suddenly appearing at his side as he was struggling to keep his morning erection under control.

'Know how you feel, know how you feel,' said Leonard apropos Duncan's penis.

'Do you mind?' said Duncan, caught unawares.

'Nope. I'd have the same problem if I'd spent the—'

'Shut up. I know you don't have much respect for women, but you'll have some for Gwynedd.'

'I do respect women!'

'How?' said Duncan, shaking off and zipping up. 'By going out in the middle of the night and fucking anything that moves? By cheating on your wife?'

'Doesn't mean I don't respect them. They knew what they wanted and they got it.'

'Like Jane Dalton?'

'I never touched her! Besides, if they go to the ceremonies, they must know what they're in for.'

'Like you?'

'No. What I mean is everyone went there for sex; others might have had ulterior motives. Anyway, each to his own Duncan: remember when we first met? The video? Besides, you got her into this mess.'

'Me? She came round—'

'Only because you fancied her when we went up to her room that first time. We were there *an hour* Duncan, but only because you seemed to have the hots for each other. You could have just walked and she wouldn't be here now.'

Duncan looked back at the house. Damn Leonard; he knew the ghost was right: now he had even more guilt to carry around.

So, choosing to avoid further discussion, he trotted back to the house to find Gwynedd coming out of the front door, wiping her eyes. Even with day-old make up and that early-morning look, he found her attractive. And he knew that once you start making excuses for things you normally find unattractive in a woman you're falling in love.

'Where's the loo?' she asked.

The bathroom had been destroyed by the fire, so he swept his arm around the summery vista before them.

'Your choice,' he said, and he went back inside, too embarrassed to talk to her. Maybe last night had just been a matter of mutual survival; a stranded climber huddles down for the night with a St Bernard to keep warm: doesn't mean they're going to settle down and raise puppies.

But as he rolled up the blanket and took it to the car they had hidden in the tumbledown barn, she walked up to him, linked her arm in his and pecked him on the cheek.

'Thanks for last night,' she said.

'What last night?'

'Whatever.'

What did she mean?

They got into the car, Duncan reversed out of the barn into the yard and then stopped. Where were they going?

'Newsagents,' said Leonard, guessing Duncan's dilemma. 'Let's see if anything's happened, take it from there.'

Seemed fair enough, as long as they kept off main roads – after their hurried departure yesterday in full view of Chief Inspector Chater, the police would be looking for the car – so he eased the Nova down the rutted path and headed for the nearest village.

The newsagent still had an Ollington *Evening Sentinel* from the night before and that, and a *Daily Mirror*, revealed a HORSE RIPPER HORROR and the death of a local bookshop owner under suspicious circumstances. Damn! The bastard hanged himself, anyone could see that. No wonder it was Chater who had come round to his home rather than a couple of uniforms. Ollington's Most Wanted he was, and Gwynedd was now his 'moll'. *Damn damn damn.*

Neither newspaper carried much information beyond 'horrific injuries' to the horse; and Fazey was only mentioned as a filler in the *Sentinel.* As Leonard had said, suicides generally weren't news.

They drove on to the next village and found the Post Office, where Gwynedd went inside and asked to borrow the local telephone directories and jotted down the addresses of all companies called Tanfeld. There were three: builders' merchant, dress agency called Tanfelds, the third just called Tanfeld Ltd which she found in the standard directory. However, it had no listings under Property Development, Property Investment, Property Management or Property Owners; likewise Accommodation – residential and Estate Agents. But the telephone number in Fazey's book matched so they had an address.

It turned out to be in a residential area to the south of Ollington, one of those rundown areas with large Victorian houses that had seen better days, but which still succeeded in maintaining a certain tainted aura. Duncan knew the area but had never seen Barnfield Road or the three houses on it. It was little more than a country lane, an unkempt private road with two large houses at its top and, about a quarter of a mile down at its dead end, No 3, the address of Tanfeld Ltd. They turned the car round as soon as they realised it was a cul-de-sac and drove back out of the road and parked out of sight behind a hedge. They were uncomfortably near to Ollington and had had to take a circuitous route to Barnfield Road when a police van had followed them for half a mile.

The house had seemed smaller than the other two, a modest Victorian detached house of standard layout – central front door with a window on either side and three windows on the first floor. A high dark roof and ornate gables completed the building. Nothing special, nothing odd, and nothing to indicate a business premises. Half the front garden was given over to a gravel driveway on which was parked a black Mercedes 200 SL but it stood alone.

'So what's the plan?' said Duncan.

Both Leonard and Gwynedd shook their heads.

'I don't believe this. Neither of you has any idea what we should do next?' he said.

Embarrassed silence.

'Fine.' Duncan took umbrage. After all, he was the one in the shit; the one who should be dead. He got out of the car and walked a distance into the field kicking at stones.

Leonard joined him. 'Don't get so het up, kiddo. We'll sort something out. Just got to be logical about it.'

'Logical? *Logical?* I fed a piece of paper to a horse and something ripped it to bits at the stroke of midnight! A bookshop owner hangs himself rather than tell us who his boyfriend is! We've got loonies running round at night, fucking dead dogs and—'

'Shut up! You're getting hysterical. Look, I'm sorry you're in this mess—'

'Too right!'

'—but you're in it now and only you can get you out. I can't do anything, neither can the police nor your mum. It's just you, Duncan. Someone, maybe the guy in that house, wants you dead. He tried once and when he finds out he failed he'll do it again. There's really only one answer.'

Duncan was tempted to say 'run and hide' but he didn't. For the first time he appreciated the magnitude of what was coming. 'You mean I've got to *kill* him?'

'Yes. And not just to help me, but to save yourself.'

'Kill someone? *Murder.* I can't . . . It's . . . No! This isn't America! It's Ollington; bloody nowhere Ollington bloody Derbyshire. People don't murder people here.'

'Oh, but they do – and one person is murdering a whole lot of people and you're next on his list. You can't go to the police, they won't listen and they'll probably lock you up as a raving lunatic, so there's no option. It's you or him. Gunfight at the OK Corral. High Noon.'

'Stop being so melodramatic.'

'It's your fucking *life*, Duncan! Look at me. I'm not going to mince words: *you were sentenced to death last night*. Someone wanted you dead. Dead like me. Only that girl's brains saved you. You owe her your life, Duncan, but more than that, you owe it to yourself to get rid of that bastard. To kill him, and stop this shit.'

'How? Shoot him, stab him, what?'

'I don't know.'

'And what if we're wrong? If it's the wrong man?'

'Then we'll have to be sure. And don't think of it as murder, Duncan. It's self-defence; he started it. You always cheer when the cops shoot the crooks on TV, don't you? When the sheriff kills the bad guys? Japs and Germans get it in war movies? It's no different. It's got to be done.'

But it *was* different. It was *real*. Duncan walked further on, Leonard deciding to leave him to his torment. He didn't want to land the boy in any more trouble but events had gone beyond the normal rules of law and order. The law didn't have any jurisdiction here, the murderer and his weapon defied rational analysis; they were having to make it up as they went along and, worse still, play by someone else's rules: rules they didn't understand.

Self-preservation was what it was all about.

Duncan leaned against a fence and stared across the field at some cows munching grass. Moo moos. His mind was reeling, Leonard's words tumbling over in his mind like some obscene tombola – words like *murder* and *kill* and *defence* – but he knew Leonard was right. There was no evidence of the piece of paper, the man, the ceremonies, nothing that could link the murders other than Leonard's word – the word of a ghost! What else? Run away? Where? For how long? And, he started to get angry, why the fuck should he?

He was minding his own business doing his crappy job and he found a murder victim. Tough, but it happens – and then all this. He wasn't to blame, it wasn't his fault, he was just trying to help out. He'd nearly been committed, he'd alienated his mother and come that close to being murdered – and all because of some wanker and his meddlings with the occult. Damn him. Damn him! Why should he die because . . .

That was it, really. Sod justice, bugger revenge: why should *he* die? But could he live with the fact that he had destroyed another human life? That he had actually been the cause of someone's death, even if that man was a mass murderer, someone who would kill him if he got the first chance. Duncan had never supported the death penalty but after all that had happened, he would gladly have seen the man hanged. But with Duncan as hangman? And without trial? Was that justice or . . .

Leonard was beside him again. 'Mindset, Duncan; set your mind. This is war. *War*. In war it's kill or be killed. Murder is legal and right and if ever it was right it's here and now with that bastard. Are you ready to do it?'

'I don't know how.'

'We'll decide what to do when we get the chance, but you've got to be ready to do it when you have to.'

'I can't promise . . .'

'I know,' said Leonard. It was his turn to stare at the cows. 'You know, I've always wondered at the mentality of people who go out looking for a fight at football matches or in pubs. And people who kill for money, who torture for fun. But now I envy them.'

'Envy?'

'Yes. They'd just get on and do it. No conscience, no worries. Just another day at the office. It's you or him; there's no option.'

Ultimately, that was it: he didn't have a choice. Only he knew what was happening and only he could stop it – or die in the process. But what if he was wrong? What if being judge, jury and executioner was based on faulty evidence? Yes, the guy looked guilty but what if it was just dreadful coincidence? How many times had he done a crossword only to find out he had put the wrong word in even though other words fitted? He wasn't a detective, he didn't have all the facts, only his opinion and that of Leonard, an interested party – and how much had he done over the last few days at his behest? What if this was all some revenge trip, Leonard convincing him about someone *he* wanted to off?

He looked at Leonard. Ugly, broken, dead. *Murdered*. Even if it was all just about him seeking revenge, surely the person who had done that to him deserved to die? Anyway, he knew Leonard wasn't in it for himself. Oh, he may have started with that intention, but he'd been as horrified as Duncan to find out what had been going on.

'What?' said Leonard, uncomfortable under Duncan's stare.

'You're right. He's going to die.' And with that Duncan walked back to the car.

Once he reached the Nova, his resolve deflated slightly. He was decided on the outcome; it was the means he was still unsure about

– and then there was Gwynedd . . . He sat back in the car avoiding her questioning gaze.

'Problem?' she said.

He couldn't help laughing, or telling her the truth. 'Leonard says – and I agree – that if the man who is responsible for all this is in that house, I've got to kill him.'

'Yes, I know.'

Duncan was stunned.

'It's logical. What he's doing can't be dealt with by the police because they could never prove he was responsible. If everyone who died was given one of those bits of paper, then he was never anywhere near the murders. And there's no reason for him to stop, so we've got to do it ourselves.'

'We?'

'Yes.'

'Why?'

As she said her next words, Duncan's world lit up then darkened, like an overloaded lightbulb. So much promise swamped by evil.

'I love you,' she said.

He'd never had anyone say that to him before, nor had he ever said it himself. It was a foreign language, but he mastered it soon enough. Taking a deep breath, he said:

'And I love you . . . which is all the more reason for you to go. Take the car and leave me and Leonard to—'

'Leonard? He's no use.'

'Charming,' said Leonard from the back seat.

'He may be with you but he can't *do* anything. I can.'

Duncan almost said 'A girl?' but decided not to. But there was no way he was going to let—

'Besides, how are you going to find out if he's the man?'

'I saw him at the farm when he found me.'

'Yes, but what are you going to *do?* Knock on his door and when he answers run away?'

'Oh, I see what you mean.'

'She's got a point, Duncan.'

'Of course she's got a bloody point, Leonard. I just didn't want her to think of it.'

'Because . . .' said Gwynedd.

'Because what?' said Duncan.

'Because he doesn't know me and I could recognise him from the photograph and he wouldn't be any the wiser. I knock on the door with some excuse and if it's him, we're one up.'

Duncan argued until he ran out of excuses but he knew it was pointless – and that's how he found himself crouching behind the hedge at the front of No 3 watching Gwynedd approach the front door. She was going to say she was lost and ask for directions.

She mounted the step into the porch and pressed the bell. Leonard was with her, ready to confirm the man's identity. There was no answer. She rang the bell again. This time there was movement behind the stained glass panel of the door and a figure appeared and opened the door.

But even as Duncan saw it was the same man and Leonard appeared at his side jabbering '*It's him, it's him!*' the man grabbed Gwynedd by the hair and dragged her into the house, throwing her past him into the hallway. He then took one step onto the porch and shouted:

'Duncan Peter Cantrill, you've got ten seconds to get inside this house or the girl dies!'

27

TANFELD WAS TALL and thin. Too thin for his frame. He had lost even more weight since his photograph had been taken with Beaumont. He stood aside as Duncan rushed in to help Gwynedd to her feet. She was unhurt but shaken and he held her to help calm her, anger and fear bubbling up in him.

Tanfeld closed the front door and gestured that they should enter the room on the right, for all the world as if they were welcome house guests. Reluctantly, they complied.

It was a large, high-ceilinged room that had been badly papered in cheap woodchip and painted white. A cold room, its lack of hospitality was emphasised by a threadworn brown patterned carpet, sagging brown corduroy easy chairs and occasional tables and wall units that looked as if they had come from some crappy DIY warehouse. The room said cheap.

'Sit down,' said Tanfeld, his voice calm. He had an accent, possibly foreign, but the years had worn it away.

Duncan and Gwynedd sat side by side on the couch, the springs having long retired so that they sank uncomfortably deep, their knees pointing up at the mantelpiece that dominated the wall in front of them. Its ornate design had been painted over in white and an old-fashioned copper-coloured three-bar electric fire stood forlornly in the space. The shelf contained souvenirs of Blackpool and Southport, as well as a cheap carriage clock, crude china figurines, two fat carved candles without stands and several coloured blown glass swans. Whatever Tanfeld was, he was not a man of any discernible taste.

Tanfeld stood to the right of the mantelpiece, five feet in front of them, and assumed a Lord of the Manor pose which, in the context of his ornaments, was about as regal as the people who must have sold him his tacky souvenirs.

'Don't speak, either of you,' he commanded. His eyes were his strongest feature, light blue and staring: they seemed fixed in space, his thin face hung on them like a disguise. His small mouth, long thin nose and short cropped grey hair emphasised his concentration camp gauntness. His clothes did nothing to improve his appearance. Well-creased, black trousers, shiny with overwear, a dark blue polo shirt, beige cardigan and worn green tartan slippers. But for all his bad taste and lack of dress sense, he seemed used to commanding an audience and being listened to, like the retired policeman or teacher he resembled. The lesson began.

'Mr Cantrill, girl, I have no intention of entering into a debate about what is to happen; you will simply cooperate. Furthermore, I will not patronise you by pretending the events of the last few days are other than as you suspect them to be. I don't know how much you know or have merely guessed, but I have to assume you are aware of the power of the runes. The death of that horse was either the wildest piece of good fortune or an understanding of the facts of the matter. I shall assume the latter, Mr Fazey's suicide being another pointer to your knowing the truth, or at least part of it.'

Gwynedd said, 'Look, I don't know what all—'

Tanfeld stepped forward and slapped her across the face so hard she flopped over sideways.

Duncan tried to stand up but Tanfeld kicked him in the face and he fell back, blood filling his mouth.

'You will sit still and listen and speak only when asked! Now where was I?' Already he had resumed his casual pose against the mantelpiece, an elbow resting on the end next to a snow bubble of Blackpool Tower, his hands clasped in front of him, one leg crooked across the other. He could have been discussing his holidays.

Duncan and Gwynedd, both concerned for the other but also in pain, could only sit and hug each other, children cowering in front of a feared parent.

Leonard was standing behind the couch and for the first time spoke up. 'Do as he says, I'll see what I can see.'

Duncan didn't acknowledge Leonard but if he had he would have used obscenities. His heart was racing and he was sure they were going to die and it was *his* fault.

'When did you find out what the rune I gave you could do?'

Duncan couldn't remember. Was it Fazey? Yes. 'Mr Fazey told me.'

'No wonder the toad hanged himself.' He smiled as if remembering the incident. 'I like to keep my little secrets. Cake?'

'Pardon?' said Duncan, swallowing coppery blood.

Tanfeld walked over to a cabinet, and pulled a squeaking door down to reveal a small Battenburg cake, plates and forks. He cut the cake and handed plates and slices to the two of them, which they accepted with shaking hands.

Tanfeld put his own plate on the mantelpiece and cut off a piece of cake with his fork and ate it.

Duncan couldn't think of anything he would rather not do than eat a supermarket Battenburg but he didn't dare refuse. He also encouraged Gwynedd to take a slice. It was dry and tasteless; they may as well have been eating bread. Despite his panic, he couldn't help noticing they were small slices.

Tanfeld took another piece, then resumed his lecture. 'You have spoiled my plans with your interference, but your coming here was not only inevitable but also extremely convenient.'

'C – convenient?' said Duncan.

Tanfeld frowned a threat then continued: 'Yes, convenient. You see, when you passed on the rune to that beast you disrupted the schedule. It was not best pleased, but there is a remedy and you have supplied it.'

Duncan wanted to ask what 'it' was, and the 'schedule', but instead forced himself to eat more cake. He thought he was going to be sick, particularly as he could taste blood.

'So, I will give you another rune and you will accept it and the consequences – and then everyone will be happy.'

'No!' blurted Duncan.

'Your desires are irrelevant, young man. I admire your resourcefulness in coming this far but, really, you should have kept your nose out of those things that don't concern you. One thing, however, still puzzles me: I care little for your amateur detective work, but how did you come to be at our ceremony the other night? I cannot believe you just stumbled on the event. Who betrayed us? Tell me their name and I shall deal with them. After all, they have caused your death, it is only fair that you make them suffer in turn.'

Duncan didn't answer. He was beginning to look at Tanfeld as an opponent, not some all-powerful ogre. He seemed in his sixties, an old man. A blow in the right place would break his leg; in a fight, Duncan's age and agility would give him an edge. All he needed was to get up off the couch with a second or two to spare. He wondered if he could—

'One more time,' said Tanfeld, his expression unchanged. 'Who told you where we would be?'

Duncan shook his head. He needed time.

Tanfeld picked up his fork, stepped over to Gwynedd and brought it down with incredible force into her left hand as it rested on her thigh, the tines penetrating a good half-inch into the flesh between her knuckles and thumb.

She screamed and Tanfeld pulled out the fork and slapped her in the face as her plate and cake fell on the carpet. 'Pain doesn't require noise, girl. We all know it hurts.'

He stepped back to the mantelpiece, wagging his finger at Duncan. 'Now, tell me.'

He looked across at Gwynedd, then at Duncan again, then at the fork – and licked her blood off the prongs and held the cleaned fork up for inspection.

'Plenty of soft flesh on her frame. Deeper flesh, too. Now, who betrayed me?'

Duncan's mind raced. He stared down at his plate, dropped during Tanfeld's sudden attack. How could he possibly tell the truth? It would sound worse than lies.

'You have one second.'

'Mr Fazey.'

Tanfeld arched his eyebrows and considered this. 'No,' he said simply and in a blur stabbed the fork into Duncan's left cheek, withdrawing it immediately and resuming his casual stance, a look of distaste crossing his face as his slippered foot ground spilled cake into the carpet.

Duncan had actually felt one of the tines enter his mouth and shock delayed the pain, but then it hit him red and raw, and tears squirted from his eyes and he grabbed his cheek and screamed as blood began to flow freely over his fingers.

'I have very limited patience, young man. The next time I shall stick this in your girlfriend's eye – and turn it. And after that . . .' He turned to his plate, cut another slice of cake and slowly ate it, the chomping of his large yellowed teeth the only sound in the cold room.

Leonard leaned in to Duncan. 'Tell him the truth. I don't think he'll be surprised. Just do anything he says.'

Duncan was wiping blood from his cheek. He looked at Gwynedd, both of them frantic with concern and impotence, unable to help themselves, never mind each other. Looking at the silent tears limping down the girl's face, Duncan needed no further incentive to kill Tanfeld.

'Leonard Halsey told me.'

'Halsey? Why?'

'I met him and he started talking about these orgies he went to, and I wanted to find out more.'

The fork was raised and pointed at Gwynedd. Tanfeld gave a little stab then slowly turned it half a circle, his eyebrows arched, his tongue on his lips, as if anticipating the removal of a cork from a bottle of fine wine.

'Mr Halsey was dead before we changed the meeting place. He couldn't have told you even if he wanted to. Besides, Mr Halsey was not entirely in favour of our little soirées. I rarely give second chances, young man, and I never, *ever* give a third. Who told you?'

Gwynedd said, 'Tell him the truth, Duncan. If he believes in his runes, he'll believe in Leonard.'

Tanfeld looked puzzled.

'Are you all right?' said Duncan, eyeing the blood on Gwynedd's hand and the pain etched on her face.

'You will speak to me.'

'Fuck off!' shouted Duncan before he could stop himself. 'You sick fucker! There's no need to hurt her.'

Tanfeld lunged for Duncan and, kneeling on top of his knees, his face inches from Duncan's, he prodded the fork into the skin at the side of Duncan's left eye. His breath smelled of curry.

'There's *every* need to hurt her. And you. And anyone else I deem worthy of suffering.' He pushed the fork harder. Duncan began to shake uncontrollably, the fork only avoiding his eyeball because the prongs were digging into the flesh on the edge of his eye socket. 'Pain is a positive force, Mr Cantrill: it gets things done. It also serves a greater cause. Pain and fear, the two components of the dark. When you were a little boy lying in the dark and you were scared, what did you fear? Many things, no doubt, but the biggest fear was the fear itself, that little light that drew pictures in your mind of hideous creatures and madmen, but what was the one thing all these nightmares had in common? They would hurt you.' He prodded harder.

Duncan held his breath, desperately trying to look away from the sliver flashing in the corner of his vision.

'Pain, young sir, is what all fear comes down to. Not death, not loss, but *pain*. Someone else dies, you carry on. You die, it's just a big sleep. Supposedly. But pain . . . That is what fear is: pain. If I were to scoop out your eye, you would still be able to see. A couple of weeks and you would have a glass eye. No-one would know except you. *But the pain*. To feel the steel prick the surface of your pupil, to experience it cutting through that precious glassy surface and entering the aqueous humor. To actually feel that unthinkable intrusion. Think what a speck of dust, an eyelash trapped under your lid feels like; now multiply that ten million fold and you'll understand that pain is all; pain is the master of emotion, of life. Pain, Mr Cantrill, *is all*. And you have but one second to tell me the truth or your remaining good eye will watch your other dead eye being fed to your lady friend.'

Tanfeld leaned back, then stood upright.

Duncan sucked in air like a drowning man, and almost fainted. His hands fluttered over his face like a poisoned bird, unable to stay still. He was crying, tears mingling with the blood from his cheek and running down his neck to stain his shirt.

'For God's sake, Duncan, tell him the truth!' begged Gwynedd, squeezing his hand and causing more blood to well up from her own wound.

'No alternative, Duncan,' said Leonard, now standing beside Tanfeld. 'Do it.'

'This is the truth,' Duncan began.

'We shall see,' said Tanfeld. 'But will you?' He allowed himself a small smile, like a crack in marble.

'I worked in a hotel. I found Leonard Halsey dead. You can check in the papers. Later that day he came back to me, as a ghost. He said he had been murdered and couldn't rest until whoever had done it had also died. At first I didn't believe him, I thought I was mad, but he proved he existed, and we began to investigate. Racimo, Beaumont, Donaldson, we realised they had all been killed by you. We traced you through a photo in Beaumont's office and an address in one of Fazey's books. You're his landlord but his rent is ridiculously low. He killed himself before . . .' Duncan burst into tears, like a child trying to tell teacher how something got broken but unable to explain it coherently.

Duncan suddenly sat back defiantly. If the truth didn't work, nothing else would – and he now knew he couldn't rush the man: Tanfeld had the reactions of an athlete.

'Interesting. And Leonard is still with you? Here?'

Duncan debated whether to say so but Tanfeld saw the indecision. 'If he wasn't there would be no need to think, so he is here.'

'You believe me?'

'I believe more than you could possibly imagine. Where is he now?'

'Stood to your left.'

Tanfeld turned to look at empty air. Leonard stared back.

'How does he look?'

'As he was when he was murdered.'

'Can you prove he's here?'

'Yes. I've proved it to . . .'

'Your girlfriend. Do it.'

'Find something I haven't seen; Leonard will tell me what it is.'

'Very well.' Tanfeld picked up one of the glass swans and turned it over. 'What does it say on the base of this?'

Leonard told Duncan and he repeated it. 'Smiddles Glass, 28 Barnet Road, Blackpool, S44089.'

Tanfeld was impressed. He picked up another ornament.

'Hong Kong.'

He laughed. Soon he was running round the room picking up papers and items, cackling with joy each time Leonard told Duncan what to say. Finally he came back to the mantelpiece.

'Fascinating, fascinating. I know it happens, of course, but not to followers of mine. They're . . . tainted, in the eyes of some. Fascinating. Nonetheless, you must die, and this Leonard will die with you.'

'What?' said Duncan, genuinely surprised that Tanfeld wasn't going to pursue Leonard any more. 'There's a ghost in this room and all you want to do is kill me?'

'I have no choice. Besides, what use is he to me? More to the point, what use is he to you? After all, if it wasn't for him, you would not be here now and your girlfriend and yourself wouldn't be in such discomfort. So, to the problem at hand. The rune serves a purpose beyond my revenge and when I realised it had not claimed you, I checked the newspaper. It has never failed so it must have been passed on.'

245

'It?' said Gwynedd through gritted teeth. The sharp pain in her hand had turned into a deep throbbing. 'You mean the black wind.'

'Oh, you *have* been busy. Splendid! I do like initiative. Yes indeed, the black wind is one name for it. "Friend" is, of course, another.'

'How about master?' said Leonard.

'What?' said Duncan.

'What?' said Tanfeld. 'Oh, your dead friend. By all means let us hear a contribution from the "other side".' He said this as if Leonard was a charlatan.

'I may be making things worse, Duncan,' said Leonard. 'So I leave it up to you, but why has he got to kill you with another rune? Why doesn't he just top you now?'

'Thanks, Leonard.'

'Well,' said Tanfeld, his tapping fingers betraying his impatience.

Duncan took another deep breath. The pain in his cheek was continuing to grow, his cheek hot and feeling as if it was swelling up like a balloon. 'He asked why I have to be given another rune?'

There was a long silence, Tanfeld's fingers suddenly frozen. Whatever he was thinking, it was clear Leonard had hit home.

'Because I wish it.'

'Bullshit,' said Leonard. 'He has to; *he's* the servant. He fucked it up the last time so he's got to make amends.'

'I'm not saying—' started Duncan.

Tanfeld's eyes blazed. 'It's rude to whisper, boy.'

'You've *got* to give me a rune, haven't you? You've no choice.'

Tanfeld took a step towards him, the fork pointing at Duncan, Gwynedd screamed and Duncan shrank back, but Tanfeld stopped and let his hand go limp.

'I am going to make you an offer, Mr Cantrill. You have no option but to accept. Yes, it is true I have to give you another rune. It is most displeased that it missed its true target. It needs to feast, and feast regularly now that it is awake. At first it was expedient, a trained dog for the killing of the unfaithful and wavering; the ones you suspect as victims were indeed souls for the eating, but they were not the first. However, once awakened, its hunger has grown. I have to feed it to keep it nourished. You disappointed it and it doesn't appreciate that; it will accept no substitutes. I am going to give you another rune, and you will accept your fate. If you do, I will let the girl live.'

Duncan laughed out loud, but the pain in his cheek quickly stopped him. 'No way!'

'As I said, you have no option. The alternative is to sit and watch as I take your girlfriend apart, piece by piece. I am a trained nurse; I have instruments. I will tie her to a table, stripped naked and gagged. I will then cut off her nipples, her clitoris, her nose, her ears. I will then slice off her breasts, inch by inch, and all the time she will be awake and aware, experiencing every exquisitely painful moment, and you will be watching, feet away, responsible. She will look at you and see not a lover or a friend, but her torturer, because you will have done this to her; you will have put her through hell. And what's more, I can make it last for *days*. No-one knows you're here, there are no neighbours – I own all the houses in this road. With the tools I have I might even be able to tackle an amputation that she would survive.' He was warming to his train of thought. 'Yes, imagine it: if she could survive the loss of a foot or a hand, why not the other? Why not all? How much could she lose before she succumbed? She's a strapping girl. And then you would *still* be given a rune and die.'

Duncan was frantic beyond rational thought. He couldn't bear the thought of anything more being done to Gwynedd because of him. 'All right, all right! But how will I know you'll free her afterwards?'

'You won't. But the alternative is in the basement, along with the rusted saws and hammers and nails.'

'Take it, Duncan!' said Leonard.

Duncan looked up at him, hatred in his eyes.

'By all means consult your accomplice,' said Tanfeld. 'Feel free to use any language you think necessary.' He smiled like an indulgent father.

'You want me to say yes?' said Duncan, deserted by the cause of all this horror.

Leonard leaned in and whispered, as if Tanfeld might be able to hear. 'Take the rune now and you've got till midnight to find a solution. Refuse and Gwynedd is dead anyway.'

'But what—'

'Shut up, Duncan!' shouted Leonard. 'Take the rune, you've got time; refuse it, Gwynedd's dead and you'll *still* get the fucking thing.'

'He might—'

'Kill her anyway? Maybe, but I think he'll keep her as a bargaining point until you're dead. It's your only choice.'

'Some choice.'

'I know.'

Duncan looked at Gwynedd. Terror lit her eyes like a reflection from a fire. Everything he did now was for her; not himself, not Leonard, not even to stop Tanfeld, but simply to save her.

'All right. I have your word you won't harm her?'

'You have my word that you will die, Mr Cantrill. Do not attempt to leave. I won't be a moment.'

Tanfeld walked briskly out of the room. Duncan immediately stood up, grabbed Gwynedd's undamaged hand and pulled her to her feet, but she was weak and he had to support her. As a result they had only just managed to get to the end of the couch when Tanfeld returned, Leonard's shouted warning too late. He didn't seem at all surprised to see them trying to escape. He punched Gwynedd in the face and she slumped back onto the couch unconscious.

'Sit down,' he said to Duncan.

Duncan squared up to him but Tanfeld looked down at a pen he had in his hand. 'A stomach wound would slow you down, and you'd be in agony until your time.'

Duncan walked backwards to the couch and stooped down to look at Gwynedd. Her nose was discoloured, the bridge oddly configured.

'You've broken her nose!'

'Quite possibly. I told you not to leave.'

Duncan gently turned Gwynedd so that she was lying on her side in case she swallowed her tongue, then he checked her pulse and her breathing. Both seemed okay. Tanfeld actually turned his back on him but he knew it would be pointless to attack him. Instead he concentrated on making Gwynedd comfortable, holding her hand and saying he was sorry over and over. Tears sprang anew and dripped onto her white face as hatred and anger welled up in him like lava, but he knew he couldn't do anything then; he would have to wait and see. Leonard kept quiet, aware that Duncan was teetering on the edge of madness and needing to keep his wits about him.

Two minutes passed, then Tanfeld turned and offered Duncan the familiar piece of paper. Duncan didn't react.

'Young man, we both know what this is, so let's not waste any more time. Take it, accept it, do not deny it.'

Duncan reached out a shaking hand then snatched it. 'Bastard!' he said.

'True, but one cannot choose one's parents. However,' he said, putting the pen into his trouser pocket, 'one can choose one's master. Well, I think we shall leave it there. You're free to go but remember, you must let the rune run its course or things will be truly terrible for your girlfriend. And don't think about passing it on to anyone else. This time an animal will not be enough; it must be a human being, and who do you want to sentence to death?'

'You.'

'Very amusing. Besides, even if you do pass it on, the black wind will still come for you. Twice cursed there is no escape.'

He walked to the door, beckoning Duncan to leave. Reluctantly, Duncan let go of Gwynedd's hand, aware that the only hope either of them had lay with whatever he could achieve in the next few hours. As he reached the front door, he looked Tanfeld in the eye. They were dead eyes, emotionless.

'I'm going to kill you,' Duncan said.

'No, you're not,' said Tanfeld. 'Not if you want the girl to live a little longer.'

And with that he closed the door, leaving Duncan with eight hours to live.

28

'*STOP THE CAR! Stop the fucking car!*' yelled Leonard from the passenger seat.

But Duncan wasn't listening. Gwynedd was in danger, he had to get help, tell the police, save her, get Tanfeld. He spun the Nova onto the main road ignoring any approaching traffic, and accelerated towards Ollington.

Leonard continued to scream at him to stop, to think about what he was doing, but all Duncan could see was that he had fucked up big time and Gwynedd was going to be hurt or worse. Time to get real and let the experts deal with it.

Suddenly Leonard was on the bonnet of the car, clinging to the roof, his bulk blotting out the road ahead. Duncan screamed at him to get out of the way but the man wouldn't move and he had to slam on his brakes, narrowly missing an oncoming Volvo, before he slewed onto the verge and rumbled to a juddering halt, the engine stalling.

Leonard reappeared in the car as Duncan tried to re-start the engine. 'Wait, Duncan! One minute! Just listen. Please.'

Duncan's fury overwhelmed every other consideration. 'Get out of my sight, you bastard! This is all your fault. She's going to die and it's all because of you!'

'No, it isn't, Duncan! It's him, Tanfeld's fault. He did all this, he's the one who has Gwynedd held prisoner, the one who gave you the rune, killed me, the others . . . Tanfeld's the enemy, not me. I'm sorry for what's—'

Duncan felt the holes in his cheek, the flesh swollen and hard, the pain spreading around the whole side of his face. Then he checked the the piece of paper in his top pocket, its fragile crispness like the shed skin of a snake bleached by the sun, and doubly loathsome.

'You're right. Sorry,' said Duncan, twisting at the ignition key. 'Tanfeld's fault. Which is why the police.'

'And what? So they go to the house, Tanfeld denies everything, they look, find nothing, leave? Or they storm the house and he kills her? Or they rescue her and charge him with kidnap?'

'Yes!'

'So what about the rune in your pocket? What about everyone who's died? Me? No way will you be able to prove any of this shit . . . and at midnight, you'll still die.'

'At least Gwyn—'

'At least? *If!* Why should you die and that fucker live? Don't you see, he's given you the perfect weapon! Slip him the rune and it comes for him – and it doesn't come back again because he's dead. Two evil birds with one stone.'

'Makes sense.'

'Course it does.'

'But what if he hurts Gwynedd anyway?' He couldn't help remembering the casual way in which he had stabbed her hand and punched her unconscious.

'She might be dead *now*, Duncan, and there's nothing you can do about it. You've no guarantees on what he'll do, I'm sorry, but you do have a guaranteed date with God knows what if you don't give the rune back to him.'

'But *how* do I give it back to him?'

'We've got to figure that out – and that means finding out as much as we can about this Black Wind he calls up.'

'Where? The only place I know is—'

'Exactly.'

'But it'll—'

'—be empty. Precisely.'

'Which means I've got to—'

'—break in. Spot on. So, easy does it, drive back to town, park somewhere quiet, and let's get to work.'

Duncan stared at Leonard. He'd become like a nagging older brother; a pain in the arse most of the time but, when the family needed to pull together, there with the right ideas and the encouragement. What he said made sense; he just prayed it was also right.

'You realise one thing, don't you?' said Duncan. 'If Tanfeld dies?'

'What happens to me, you mean? Yes, I know.'

'Are you scared?'

'No. I'm dead already.'

'What about what's going to happen, you know, after . . .?'

'Don't know. Not much I can do about it anyway, let's be realistic. All I can think is, if I've been given the chance to come back and get Tanfeld, someone somewhere must like me enough to, well, keep me out of the cauldron.'

'Do you believe in . . . I don't believe I'm saying this – asking a dead man about heaven and hell.'

'Well, I hope there is a hell, because that's where that bastard is going. As for heaven . . .'

Duncan thought about Leonard's marriage and his sexual proclivities, and couldn't help wondering if, perhaps, there might be a third destination.

They parked the Nova in the multi-storey car park behind the Peak Shopping Centre to limit the chances of it being spotted, then they walked the two hundred yards to Tyler Cop and Fazey's shop. Duncan insisted on taking the shotgun with him – 'just in case the car got nicked' – and stuffed the barrel down his trousers, the stock under his armpit. It gave him a slight limp but was surprisingly undetectable.

The door to Fazey's shop had been boarded up and sealed with police tape, presumably as it was still the scene of an investigation.

As soon as the street was empty of shoppers, Duncan ripped off the tape that ran the length of the door and shoulder-charged it. Two goes and the door burst open. He immediately shut the door and dropped the latch. Apart from the missing tape, anyone checking from the outside would find a boarded door that was locked.

Satisfied that they could work undetected, Duncan headed upstairs. Remembering that the only visible proof of the shop on the street was the front door – which was now boarded up – it was safe to turn the lights on.

The shop was pretty much as they had left it, apart from a sprinkling of dust on most touchable surfaces – fingerprint powder. The office had been systematically searched, and a good deal of its contents taken away for examination. Luckily, the books appeared undisturbed.

Extracting the shotgun from his trousers and leaning it against the tables in the middle of the room, Duncan took the first half of the main room, Leonard the rest. They searched the shelves until they had narrowed their investigation down to a series of shelves on the right hand side of the shop running from half way along the wall to the office door. Perhaps two thousand volumes in all, under sections headed Witchcraft, Demonology, Cults, Paganism, Legends and Folklore, and, intriguingly, Proceedings – several hundred paperbound volumes of reports, papers and essays from various societies and organisations dealing with the occult.

Duncan started with the top shelf nearest to himself and slowly worked his way along, picking out any books that looked to be of help, and piling them on the central table. Having checked two shelves, he pulled up a chair and began to work his way through the thirty or so books he had selected. It was going to be a long job.

They discovered several references, but it was several hours until they had found all they could. Although it told them what they had been looking for, and threw some light on Tanfeld, it was like a prisoner managing to translate his death warrant just as the firing squad cocked their triggers.

The reference they had found the previous day in one of Jane Dalton's books had been near the mark. From what they could glean, the Black Wind was an ancient legend from hill areas in several parts of the country, including the Welsh borders. It was some kind of natural force that jealously guarded its native domain from intruders. Regular appeasement, by way of offerings, ceremonies and, on occasion, sacrifices of animals, were believed to keep it quiet. As is so often the way, the Christian church had adopted pagan rituals in these areas and the priest's blessing of doorways and windows of new homes was one such of these. They discovered that Tanfeld had been a respected authority on local legends, including that of the Black Wind, in the 1940s and 1950s, until he had made a discovery and from then on he became an outcast, subject to ridicule at first, and then ignored. But, clearly, he was having the last laugh . . .

There was a noise downstairs. Duncan stopped dead, and looked at his watch. 8.45pm. Good grief. He'd never spent as long in a library in his life! Mind you, he'd never had the motivation to . . . He looked up at the roof. Night had fallen, darkness lying across the skylight like a blanket. He could see his own reflection, a white-faced figure surrounded by piles of open books.

Duncan stood up and edged towards the door. What could it be? Someone in the street? Suddenly there was a crash and the sound of running feet on wood and before he could think where to run, a young policeman burst into the room, his truncheon raised.

Duncan backed towards the narrow aisles that ran behind him, but the constable saw the movement.

'Don't move, you. What's going on?'

He looked at the books open on the table. 'This isn't a bloody library. Looking for something to steal?'

He stepped towards Duncan, then saw how scruffy and pale he was; saw the livid purple swelling of his cheek; smelled his sweat. 'Or were you looking for somewhere to kip?'

'Agree with him,' said Leonard, standing beside the PC. 'I'll see if he's alone.'

'Yes,' said Duncan.

'No-one else,' said Leonard, stood at the top of the stairs. 'The door's shut, too.'

Duncan nodded but the police constable saw his glance and spun to look over his shoulder but, of course, there was nothing for him to see.

He turned back, but now he did see something else. The shotgun that Duncan had retrieved from beside the table pointed at his stomach.

'Oh shit,' said Leonard. 'That's blown it.'

'No choice,' said Duncan. 'He'd have seen it.'

The policeman went pale, his mind plainly torn between his terror at the gun and his puzzlement at Duncan's words. For a moment Duncan felt sorry for him and almost faltered.

'Three hours, Duncan. And there's Gwynedd,' said Leonard, seeing his reaction.

Duncan nodded and the policeman panicked. Who else was there? Were they armed? 'What? What? Don't shoot, please, don't shoot.'

'Shut up, let me think.'

'Duncan, tie him up, leave. We've found all we're going to get.'

'Okay,' said Duncan. 'Drop the truncheon. Now! And get your handcuffs out. How did you know we . . . I was here?'

'Okay, okay, just be careful. No need to shoot. The skylight,' he said fumbling for the handcuffs. 'Could see it from the multi-storey.'

'Did you find the car?'

The policeman was going to say no, but Duncan pushed the barrel towards him.

'Yes. The Nova. Checking a mugging. It was sat there on its own. Checked the licence just in case. They said it was stolen by someone wanted in connection with the suicide of the shop owner. I saw the skylight from up there, thought I'd see . . .'

Duncan didn't like the terror in the man's eyes, but they were an effective reminder of his own and Gwynedd's terror of a few hours before. His swollen cheek was making him slur his words. God knows what the cop thought he was.

He marched him over to one of the radiators. He got the man to handcuff himself to the inlet pipe at one end. Using the man's tie as a gag, he then followed Leonard's advice to use the clothesline in the bathroom to tie the man's arms and legs. When the PC was finally trussed up and unable to move, Duncan sat back sweating, the pain in his cheek excruciating. He had dabbed at his face with cold water but it had done no good. He checked his watch again. Just over three hours left. He knew what he had to do but he was still no closer to finding a way of doing it.

He pressed the inside of his cheek with his finger. It felt impossibly thick. He wondered what Gwynedd's hand would look like – and her nose! That bastard. Then he remembered the film *Marathon Man*, the way Dustin Hoffman's character had used the pain in his tooth to remind him of the reasons for his violence. Duncan's damaged face now served the same purpose; he prodded it and nearly shrieked with the pain. He didn't need that much reminding!

The constable's radio suddenly crackled into life. Shit!

'He might have radioed he was coming here,' said Leonard.

'Should have thought of that.'

He unclipped the radio and threw it into the office.

'Wheels,' said Leonard. 'We need a car.'

'Where are you parked?'

The man didn't answer. Duncan jabbed him in the back with the gun. 'Your car, where is it?'

Still no response, other than the man peeing himself.

'He's gagged, you prat. He can't answer.'

Fuck! Duncan bent down, and pulled the gag aside.

'It's on the Cop. It's outside. Outside!'

Duncan felt for the man's car keys, pulled out a Ford keyring with three keys, then put the gag back on.

He ran down the stairs of the shop to the street where, checking there was no-one about, he got into the Escort panda car. But instead of driving off, he stared at the keys in his hand.

'What?' shrieked Leonard. 'Let's get going. When he doesn't answer, they'll have every—'

'Shut up, I'm thinking.'

'Oh, that's okay then. For a minute I thought we were sat here like sitting ducks wait—'

'Shut up! Tanfeld had a Mercedes parked in his drive, didn't he?'

'Yes, but—'

'And we really need to slip the rune to him as close to midnight as possible.'

'So he doesn't pass it on. Yes, but—'

'Will you shut up with your bloody "buts"! I swear if I don't get through tonight alive, I'm going to come and haunt *you!* Now shut up!'

He turned the keys over and over in his hand, pulling faces and mentally counting through the options.

Finally he put them in the ignition. 'Right, we go find mum's BMW.'

'At the college? But what if it's been recovered?'

'Then things will have got even worse than they are.'

'Not possible,' said Leonard.

'He says in a stolen police car with three hours to go.'

Leonard remained silent as they drove off towards Ollington College.

29

DUNCAN SWITCHED OFF the BMW's engine, let the car coast to a halt in the road outside Tanfeld's house and got out, shotgun in one hand, carrier bag in the other, leaving the door open.

Bent double, he trotted over to the parked Mercedes and, stooping down, pulled a screwdriver from the bag and stabbed the front nearside tyre. There was a gasp and then a long hiss as the tyre deflated. He edged along to the rear tyre and repeated the procedure, then lay on his back and, squirming under the back end of the car, pierced the other rear tyre and waited as that too emptied of air.

He then rolled out from under the car and sat on his haunches, his back against the rear passenger door facing away from the house. He waited a minute then, sure his vandalism hadn't been detected, carefully emptied the contents of the carrier bag onto the ground next to him.

'Right, Leonard, I need to know where Gwynedd is.'

Leonard didn't reply. Instead he disappeared from Duncan's side and reappeared immediately by the window of the room in which they had met Tanfeld. Having scanned the sitting room through a gap in the curtains, he returned.

'Not in there,' he reported, gone again in an instant.

He stared into the room on the other side of the front door. It was a dining room, with a large table, chairs and cabinets and a dresser. As with the room they had been in earlier, the furniture was cheap, the ornamentation brash, the decorations tacky, but Gwynedd was there. Alive, thank God, and . . . polishing.

Leonard was at Duncan's side. 'She's there – and she's cleaning.'

'What?'

'The weirdo's got her polishing the bloody furniture – Mr Sheen and all! There's a Hoover out as well. He's probably had her doing the entire house.'

Duncan made to rise, his anger all the greater for the bizarreness of Tanfeld's behaviour.

'No!' urged Leonard. 'Look, she's alive; it's more than we bargained for, be honest. She's in the room on the left, which means the other room's empty. Stick to the plan.'

Duncan looked at his watch in the dim light from the house. 11.40pm. Stick to the plan.

'Any chance of getting round the back?' he asked anyway.

Leonard looked to the right. 'Metal gate. Make a hell of a noise. The other side? Bushes all the way to the house wall. And there's no time to try round the back, even if there's an easy way in. No, Plan A it is.'

'Right. Let's do it. And remember, keep out of it. No distractions.'

Leonard nodded as Duncan picked up the first bottle and, flicking his Bic lighter, set fire to the petrol-soaked cloth hanging from its neck. He took two steps back from the car, pulled his arm back, and hurled the petrol bomb through the right hand window.

There was crashing glass, a pause, then a low *whump* and light started dancing on the inside of the curtains. He lit a second bottle and threw that after the first, but his aim was out and it hit the brickwork above the window, spewing a flaming fountain across the right side of the house. Quickly, he lit his third and final bomb and threw it dead centre of the window and smiled as it exploded inside.

He stepped back into the centre of the driveway, raised his shotgun and aimed at the front door, but then he changed his mind and crouched back down behind the car.

'The plan, the plan!' hissed Leonard.

'If he sees me he might go back inside. We don't know about the back, remember?'

Leonard saw the sense of it and shut up.

The fire took hold incredibly quickly, but remembering the cheap furniture and the foam seating, it was not that surprising. Then he heard a scream – Gwynedd – and a shout from Tanfeld.

There was an explosion in the burning room strong enough to blow out what remained of the glass in the window – what the hell could have caused that? – and just as Duncan decided he would have to go in, the front door burst open and out stumbled Gwynedd, followed by Tanfeld, amid a cloud of choking smoke. Both tripped down the two front steps and skidded onto the gravel.

Judging them to be far enough from the house to make Tanfeld's retreat impractical, Duncan jumped up and, leaning over the car roof, pointed the shotgun at Tanfeld's chest and shouted:

'*Tanfeld! Stop right there!*'

Squinting his eyes against the smoke, the man turned to look at Duncan and saw the shotgun. He twitched, as if about to run, but stopped. Instead, his eyes staring straight at Duncan, he reached out for Gwynedd. Duncan shouted at her to run but too late; she was coughing and her hideously bruised eyes were blinded by tears and she walked straight into his grasp.

Tanfeld immediately pulled her in front of him, his arm across her throat.

'Duncan! Duncan!' Gwynedd cried, but Tanfeld tightened his grip and choked off her pleas.

'An interesting dilemma, Mr Cantrill. Aim is an irrelevancy with a weapon such as that; shoot at me and you hit the girl. Stalemate, I believe.'

'But you're not going anywhere either. Your car's fucked, and your house is burning down.' As he said this, flames reached the hallway, lighting up the stained glass in the porch windows yellow and orange.

'So what if I choose to stand here? Come midnight, you die anyway. And then the girl.' He pulled harder on her throat, her arms flailing uselessly at his elbows.

Duncan was appalled at the damage that had been inflicted on her pretty face, but knew there was more at stake than a busted nose and black eyes. He had to keep his cool, whatever the provocation, and however much his heart reached out to her.

'Okay, we wait,' said Duncan, checking his watch but not registering the time; his attention was held by Gwynedd's struggle for breath.

'If I don't get bored.' Tanfeld looked back at his house.

The fire was spreading quickly, already licking out of the front room at the windowsill above. Duncan could see Leonard standing by Tanfeld, his fists clenched in anger at his impotence. Duncan nodded at him to move out of his line of sight and he disappeared,

Tanfeld not noticing the contact as he glanced over his shoulder at the blaze.

'There was no need for this wilful destruction. Another fifteen minutes and what would it matter?'

'Well, let Gwynedd go and you can call the fire brigade.'

Tanfeld didn't reply.

'Don't want to call anyone, do you? Don't want anyone seeing what's going to happen when your Black Wind comes.'

'Perhaps, but whilst I may lose one of my houses, you will lose your existence. I think one outbalances the other a tad. Don't you agree, my dear?' he said into Gwynedd's ear, tugging his elbow tighter around her throat, so that her legs left the floor and kicked lamely at his shins.

Duncan walked out from behind the car, shotgun at the ready. 'Stop it. Don't hurt her.'

'Leave.'

'You know I can't do that.'

'Oh yes, you can. We both know you still have the rune, otherwise you would have shot me as soon as I came out of the house. You want to pass it on to me, but obviously I'm not going to accept it.'

'"If the Black Wind consumes its master, it consumes itself."'

Tanfeld laughed. 'You have been doing your homework, haven't you? Was it McGill's *Demons of England*, or my own *Researches into the Legends of Shropshire*?'

'Yours.'

'In Fazey's shop, I suppose. I always wanted him to remove the volume but, well, vanity . . .'

He talked as if they were enjoying a pleasant drink in a snug pub nearby, rather than threatening each other with death in front of a blazing building.

Duncan had found a paper written by Tanfeld in a bibliography. It was a paper published in the archives of the Society for Occultic Research in November 1958. He had been researching a local legend in west Shropshire, barely a mile from the Welsh border, and had uncovered a book written sometime in the fifteenth century hidden in a vault of a local church. From previous researches he stated that he believed it be a guide to summoning demons and he intended to translate it. At that time he had confessed that even if he failed in his task it was still an important find. The president of the Society had congratulated him on his discovery and welcomed correspondence on it. Subsequent issues had thrown additional light on the local legends of the Black Wind, one recurring theme being its invocation as a means of defeating invading armies during the 8th and 9th centuries AD. The Society being staffed by believers, all suggestions were taken seriously. It would have been silly if it hadn't led to such desperate results.

'Over thirty years I laboured on the book. Thirty years, day in, day out, dedicated to its understanding. I found it required the power of a coven to help tap the source, so I founded the society to which your friend Halsey – whom I presume is with us – became an unwitting and eventually unwilling participant. I finally succeeded in understanding the ritual, the invocation and its consequences.'

'And you lost control.'

'Control? An interesting word. Let us say it was more determined than I was led to believe. After slumbering so long it was hungry. I fed that hunger but I also discovered that it was greedy; it wanted more than it needed. You will make it very happy; a recovery of something it had lost. And then . . .'

'It's your master. You're just like fucking Renfield, aren't you, doing what the master bids!'

Tanfeld smiled indulgently but even in the flickering light from the fires, Duncan could see that there was no sincerity in it.

'Who . . . cares?' he said, pulling even harder on Gwynedd's throat.

'Stop it!' shouted Duncan.

'Shoot then!' shouted Tanfeld.

Duncan fingered the triggers, but instead ran at the man, swinging the shotgun like a club, trying to crack him in the face.

He swung round, pulling Gwynedd with him, but her weight was too much for him and she slipped from his grasp and fell to her knees. Duncan's wild swing missed and as his momentum twisted him round, Tanfeld lashed out and grabbed the barrel of the gun. Duncan felt his fingers fly loose of the trigger guard and the gun took flight. Too late he reached for it with his other hand, only to see Tanfeld spin it in the air before him until he held it pointed at Duncan's head. He screamed in frustration but Tanfeld simply nodded.

'Well, well, well,' he said, cocking the hammers. 'Something seems to be amiss here, doesn't it, Mr Cantrill? Could it be that I have the gun, you still have the paper and midnight approaches?' He found this very amusing.

Duncan slowly edged down until he touched Gwynedd's shoulder. She gave a start as she struggled for breath, then a shaking hand grasped his and he hauled her upright, all the time his eyes fixed on the barrel of the gun barely six feet from his face. The two of them huddled together. Gwynedd shook with fear and relief, but upon spying the shotgun pointed at them began crying.

'It's all right, it's going to be all right,' Duncan said, trying to hush her, but his attention was locked on Tanfeld's face, watching for any emotion. There was none.

'So, what now you bastard?' Duncan finally said.

Tanfeld shifted uncomfortably. The heat from the fire was making him sweat, the flames now appearing inside the left hand room and upstairs right bedroom. It must be visible for miles.

'You die.'

Gwynedd whimpered and buried her face in Duncan's chest. The poor girl must have been terrified all day.

'No, I don't,' said Duncan calmly. 'I can't die, not unless it's because of the Black Wind. Disappoint it again and you'll be in serious shit.'

Tanfeld twitched a bead of sweat off his eyebrow. 'You are correct. But there is nothing to stop me maiming you beforehand, or shooting the bitch.'

'But you won't. Look at your house. Someone somewhere will have called the fire brigade by now. Police'll turn up, too. How would you explain our bodies outside your house?'

'Give me the keys.'

'What?'

'The keys! The keys to the BMW.'

'No.'

'Give me the keys or the girl dies.'

'No. You know you can't.'

Tanfeld gave off a strange smile. 'Patience is a virtue I have never found time for.'

Then laughing at his little joke, he shifted the gun so that it was pointing at Gwynedd's stomach and pulled the trigger.

Gwynedd shrieked and fell from Duncan's grasp onto her knees and vomited onto the floor.

Tanfeld looked at the silent gun, aimed it at Duncan and pulled the second trigger. Again it didn't fire.

Duncan smiled. 'I might be stupid but I'm not an idiot.'

With amazing speed, Tanfeld lunged forward and swiped the barrel of the gun across Gwynedd's head. She crashed onto her side, blood oozing from her scalp.

Leonard shouted a futile warning as Tanfeld ran at Duncan and pushed him onto his back, kicking him in the testicles and raising the butt of the gun above his head.

'Worm,' said Tanfeld.

'You can't kill me!'

'But I can hurt you.'

He raised the gun to its highest point but then stopped. Duncan squinted against the smoke and saw the man's attention was held by something in the distance. And then he heard it: a siren. Emergency services were on their way.

Tanfeld shifted his gaze to the watch exposed on his wrist. Duncan saw his chance and lunged out with his feet at the man's crotch.

Tanfeld let out a little gasp but otherwise didn't react. 'What you haven't got, you don't miss,' he said, smiling as he brought the gun crashing down onto Duncan's shoulder.

Pain creased his body like a shaft of steel. He tried to scream but his throat wouldn't work. Leonard screamed abuse at Tanfeld, but it was as futile as Duncan's defence.

'Minutes left, boy. Minutes of pain—'

He hit him in the chest with the butt of the gun.

'—Minutes of misery—'

Again he hit him in the stomach.

'—Minutes of regret.'

Duncan flinched, expecting another blow, but instead Tanfeld turned and whipped the moaning Gwynedd across the head again and she juddered and stilled, even more blood on her hair and face, its scarlet all the ruddier in the glow from the fire.

Something in the house collapsed, sending a shower of sparks into the night and, as the crackling lessened, the familiar two-tone fire engine horn could be heard even louder.

Tanfeld raised the butt of the gun above Duncan's face. 'The keys to the car. Now.'

'No.'

'I have nothing to lose, boy. You still have precious moments of life – and where there's life there's hope.'

Duncan tried to spit at him but the phlegm clogged his throat and made him cough. When his eyes cleared, he found Tanfeld had walked over to Gwynedd and had her head held up by the hair.

'The keys, boy, or I'll snap her neck!' He jerked her unconscious frame to emphasise the point.

Duncan eased himself up, fighting the pain in his shoulder and stomach, and, reaching a shaking hand into his trouser pocket, pulled out the keys attached to the BMW car alarm remote. He held them out to Tanfeld.

The man started to let Gwynedd drop, but then stopped.

'Show me the rune.'

Duncan tried to protest, but he could see the man's grip tighten on Gwynedd's hair, twisting it round his hand like a dog's lead. Duncan reached into the top pocket of his shirt, fumbled open the button, and pulled out the piece of paper.

'Eat it!' barked Tanfeld.

'What?'

'Eat the rune. Now!'

Duncan looked at the piece of paper. He could see a smile spreading on Tanfeld's face as he edged the paper to his trembling lips, both of them aware of what it would mean.

Duncan hesitated, hoping the siren in the distance would suddenly burst into the lane, but there was no time left. Tanfeld raised his fist, ready to smash it into Gwynedd's face. Duncan had no choice. He put the rune in his mouth and closed his lips, pretending to chew.

Tanfeld stared at him, then realising Duncan might not swallow it, he dropped Gwynedd and dashed over to him, grabbing him by the lapels and shouting into his face:

'*Eat it, boy, eat it!*'

Duncan tried chewing but his mouth was dry. Tanfeld screamed, inches from his face, spit peppering his hot cheeks, and eventually Duncan managed to condense the paper into a pellet which he swallowed with great difficulty.

'Open your mouth!'

Duncan did as ordered and Tanfeld checked he had ingested the rune. Satisfied, Tanfeld kissed him on the forehead then pushed him to the ground.

'You're so privileged.'

He stamped on Duncan's wrist so the car keys fell out of his fingers, then he picked them up.

'Take them,' Duncan managed, but pain caught his breath.

266

Tanfeld turned to walk to the car, then paused and kicked Duncan with extreme force in the ribs. As Duncan's world exploded into a raw red inferno of pain, he heard Tanfeld say, 'And that's for my house.'

With that, he ran over to the BMW, jumped inside, fired it up and roared off down the lane, gravel spraying Duncan and Gwynedd like a spit of contempt.

Duncan was doubled up in pain, every bone in his body feeling as if it had been broken. He was sure his shoulder and ribs had been seriously damaged, maybe even broken, and the pain between his legs still offered an intensity that denied movement. Leonard knelt down next to him. Duncan looked up at him and shook his head.

'Say nothing,' he said. 'Say nothing.'

Duncan managed to drag his stamped wrist into view and looked at his watch in the light from the fire. It was broken, the hands frozen at 11.54. There was still time, but he had to get Gwynedd to safety.

He rolled over on his front and crawled over to her limp body. Smoke rose into the night sky, grey on black, the trees and bushes cavorting in the yellow light, the house cackling at its own destruction.

He reached Gwynedd and checked her pulse. She was still alive despite the blood on her face. He edged himself onto his knees, the pain in his groin sucking the breath from him. Using his good arm, he reached under her armpit and hoisted her into a sitting position. He then forced himself to stand, pain exploding in his head, his left side virtually immobilised by Tanfeld's blows.

He looked down the lane. Blue lights creased the night, but they were still some way off. The BMW's rear lights had disappeared.

He reached under Gwynedd and, grabbing her jumper, slowly pulled her towards the Mercedes, her feet dragging in the gravel like broken branches. He chose to ignore his own pain – there were only minutes left – and he slowly got her to the car where he propped her up against the driver's door, shielded from the heat of the fire. He looked around for the shotgun, limped over to where it lay discarded, and returned to the Mercedes.

It took two swings to smash the driver's window. Reaching inside, he unlocked the door and pulled it open. He had spotted what he was after the first time they had visited Tanfeld's house.

Checking Gwynedd was still breathing, he sat in the driver's seat and picked up the mobile phone clipped to the dashboard. Surprised at how bloody his hands were, Leonard reminded him of the number and he punched it in and waited.

The clock on the dashboard ticked close to midnight.

He heard the phone ringing and waited, its insistent beeping in his ear counterpointing the fire engine's approaching siren in his other, both sounds laid on a backing track of whooshing flames and crackling wood.

The *beep-beep* continued.

'Come on, you bastard. Answer me, answer me.'

Finally the receiver was picked up, but there was no answer.

'Tanfeld!' shouted Duncan. 'Answer me, Tanfeld!'

'Cantrill?' came the reply. 'Of course, you would know this number. Surely you have better things to do than talk to me. Like praying. Or running?'

'I don't need the prayers, you fucker – you do.'

'Ha! Keep it up boy. It will be amusing to hear you scream as it comes for you.'

'And when will that be?'

'About a minute. Do stay on the line.'

'Oh, I will. What will happen?'

'Sixty seconds and you'll be able to tell me.'

Duncan coughed, smoke infiltrating the car.

'Dear me, you should watch that cough. Could turn into something nasty.'

'What will happen?'

'It will get cold. Very cold. Then dark. And then . . .'

'How warm are you, you bastard?'

For the first time Tanfeld faltered. 'I'm . . . what do you mean?'

'Whoever willingly accepts the rune dies?'

'Indeed, dear boy. Did you enjoy your snack?'

'Did you take the car keys?'

'Obviously . . . why?'

'Getting cold, is it?'

'I . . .'

'The key fob, Tanfeld. In the alarm remote. You willingly accepted it – and I willingly gave it. What's the time?'

No answer.

'Time to die, I think,' said Duncan.

He heard the telephone drop and, above the clatter, a screech of brakes and then another, higher pitched scream of terror – '*Mother!*' – then the line cut dead.

Duncan dropped the phone to the floor and slumped back. Even in his pain and fear he managed a smile. It had been a risk, but he'd had no alternative.

Although it hadn't all gone as planned, the man had accepted the rune he had hidden in the BMW key fob, knowing that ultimately it would be his only means of escape. The false rune in his pocket had just been in case Tanfeld had become suspicious. And now, it was over.

The fire brigade would arrive, and soon an ambulance, and then he and Gwynedd would be whisked off to hospital, their injuries tended to, the rest of their lives waiting to be completed. So there would be the police and explanations, but so what? After you've survived an aircrash the last thing you worry about is the mortgage.

He forced himself to roll out of the car where he slumped down beside Gwynedd.

'I'm sorry,' he said. 'Sorry you got hurt but it'll soon be over. I'm just so sorry.'

He started to cry, cradling her head on his chest, sobbing with relief. He could see the fire engine now at the head of the lane, its siren blaring, electric blue lights slicing through the darkness. Thank God, thank God. Leonard tried to speak but Duncan ignored him, instead hugging Gwynedd to him, rocking back and forth, his chin and hands sticky with her blood. But then the fire engine's lights dimmed and its horn receded as darkness enshrouded the lane, blocking their rescue from sight.

Then the wind began to howl, cold and angry, and blackness approached up the lane like a solid wall, a tidal wave of ink, swamping and swallowing everything in its path. The fire engine disappeared completely as if drowned, then trees and bushes on either side vanished into the maw that roared towards him. The cold intensified, chilling Duncan to his bones, the air hazed with his panicked breaths, fresh blood giving off stripes of vapour.

Leonard knelt down beside him. 'It didn't die with Tanfeld,' he said, tears in his eyes. 'It's still coming. I'm sorry.'

Duncan didn't have any time for apologies. He crawled round in front of Gwynedd and hauled her up the side of the car until she was propped upright, though still unconscious, her hair blown back across the roof of the car. He pulled open the driver's door, fighting the pressure of the wind, horrified to see the window frosting, the doorhandle icing to his fingers. Finally he tugged it fully open and slid Gwynedd inside, her head falling across the passenger seat. As he lifted her legs into the footwell, he glanced over his shoulder.

He could see Leonard silhouetted against a growing black circle that shrieked towards them, growing bigger every second, as terrifying as any film Duncan had seen of a tornado; an implacable, unstoppable force dedicated to mindless destruction.

Leonard was saying 'Sorry' over and over as he started to disappear, first becoming transparent and then vanishing altogether. Evil was approaching. Duncan's only hope of saving Gwynedd was to let the Black Wind take him away from the car.

Slamming the door, he edged along the bonnet, the wind pounding at his back, the unholy screaming tearing at his ears. He felt his legs and body going numb as if he was naked, and his hands kept sticking to the bonnet of the car the way ice cubes stick to wet fingers; he had to pry them loose with each move, convinced he would soon be tearing skin. As he reached the end of the bonnet, he pushed himself upright and stepped sideways.

Immediately the wind blasted him forwards. He managed to keep his footing for a couple of seconds, but the hurricane at his back was impossible to resist, so he set his feet in motion and started to run. But however hard he twisted his body, or tried to aim his legs, he was forced inexorably towards the burning house, right for the front door which was now a sheet of fire, fanned by the wind.

Duncan couldn't change course, couldn't even turn round; he was a tumbleweed heading for an inferno. Then he lost his footing and started to fall forwards, but even as he braced himself for the impact, he found himself whipped into the air and tossed end over end.

Orange-black-orange-black his eyes registered as his ears were shredded by the shrieking cacophony of the wind that batted him like a giant hand of ice. There was a brief breath of heat then he was crashing into the darkness, objects shattering about him, his limbs hacking through carbonised wood, his mouth filling with ashes, the bitter taste of smoke invading his lungs and needling his eyes. He was inside Tanfeld's burning house.

With *it*.

30

DUNCAN'S WORLD WAS a kaleidoscope of heat and ice, dark and light, hope and despair. It was if all his emotions, sensations and memories had been thrown into a mixer and whirled into a phantasmagorical blend and had then been doused over him, with a shock as strong as exiting a sauna into an icy pond. And it was this sensation of hot and cold that came to predominate, the interchange between the two becoming faster and faster until there was no difference: ice burnt, flames froze. He forced open his eyes and looked about him, his breath stolen by what he could see.

He was lying on his back on a jagged tumble of debris, most of it burned or smouldering wood. On all sides rose blackened brick to a ragged open space above him that glowed red about the edges, smoke swirling upwards, sucked out by the night air.

He sat upright. He had fallen through the burning staircase into the cellar, his descent broken by the fragile wood of the steps. Above him the house still burned, but the flames had not intruded into the basement. The air was rank with smoke but breathable. The room was twenty feet square, the bare walls rising to a high ceiling, half of which had fallen through with him. There appeared to be no way out – it was at least twelve feet to the floor above and, even if he managed to get up there, the house was still ablaze. He could see fire licking its way up the wall to the first floor, and hear hungry flames racing to consume every inch of the old house's heart.

He stood up, his footing unsteady, alarmed to find his clothes smoking and in a flurry of hands he flapped at his limbs and back and front in case he was still alight. Then he scrambled over to one wall but, touching it, found it burned his fingers. He was in an oven.

Heat suddenly invaded his world with a vengeance, causing him to sweat and tear at his clothes to get air to his scorched skin.

What comfort he might have taken from the Black Wind expending itself in forcing him into the house was more than defeated by the desperation of his new circumstances. Even as the air turned hot enough to taste and his throat dried, making breathing painful and laborious, he understood he could measure his future in minutes. If the upper floor of the house or walls collapsed into the cellar with him, he would be crushed or burned; if the house remained solid as it was eaten by fire, then he would be cooked: dry roasted in a fire of his own making.

He ran over to the opposite wall; it also was too hot to touch, and now the wood littering the floor began to crack and splinter with a sound like rifle shots. Burned timber was easily re-ignited; the floor beneath his feet could explode into flame at any instant.

He frantically tried to kick himself a clear space in the corner but the energy it required was soon exhausted by the super-tropical heat that was enveloping him like dragon's breath.

He fell to his knees, too weak to stand, sweat stinging his eyes, his dried lips stuck together and commuting his scream to a pathetic whimper that died somewhere on the back of his tongue. His thoughts ran to Leonard and Gwynedd and all that had happened but, facing death for the second time, he could find no comfort in his helping Leonard or saving Gwynedd. No, all he could see was how much of his own life he was going to miss when he died; and how much of it he had wasted growing up, for that was what he had never properly done: grown up. His life had been a pointless exercise in gesture and bitterness, a waste of talent and time and wealth. By pursuing his own agenda he had destroyed his own future – and the irony that it had taken the death of a stranger and his own imminent demise to show him the truth of it provoked bitter tears that mingled with his sweat to sheen his face in a curtain of misery. He had never done anything worthwhile in his life and only had himself to blame. He deserved his fate. He deserved to die.

Suddenly the heat halted, as if it was a fan heater that had been switched off, and the world which had been the blackest black and fiercest yellow now turned a frigid, electric blue that cooled him as effectively as if that very same fan heater had been switched to Cold. And then there was a voice; a voice he recognised.

'Not yet. There's time.'

Duncan looked around him. The smoke had cleared; the cellar was cool and calm, the fire above a slow motion twinkling in the distance, the sounds of destruction barely a whisper. He shook his head. He must have gone insane . . . thank God! If he didn't know what was happening, perhaps death wouldn't be so bad.

'You're not insane.'

What? Who said that?

'I did.'

Duncan turned to face the other way. Someone was standing in front of him, their back against the wall at the rear of the cellar ten feet away.

Who? What? *How?*

'You'll understand soon enough,' said a voice.

Duncan stood up and edged towards the shadowed figure. A fireman? The smoke had thinned but it still lent the light in the cellar a deceptive vagueness.

'Who are you?' he coughed. 'How are we going to get out of here?'

'We aren't, boy.'

'Why? You must have got in somehow. Who the – how do you know my name?'

'Simple. Look.'

The figure took a step forward and the sapphire light from the flames caught his face. Duncan let out a cry.

'Yes, boy. Credit for your ingenuity but not for your execution.'

Duncan stumbled back, clasping his head, his mind as blurred as his eyesight, and found the strength to scream.

The man stepped forward and looked him straight in the eye, barely a foot from his face. 'Terror doesn't require noise. We both know you're scared.'

Duncan tried to scrabble away over the debris, but he missed his footing and, overbalancing, toppled forward. The man stepped aside and let him crash to the ground. Duncan rolled over on his back and stared up at . . .

Tanfeld.

Duncan shook his head, madness a blink away. 'No! You can't be – you're dead!'

Tanfeld sneered down at him. 'True – and I must thank you. Without your assistance I would never have taken that final step for myself. How wrong I was to doubt my own work; how foolish, how . . . *human*. Well, no more.'

Tanfeld was dressed as he had been when he died, but he looked even more wasted, as if something had sucked the life out of him. He leaned forward and offered Duncan his hand.

'Death was such a small price to pay for this . . . joy. And such a small price for you to end your pathetically meaningless existence.'

'No, it killed you! The Black Wind killed you!'

'A mere detail – and I thought you knew something about my work.' Tanfeld edged closer, his pupils swallowing his irises as they bore into Duncan. 'That which consumes its master is released, not destroyed, for who is left to contain it? If the genie in the lamp kills its master, the genie remains free – as we are free; as I am free. Now, behold your redeemer . . .'

Duncan began to sob uncontrollably as Tanfeld raised his arm and, before his disbelieving eyes, he saw it transform into a scythe.

Starting at the shoulder, Tanfeld's cardigan dissipated and old metal grew from flesh and bone as natural as hair, and as ugly as cancer. The blade formed a perfect crescent and glinted dimly in the blue light, blood streaking its inner edge, purple and thick. Suddenly it swooped down and Duncan felt the blade miss his face by millimetres.

Duncan tried to roll away but the debris held him firm. His scream was also stilled as his mind struggled to accept the metamorphosis before him. The thing that was Tanfeld laughed, his yellow teeth greened by the blue firelight.

'Imagine the pain, Duncan. The feeling of your flesh parting as tissue and muscle are torn asunder; and your veins and arteries are slashed to let your blood pump into the night. Picture your very essence spurting onto the ground like that of a dying pig in a slaughterhouse . . .'

The blade whistled upwards, its cold wake stinging Duncan's eyes and rustling his lank hair.

'Cartilage, bone, marrow, cleaved in two . . . Think of dismemberment, of seeing your arm twitch its last on the floor in front of you, your shoulder an unstoppable tap, fountaining your life away . . . ah, *poetry*.'

Duncan stared up at the blade above him, unable to breathe, his whole being focused on it. Then, just as he expected the blade to deal the fatal blow, it shrank back into the shoulder socket, and the rest of the it-Tanfeld darkened, the clothes melding together into a dark, tarlike covering. His face swelled in a series of rapid jerks, swallowing his mouth and nose and ears and cheeks, until it was several times its original size and only the eyes remained recognisable. Suddenly a big lipless snout opened and let out a horrifying howl, its dreadful teeth gleaming in the dark, row upon row of short sharp incisors as full as the keyboard of a church organ. It then raised its remaining hand to the ceiling where it turned into a huge hairy paw equipped with a dozen claws that splayed out like a fistful of hypodermic needles. There was no mistaking its base design; the mouth, fur and giant clawed paw were all derived from a dog. And all the time that it scrabbled at the ceiling above, freckling Duncan's face with particles of charred wood, it waved its awful cavern of a mouth from side to side and howled and howled, a noise as earsplitting as any air raid siren.

Then, as quickly as it had appeared, the bulk of the huge beast collapsed like a discarded cloak and became a wriggling black carpet on the floor. Duncan could still see the man's eyes staring back at him out of the struggling mound, but then there was a muffled giggle as the two bright orbs were overrun by the hundreds of little black snakes that Duncan could see made up the heaving black mass. Other snakes scurried away from the main body and up the wall towards the flames above, where they spluttered and hissed and popped as they were consumed.

Duncan was unable to comprehend what he was seeing, his mind on the very edge of shutdown, his bladder long having given up its ability to retain urine.

The mass spoke, a thousand little voices combining in one mocking tone: 'This is *wonderful!*'

Suddenly they all rushed back to the centre, their bodies piling on one another and rising up from the ground until they tottered a full six feet high.

'Black magic!' said Tanfeld's voice. Then slowly, starting from the ground up, the black writhing mass stilled and turned a brilliant, crystalline white; a white that shone out clean and pure even in the blue glow from the unearthly flames above. Finally the transformation was complete and the white statue of Tanfeld stood silent and unmoving before its terrified and bemused victim. Then its eyes opened, and so did a slash of a mouth:

'Oh sweetness – and you thought I had *lost?*'

Then the monstrous sugar sculpture collapsed into a heap on the floor, turning into a muddy grey liquid as if immersed in water, quickly surrounding the pile of debris Duncan kneeled on, turning the broken wood into an island.

'We are what we eat,' said a voice in Duncan's head. 'Say hello to nightmares.'

Then it was gone.

Gone! Duncan looked around him. The flames above were still coiling and uncoiling in slow motion, still shaded blue, but the it-Tanfeld was nowhere to be seen. Duncan could barely trust his legs to move, but slowly he edged back across the cellar, careful not to step in the mushy water, until be butted up against the wall. Gingerly he turned and tested the surface, his hands shaking uncontrollably. The bricks were warm, but safe to touch. He started to look for toe and handgrips, to see if he could pull himself out of the pit.

He found a broken brick about eighteen inches off the floor, pushed his toe into it, then reached up a trembling hand to find a fingerhold. He managed to establish a tenuous grip just over half way up the wall, but as he heaved himself up, the voice came again from behind.

'Where are you going, my sweet?' It was higher pitched than before, and less threatening – and all the more ominous for that.

Duncan glanced over his shoulder and what he saw made him lose his grip and stumble back onto the broken wood, his feet two-stepping frantically before he could steady himself.

Lying on top of the debris was an old woman in a tatty blue floral print dress. She was tall and emaciated, with waist-length grey hair that hung around her head like a shroud. Her long face had ivory-coloured creased skin and sunken bruised eyes, her down-turned mouth offering a smear of vibrant scarlet gloss like a fresh wound. Her heavily varicosed legs were matched by the veins on her scrawny scabby forearms, and she had pencil-thin fingers, their long nails yellowed like toenails.

She splayed her legs, and her tongue began exploring the red halo of her mouth like a naked snake. She was obscene and disgusting, a mockery of womanhood and sexuality, but it was her eyes that shocked the most. They were the same as Tanfeld's, and as deeply deranged. As her hands stroked up and down from the emptiness of her breasts towards her crotch, she spoke in an ugly cracked whisper:

'Come to mummy, boy. Come and show mummy you love her.'

She seized the hem of her dress and slowly pulled it up her skinny white thighs, bones showing through transparent skin. The action was supposed to be provocative, but it was like the slow revelation of a corpse in a mortuary. Finally she tugged the dress up to her waist to reveal a grey-haired pubic mound like a dead mouse. Duncan felt sick, and the woman smiled evilly as she saw his reaction.

'Mummy knows what's best; knows what her little boy really wants. Come and show me.'

She pulled her legs wide, allowing her labia to be seen, another wrinkle among many.

Duncan forced himself to look back at her face and her smile broadened.

'That's a good boy. Show mummy what you've got.'

Duncan shook his head, words a mystery.

'Don't think,' interrupted Tanfeld's voice, oddly at home in the old crone's face. 'Just do. Do me, do us, do *it*.'

Then the woman's tongue began to grow, first falling out of the side of her mouth like a spat-out sausage, then slowly squirming across the timber beside her, to crawl across her thighs to her vagina where it eagerly insinuated itself between the folds of her cunt and steadily worked its way in, impossibly deep. The woman's eyes rolled in pleasure and she moaned. Then the tongue pulled itself out of the vagina and began moving towards Duncan.

He was rooted to the spot with terror as the tongue-snake reached his foot, caressing the dirty canvas of his trainer, licking away at one of the eyelets of his laces as delicately as if it was his urethra. Then it began to move up, touching the cuff of his jeans, sneaking in between his jeans and his socks.

Duncan gave a cry of horror and stepped back; he had always had a phobia about old women, stemming from infant encounters with his great aunt Edwina; the smell of her stale perfume, those dry lips, thin hair, liver spots . . . and Aunt Edwina had always insisted on kissing him on the lips. But this creature didn't look like Edwina Cantrill, it looked like nothing on Earth. It was so repellent, Duncan was overwhelmed by revulsion; he shivered and squirmed as if he had been doused with a bucket of mucus.

The disappointed tongue slithered back towards its owner's mouth, a giggle of satisfaction shaking her brittle frame. It snapped back into her mouth with a crack like a whip, and she spoke again with Tanfeld's voice.

'Mother wasn't such a bad sort after all,' said Tanfeld. 'I was just too young to appreciate how creative she was. Even waited till I'd reached puberty before she took my balls. She kept them, you know; as she said, what was mine was hers. And now we're together, and what's yours is ours as well. So come on, boy, pleasure us. Now.'

The woman-thing threw its legs even wider and humped its hips at him rhythmically, a lascivious grin on its face. 'Take us boy, before we take you.'

Duncan couldn't move, his mind struggling to understand what was happening. Tanfeld had said 'Mother' as he died, and here he had transformed into an old woman who called herself mummy. The scythe, the dog, this woman, snakes . . . why the changes, what was the it-Tanfeld trying to do?

But before he could make sense of it her hands were parting her vagina. Duncan looked down at her cunt and as he did her hands jerked sideways, expanding the entrance until it was a large gaping hole, suddenly dark and threatening. Then her body juddered as if in orgasm and her legs gave a convulsive kick and she pulled her knees right back to her chest as something emerged from her vagina. It was a head, slick with blood like a newborn child's but too big for even the biggest of babies. The woman screamed with the effort and opened her legs even wider, then the head shivered and pushed itself out to look up at Duncan. It was Tanfeld.

'Come in,' he said. 'Come in and join the fun. We're all here.' It licked blood from its chin.

'Indeed,' said another voice.

Duncan looked up. The old crone had opened her mouth so wide her face had disappeared and Beaumont's head was poking out of it, smiling and friendly, his neck ringed by her pale stretched gums.

'Come on, boy, join us. It's so . . . different,' he said.

In that instant Duncan realised how Leonard had died, why his neck had been so constricted, and what had caused the smell. It had come into his hotel room as a woman – the one thing Leonard feared so much he could never make a commitment to; his addiction – and lowered itself over his face and devoured his head with her vagina, choking the life out of him. Duncan sat back on his haunches and screamed, then he stopped. What was the point? Only he and it could hear him, and it clearly enjoyed his fear.

'No,' Duncan said simply. Something was wrong here. He laughed when the thought occurred to him. Something wrong? Are you kidding?

'Yes, you may be,' the Tanfeld and Beaumont heads said together. 'But we'll forgive you.'

It could change its shape, it could read his thoughts – so why hadn't it killed him yet? Why play all these tricks?

The instant the question occurred to him, both heads retreated back into the body of the woman, her jaws and legs snapping shut with a loud slap. Then, remaining on her back, she raised herself onto her hands and legs so she was crab-shaped. Her face lost its features, the nose, eyes and mouth sliding into one featureless pink ball which rolled down backwards until it could touch the floor on its elongated neck. The head then wormed its way under the body towards Duncan. By the time it stopped the neck must have been fully six feet in length. The taut pink ball then rippled and the skin peeled apart with a sound like sandpaper on glass and an enormous eye twelve inches across opened and stared at Duncan, green and yellow with a black slit of an iris running from top to bottom. Its lashes were worms, wriggling and cavorting in the air and occasionally making hungry stabs at the flesh of the eye.

'Why haven't you killed me?' Duncan asked calmly.

'Call this living?' said a voice in his head.

'Why haven't you killed me?'

The eye blinked at him.

Duncan repeated the question.

'Toying. Playing. Game,' said the voice.

'So why haven't you killed me?' Duncan stood his ground. For the first time he had something to cling to; it was only a question, but it was something: why was he still alive?

The eye closed and the neck retreated, only to rise up above the body at the other end. As it did so, its skin visibly darkened and became more angular and segmented, and is centre became pinched and stretched, soon forming into a vicious curved spike. At the same time, its legs and arms turned black and shiny, as if it was growing armour. Then out of the vagina squirted two huge black claws which rose up until they clacked against the ceiling that remained. Four more legs sprouted from the body, two on either side, and took up position on the rim of the room. The scorpion's stinger swung down until it hovered inches from Duncan's upturned face, dripping dark liquid that sputtered and fizzed as it splashed on the burnt wood. Finally, two eye stalks popped up from out of the beast's belly and swivelled round to look at him.

There is a moment when fear stops, when the desperate need for continued existence, for life itself, stops being a priority. A time at which the brain says: enough, what will be will be. Duncan had reached that point, literally too scared to be frightened, his mind simply taking in what was happening for all the world as if it was an everyday occurrence – and with this came renewed clarity.

For the first time since he had been thrown into the house, Duncan was able to look at things from a perspective that didn't rely on his need for survival. For all he knew he was already dead and in hell, so what the hell. But when those two eyes popped up, like a bad special effect, the action struck him as rather comical; it was an afterthought, as if it had forgotten that it would need eyes in order to look at him. It broke the spell; it was fallible, whatever it was.

'No, I'm not,' Tanfeld's voice said.

'Yes, you fucking are! Kill me, then. Here, now. Do it!'

The stinger edged forward an inch, but didn't strike.

'You can't kill me, can you?'

'No, I choose to toy.'

'You're lying. You can't kill me. I'm not cursed, the rune has been fulfilled.'

It laughed. 'I toy.'

'No, you can't kill me . . . unless . . .'

There was no answer, just the sound of a distant wind driving the silent blue flames above him.

'You can't kill me unless *I let you*.'

The wind howled louder, like a cry of frustration.

As Duncan conceived that very simile, the sound ceased.

'I'm in control. You've tried to scare me with other people's fears. Is that what the Black Wind uses? Its victims' fears?' He assigned its transformations: the blade that beheaded Racimo; the woman that killed Leonard; it probably killed the horse in the guise of a pack of dogs; Tanfeld's mother; and now, in front of him, the scorpion that would have appeared on Beaumont's boat. But what about the snakes? No, not snakes. *Eels*. Donaldson was drowned . . . His understanding brought elation. 'Well, their fears don't scare me, they're not real. Whatever you change into it will always be *you*.'

No answer. No noise. Duncan followed his train of thought.

'The Black Wind lives on fear. It terrifies its victims with their worst fears, feeds off the terror then kills them, like a poultry farmer kills a fattened turkey. You haven't killed me yet, just tried to scare me.' The logic suddenly blazed in Duncan's mind like a guide to survival. 'As long as I'm frightened of you, you'll continue to exist. You're feeding on my fear.'

'No.'

'And you're keeping me frightened with your tricks – changing your appearance, using the fears of those you have destroyed – but why haven't you used my own fears? Why?'

Suddenly, like a blast of cold air, Duncan could feel its own fear. '*You're* afraid. You haven't got the power to kill me. You need my terror to exist.' He was nearing a truth the it-Tanfeld didn't want him to appreciate and, as if in answer, it changed again.

It retracted its claws and legs and slumped to the floor, changing colour as quickly as a cuttlefish to a pinky-yellow white, and blew itself up like a balloon until it was a ten-feet-long grub, its bloated body shaking and shimmering as it squirmed at Duncan's feet. It then lifted its head and spat at him with a small, harsh mouth that opened and closed like a valve in time with Duncan's hammering heartbeat. His mind flashed back to a horror from his childhood.

He had been five years old and a group of older boys had promised to show him some treasure hidden under a rock and when he had cautiously pulled up the large slate they had led him to, he had found a dead cat alive with maggots and the boys had pushed his face into it and for weeks after he could still feel the wriggling white grubs in his mouth and nose and hair. It was a memory he had long suppressed but it had dug deep, opening a schism in his defence through which he knew it would now attempt to pour its full venom.

Duncan fought for breath, his concentration broken, like someone bursting out of water after being immersed too long, gasping for breath and light, aware only of their need for air. He felt dizzy, heard it laugh . . .

He focused on its eyes, ignoring its corpulent body. Its eyes were a man's, a *man's*. Tanfeld's, not a monster, no demon, just a dead man who stabbed you in the cheek and bought shitty souvenirs from Blackpool. Concentrate, concentrate . . .

Duncan spoke aloud: 'If you . . . can trick me into . . . giving in, you might stay alive . . . long enough to feed on other people.' Yes, yes, think it through. Others' lives were at stake, not just his own. If it killed him it would go for Gwynedd and after her, anyone who came across its path – and each terrified death would fuel its lust.

'No,' it said.

'Yes! You'll kill and kill until . . .'

'Until?' it taunted.

Duncan could feel his thoughts being led down a deep tunnel of despair; he forced himself to switch on the light of hope. 'As long as you scare me you live. You haven't the power to kill me, have you? Not unless you terrify me. Fear is the food that gives you your power to be and to kill. So, the answer's simple.'

'No.'

'I'll not fear you.'

'You cannot.'

'You can't scare me.'

'You cannot. No.'

'Yes, I can. No matter what you look like, you can't kill me. You *daren't* kill me or you'll cease to be, but *I* dare kill *you*.'

'No!'

'Yes.'

Duncan stepped forward to the loathsome creature. The giant grub squirmed back out of his reach. Duncan smiled as he realised he had hit on the truth.

'I'm going to kill you,' he said.

'No! You fear me! I have untold terrors at my call!'

'No, you don't. Prove it, show me . . .'

It screamed, the sound grinding its way around the inside of Duncan's skull, but he didn't care. He didn't care – and it knew it.

'I've won. *You're* afraid.'

It stood its ground.

'I'm so unafraid of you, I'm going to . . . touch you.'

The obscene maggot shuffled back another yard, then started to shake. Duncan advanced towards it, choosing his words with almost ritual-like care.

'You need my terror to live, but I'm not frightened. If you kill me you die, but you're too weak to stop me. You're dying.'

The maggot shook even more violently and darkened as if consumed by fire, then up-ended itself and stood erect, looking like a giant black pea-pod.

'It doesn't matter what you look like,' said Duncan. 'I'm not afraid. *You're* afraid – and you're going to die.'

The pea-pod quivered, then split down the middle and out stepped a naked Duncan, sloughing off the two pod halves like a bath towel.

The it-Duncan spoke with Duncan's voice: 'Too late. Touch me and you die.'

'Touch me and *you* die,' said Duncan stepping towards it.

They looked into each other's eyes. The it-Duncan smiled, but its eyes were still those of Tanfeld: proof, if Duncan needed it, that it wasn't in control any more.

'You fear yourself, don't you, Duncan?' it said. 'Your wasted education, your pathetic life, the endless succession of pointless jobs, the misery you bring your parents.'

'True,' said Duncan.

It smiled.

'But not any more. Now I know better. It may have taken the death of a good man to teach me about living, but now I know better and I intend to do better, and I'm going to start by getting rid of you. Whatever faults I might have, I can correct them. You won't have that chance. I'm me and I'm not afraid. You are . . . a figment of a madman's imagination, a dead man – and you're going to die again, for good.'

Duncan raised his hand and held it in front of the it-Duncan's face. 'Die, fucker.'

As he touched its face, somewhere in his mind he heard *Please* and then something hit him with the force of an explosion and he felt himself rising up through fire. Soon blackness beckoned and Duncan couldn't resist its soothing embrace.

31

DUNCAN WAS BEING dragged through smoky darkness, feet clumping into his head as he was hauled over jumbled debris and burning embers. His agonising journey was made worse by his hands trailing in ashes that clung to his sweat like phosphorous, burning into his skin, while his shirt was rucked under his throat, making breathing even more difficult. He tried to reach up and grab at whatever held his collar but couldn't reach. He couldn't imagine what it looked like now or where it was taking him – all was darkness, sound stifled by a roaring in his ears, and he was simply a rag doll at the mercy of his captor.

Suddenly he was pulled to his feet and thrown into the air, his world spun upside down and he found himself coughing blood, tears blurring his eyes, his stomach jarring as he was bounced up and down. He tried to protest, but his raw throat was strafed with smoke and all he could do was hack up more red phlegm.

Then there was light – white and flashing blue – and voices. Cold air slapped his face and hands and he found himself being fumbled through the air again, this time to be laid on his back and look up at creatures with yellow heads and single giant eyes prodding him. He tried to struggle but something was pushed onto his face and cold air forced into his lungs.

After he had finished coughing and brushed the oxygen mask aside, he sat up, the two firemen who had pulled him out of the house squatting down on either side of him, checking him over.

'Gwynedd,' he managed to gasp.

'Shush up, kid, you're damn lucky. We'll get the paramedics to sort you out.'

'Gwynedd?' he repeated. He tried to struggle up but one of them held him down.

'Best not move, mate. Wait till the—'

Duncan pushed the man's hand aside.

'Gwynedd!' he shouted, his concern now apparent.

'Where? In the house?' shouted one through his mask.

Duncan shook his head. 'No. The car, the car!'

One of the men turned and looked across the chaos that surrounded the front of the house. Duncan followed his gaze. There were two fire engines, a police car and, edging through the melée, an ambulance. The ground was littered with hosepipes and rescue gear, and firemen hunched over two hoses being played on the upper storey of the house, with a third hose leading inside the house through the front door. Over by the edge of the drive, the Mercedes 200 was lying on its side, the rear end towards the house.

Duncan screamed and scrambled up, the lightness in his head and the pains in his body ignored as he pulled free of the restraining firemen and dashed across the soaking gravel to the wrecked vehicle.

Standing on tiptoe he tried to see inside the car but he couldn't see anything, so he heaved himself up onto the car's nearside and pulled open the passenger's door. It wouldn't stay open on its own and he had to kneel down and let it rest on his back as he tried to see if Gwynedd was still in the car. The light from the fire didn't help as it only provided flickering reflections on metal and glass, distracting his gaze. But then he saw her, huddled against the rear passenger door, curled up in a ball, her head hidden under her arms. He immediately lowered himself onto the front passenger door, careful not to let the car door fall on him.

One of the firemen appeared above him, and saw the problem. 'Hey kid, wait on, we'll get her out.'

Duncan ignored him, struggling between the front seats to the rear of the car, cursing the head restraints that dug into his back and thighs.

He was lying between the two seats, his feet under the dashboard providing anchorage and, ignoring the pain in his side where the driver's seat bruised his ribs, he gently placed his shaking hands under the girl's head to lift her face up.

'Careful,' shouted the fireman. 'She might have neck injuries.'

Duncan realised he was right and instead felt for a pulse in her wrist. He wasn't sure there was one, so he instead pressed his hand to her chest and after a few anxious moments felt her bosom rise and fall, rise and fall. Good, she was alive.

He looked up at the fireman. 'What do we do?'

'You get out and we'll right the car. Get to her through the door.'

Duncan nodded. It made sense. The fireman edged back from

the door and Duncan squirmed back onto the front seats, then stood up poking his head through the passenger's door held open by the fireman.

As the man offered a hand to help him pull himself out, Duncan looked past him and saw someone being walked towards a police car by a policeman and another fireman. It was a girl, dazed and limping: Gwynedd.

No, it *couldn't* be! Duncan looked up at the fireman, then back down at the person in the car. The girl there looked up at him, her face ruined by a wide smile that showed rodent-like teeth and eyes that were solid black orbs. A thin purple tongue edged out the corner of her mouth and slowly licked its way across her top lip.

Duncan let out a yell of horror and heaved himself up, but his unexpected movement overbalanced the fireman and he fell backwards off the car and let go of the door. Duncan saw it closing and, pulling his hands out of the way of the crashing weight, fell back inside the car, the door slamming above him, his left knee popping as his leg bent under him and, as he came to a stop, his scream of pain turned to a scream of horror as the it-Gwynedd insinuated its head between the two front seats and screamed into his face, its hot foul breath scouring his face.

Duncan huddled back as best he could, praying the seat would keep the creature from him, but it was little defence. He screamed at it:

'You're dead, you're dead, I killed you!'

Its yowling turned into hysterical giggling that rattled like a machine gun in his ears. It leaned closer, the eyes bulging bigger like snooker balls, the only highlights the twinkling light from the outside world playing like a movie clip on the top right of each eye. The tongue stilled and pointed at Duncan's face like an accusing finger. Suddenly it silenced, then spoke, its voice high and rough, like a bad female impersonator.

'You want to lick my cunt, don't you, Duncan? You want to suck my big fat tits and come in my mouth and finger my arsehole, don't you, Duncan? Dearest.'

Despite what he was seeing, Duncan's mind showed him what the it-Gwynedd was saying. He could picture Gwynedd naked on a pure white bed, her legs open, her hands holding her breasts up towards him, the nipples engorged, her mouth open and rounded, her body swimming in a sweat of desire. His girlfriend, his lover, wanting him, pleading with him for satisfaction – and he wanted her. He needed to cross the space between them and sink into her flesh and wallow in her supple curves, feel her heat and her longing, and taste her and enter her, again and again and again. Yes, he could hear himself saying, yes yes yes . . .

He leaned forward, his face edging towards the monstrosity in front of him which, even though he could see and smell it, meant nothing compared to the pornography that was unreeling in his unhinged mind. It didn't matter: all he wanted, all he had ever wanted, was Gwynedd: her body, her sweat, her smell . . . he lusted for her, to penetrate her as deeply as his cock would let him, ball-deep, their public hair tangling like velcro, pulling and stretching even as they humped against each other, pumping and pistoning . . . Yes, yes, yes, he heard himself say, his mouth open to meet the beast that waited to devour him. And he didn't care! He didn't *care!* He wanted Gwynedd: wanted her body, her vagina, her breasts, every part of her.

He poked out his tongue, desperate to touch the pencil-like tongue of the it-Gwynedd, assured of sexual ecstasy whatever the cost, the pain in his cramped erection already superseding the pain in his broken knee cap. His balls were hot orbs, desperate to unload, his mind fevered, his being dissolving into a dammed pool of need, all focused on breaching the one last barrier that held his existence in check. One touch and the flood would be unleashed.

The mouth gaped before him, the eyes boring into him, its tongue, scaly and dry, edging closer, inches from piercing his own tongue and tapping into his essence.

Yes yes yes echoed round the car, but now they were the desperate pleadings of the it-Gwynedd, its need even greater than Duncan's. It had prompted his basest desires until he had lost his will and was ready to be sucked dry of the nourishment it needed to escape to feed on the other souls outside the car. One more inch, one more lustful implant in the pathetic, under-used organ the boy called his mind and it would be free.

Yes yes yes, it begged. And yes yes yes came the equally eager reply. Surrender was so easy. It had him – and soon it would have them all and then . . .

'No!' a voice shouted.

Duncan ignored it. Like a call from the street during a passionate embrace in bed, it was an irrelevancy. He must—

288

'No!' shouted the voice again. 'Duncan, don't! Stop it, stop it!'

Duncan paused. The it-Gwynedd begged him to kiss it, to touch tongues, to share spit, but the voice shouted again.

'Duncan, stop! Think! Sex isn't everything. There's more to life.'

'Like what?' said Duncan's fevered mind.

'Love,' came the simple reply.

Ha! shrieked the it-Gwynedd, but Duncan had stopped, his eyes wandering as he sought to distinguish between what he could see and what he saw.

'You love Gwynedd, don't you, Duncan? You may want her, but you also need her. And she needs you. *Think*, boy. Love is what you want, not sex. Sex comes after, love should come first – and you love Gwynedd.'

Duncan leaned back, seeing for the first time what he had sought to kiss but, instead of screaming his horror, he looked blankly at Leonard who was kneeling in the space next to him.

'Don't you see, it's desperate,' said Leonard. 'It hasn't the power to scare you now, to tap into your fears. Terror is too deep-seated; it needs hunting out and then mining. But desires, love . . . they're obvious; plain for anyone to see. For *it* to see. It can't frighten you so it's using the obvious wants you have to trap you. It knows you want Gwynedd and it's going to give you her – but only in your mind, Duncan, but I'm here, its evil can't contain me now – and that proves it's dying.'

Duncan looked back at it, the struggle for sanity plain on his face.

Leonard leaned into his ear. 'One last stand will end it. Don't give in, don't give up. Fight it, Duncan, control your desire.'

Duncan, his eyes fixed on it, nodded slowly.

'No,' he said to it. 'No more tricks, no more time. You . . . are . . . dead. Die!'

The thing looked at Duncan, its mouth slowly closing, its eyes receding until it looked more or less like Gwynedd.

'Love me,' it said plaintively.

'In your dreams,' said Duncan and he spat at it.

The spit never landed. It disappeared, gone as if it had never been.

Duncan leaned back, and the pain in his shattered knee jolted him speechless.

'Has it gone?' he finally managed between gritted teeth.

'Yes.'

'And you?'

But Duncan could see already that Leonard was fading.

'Oh God, no!' he said. 'Don't go, Leonard, please.'

'No choice, kiddo. Tanfeld's dead and so's his Black Wind. It's all over.' The man's voice was fading as well.

'Oh God, no,' cried Duncan. 'Don't leave me, please.'

'You've got Gwynedd. Go to her. Love her. Do something with your life. Use your brains.'

'But there's so much I haven't said!'

'You've said enough. Done enough. Learn from my mistakes, Duncan. Learn before it's too late.'

'Learn what?'

But Leonard had disappeared.

'Learn what, you bastard?'

'Charming,' came the final distant echo.

Duncan began to cry and soon was bawling like a baby. Even as the firemen slowly righted the car and carefully extracted him, taking care with his shattered knee, he continued to cry. All thought he was crying at the pain and did their best to calm him but it was no use.

Only when he was ensconced in the ambulance, with Gwynedd on the stretcher across the aisle, did he stop. He reached out to her and their hands touched.

'I love you,' he said, tears welling anew at the sight of her bloody and bruised face.

'I love you,' she said, forcing a smile through her pain.

The ambulance set off, siren blaring. Over the noise, she asked him about Leonard.

He shook his head. 'Gone for good.'

'So Tanfeld's . . .?'

'Dead. And that thing . . . so no more Leonard.'

She squeezed his hand, trying to hide the pain it caused her stabbed hand. He saw the wince and smiled and let her take it back to have it tended by the paramedic.

He looked up at the ceiling of the ambulance. In saving Leonard he had killed the man a second time. Or had Leonard killed himself saving Duncan from *it?* Whichever, he was alive, so was Gwynedd, and they had their lives in front of them – and life was for the living.

Goodbye, Leonard, I'm glad I knew you – and thank you.

PART FOUR

Incriminations

Our remedies oft in ourselves do lie,
Which we ascribe to heaven
                    William Shakespeare,
             All's Well that Ends Well

32

THE CEMETERY WAS quiet, rain and the late hour keeping people away. Duncan usually visited the grave earlier in the day but his car had been giving him trouble and he'd had to wait for a new exhaust to be fitted.

He sorted through the broken flowers and, realising none could be saved, threw them all away and repositioned the small stone vase in front of the headstone. He checked his watch. 4.35pm. He'd have to go soon, but he didn't feel guilty about rushing his visit; after all, he had been coming every week for the last eight months.

He reached into his pocket and pulled out the card and looked at it, and smiled. He could imagine the comments now. He knelt down, brushed aside the pebbles along the base of the headstone and placed it with the others. Soon have the complete set. He covered it over, muttered a few words, then stood up.

There was a quiet cough behind him which made him jump. He spun round to see Chief Inspector Chater standing two graves away under an umbrella. It was only then that Duncan realised just how hard it was raining. Still, it was only water; he'd soon dry out. Others would never enjoy that luxury.

'Good afternoon, Duncan,' said the detective. 'I thought it was you.'

'Of course it's me. It's thirty-odd miles from Ollington; it's not a coincidence.'

'No. Sorry. I know you come here every week.'

'And they say the police haven't enough resources. What the hell are you following me for?'

'Day off, my own time; taxpayers'll never know. Just curiosity; there were a lot of unanswered questions and I want some answers.'

'You had all the answers when you got me out of Tanfeld's house.

'Told you the story half-a-dozen times; not my fault you chose to disbelieve me.'

'It was fantastic.'

'It was true. Anyway, you got your pound of flesh. Two years suspended.'

'You did some stuff I couldn't ignore.'

'I had my reasons.'

'They weren't good enough—'

'I had—'

'—in the eyes of the law.'

'Fuck the law. It didn't help me.'

'I'm on your side, Duncan. You have to see—'

'See? See what? I stopped that loon *killing* people – and I get charged with umpteen offences. How many was it?'

'I don't—'

'Sixteen! Sixteen bloody charges. Only my dad's lawyers got it down to four. If it wasn't for them I'd be in prison now, serving God knows how long.'

'It wasn't your dad's lawyers.'

'Oh, do me a—'

'It was me. I went out on a limb for you; almost got myself fired. I got the charges dropped and reduced. Me. Stealing the girl's car, breaking and entering into the bookshop, assaulting that policeman. Christ, if it wasn't for the shotgun you might have got away with that, but the Chief Constable has a thing about firearms. My insistence and your defence of having a breakdown after finding the bodies – that's what saved you. Besides, you got a suspended sentence.'

'Thanks a lot. And how long before it's wiped off the record? Seven years? I didn't do anything wrong!'

'The ends justified the means?'

'Too fucking right.'

Chief Inspector Chater walked up to the grave, read the inscription, then knelt down and picked up the card Duncan had hidden.

'Eight of Spades. Mean anything?'

'No. The tits do.'

The policeman looked at the naked girl on the playing card; a big breasted blonde. He ferreted in the gravel and pulled out half-a-dozen others, all pneumatic naked girls.

'I heard he had a reputation with the ladies.'

'One way of putting it.'

'But he's dead. What's the point?'

Duncan looked at the headstone.

IN LOVING MEMORY OF LEONARD HALSEY.
JANUARY 8 1946 – JUNE 16 1994. R.I.P.

'He wasn't as dead as some people thought then – and who knows now? But you don't believe me, so what's it matter?'

'I want to understand.'

'Bit late now.'

The detective idled a finger in the wet pink pebbles. 'How's Gwynedd?' he finally asked.

'She's fine,' said Duncan, his impatience making him notice the relentless drizzle. 'She's in the car; got a bad cold, didn't want her out in this.'

'Are you living together?'

'Yes. Engaged, actually. My mother helped us get a flat near the college. Don't know what we'll do when she graduates; I'll still have two years to do.'

'And you're studying . . .?'

'Art. Going to teach design, I hope.'

'Good.'

'What's it to you?'

'Look, you ungrateful little sod. Saving your hide probably cost me promotion; I helped you, if you did but know it, and the least I deserve is to be able to talk it through with you.'

'But I'll only tell you the same as before. Nothing's changed.'

'I have.' Chater bent down and covered up the cards. 'My father died last week. I need to know everything I can. Do you understand?'

Duncan looked up at the slate sky. Shit. He nodded. 'Yes . . . I'm sorry. Was he a good man?'

'The best.'

'You've got no worries, then.'

Chief Inspector Chater looked back at him, then stood up. 'Good. Come on, I'll buy you both a coffee.'

Duncan nodded. If his own father died, he didn't know how he would react – the man was almost a stranger – but Leonard's final departure had affected him deeply.

That they had only become friends through circumstance and *after* Leonard had already died was irrelevant. Duncan's only regret at the death of Tanfeld had been that it spelled the end of Leonard's time with him; for all his faults, he would have liked to have kept his friendship. But Leonard had actually left Duncan with more than just a memory: he had made him realise how precious life truly was. And if Inspector Chater wanted to talk because his father had died, what would it cost Duncan to listen?

THE END